THE CAVANAUGH HOUSE

Elizabeth Meyette

Author of *Love's Destiny* and *Love's Spirit*

To my family and friends in Rochester, NY who dance and sing in my childhood memories, and to the Sisters of St. Joseph who taught me to love reading and writing.

This house held secrets. Secrets that wafted through rotting window sashes on the winter wind. Secrets that spiders wove into webs anchored between the ceiling and walls. Secrets that scuttled on the feet of cockroaches across stained kitchen linoleum and scurried into its cracks. Secrets that peered from holes in the baseboard from glinting mouse eyes. This house held the secrets close to its bosom where they had slept for decades. No one had disturbed these secrets in all the years the house sat decaying from neglect. There was no reason to, and there was no desire.

-ONE-

June 1968

This might be the biggest mistake I've made yet, thought Jesse Graham.

She climbed out of her three-year-old yellow 1965 Volkswagen Beetle and waded through tall grass and weeds that scratched at her sandal-clad feet. Looming before her, the two-story house—her house—hovered, insinuating more height than it could actually claim. Wrapped in chipped and peeling greenish-yellow paint, the house looked weary, and the once-red front door had faded to a dull russet. The roof sagged, and the tiny porch appeared to be giving up the fight to support the small roof above it. She stared at the house, and the windows stared back, blank. Above the front door, two windows mirrored her dismay as the wood trim above them bowed down. In her twenty-eight years, she had never seen a sadder looking house.

"Oh my God, what have I done?" she breathed.

She closed her green eyes, as startlingly brilliant as her mother's. She suspected they were all she had inherited from the aloof, career-focused woman, for she could see no other similarity. Once again the fear that she had been the cause of her parents' divorce in her early childhood crept into her mind: did her father leave because of her? Jesse always supposed that her father had wanted a boy, and when she arrived, his disappointment caused him to flee. She shook her head.

"That's nonsense. People don't run away because of the gender of their baby," she said aloud.

She combed her fingers through her thick auburn hair, a gesture she made when concentrating or trying to work through a difficulty. So much sorrow had entered her life recently both on a personal level and a national level with the assassination of Robert Kennedy two weeks earlier and Martin Luther King just months before that. Too much sorrow, and now she faced the consequences of her recent break-up with her fiancé, Robert.

She scanned the yard, which deepened her apprehension. Overgrown bushes hugged the house as if begging it to remain and the lawn had conceded the fight with weeds years before. Now crabgrass, nutsedge and dandelions grew knee-high, hiding even a path to the door. Age-old maple and oak trees dotted the property, providing shade from the June sun, their leaves motionless in the early summer air. The few houses on this road weren't adjacent as they would be in the town, but they were close enough to view this forlorn yard that perched at the dead end of the street. Anything she did would be an improvement.

Jesse's shoulders shook as she began to laugh, silently at first, then shaking with mirth. At first she feared she might be descending into hysteria, but she didn't feel out of control. In fact, she felt very much in control knowing that if she didn't laugh, she would cry. What had she expected? Valet service and a mint on her pillow? The house had been abandoned for over twenty-five years—weeds were going to grow, paint was going to chip. But they were *her* weeds and *her* chipped paint; no one was going to tell her what to do about them. And no one was going to take them away.

Circling the house, she was pleased to see that the windows, with the exception of one that was cracked, were intact, albeit the originals from when the house was built circa 1920. They would not keep summer heat and winter cold at bay.

"No, they're not 'bay' windows," she laughed, then groaned. "Geez, I even make lame jokes when I'm alone."

The house was wider than it was deep, although an addition at the back accommodated a kitchen. Two outbuildings stood farther back on the property, one an outhouse, the other a small carriage house.

"Oh, Lord, I hope there's indoor plumbing."

Plumbing! Not yet; she hadn't contacted the local utility companies to have water or gas and electricity turned on in the house. She checked her watch, relieved to see that it was just 1:30 p.m. She still had time to make it into town and take care of that.

Returning to her car, she rustled through her purse in search of the keys her mother had given her. Her fingers found the horseshoe-shaped key ring, smooth brass worn down by years of use holding three keys: a standard Yale lock key, a smaller brass key and a skeleton key. She headed for the front door and tested the first of three steps leading up to the porch. Feeling confident that they would hold her, she climbed them and faced the door. Her body tingled as if ants crawled beneath her skin; what would she find in there? This was the first step to her new-found independence. No one was coming to her aid if her plans failed. The house was a tumbled-down mess, but wasn't she as well? She had burned many bridges in Rochester, and the bridge with her mother was smoldering. Her father had been out of the picture for years, and she was an only child. Her dear friend Maggie was her sole support system.

Whatever existed on the other side of the door was now a part of her existence, too. This abandoned and rejected house was all she had. And she was all this house had. *We're in this together*. Straightening her shoulders, she took a deep breath and selected the key. She was surprised that the Yale key worked so easily in the old lock. Her heart pounded as she turned the doorknob and entered the house.

It took a moment for Jesse's eyes to adjust to the dim interior, for the windows were thick with grime, and the trees filtered out most of the sunlight. The centrally located door opened into a small foyer, a room on either side. Straight ahead was a staircase, and beside it, a hall led to the kitchen. Musty air invaded her nostrils, dust turned everything a dull pale gray, and she felt ancient, powdery motes settle upon her like a second skin. Lacy cobwebs stretched from the high corners to the brass light fixtures hanging in the middle of the ceilings. She heard scurrying at the far end of the hall and resisted the urge to run outside.

To her right was the dining room with a door on the far wall that led back to the kitchen. Turning left, she entered the living room, sparsely furnished with drop cloths draped over the pieces. A chair sat perpendicular to a sofa with a round coffee table in front. A floor lamp hung its head in the space between the sofa and chair, and nestled in a far corner was an oak secretary with a drop-down desk. Drooping at the windows were barkcloth drapes that once had boasted white gardenias on a rose background, but now hung in faded tatters, eaten away by dry rot.

Jesse turned slowly, surveying the room.

"Wow," she said. "Wow, wow, wow."

Her thoughts traveled to Robert's apartment with its white leather furniture, glass and chrome accent tables, and carpeting so thick it was like walking on moss. It was as though she was on a "Rat Pack" set when she was there; everything was sleek and modern, tasteful and expensive. She had lived in that world for the past two years. And like its furnishings, that world had turned out to be less ideal than it appeared. A world more than just miles away from this dilapidated house.

Mustering her courage, she pulled the fabric off the sofa. She shrieked as a flurry of grey shapes scattered in all directions—one straight toward her. She panicked as paws scurried across her sandaled foot. Mice! Goosebumps prickled her skin and adrenalin shot though her body. Heart pounding, she ran out the front door, off the porch and bolted to her car. Her knees gave out and she collapsed, trembling.

"Are you okay?"

Grabbing the door handle, she pulled herself up and looked around for the voice's owner.

"I'm over here," he said.

She looked toward the road and saw a blue pickup truck at the end of the driveway. Leaning out the driver's-side window was a man about her age, with tousled red hair. Humor lit up his mouth and softened his strong jawline and rugged face.

"Are you okay?" he repeated as he climbed out of his truck and started toward her.

Jesse brushed herself off and ran her fingers through her hair.

"Oh, yes, I'm fine," she said.

She saw his hazel eyes twinkle with amusement.

"I can see that. In a hurry to get somewhere? I noticed your quick exit."

She looked at her watch and gasped. It was after 2 p.m. If she were going to get any utilities started, she needed to get to town.

"I need to get my utilities started."

Oh, that sounded intelligent. She was a little off balance, and not just because of the mice encounter; this man's gaze was warm and unsettling. He chuckled.

"Well, I would never want to keep a woman from that."

"What I mean is…"

He held out his hand.

"Joe Riley."

She shook his hand and smiled.

"Jesse Graham."

"Nice to meet you, Jessica," he said.

"Not Jessica, just Jesse. The nickname for Jessica is J-E-S-S-I-E. I'm J-E-S-S-E. Pronounced the same, spelled differently."

"Oh, like Jesse James," he said.

"Yeah, I've never heard that one before," she tossed back.

"Sorry. Wow—I'm making a great first impression," Joe said as he scanned the property, avoiding her eyes. "So you bought the old Cavanaugh House, 'Just Jesse.'" It was a statement more than a question. His eyes studied the place, traveling over the roofline, down to the foundation and back to the outbuildings. "Mighty brave."

"I didn't buy it; I inherited it from my Aunt Helen."

He raised his eyebrows and nodded but didn't say anything.

"I just met the current residents—all one million of them, I think—when I pulled the drop cloth off the sofa. The mice took me by surprise. I panicked and ran."

He laughed and looked back at the house.

"If there were a million, I'd probably do the same."

"Okay, maybe a thousand. At least a couple hundred." Jesse laughed, feeling at ease with him. "I think a call to an exterminator is also in order. I'd better head into town and get things started."

"Can I help?" His face was earnest, his smile genuine.

"No, thank you. I can handle things myself," she said.

"Well, you can't stay here tonight with a million mice living in there. You'd be welcome to stay at my place."

She lifted her chin and looked at him sideways. "Right. Your place."

"No, no, no. You don't understand. I live with my mother less than a mile from here." His face was the color of summer tomatoes. "It's all legit. Mom would be a proper chaperone, and we have a spare room. I'm sorry. I didn't mean to imply…"

Jesse was touched by his sincerity. He was falling all over his words.

"No offense taken. And that is a sweet offer. It's just that…well…I need to take care of things myself. It's important to me."

"Oh, got it." He took a step back and looked around the yard. "Well, then, I'd best be leaving."

She saw his discomfort and rethought her words.

"No, Joe, it was very kind of you to offer, and truly, I take no offense. I'm just at a place where I need to depend on myself right now." She smiled at him, and he nodded and turned to leave.

"Wait, there is something you could help with."

He turned back to her.

"I do need a place to stay, but I have a friend in town who may have room for me. May I use your phone to call her?"

"Sure, follow me." He hopped into his truck as she locked the house and then backed her Beetle out to follow him. Looking back at the house, she was filled with ambivalence. On the one hand the house scared her, on the other, she already felt like she belonged there.

As she drove, Jesse remembered the day she found out about her house. On her twenty-first birthday her mother had presented her with a large manila envelope.

"You will probably want to sell this as soon as possible. Oh, and happy birthday," Eileen Graham said as she tossed the envelope to her daughter.

Opening the envelope, she sensed her mother's green eyes on her. She pulled out a sheaf of papers and leafed through them. Her Aunt Helen's will, the deed for the house, and the mortgage forms created a thick stack that intimidated her. Something else was in the envelope; she tilted it and a set of keys slid into her hand. She looked at her mother who shrugged, lit a cigarette and then examined her manicured nails. Breathing smoke as she talked, she gestured at the papers.

"For some reason, my sister wanted you to have the house. There was nothing I could do about it."

Jesse wondered at her last statement, but dismissed it as she looked through the documents.

"I own it free and clear. Aunt Helen has a trust that will pay the taxes," she said.

Her mother stubbed out her cigarette and left the room.

Jesse had never sold the house and, according to her mother, it had stood vacant for all twenty-eight years of her life. She'd had no idea what she would find when she arrived, but it would be hers and the house would be away...far away.

Joe opened the door for Jesse, ushering her into a modest Cape Cod. The living room was decorated in yellow and white with French blue accents. Chintz curtains framed the windows, and the hardwood floors gleamed in the afternoon sun.

"The phone is in the kitchen," he said leading her toward the back of the house.

She heard a woman humming "Fly Me to the Moon."

Upon entering, she saw a petite woman working at the sink. Her light brown hair was pulled up in a smooth chignon with a few wisps escaping in soft tendrils. Joe crossed to her and placed a kiss on her cheek.

"Meet our newest neighbor, Mom. This is Jesse Graham. Jesse, Susan Riley.

His mother wiped her hands on her apron and smiled up at Joe before she turned to greet Jesse. On seeing her, the woman stopped, her hand fluttering to her open mouth. Her eyes, a deeper hazel than her son's, were wide, eyebrows raised. Jesse had already moved forward to greet her.

"How do you do, Mrs. Riley?" she said holding out her hand.

Slowly Mrs. Riley took her hand and peered into her eyes.

"Jesse, you say?"

"That's right, Mom. She's moving into the Cavanaugh House."

The woman continued staring at her, still holding her hand.

"Of course she is," she murmured.

Jesse almost laughed at the way she said it, as if someone moved into the house every day.

"Mom, she needs to use the phone."

Mrs. Riley looked at Joe and dropped her hand.

"Oh, of course," she repeated. "Here, dear, have a seat and I will make you some tea."

"No, I don't want to be any trouble,"

"She needs to make arrangements for a place to stay tonight, and then she needs to get her utilities started." He winked at Jesse and they laughed at the shared joke. Opening a drawer, he pulled out the phone book and she laughed again.

"Phone books amuse you?" he teased.

"Sorry, but I just moved from Rochester, and our phone book is ten times thicker than that."

"You live in hyperbole, I see," he laughed. "Mom, she lives with a *million* mice in that house."

"I guess I do," she admitted.

As she loaded them into her Beetle, Jesse inventoried her purchases: flashlight, batteries, candles, matches, some groceries including paper products and beer. She would definitely need beer. Seneca Gas & Electric could not promise power to her house for at least two days, and she did not want to overstay her welcome at St.

Bartholomew's convent. *Face it. You're afraid you'll catch a vocation if you stay there too long.*

She had never considered entering the convent like her friend Maggie had after graduation from St. Cecilia Academy. She had teased Maggie about living a celibate life as Sister Angelina and bet her a new cashmere sweater that she wouldn't last. That had been nine years ago, and they had remained best friends. Different life choices left them few reasons to socialize, so they telephoned often and vowed to meet for dinner on their birthdays, Jesse's in July and Maggie's in February. Sitting across from her friend at their last birthday celebration, she again envied Maggie's black hair, wild if the curls were left untamed. Now that she was in the convent, Maggie's hair was short, but the curls continued to dance around her heart-shaped face. With her large brown eyes and short hair, she grumbled that she looked like a pixie, but Jesse countered that she could be a stand-in for Audrey Hepburn.

"Except for the curls, Jess. Audrey Hepburn doesn't have to deal with this tangled mess," Maggie said trying to tamp down her hair.

It was during this birthday dinner that her life changed. She remembered Maggie's shock at her announcement that night.

"I've left Robert."

Maggie looked at her friend, searching for the exaggeration she often found in her conversation. She saw only determination in Jesse's eyes. Determination and deep sadness.

"Jess, what's going on? I thought you were engaged," Maggie said.

"I thought so, too, but apparently Robert forgot. At least I suspect he wasn't thinking about it when he was rutting on Peggy Stewart."

"Oh, no. Jess, I'm so sorry. Are you sure?"

"I walked in on them when I went to his apartment to pick up my students' graded papers I'd left there. He was supposed to be in New York City for the weekend, so I let myself in with my key. The papers were on his desk in the study. As I walked down the hall, I heard music coming from his bedroom. I figured he'd forgotten to turn off his clock radio, so I went in to do that. There was his butt jiggling up and down like a fishing bobber with a twenty-pound bass on the end of the line. Peggy was moaning like a dog in heat, and I yelled, 'What the hell is going on?' I suppose someday I'll look back and laugh at the ridiculous scene, but right now it just hurts."

She snifled; Maggie handed her a tissue.

"Sweetie, I am so very sorry," Maggie said, her own eyes glistening. She reached over and took her friend's hand. "That must have hurt more than I can ever imagine."

Silence fell between them as Jesse regained her composure.

"Thank you,"

"For what?"

"For not saying, 'You're better off without him.' I know you never approved of our relationship, but you've always been supportive when things got tough between Robert and me. As you know, I couldn't go to my dear *mother* for comfort. Thanks for that, Mags."

Maggie patted her hand.

"What *I* thought wasn't important as long as you were happy, Jesse. And what your mother thinks has never been helpful. I'm sorry you went through this. How are you doing now?"

"I'm in run-away mode. I just want to leave town. It's so hard when I bump into our friends, catch them off guard, watch them squirm and try to make small talk. I just want to scream at them, 'I didn't do anything wrong! Your rotten friend Robert did!' But they were his friends first, and loyalty runs deep. I can't go to any clubs because all of the musicians know him, and know me through him. We were always in the newspaper for this gig or that benefit—the perfect couple smiling at each other. *Ugh.*" Jesse buried her face in her hands and squeezed her eyes to stem more tears. "I've given notice on my apartment, and I want to leave Rochester in June right after exams. I just need to be anonymous. I want to go to some quiet place where no one recognizes me, shut the door and be alone."

Maggie twirled the swizzle stick in her rum and coke. She looked up.

"Are you sure that's what you want, Jess?"

Jesse was alert to the softness of Maggie's voice and the intensity of her question. They had been friends since freshman year at St. Cecilia High School and knew each other well—well enough for her to recognize a deeper meaning behind Maggie's question.

"What, Mags? What's going on in that devious little mind of yours?"

"You would speak that way to a member of the Sisters of St. Joseph? You could be excommunicated." Maggie's eyes were dancing, and her mouth fought to hide a smile.

"I think the Catholic Church kicked me out a long time ago. Probably when I surrendered my virginity to Scott Carlson behind St. Cecilia's Home Ec building," she snickered.

The women's laughter attracted attention from nearby patrons, and in an effort to calm down, Jesse snorted. Both erupted in laughter again bringing disapproving glares.

"I'm glad I didn't wear my habit tonight," Maggie said as she wiped her eyes.

Jesse sobered. "But, you see, Mags, they recognize me," she said as people continued to stare at her and whisper. "At least they aren't pointing and asking, 'Isn't that the woman Robert Cronmiller fooled around on?'"

"Okay, now you're getting maudlin. Enough, Jess. Listen, I have an idea."

"Uh, oh. Your ideas used to get us into a lot of trouble, Sister Angelina. I can't believe they let you into the nunnery…"

"Hamlet means a brothel when he says, 'Get thee to a nunnery.'" Maggie's eyes twinkled.

"Well, career paths do change, Mags. Maybe there's hope for you yet."

"Which brings me to my point. If you are serious about getting away, we have an opening for an English teacher at St. Bartholomew's next fall. The pay stinks, you work with snotty girls, you live in a hick town, but you get a free lunch every day."

Jesse's eyes bored into Maggie's looking for any trace of teasing.

"You're serious."

Maggie nodded. "Yes, I am."

She continued to stare at her friend, but her eyes were seeing possibilities, not what was in the room before her.

"Maggie, your school is just a few miles from the house my Aunt Helen left me. I could live there. I could get away from all of this."

"At least for a while, Jess. It would give you time to sort through it all."

And Jesse's life changed that moment.

Jesse gazed at the huge stone buildings that lined the curved drive of St. Bartholomew Girls' Academy. The first building along the drive was a Gothic revival style dormitory. Arched leaded glass windows perched in the bluestone structure, the clear smooth glass complementing the blue and brown hues of the architecture, and thick sturdy walls rose three stories high. Lounging on the large front veranda were several girls in gray plaid jumpers over white blouses. Jesse smiled to herself, *Ah, the days of wearing a uniform.* She noticed athletic fields behind the building and saw girls in bright red gym shorts and tops playing field hockey.

"Bright red makes it harder to disappear into the trees for a smoke, my pretties," she murmured.

Matching in architecture but dwarfing the dormitory, the academic building came next. At once foreboding in its massiveness, it also commanded an atmosphere of scholarly purpose and she instinctively sat up straighter. Directly across from the school was a parking lot, and she maneuvered her VW into a space nearest the next building: the convent. Smaller than the dormitory, it appeared stately, but more welcoming. She turned off the engine and sat staring at the building. *What the hell am I doing here?*

Resigning herself to her fate, she slid out of her car and climbed the steps to the convent's front entrance. The doorbell sounded deep within the building, and Jesse identified the tune: "Pange Lingua." *You've got to be kidding me.* She fought the urge to run. The door opened with a *whoosh* and a tall, thin nun dressed in full habit leaned into her face and demanded, "Yes?"

Startled, Jesse took a step back, recovered herself, and examined the woman who had barked at her. Dressed in the traditional habit of the Sisters of St. Joseph, the nun looked medieval in a full length black habit tied at the waist with a cincture. Stiff white linen that formed the gimp and coif framed her face, and a large white wimple looked like a giant baby's bib. The rosary beads that dangled from her cincture rattled and swayed with her movement. Her long, black veil fell around her face as the nun glared at her.

"Good afternoon, Sister. I am here to see Maggie— that is Margaret—that is Sr. Angelina."

She watched as the nun's expression changed from merely rude to shocked. The woman scrutinized Jesse and her nostrils flared.

"What did you say your name was?" Her voice challenged.

"Jesse Graham." She thought she should be carrying Toto in a picnic basket.

She took in Jesse's shorts, t-shirt and sandals and scowled at her.

"She is expecting me..." she began, but the nun cut her off.

"Wait out here."

The door slammed in her face.

Seething, Jesse started to descend the steps, but stopped when she heard Maggie's voice.

"Did you like that warm welcome to St. Bart's, Jess?"

She turned and looked at her friend. She flinched at seeing Maggie in her habit, for when they met for birthday dinners, her friend dressed in what she called "street clothes." Jesse was still fuming over her rude treatment, and seeing her friend in her religious habit unsettled her further.

"See what happens when you don't have sex, Maggie? I worry about you," she said.

Maggie laughed. "Even if she hadn't taken vows, I doubt there would have been much sex for Sister Alphonse. Sorry your first taste of St. Bart's was so sour. Most of the sisters are quite nice. Come on in. Where is your suitcase?"

"Let me look around first, Mags. I may decide to sleep with the mice tonight after all."

"Come on, Jess. I'll protect you from Sr. Sunshine. But don't do anything rash, her brother is the sheriff in town."

Laughing, the women headed to Jesse's car to get her suitcase.

"I've got some groceries, too. Can I put them in your refrigerator?" she asked.

"Sure, anything you need. Oh, I see you want to put some demon beer in our sacred refrigerator, too," Maggie said as she lifted out a grocery bag and a six pack of Genesee Cream Ale.

Jesse struck her head with the heel of her hand.

"Crap. I never thought of that, Mags. Just leave it in the car."

"Are you kidding? We love Genny Cream Ale!"

Jesse looked at her in amazement. "They *drink*?"

"You are in for a few surprises, my friend," Maggie laughed.

Dinner was far more interesting than Jesse had expected. She scanned the room counting forty-six sisters total and saw Sr. Alphonse at a far table. She breathed a sigh of relief. During grace she whispered a prayer of thanksgiving for the distance between her and Sr. Sunshine. The nuns sat at round tables of six, and the postulants (Maggie called them "baby nuns") served them. After the salad course, steaming plates of roast beef, potatoes, carrots, and onions were placed in the middle of the tables. During dinner, postulants refilled water, wine and coffee. Jesse savored the beef; the phrase "melt in your mouth" came to her mind. This was food that did more than nourish—it comforted, and she needed a lot of comfort.

The conversations centered on students, curriculum and results of final exams for a while, and then ranged from books currently being read to the local news. Finally, one of the nuns turned to her.

"Sr. Angelina tells us that you have been friends since high school, Jesse."

"Yes, we met in biology class when neither of us had the heart to cut into our frogs. Sr. Catherine was not pleased with us, and we had two detentions cleaning pipettes and slides," she laughed.

"Those weren't our only detentions. Remember the time we had slam books and Sr. Marcus reamed us out?

Our defense was that we were merely saying nice things about people in our slam books," Maggie laughed.

"Yes, things like 'Susan Foreman doesn't look as fat as she did last year.' What wasn't nice about that?" she said feigning innocence.

The nuns at their table laughed as they continued to regale them with tales of their mischief. When the plates were cleared, chocolate torte with raspberries materialized much to her delight.

"You nuns surely do eat well!" she said as she dug into her dessert. Noting the silence, she glanced up, the heat rushing to her face. Scanning the stern faces, she realized she had offended them.

"I apologize, sisters. I meant no insult."

The eldest of the nuns, Sr. Roberta, nodded.

"I am afraid that remark calls for a penance, Jesse," the nun said.

"Yes, sister." She bowed her head. She felt like she was seven-years-old again. How could these women wield such power?

"You have to deal first for poker tonight," Sr. Agnes scolded.

The words didn't register at first, and then she looked up and saw the merriment in their eyes. She felt a rush of relief, and a blush rose to her face again. They all laughed.

"Oh, my God—gosh. You really had me there." she laughed.

Sr. Roberta patted her hand.

"We always have to initiate our guests, Jesse. You handled it very well."

Jesse laughed, warming toward these women who were so dedicated to God, to their students and to each other.

Exhausted, Jesse lay in bed staring at the ceiling, one arm flung over her forehead. She examined the room, noting how it smelled of beeswax and freshly ironed linens. The cherry dresser and small desk gleamed to a high polish as did the hardwood floor. A small rug rested on the floor by the bed, and a crucifix hung above the headboard. It was more comfortable than spartan, but certainly not luxurious.

Had it been just this afternoon when she entered the Cavanaugh House? She wiggled her feet beneath the blankets as she recalled little mouse paws scurrying across her foot. It was going to take a lot of work to get the house into habitable shape. Paint and décor were the least of her worries; she wondered if she would fall through the floor because of rotting wood. The contrast between her house and the tidy room she now occupied made her chuckle.

She reflected on the evening. The nuns had played Scrabble rather than poker, and even as an English teacher, she was challenged by their vocabulary skills. She had flinched when one nun changed EAT to CHEAT, and Maggie caught her eye and winked. Wounds were still fresh, and healing from the pain of her broken heart would take time. But she winked back and recovered by earning a triple word score when she extended CHEAT to CHEATER. Maggie's laugh confused the other sisters, but they attributed it to Jesse's good fortune. She knew it was irony. Yes, somehow Robert's rejection was going to turn into triumph for her. She believed it in her bones.

-TWO-

The Seneca Gas & Electric Company truck pulled in behind Jesse's VW at 10 a.m. on Friday, two days after she had called. Reluctant to enter her house alone again, she had waited for the workman to arrive. He was a slight man in his fifties with a quick smile and bright blue eyes. Together they walked to the back of the house in search of the meters, finding them below the kitchen windows. The man whistled.

"Man, these are old! I'm not sure I'll be able to use them as they are. Could be a replacement job."

"How long would that take?" Jesse asked.

"Well, first we have to see if the wiring can even stand an upgrade to a new meter. Let's take a look-see inside," he said.

She led him to the front door and unlocked it. Today she had worn sneakers and socks just in case. As she opened the door, the man hesitated.

"They say this place is haunted. I don't believe in that sort of stuff myself." His eyes scanned the interior. "No, I don't believe in that baloney." He strode inside. Upon entering, the workman looked around and whistled again.

"You've got your work cut out for you, little lady."

She shuddered at the term and frowned at him.

"Ooops. Sorry, lady—ma'am—uh," he tipped his cap.

"Jesse, just call me Jesse."

"I'm Wes, Jesse. Pleased to meet you. Joe told me you plan to move into this place. You have a lot of pluck taking on a project like this. I suspect you will need new wiring, plumbing, maybe flooring or foundation work. I'm happy to help you, and Joe might be able to help with some of the other." He glanced at her. "It'll get expensive."

Jesse gave a dismissive wave. She had significant savings that would allow for a total rebuild if necessary. All she needed to do was run up to Rochester to make the withdrawal. Her mother had offered little nurturing, but Eileen Graham had provided her a very comfortable life. Besides, she'd be earning that huge salary from St. Bart's pretty soon.

"Can you fix it enough to live in for a while?" she asked.

Wes's face softened. "We'll get you fixed up, pretty lady—damn—I mean, darn. Sorry, I can't get used to this women's libber stuff. I mean no offense."

She smiled at his awkwardness, appreciating his sincerity.

"Don't worry about it, Wes. I'll train you."

"Can't teach an old dog new tricks, Jesse."

"I hope you're wrong there, or I'm in big trouble." She grimaced as she looked around.

The plumber arrived while Wes was still working, and he was equally pessimistic about the condition of the plumbing in the house. He examined pipes for leaks, and fortune shone down when he pronounced them sound. Rusty water ran for 20 minutes before he thought it would be potable; he took a test sample. Jesse had been smart enough to buy distilled water for drinking and cooking, so all she needed was plumbing for bathing and flushing.

Descending to the basement with the workmen had been unsettling for her; she had a strong aversion to cellars. Something about being below ground level gave her the heebie-jeebies, giving rise to claustrophobia and panic. When she had told Maggie that she attributed it to a past life where she was buried alive, Maggie had pretended to be scandalized and made the sign of the cross.

At least she had the workmen with her for her first foray into the underworld. Evidence of mice, both living and dead, produced an acrid odor; she held her hand over her nose and mouth to stifle the stench, but to no avail. The possibility of mice running across their feet didn't seem to worry the men as they went about their business. Keeping a sharp eye out, Jesse examined the basement, which was easy since it was open and unfinished. Cement foundation blocks rose up nine rows which made for a high ceiling. A converted coal furnace stood at the center, its heating ducts running out in all directions like a giant octopus lurking in its lair. Three bare light bulbs hung suspended in a line from the ceiling. Wes laughed when he found the antiquated fuse box.

"I might have some replacement fuses for you, Jesse, but I'll have to dig deep to find them. I think they're in with some dinosaur bones," Wes chuckled. He had examined the wiring and pronounced it safe. All in all, the inspection had been better than she had expected, and both men said they could reinstate service. Wes cautioned her to use nothing higher than a 60 watt light bulb and to update the electrical wiring as soon as possible.

"You'll be able to live here, Jesse, but it will seem as if you're living in the 1940s," Wes said, stroking his chin. "You gonna be comfortable with that?"

She warmed to his sincere concern and flashed him a brave smile.

"I've just left some "vermin" behind me, Wes. Some "vermin" with all the trappings of modern life. Maybe a little old-fashioned living is just what I need."

Now Jesse was alone in the house, looking at the coverings on the rest of the furniture. Frozen in place, she contemplated pulling the drop cloths off and facing the onslaught of more mice. *Nuns or mice, that's my choice,* she thought. She had spent two nights at the convent, and, as nice as the sisters were, she was ready to start her own adventure. Even though the house was dilapidated and the exterminator hadn't arrived yet, she was excited about living here. Something rolled around in her gut sending out rays of excitement—like standing in the roller coaster line. Fear mixed with exhilaration.

She eyed the cover draped over the chair; surely this is where all the mice who fled their sofa home were hiding. Just as that thought struck her, a gray form skittered out from under the couch. Her stomach dropped to her knees, and she began to tremble.

You can do this, Jess. You're much bigger than they are.

Stepping into the living room, she approached the furniture. Why was she so afraid of these little creatures? As she slowly reached forward, her heart leapt at the sound of a loud knock on the front door. Quickly self-assessing, she was grateful she hadn't soiled herself. She pressed a hand to her heart as if trying to slow the beating as she returned to the foyer.

Opening the door, she was greeted by a tall, skinny man with dusty colored hair and goggles that magnified his eyes to twice their size.

"Are you Miss Graham? I'm Erik. You know, Erik's Extermination Service."

Jesse still clutched her chest as her heart began to slow its pounding. It took a moment for his words to register, and when they did, relief mixed with her addled emotions.

"Great! Come in, come in, Erik." She gestured as she opened the door wider.

Erik entered and looked around. "I've got my job cut out for me!"

"Indeed you have. I've already met some of the residents, and I'm hoping you can evict them all— including spiders," she said.

She led him through the rooms on the first floor and then ascended the stairs. Thinking that she and Wes had cleared out all the cobwebs on their excursion to the second story, Jesse plunged ahead running right into the diaphanous strands across her face.

"Oh, crap!" She swept the web from her face and hair. "I thought we got through all of these spider webs!"

"Nature will take her course, Miss Graham," Erik laughed.

The second story consisted of three rooms and a hall. At the top of the stairs to her right was a bathroom with black and white octagonal floor tiles, a sink, toilet with a pull chain for flushing, and a claw-foot bathtub. Its window looked out to the east through the overgrown trees and hedges. To her left, the door opposite the bathroom door opened to a bedroom furnished with a double bed, nightstand, chest of drawers, old leather-strapped trunk and a wooden rocking chair with a reading lamp beside it. She looked over her shoulder at the hall that ran alongside the stair railing. It led to the door of a larger unfinished room that ran the width of the front of the house. Walking to it, Jesse pushed that door open and felt cold; she shivered and looked toward the windows where the bright June sun was struggling to break through the dust and grime. It was a beautiful warm June day, the windows were closed, and there was no draft.

This room was empty save for a chair that sat forlornly in the center of the floor and to the right a tall armoire against the wall. The space seemed to have served as an attic. Unlike the flat eight-foot ceiling in the bedroom, the ceiling in this room opened to a central beam and followed the pitch of the roof. Two narrow windows sat side by side in the front wall of the house.

Jesse rubbed her arms against the chill. A heavy sadness had settled upon her as if emanating from elsewhere. She shook her head and scanned the scene, fearful and elated at the same time. She looked at Eric whose eyes were darting around the room.

"Did anyone tell you that the Cavanaugh House is haunted?" He shivered.

"So I hear," she said. "I don't believe in ghosts. But I do believe in mice and spiders. Can you get rid of them?"

They exited the room and both relaxed a little. Heading down the stairs, Erik got back to the business at hand.

"Well, Miss Graham, you have a lot of places to house critters. I think I'm going to have to bomb your house."

"Bomb my house? Isn't that a little extreme?"

Erik laughed. "I don't mean bomb it as in blow it up; I mean bomb it with insecticide and mouse repellent. You've got mice, spiders, cockroaches, chipmunks—hell, you're running a critter hotel here. I'll come on Monday morning first thing. Then you'll be able to move right in on Wednesday, well, after the clean-up."

"Wednesday? You mean I have to go back to the nunnery? And what do you mean by 'clean-up'?" she asked.

"Well, think about it. There are a lot of unwanted guests here. Once I bomb the place, they will all be deceased—probably right where they are. That's going to be a lot of bodies, and considerable sweeping up."

Jesse's face paled, and her hand flew to her throat. "Oh my God."

"Hey, look. I'll come back on Tuesday and give you a hand. I can haul all of the carcasses to the furnace at the dump."

Lightheaded, she steadied herself with the doorframe.

"Thanks. That would be great." Her thin voice trembled. "I'm sorry to be such a sissy, but I have an aversion to mice and spiders more than anything. If this house had been full of snakes and lizards, I would be okay."

Erik smiled at her.

"All right, maybe not okay, but not this bad."

They laughed as she walked him to the front door. Closing it behind Erik, Jesse turned and surveyed the rooms before her. Sad rooms dimmed by years of neglect, by dust and grime, by a pervading sense of waiting. She felt that as surely as she felt the comfort of sneakers on her feet. Waiting.

Jesse stared at the candles flickering on the altar. Allowing herself to surrender, she was immersed in the sweet voices of the sisters who surrounded her, altos and sopranos mingling in pure harmony. Engulfed in serenity, she wondered if this was what heaven was like. Then she wondered if there was a heaven. Then she wondered if there was a God. When she had returned to her apartment after finding Robert with Peggy, she had collapsed on the floor next to her bed and sobbed. She had pleaded with God to make it all a bad dream. She had prayed that she would awaken and find him beside her, gentle and loving. God did not hear her, or at least He did not answer.

Maggie tugged on her sleeve. The sisters were all sitting down, and she still stood. Dropping to her seat, she gave Maggie a smile of gratitude.

"You were lost in prayer, there, Jess," Maggie whispered.

"I should not be here, Mags. This makes me a total hypocrite. I don't believe in God anymore," she hissed.

"That's okay, Jesse, God still believes in you. Just think of this as a shower of nun prayer washing over you and helping you through this. They are all praying for you, you know." Maggie smiled.

"Shhh!" Someone poked her shoulder, and she and Maggie turned to find the owner of the voice. Sr. Alphonse glared back at them.

Turning back Maggie whispered, barely audible, "Even Sr. Alphonse is praying for you."

"Yeah, she's praying that I leave," shot out the side of Jesse's mouth.

Another poke urged her to silent meditation again, but not about what the priest was saying in his homily. Her mind wandered to the good times she and Robert had enjoyed. When he played the piano and sang to her, she felt like she was the sole person in his world. That was how he had seduced her initially, after a benefit she had attended with her good friend, Marcia. Wandering away from the party and finding herself alone in the library of the host, she had sat at the piano and plunked a few keys of "Twinkle, Twinkle Little Star."

"I see I have some serious competition," spoke a voice from behind her. Startled, she turned to see Robert leaning against the door jamb, arms folded across his chest. His white shirt was open at the collar, tie loosened, his black suit cut to perfection. Jesse thought he should be on the cover of GQ; she also thought her innards had turned to Jell-O.

"Hello," was all she could manage. She watched as he pushed off from the door jamb, a smile playing at his lips, eyes crinkled in mirth, and walked toward her moving like a jaguar, fluid and muscular.

"Hello. I have wanted to say that to you all night," he replied. Standing next to the piano bench, he indicated the space beside her. "May I?" His voice flowed over her like a warm rush of water, and she began to understand what those novels meant when women got "the vapors." Smelling salts—or a stiff drink—were in order. Obligingly, she scooted over and he sat beside her and began to play as if caressing each key. She had no trouble transferring the joy the ivories must have felt to herself. His hands floating across the keyboard, his eyes never left hers and he began to sing.

Oh, yeah, he nailed it—the love song from her favorite movie, *Casablanca*.

"And we know how that ended for Bogey and Ingrid," she murmured breaking the spell.

And it had ended just as badly for us, she thought returning to the present. How could Robert betray her like that? Worse, how could she not have known?

An altar boy rang the bells three times, interrupting her thoughts. Since she was kneeling with the sisters, some part of her brain had attended to the requisite postures during Mass. When it dawned on her that it was almost time for communion, she panicked.

She leaned over to Maggie and hissed, "I can't go to communion. I haven't been to confession in *years*."

Maggie patted her arm. "Are you sorry for your sins?"

"What are you Father Angelina now? You're going to give me absolution or something?"

"Have you committed a mortal sin, Jess? Have you killed anyone lately?"

"Mags, I can't. I can't do this." Her voice was desperate.

"Okay, Jess. Just stay here. It'll be okay."

Maggie rose to follow the nuns in her pew up to the communion rail. Watching her friend, she caught sight of Sr. Alphonse out of the corner of her eye. The woman's glare would shrivel an elephant, and Jesse turned away. Man, those nuns had power in their eyes. They could make you feel like a ten-year-old caught shoplifting.

She suspected all eyes watched her as they passed. *They're wondering what grievous sin I've committed. Oh, if they only knew the wild and wanton life I've been living.*

Maggie returned and knelt beside her, placing her face in her hands. Through her fingers she whispered, "I'm praying for your blackened soul, Miss Graham." Then she turned her head and winked at Jesse.

Jesse wandered the aisles of the hardware store; she found something appealing about this place. Even if a person didn't know a nail from a screw, shelves lined with little drawers full of tiny metal objects meant somebody knew the difference and knew how to use them. That was solidly reassuring. Running her fingers along different brushes with bristles ranging from soft to almost brittle, she wondered which kind would work best for all the scrubbing soon to be in her life. One of each kind joined the heavy work gloves, mop, broom and dustpan in her shopping cart. She wondered if they sold work boots—good sturdy ones that could deflect a fleeing mouse. Distracted by thoughts of mice, she rounded the corner and smashed her cart into another one pushing it into its owner.

Joe turned and grinned at her.

"If you're trying to get my attention, Just Jesse, you could call out my name."

She knew she was blushing. With her skin coloring, there was no hiding the fact, and the more she tried to stop it, the hotter her face grew.

"Hi, Joe."

He glanced at the items in her shopping cart.

"Looks like you're going to be a busy lady—woman," he corrected. "I can't get this new terminology down."

Pleased that he tried, heck, that he even was aware of it, she smiled.

"I'm getting ready for Erik to bomb my house. He said the subsequent clean-up effort could be daunting."

"When is he coming to do that?" he asked.

"He's bombing on Monday, we're cleaning up the carcasses on Tuesday and I can move in and start to clean on Wednesday."

Joe stifled a grin. "Wow, it used to be laundry on Monday, ironing on Tuesday, shopping on Wednesday. This women's lib thing is really working."

Annoyance flared and she leaned her face into his. He held up his hands in a defensive motion.

"I was just pulling your chain," he laughed. She realized he had anticipated her scolding.

"You were earning some brownie points a minute ago, but you just lost 'em." She scowled at him.

"Let me earn them back. I'll come and help with the clean-up of a million mice on Tuesday," he offered.

Jesse saw the twinkle in his eyes and couldn't stay mad, but did she want him to help her with this? She realized how much she enjoyed his company as they stood together in the aisle, and a red flag went up. Being attracted to another man this soon after her break-up with Robert was neither wise nor a part of her "newly independent" plan. She hesitated, wanting to be independent, but dreading the aftermath of the bombing of the Cavanaugh House. She sensed his eyes on her as she tried to decide whether or not to accept his invitation.

"I promise I won't make any more inappropriate 'cave-man' statements." He placed his hand over his heart and looked solemn, but his hazel eyes danced with amusement.

Jesse let a half-smile break as she thought about her decision. It would be great to have his help, and she was strong; she could control any attraction she had for him with common sense.

"Okay. If you want to come and scoop up a million dead mice, you can. But if you don't behave yourself, I'll kick you out and you won't be able to have any more fun."

They laughed and their gaze held a bit too long. Both straightened and looked around at items neither needed.

"Well, then, I'll see you on Tuesday," she said.

"See you then." He pushed his cart down the aisle and disappeared around the corner.

Watching him, Jesse realized she would need a lot more common sense.

As promised, Erik had arrived on Monday and set off bombs throughout the house. Standing next to her Beetle wearing her new sturdy work boots, Jesse had watched him enter the front door. Tensing for an onslaught of rabid mice, she'd grasped the door handle poised to jump into her car if needed. No wrathful herd had exploded from the house, and she had begun to breathe easier despite the acrid fumes wafting her way. Lugging his equipment, Erik had emerged from the house looking like an astronaut with his bulky suit on.

Today he was back with brooms, dust pans, shovels, and a wheel barrow.

"You ready, Miss Graham?" he asked handing her a white face mask.

"I don't think I have a choice, Erik," she said as she pulled her hair back into a pony tail.

Hearing an engine behind them on the street, Jesse turned to see Joe pull up in his truck. He hopped out and plonked on a New York Mets baseball cap.

"Joseph P. Riley reporting for duty," he said slapping a smart salute.

"Hi, Joe. You don't have to do this, you know," she said, but grateful nonetheless.

Joe shook hands with Erik and exchanged greetings.

"Oh, it'll cost you, Jesse." He smirked.

"What does that mean?" she asked.

"This isn't a free service from me. Erik's getting paid, so I should reap some reward as well." He winked at Erik who turned and examined the tree tops.

She jutted her chin.

"Just what do you expect from me? What *reward* did you have in mind? Is this how you treat friends? Now I *owe* you something? Just forget about helping." Jesse's face burned and she clenched her fists in rage.

"Whoa, whoa, whoa! This is my payment: Come to Tony's with me this Friday. The perch dinner is the best around, and they push all the tables back to clear a dance floor at nine."

Hearing Erik chuckle behind her increased her fury. Now she felt foolish as well as angry. She swung around and scolded him.

"This isn't funny, Erik," she seethed. "You both should be ashamed of teasing me when I'm going in to face death and destruction!"

Trying to control their mirth, both men fought the grins breaking across their faces. Finally they burst out laughing. Watching them double over and slap each other on the back, she crossed her arms and tapped her foot.

"Well, if you're not going to join me Friday night," Joe said trying to catch his breath, "I'll head home and try to find something constructive to do."

He started for his car.

"No, wait. Please."

The men stopped laughing and Joe looked back at her.

"I need…I need…," she couldn't say it. She wanted to be independent, standing proud and strong on her own two feet facing whatever challenges life threw at her. But she wasn't strong at that moment. She felt small, alone and afraid. Asking for help was like cutting out her heart.

Joe walked to her and draped an arm across her shoulders.

"I'm here for you, Just Jesse." His voice washed over her like a warm rain. Her throat tightened with emotion as she stifled a sob.

He squeezed her shoulder and dropped his arm. "What you need are two manly men who will face death and destruction with you."

She glanced at Erik, skinny and shy with eyes magnified by his goggles, peering over the mask he wore. Manly indeed.

Finally, she laughed and they grinned.

"You two are terrible! I'm an emotional wreck and you set me up for an eighth-grade boy joke?" she scolded through her laughter.

Her knees wobbled a bit as they all approached the house. It seemed to lean toward them, appearing larger than it actually was. A looming presence. She squared her shoulders and followed Erik up the steps and into the front foyer.

Jesse was not prepared for the scene before her. Lying scattered about as if tossed into the rooms at random lay hundreds of mice. Pungent odors hung in the air, and dust motes floated in the sun filtering in through the grimy windows. Suspended from the ceiling and walls as if caught in a snapshot drooped webs containing spiders, insects and insect parts. Nothing moved in the heavy stillness. A shiver zigzagged from the nape of her neck down her spine.

"Nicely done, man," Joe said patting Erik on the back.

Erik crossed his arms and smiled as he surveyed the job. "I take pride in my work."

Jesse wondered at their nonchalance and chalked it up to men's cold hearts. *Not fair. These were vermin and bugs, not people.* And she wondered if Robert had cared at all when he saw the destruction he had caused in her life. *All men are not Robert,* she reminded herself for the hundredth time.

"Let's get to work," Erik said heading out the door to get the wheelbarrow.

They spent the morning scooping up carcasses and dusting down cobwebs. After inspecting the upholstered furniture, they agreed it wasn't salvageable after serving as a mouse hotel for more than a quarter of a century. Erik and Joe carried the sofa, chair and mattress to Joe's pickup truck and tossed them in the back.

After collecting his check, Erik bade them farewell and hopped in his truck. As he drove away the silhouettes of mice, termites and bugs painted on the back of his vehicle shrank and disappeared.

"How are you doing, Just Jesse?" Joe asked brushing a wisp of cobweb from her hair. She flinched. "Sorry," he said dropping his hand.

She lifted her mouth in a half-smile. "I'm doing."

"This was a tough day. How about some lunch? Trudy's diner has a great tuna melt," he offered.

"Thanks, but I think I need to keep going on the house while I've got the motivation." She was tempted to accept his offer, but knew she had to stay with the tasks at hand or this house would conquer her and freeze her in fear. She glanced up at it again, opposing attraction and repulsion filling her.

"You're a pretty brave lady."

"Woman," she corrected.

"Woman," he repeated, smiling.

Jesse sensed his reluctance to leave as he put his hands in his pockets and scanned the yard. If she were honest with herself, she wanted him to stay, but she had to do this on her own. And she was not ready for entanglement with someone—not yet. She had a lot of healing to do before she could open her heart to someone new. Her eyes followed his across the high grass and weeds.

"I could help with your lawn...yard...," he said.

"Joe, I think I need to work on my own right now."

He turned and looked at her, then squinted toward the sun.

"Cool," he said as he turned toward his truck.

She looked at the yard again realizing what a Herculean task it would be. Joe was offering help not a marriage proposal. It would take her weeks to do this on her own, and she wanted to move in as soon as possible.

"Tomorrow?" she asked.

He stopped and turned back to her.

"I don't want to push myself on you, Jess. I get it. You need space." His eyes searched hers. "Someone hurt you very badly." He turned and walked toward his truck. Waving out the window, he pulled away from the curb.

Jesse watched the dust kick up behind him as he drove down the road.

Indeed, she thought.

On the counter next to the sink sat a radio from which music floated out, blending with the soft hum of the ancient refrigerator. Jesse had been relieved at the cold interior of the appliance when she loaded in her groceries, but she grimaced at the sight of the small square freezer compartment that cradled her pint of Neapolitan ice cream. She couldn't store anything atop the refrigerator since it sloped downward rather than having a flat top. But the groceries and the beer fit just fine, and she was planning the first meal in her new home: Zweigle's white hot dogs, Charles Chips potato chips and Genny Cream Ale. Not her usual healthy diet, but stress had a way of determining what went into her shopping cart.

The bathroom and kitchen had been her immediate targets for a thorough cleaning. She was just finishing up scrubbing the last of the kitchen countertops when she heard a pleasant ringing tone. Looking around, she spied the chimes of the doorbell hidden behind the open kitchen door. Hurrying to the foyer, she opened the door to find a large red bean bag chair that appeared to have arms floating in front of her. Maggie's face peeked around one side.

"Happy New House," she cried.

"Maggie! How did you know I was seatless?" she laughed as she grabbed the bean bag chair from her. Maggie bent down to retrieve another that sat on the porch next to the door.

"Are you kidding? Generations of mice must have taken a toll on your furniture," she laughed.

"This is so cool. Hey join me for dinner—Zweigle's white hots!"

"You sweet-talker! How can I resist? I'll need to call the convent and let them know, though. Oh, do you have a phone yet?"

"Yikes, I hadn't even thought of that! I was happy to achieve dead mice and running water. I'll contact the phone company tomorrow. Hey, I'll bet you could use Joe's phone; he lives less than a mile away."

"Let's go," Maggie said.

Susan Riley answered the door, explaining that Joe was out for the evening. Jesse was surprised at her disappointment on hearing that; what difference should it make to her if he was out for the evening? She brushed the feeling aside and introduced Maggie to Susan who was startled to be welcoming a Sister of St. Joseph into her home. A sister who did not wear her habit. Susan made a pot of tea while Maggie phoned the convent. Jesse often felt Susan's eyes on her making her uncomfortable.

The women made small talk for a while, and then Susan turned and faced Jesse.

"Jesse, I must tell you that your Aunt Helen was my dear friend. I can't help staring at you because you are her spitting image."

Jesse was relieved at that explanation, which made perfect sense. Her mother always threw it in her face that she looked like Helen instead of her. She suspected that was one of several reasons why her mother had always been so cold toward her. For as long as she could remember, she had never measured up to Eileen Graham's expectations, and Eileen never missed an opportunity to remind her of that. She had inherited the auburn-hair and fair-skinned ancestral genes, not the raven-haired beauty genes of her mother. Combined with her emerald green eyes, Eileen looked exotically beautiful. In contrast, Jesse always believed that her own combination of reddish hair and green eyes made her look like an orange cat. The only year she ever remembered her mother dressing up for Halloween, Eileen was a beautiful, sensuous witch, and she dressed Jesse as her "familiar." She rubbed a finger along her upturned nose, another point of contention which her mother had encouraged her to alter with plastic surgery. Susan patted her hand.

"I'm sorry about what happened to your aunt," Susan said.

"Thank you, Susan. I guess it was a terrible accident," she replied.

The ticking wall clocked measured the silence. Finally Susan spoke.

"Accident?"

"Yes, the car accident that killed my Aunt Helen," she said, apprehension forming as she watched Susan's face. The woman's eyes flicked away from Jesse's.

"What is it, Susan?" Maggie asked.

Susan looked from Maggie to Jesse. Leaning forward, she took Jesse's hand.

"Jesse, honey, your aunt didn't die in a car accident." She looked at Maggie as if asking for help to reveal the information she alone knew. She looked back at her. "Sweetie, your aunt committed suicide."

Ears ringing, Jesse couldn't comprehend the words Susan had uttered. Her mother had told her about her aunt's automobile accident once, and that was about all she ever said about it. Looking for photos for a fourth grade project, she had come across a picture of the two sisters when they were quite young.

"Who am I with here, Mother?" she had asked pointing at the photo.

"That's not you, Jesse. That is me with your Aunt Helen."

"I have an Aunt Helen? Can I meet her?"

"No, she died years ago." Eileen lit a cigarette and blew out the match.

"How did she die? Was she sick?" she had asked, staring at the photo.

Her mother puffed out a cloud of cigarette smoke, rolled her eyes, and explained that a winter storm had come up as Aunt Helen was driving home from the hospital where she worked as a nurse; another driver slid across the road and hit her head on.

"No, my aunt was killed in a car accident. My mother told me about it..." she looked up at Susan and stopped. The realization hit her. "My mother lied."

The look in Susan's eyes confirmed her statement.

"But why would she lie to me about that? Maybe it was just too messy for her ideal world. Having a sister who committed suicide would mar her own perfection, thus the lie."

She tried to digest this news, to make some sense of it. Her mind hopped around like a crazed rabbit, ultimately settling on one thought.

"How?"

Susan looked at Maggie as if she would help her escape this question.

"Before you ask questions, Jesse, be sure you want to hear the answers." Susan's voice was soft and gentle.

Jesse looked out the window as the clock ticked on. She looked back at Susan.

"How?"

"She hanged herself, Jesse,"

"In the Cavanaugh House?"

"Yes."

-THREE-

Jesse lay on top of the sleeping bag in the middle of the living room staring at the ceiling. Dinner with Maggie had not been the celebration she'd intended as conversation had centered on the news of her Aunt Helen's suicide. They sat in her new red bean bag chairs, sipping Gennys and discussing Susan's revelation. The reasons she had come up with for her mother's deception made sense. Mother wanted everything neat and tidy, abiding no distasteful situations, let alone a skeleton in the family closet.

Jesse's thoughts turned to her aunt. Was she a perfectionist, too? Somehow, she didn't think so. This house did not reflect the personality of a perfectionist even as it must have been when it was fresh and lived in. Her mother's house was spotless, tastefully decorated in the latest style with the most expensive furniture. Decorated in scuffed antiques and mismatched furnishings, Helen Cavanaugh's house suggested a woman of simple, even eclectic tastes as revealed by some items Jesse had found upstairs like a cowgirl outfit and old six-shooter. Neither item would have made it past Eileen Graham's solid oak front door with the artist-commissioned stained glass window.

What had caused Aunt Helen to take such a drastic action? Was her life so unbearable that she had no alternative but to end it? What brings a person to that decision? Thoughts flitted through her mind, sleep evading her. She thought about getting up and reading for a while when she heard a soft scraping noise.

Oh no, Erik missed a mouse.

She heard it again, and it seemed to come from the room directly above her. Too big to be a mouse. Was it a bigger animal?

She turned on the table lamp, grabbed a hammer that she'd been using earlier, put on her sneakers and crept up the stairs. She stopped to listen when she reached the top.

Scritch. Scritch. Scritch.

The noise slid under the door of the front attic room and slipped up to reach her ears. Gripping the hammer, she moved toward the door. She grasped the glass knob and turned it, pushed the door in and switched on the light. The 60-watt bulb in the ceiling fixture lent a soft glow to the room and cast shadows in the corners. Her eyes travelled across the room peering into places that might conceal a critter. Nothing.

Scritch.

She turned toward the window and saw a tree branch that appeared to brush against the pane. Letting out a breath, she realized she'd been holding it in since entering the room.

"Jesse Graham, you have a vivid imagination," she said aloud. Smiling she turned off the light and closed the door.

Scritch. Scritch. Scritch.

She paused. That noise came from the side of the room where the armoire was, not from the window where the tree stood. She shook off her suspicion and went down the stairs.

A loud knock woke Jesse from a restless sleep. She stumbled to the front door to find Joe standing on her porch with a scythe in his hand.

"Great way to start the day," she yawned. "Awakened by the Grim Reaper."

"At your service, ma'am," he said, bowing. "I see you were in the arms of Morpheus."

She yawned again and scratched her head.

"Rough night," she said.

"Well, this is a noiseless chore, so sleep away," he laughed.

Jesse squinted at the sun. "What time is it, anyway?"

"Ten."

"Holy crap, I'd better get moving! You get started, and I'll be out in a few minutes." She slammed the door in his face and heard his chuckle on the other side. A ticklish sensation in her belly told her she was glad Joe was here, but she dismissed it.

The memory of the odd sounds of the previous night crept into her mind, and in the bright sun that streamed through the newly washed windows, she discounted it as midnight sillies. Her bare feet slapping on the hardwood floors, she sauntered into the kitchen and poured a bowl of cereal, eating it over the sink as she watched Joe walk, swinging the scythe. He methodically hewed a path along the back of her property, the tall grass and weeds flying along either side of him. She was well aware of the warmth he enkindled in her, and she chalked it up to gratitude for how helpful he had been since she arrived.

That's all—gratitude.

The sun baked Jesse as she walked the lawn, creating rows of cut grass covered with the long blades that toppled out of the old push mower. Captured within the red-bandana fabric of her halter top, her breasts swung with her gait, her pony tail bobbing in rhythm. She loved the freedom of anonymity that required no preening. The muscles of her long, tanned legs flexed as she pushed off driving the mower forward. She knew she would pay for the exertion tomorrow, but she hoped a hot bath and some Ben-Gay would ease the anticipated muscle aches.

A far-off memory of walking with her father as he mowed their lawn with a similar machine came to her; he had made it seem so easy. Her hands had gripped just inside his, barely reaching the handle; he walked slowly so she could see how the lawn mower worked. She remembered the smell of fresh-cut grass, a smell that always had reminded her of her father and how secure and safe she had felt with him. A thick twig caught in the mower, halting it.

"Oooommph," she cried, surprised as the handle slammed into her stomach.

"Are you okay?" Joe called.

Jesse gave him a thumbs-up, removed the twig and kept mowing. The recollection of her father persisted. She hadn't seen him in the 23 years since her parents' divorce when she was five-years-old, yet every memory of him brought with it a warm, sweet emotion.

Joe had worked all morning, swinging the scythe to cut the grass and weeds back to a mowable length. He'd brought the push-mower to follow up, but Jesse insisted on managing that chore. Now she followed the swaths he had cut and mowed them down to size. They had worked steadily, breaking for a quick sandwich at noon. The afternoon sun was arcing toward the west as they covered the last part of the yard, and her hands burned with blisters through the work gloves she was wearing.

Joe had taken off his shirt earlier in the afternoon, and it was all she could do not to stop and watch the muscles ripple across his back as he swung the scythe back and forth hewing the tall growth. Sweat glistened off his shoulder blades and ran in rivulets down his spine to the top of his cut-off jeans shorts. His freckled skin was smooth and tanned, and Jesse stole more glances than she'd like to admit.

Susan stopped by at suppertime with a picnic basket full of ham sandwiches, potato salad, fresh radishes and tender lettuce from her garden. They moved the kitchen table and chairs to the backyard and enjoyed the feast beneath the trees, admiring the newly reclaimed lawn.

"Jesse, let me see your hands," Susan cried, noticing the blisters.

She examined Jesse's hands and declared them in danger of infection.

"I have some ointment I'll bring over; you need to keep these clean and apply the ointment often."

"I'm fine, Susan, honestly," she protested.

"I insist." Susan dropped Jesse's hands indicating the discussion was over.

Joe grinned. "That's what comes from having a mother who's a nurse. You're never safe from mercurochrome and peroxide." Susan winked at him and a pang shot through Jesse as she remembered her own mother's indifference to any injury, or Eileen's anger if Jesse's needs interfered with her schedule. Then a memory stirred.

"Susan, my mother told me Aunt Helen was a nurse. Is that how you knew her?"

"Yes, we met working the same shift in the maternity ward at the hospital. Oh, how Helen loved those babies, and when...," Susan stopped. "Oh, look at the time. I need to get back to the house for my bridge club. I'll just have time to run the ointment over and show you how to apply it."

"Susan, don't go to any trouble...," she said.

"No trouble at all, Jesse." The woman smiled at her. "I'm happy to help."

By dusk, Jesse and Joe had salvaged what they could of the shrubs that surrounded the house and outbuildings.

After loading the equipment into Joe's truck, she was reluctant for him to leave.

"How about a nice cold beer?" she asked.

His smile was quick, and her heart fluttered. Fearing he would somehow see that in her eyes, she looked away and led him to the porch.

She brought out two bottles of Genesee beer, handed one to Joe, and they clinked them together in a silent toast to a job well done. Sitting on the porch steps in the twilight with him seemed so natural. The incessant call of peepers mingled with the chirp of crickets in the fresh-cut-lawn-scented air. Jesse savored the moment of peace. Leaning against the post, she closed her eyes and let the nightfall envelop her. When she opened her eyes, he was looking at her.

"What's your story?" she asked, her voice soft in the darkening night.

"Well, I was born in—," he started. She punched him in the arm.

"Owww! I've been slaving all day and now you beat up on me?" He feigned outrage.

"Oooh, sorry," she cried. "Did I hurt you?" In her concern she rubbed his upper arm. Then looking up at him caught the twinkle in his eyes. "Oh, you're fine," she said slapping his arm.

"Geez, Jesse, take it easy," he laughed. "Seriously, what do you want to know? I'm pretty boring."

"I doubt that Joseph P. Riley," she laughed, then sobering asked, "How long have you had your own construction business?"

"I took it over when I returned from Vietnam. I'd studied mechanical engineering and earned my B.S. before I was drafted, but when I got back from Nam, I knew I wasn't suited for a desk job. My dad owned the business and couldn't run it any longer, so I bought it. I like working with my hands, creating with wood, building, and I like the freedom of being my own boss. For big jobs, I hire a crew."

"Master of your own destiny. I like that," she said.

"How about you, Jesse? What's your story? How did you end up moving into the most run-down house in this county?"

"It's complicated." Jesse stared across the yard toward the road, her chin cupped in her hand, elbow resting on her knee. She avoided looking at him.

"Cool," he said after a moment of silence.

Turning, she looked into his eyes. "I don't think I'm ready to talk about it yet."

"It's okay, Jess. When you're ready, I'm here if you need me."

Struck by the soft understanding she saw in his eyes, she recognized how easily she could melt into him at that moment. She stood, breaking the spell. Joe stood, too.

"It's been a long day." Her voice shaky, she looked up at him and continued. "Don't be too nice to me, Joe. I can't take tenderness right now."

She took his empty bottle, turned and went into the house.

"Good night," she called as she closed the door.

Jesse slept deeply until just after midnight when she was awakened by the same noise she'd heard the previous night.

Scritch, Scritch, Scritch.

There was no wind. In fact the night was still and no breeze came through the open windows. She tried to ignore the fear that pricked at her. Surely there was a logical explanation for the sound; she needed to figure this out once and for all. She turned on the lamp by a red bean bag chair and started for the stairs. Again, the noise came from above her; that would be the large attic room. She climbed the stairs and moved toward the door registering every creak the floorboards made. *Funny how you don't notice noises like that during the day*, she thought.

Her hands felt sweaty as she grasped the doorknob, and they slid around the glass ineffectively. She wiped her palm on her t-shirt, grasped the knob tighter and turned it; the catch released. She inched the door open, switched on the light and stepped into the room.

Nothing. Nothing moved, nothing made noise, nothing seemed out of place. Jesse scanned the room, then knelt down to look under the armoire, holding her breath lest any critters survived Erik's full-fledged attack. All clear. Glancing at the window, she observed that the tree branch didn't touch the pane at all. When she turned to leave, she noticed that the door to the armoire was ajar; she was sure she had closed it after inspecting the clothes hanging inside. She approached it and yanked both doors wide causing the fringe on her aunt's cowgirl jacket to swing making a swishing sound.

"You certainly had curious taste, Aunt Helen," she said aloud.

She heard a sigh. Her scalp tingled and she broke out in a clammy sweat. Closing the doors of the armoire, Jesse hugged herself against the chill. As suddenly as she felt it, it was gone. She trembled as she looked around for the source of the draft. Finding nothing, she turned off the light and hurried out of the room, closing the door behind her.

Returning to her sleeping bag on the living room floor, she lay down and pondered what had just happened. Not only did she inherit a dilapidated, abandoned, old-fashioned house, apparently it was haunted as well. Haunted by her dead aunt who hanged herself. Probably in that upstairs attic room.

Great.

Joe had said he would pick her up at six on Friday. She spent more time than she intended getting ready. After all, they were just going to a fish fry. It wasn't like they were going to The Rochester Club where she used to wear glamorous gowns and real jewels for evenings out with Robert—rich, gorgeous, talented Robert. Every woman's dream with his jet-black hair often tumbling over his clear blue eyes—eyes that seemed to look into your soul—and a fantastic build. If his looks were not enough, he was a gifted musician who beat the odds and made it big—big enough to live a life of luxury. While often in New York City playing gigs, he preferred to be in Rochester, where life was less hectic and he was just a home-town boy. Well, not exactly—he was always recognized and adored, and Jesse knew that was the elixir of life for him. Putting on a show of humble acceptance of his gift endeared him even more to his public, but when alone, he would mock the people who jostled to be near him or invited him to social events so their names would appear with his in one inch of column space on the society page of the *Times Union*.

Her thoughts returned to the present as she checked her appearance in the mirror. She wore a pink and orange paisley dress with an empire waist and baby doll sleeves. Choosing taupe flats over sandals, she then put on a headband the same orange as in her dress. Pale pink lipstick glistened on her lips and a dusting of teal eye shadow enhanced her green eyes. She added a little more blush and fluffed her hair, dismissing the idea that she wanted to look good for Joe.

At the sound of the doorbell, she hurried down the stairs and opened the door. Joe whistled viewing her from head to toe.

"Tony's will move up the ranks with you there tonight, Jesse."

"Am I too dressed up? I can change."

"You look pretty…uh, great. Is it all right to say pretty?" he asked, his puzzled look eliciting a laugh from her.

"It's all right with me! Thank you, Joe." Her heart felt lighter than it had in months. "You look great, too," she added. Indeed he did with a buttoned-down-collar blue oxford shirt tucked into khaki pants and brown leather boat shoes. They smiled at each other and then wavered in their awkwardness. Jesse was at a loss for words; Joe finally spoke.

"Let's go! The fish are frying and the music is loaded in the juke box."

Tony's was a low-slung building with a wide veranda holding several round tables snugged with ice cream parlor chairs. Stepping inside, Jesse was transported back to the 1950s; the floor was a black and white checkerboard, and red padded booths lined the walls. Each booth's table had a jukebox selector attached to the wall, the large jukebox itself holding court at the far end of the room. Tables and chairs scattered across the floor, many cobbled together to accommodate parties of eight or ten. A counter formed a J along the wall to the left, and metal stools with matching red seats swiveled beneath their occupants as they turned to chat with a neighbor.

Jesse sensed a lull in the lively conversations as they entered. Patrons glanced in their direction, and then leaned in to speak to others nearby. Taking her elbow, Joe guided her toward an empty booth near the back of the room. Like a wave, conversation resumed and many called out greetings.

"Hi, Joe!"

"Hey, Joe, how're you doing?"

Comfortable, he moved among the tables shaking hands and patting backs. Jesse sensed a vitality in him, an energy that shimmered off and floated back to her, reassuring and solid. She knew he felt proud to be seen with her. She was uncomfortable at how comfortable she felt by his side. He introduced her as they moved along. The sea of faces and din of names rolled through her head then immediately deserted her. She smiled and acknowledged the welcomes and greetings, noting that people reacted with varying degrees of disbelief at her living in a reputedly haunted house.

If they only knew, she thought.

Settling into the booth, Joe pushed aside the menus and folded his hands on the table in front of him.

"I thought you'd like to try the all-you-can-eat perch dinner. It's the house specialty on Friday nights," he said adding, "but if you want to try something else, it's A-okay."

"I'll trust your judgment on this one," she laughed as the waitress set two glasses of water before them. They ordered beers and Jesse looked around the room seeing people still glancing her way. A man sitting at a table with a large group rose and came over, sliding into the booth next to Joe. She noticed a subtle shift in Joe's demeanor, not anger but a quiet disdain that simmered just below the surface.

"Joe, please introduce me to your new friend," the man said as he looked into Jesse's eyes. Blue eyes with flecks of gold held her gaze, direct and almost demanding, causing her to catch her breath. A sense of déjà vu overtook her. She somehow knew this man, and her attraction was immediate but more curious than amorous. He held his hand out across the table; wrapped in his smile was a legacy of confidence and privilege.

"I'm Al Wyndham, and I believe you are Jesse Graham."

"News travels fast in Seneca Corners," she said, shaking his hand.

"News of pretty girls travels fast."

Joe ducked, waiting for Jesse's women's lib tirade, but none came. Instead she smiled at Al with a faint hint of amusement. Joe looked from one to the other.

"So you're a friend of Joe's?" Jesse asked.

"We go way back, don't we, Joe? We were classmates all through school and played football—took our team to States, didn't we?" Although he directed his remarks to Joe, his eyes never left hers. She shifted, uncomfortable under his scrutiny. "So what possessed you to buy that dilapidated old house? Surely there were other more desirable properties out there to choose from, Jesse."

"Actually, I didn't buy it; I inherited the house from my Aunt Helen Cavanaugh," she said, watching him. She noticed a flinch and wasn't sure if it was from sympathy or disbelief.

"I'm sorry. I didn't know that," Al replied, his voice sincere.

"No problem; no apology needed." Jesse sat back as the waitress set their beers in front of them. The waitress beamed at Al before turning back to another table.

"I mean, it's tragic how she died…how they found her…I mean, I'm sorry," Al stumbled over his words. "You know that house is …"

"Let it go, Al." Joe's voice was low, a veiled threat. Al looked at him as if he'd forgotten he was even there. A challenge passed between them. Al stood.

"Save me a dance later, Jesse?" His eyes flicked to Joe and back to her. Unsure what the local custom was, she glanced at Joe who shrugged.

"Sure, Al, I'll save you *one* dance." Glancing sideways, she saw a corner of Joe's mouth turn up for an instant.

The waitress returned with two plates loaded with hunks of golden fried fish, crisp cole slaw and a stack of steaming french fries. Jostling more than seemed necessary, she playfully pushed her hip into Al and then bent over the table to set down the plates. Al moved aside and nodded before he returned to his table. The waitress looked over her shoulder at him, her disappointment as tangible as the food before them.

"Need anything else?" she sighed.

"No, we're good. Thanks," Joe replied.

"There's a story here," Jesse ventured.

"For another time, Jess. We're here to eat and drink and dance too much; we need to conserve our energy for that."

Digging into their dinners with gusto, they limited conversation to progress on the Cavanaugh House. Gradually, they began the slow process of revealing themselves through childhood stories of little matter, edging down the road toward trust. A road Jesse wasn't sure was on her map anymore.

As their enthusiasm for fish waned and forkfuls were less plentiful or frequent, another man sat down beside Joe.

"Where's the money you owe me, Riley?" The man was tall and muscular, his shirt tight around muscled biceps and pecs. His deep bass voice added danger to his appearance as if his size were not deterrent enough. Thick black hair waved wildly above his face like he had run his hands through it many times since the last combing. Jesse set her fork down and wished she hadn't eaten so much since her stomach was knotting up.

"You'll get your money, Bugsy, I just need time," Joe answered.

"You'd better not call the coppers, Riley," the man said thrusting his face into Joe's.

"You ARE the coppers, fool!" he spat back.

Jesse froze. Then the two men threw their heads back and guffawed like schoolboys.

"Oh my God, you scared the crap out of me!" Her eyes sparked.

Wiping his eyes, Joe slapped his friend on the shoulder.

"Sorry, Jesse. We do that all the time." He paused to catch his breath. "You should have seen the look on your face. It was better than the mouse day."

The other man wiped his eyes, too, his large frame still shaking with laughter. He stuck out his hand and said, "Marty D'Amato."

Jesse broke into a smile as her hand disappeared into his grasp. His eyes crinkled with delight, and his boyish grin made it hard not to like him immediately.

"Marty is our local law enforcement," Joe said.

"Keeping Seneca Corners safe is the name of my game," he laughed.

"Then where were you during my home invasion?" she asked, suppressing a smile at his startled look. All business, he took out a small notebook and flipped it open taking a stub of a pencil from his shirt pocket. Joe's shoulders shook with mirth.

"When was this break-in, Jesse?" he asked.

Keeping a straight face, she tapped her chin as if garnering the precise moment. "Um, I think it was Wednesday, June 26."

"Do you know the approximate time?" he asked as he scribbled.

"Around 1 p.m. Oh, they were animals" she answered, pulling the corners of her mouth down.

"Did they take anything?" His eyes were locked on his notes.

"They took my breath away," she answered.

Joe was curled into the corner of the booth holding his stomach. Marty looked up at her.

"What?"

"My breath. I couldn't breathe for a few moments."

He shot her a quizzical look then looked at Joe.

"Okay, you two. What's going on?"

Joe exploded into laughter and Jesse released the smile she'd been fighting.

"They were mice."

Marty stared at her processing her words. "Mice?"

"My house was invaded by mice."

"Millions of 'em," Joe added.

He flipped his notebook shut and grinned. Shaking his finger at her, he said, "You got me good, Jesse."

"She did, man," Joe agreed.

"Where are you living with a million mice?" Marty asked.

Jesse sighed, knowing the answer would bring the same reaction from Marty as everyone else. Joe answered for her.

"Jesse moved into the Cavanaugh House."

"You're pretty brave to live there regardless of a million mice...in fact, why are you?"

"I inherited it from my Aunt Helen."

He looked at her for a full moment; she saw the quick intelligence hidden behind his brawn. Whatever he was thinking, he was following a long line of ideas. She watched his eyes as they focused, not on anything in the restaurant, but on information and data. When he returned to the present, he looked at her.

"Sorry about your aunt," he said softly.

Of all the condolences she had heard, this one especially touched her and tears stung her eyes. Surprised, she shifted in her seat and looked down at the remains of her meal.

"Thanks," she answered.

"If there is anything I can ever do..."

"Thanks," she repeated.

As if on cue, everyone rose from the tables and began pushing them into the back wall. Chairs were distributed along the remaining walls, and a young man came out of the kitchen and began sweeping the floor.

"Time to dance!" Joe announced.

The evening flew by in a flurry of the Twist, the Pony, the Locomotion and slow dances during which Joe achieved a balancing act of distance and interest, boosting Jesse's comfort with him. During a Beach Boys ballad, Al claimed his promised dance and swept her away from Joe.

"Are you enjoying the night life of Seneca Corners?" he asked with a smile playing at his lips. While his question did not seem sarcastic, it carried a hint of derision.

"I'm having a great time," she replied, realizing as she said it that she was, indeed, enjoying herself. There was a sense of freedom here that she had not experienced for the last several years in Rochester. Nights out on the town with Robert meant flashbulbs and reporters not to mention people who wanted to get "next to" him— especially the women. He always took it in stride, exuding patience with the lowliest of them all only to scorn them back at the apartment when they were alone. Looking around, Jesse appreciated the paper decorations, the strung Christmas lights and the time-worn seats mended with gray duct tape. Simple surroundings, simple fun—it was heaven on earth to her.

"You and Joe have hit it off very well. Are you...uh...going steady?"

Leaning back to look at him, she tried to determine if he were joking. His face was deadpan, and she believed he was serious.

"Gosh, Wally, did the Beaver tell you that?" she asked looking at him out of the corner of her eye.

He tilted his head and scrutinized her, then broke into a boyish grin.

"I think my life-long residency has stunted my social graces," he laughed.

Jesse believed he was blushing. She decided he could be charming if he didn't realize how charming he was.

"Joe has become a friend who has helped me out of a couple of tight spots," she remarked. "We are not dating, and I am not interested in dating at present. I have enough on my plate just whipping my new-to-me house into some order."

"So no dating, but you do eat dinner don't you?"

She saw what was coming but wasn't quick enough to deflect it.

"Will you have dinner with me one night, Jesse? I would like to become a friend, too." He said it so gently that she could not refuse. Looking up at him, she saw his smile and wondered how many times he got out of mischief with that sweet face.

"Sure, I'll have dinner with you sometime, Al," she said.

The music stopped and Joe was quick to reclaim her for the next dance—The Twist this time.

"Soooo…" he implied a question.

Jesse scanned the room aware that he was dying to know what she and Al had discussed.

"So, what?" she asked, her eyes wide.

"So what did you two talk about?"

"Not much." Feigning indifference she looked at the dancing couples around them. She slid her eyes up to him and saw his dismay.

"Al wanted to know if we were going steady."

Though the music continued for several more beats, Joe stood still.

"What?" His face was screwed up as if she had spoken to him in a foreign language.

"Steady. Are we steadies."

"Are you serious?" He tried to get back to the rhythm of the song but looked more like a Raggedy Andy doll being tossed around.

"I'm not ready to get serious," she teased.

Joe stopped his pretense of dancing.

"He asked you that?"

She nodded.

"So what did you say?"

Jesse noted his keen interest in her reply.

"I said you were my good friend."

He straightened a little at that. "*Good* friend, huh?" He looked pleased. The music stopped and they returned to their booth for a beer.

"I'm honored to be your *good* friend, 'Just Jesse.'" His crooked smile caused that stirring in her that she wanted to avoid.

"He also asked me out for dinner. I said yes."

Joe's face fell.

Jesse slept soundly that night and awoke refreshed, excited about fixing up her house. Her home. She needed to think of it as her home, because truthfully, she had nowhere else to live. Returning to her mother's house was out of the question; she shuddered just thinking about it. Looking around the living room, she folded up her sleeping bag and stuffed it in a corner. She rather liked this house. With the old peeling wallpaper gone, the soft sage green on the living room walls lent a cheery atmosphere. Cream drapes hung in simple lines framing the windows, and a taupe and forest green rug gathered her two bean bag chairs and the table into a cozy area. Soon her sofa and mattress would arrive and she would finally be able to sleep in a bed upstairs.

Next to the room where the scraping always echoes.

Hearing an engine, she went to the front window expecting the furniture van, but saw a police car pull into her driveway instead. Static from the two-way radio carried through the front window as Marty emerged dressed in his police uniform. Settling his hat on his unruly hair, he hitched up his belt and walked to the door. Jesse opened it and greeted him.

"Hi, Marty. Should I be worried?"

He grinned and stepped inside.

"Hey, Jesse. I was patrolling around here and thought I'd come see about your home invasion." Eyes crinkled with mirth, his laugh was infectious.

"Come on in and check the place out," she said.

He took in the fresh paint and polished wood floors in the rooms and let out a whoop.

"Wow, Jesse, you've been working hard! I can't believe how much better this looks."

"Oh, have you been inside before? Should I notify the police of trespassing?"

He took off his hat and circled it in his hands; he looked like a little boy caught stealing from the cookie jar. He looked back up at her.

"Well, you know how kids are. We never actually came inside, but we always tried to see in the windows. As young kids, we'd dare each other to come up on the porch—real Boo Radley, you know what I mean? We'd ride our bikes down on summer nights and climb trees trying to see through the upstairs windows where she…" He stopped speaking and looked at her. Her eyes were locked on him. "Man, I'm sorry, Jesse. I'm so used to just thinking of this as the Haunted House with no personal connection to Miss Cavanaugh. I apologize… I didn't mean to…I should have thought…" Embarrassment caused his words to tumble out. She put a hand on his sleeve.

"It's okay, Marty. I get it. I want to know more about what happened. I just found out that my aunt committed suicide; I'd always believed she died in an automobile accident."

He shifted and looked around the living room. Jesse suspected something more to the story.

"What can you tell me?" She whispered as if she did not want to scare away any hope of his sharing information with her.

"Just rumors, Jesse. You know how legends spring up and stories grow and get bigger than they actually are…" His voice trailed off. "I'd better get back on patrol."

"What are you not telling me? Honestly, it's okay. I've been lied to so often lately that I'd welcome any morsel of truth that came my way, no matter how painful. Truth never hurts as much as lies do." She felt his eyes on her as she fought back unexpected tears.

"Some say she didn't commit suicide. Some say she was involved with—well, with people who could endanger her life. There are rumors that she… Jesse, what good will it do to rehash rumors? Those aren't truth, and besides—,"

"You mean she might have been murdered?" she gasped, realizing the meaning behind his words. "My poor Aunt Helen."

"Now I didn't say that, Jesse. I said there were rumors—nothing was ever proven." he protested.

"I'm like Alice down the rabbit hole. It just gets curiouser and curiouser," she said as if to herself.

"I'd better get back to work," Marty said as he covered his mop of hair with his police hat. "Sorry I ever brought any of this up, Jesse."

She murmured goodbye as he closed the door, her thoughts drifting back more than twenty-five years.

"So Marty hinted that your aunt's life had been in danger?" Maggie sat with her feet curled under her on Jesse's new couch. Sipping the chardonnay as she contemplated this, she twisted a lock of hair around her finger. Rain pattered against the windows, competing with the Chuck Mangione album playing in the background.

"He said something about her being involved with people who could do her harm, or something like that. Put her in danger. It blew my mind, Mags. First I find out she didn't die in an accident, then I think she committed suicide, now it sounds like she could have been murdered. It's like my world is getting crazier by the minute. I don't know what's real anymore. I'm feeling pretty...not weak, but fragile. It's been less than a year since I found out about Robert cheating on me. Now I find out my mother's been lying to me all these years. I don't know who to trust anymore."

"You can trust me, Jess. I will always be here for you," Maggie said.

Jesse smiled at her. "Of that I have no doubt, Miss Maggie-pants."

"Besides, who else do I have that will allow a nun to come over, drink too much, and crash on her couch? We need each other, Jess. And we know too much about each other!" Maggie laughed and clinked her wine glass against Jesse's.

"Maggie, I want to find out the truth about my aunt's death. You've lived here for what, seven years now? Would you help me? Would you nose around a little and see what you can find out? Too bad you can't hear confessions—hey, maybe Father Steve knows something. How long has he been at St. Bart's? He hears confessions at Sacred Heart in town, doesn't he? Maggie—maybe he knows something!"

"Even if he did, the seal of confession prevents him from even going to the police, Jess. You know that. He can't tell anyone what he hears in confession. Besides, we don't even know that anything like that happened to your aunt. It was reported as a suicide, wasn't it?"

"That's what Susan said. I think I'll ask her about it. She knew Aunt Helen—they worked together, so she probably knows more than anyone." Jesse stared at the candle burning in a Chianti bottle on the table. Various colors of wax had dripped down the neck and followed the straw covering around the wide base. She watched as the current red candle dripped down to join the others, mingling red with green, blue, yellow and white. "It will all come together, I just know it."

"I think your nocturnal noises have you imagining things," Maggie said. "Have you heard any more of them?"

"Not for a while. Hey, maybe Aunt Helen will show up tonight while you're here," Jess laughed. "Are you sure you want the couch tonight? I have a huge double bed now, so you're welcome to bunk with me."

"You know I snore, Jess. You'd never get any sleep, let alone hear Aunt Helen," Maggie said rising to carry her wine glass to the kitchen. She set the glass in the sink, yawned and stretched. "I am ready to catch some z's. How about you?" She padded back into the living room and started spreading a sheet over the sofa.

"Sounds good to me."

Jesse turned off the kitchen light and headed upstairs.

Slowly rising to consciousness, Jesse became aware of the sound.

Scritch, scritch, scritch.

Sitting up, she turned on the lamp next to her bed and listened. A few minutes later, she heard it again.

Scritch, scritch, scritch.

As usual, it came from the attic room. She threw back the covers and headed to her door. She walked down the hall and paused outside the room to listen. No breeze blew tonight, and the rain had stopped earlier. Nothing was causing that tree to brush against the window; besides, she had already confirmed that the tree didn't reach the pane. She shivered. What could be causing this? There had to be a logical explanation. Her quips about Aunt Helen haunting the house had been half-joking, but deep inside she wasn't sure it was a joke.

She had never thought much about ghosts before. Sure movies made millions off scary stories and books had loyal followings of readers who loved to be scared as they read late at night. Jesse was pretty practical and believed in what she could hear and see and touch. That was part of the reason she had fallen away from the Church; if faith in the unseen was what you needed, she was out of luck. She often envied Maggie for her complete devotion to her faith because more and more Jesse had little to believe in.

There it was again.

Scritch, Scritch, Scritch

She tried to pinpoint the location of the sound before she opened the door. Previously, the minute she entered the room, the noise would stop. Maybe if she knew exactly where to look when she entered she would catch sight of something...she hoped, not a critter. *So you would rather see a ghost than a mouse? Yes, I would.*

Scritch, Scritch, Scritch

She determined that the noise came from the middle of the room right in front of the windows. Gathering her courage, she stepped forward to open the door when a hand touched her shoulder.

Jesse screamed and Maggie jumped.

"It's just me, Jess!" Maggie cried.

Jesse saw the fear in her friend's eyes and knew that she had heard the sounds, too.

"Oh my God, Maggie. You scared the shit out of me!" Too late, she realized she was mixing prayer with vulgarity. "You heard it, didn't you?"

Maggie nodded, her eyes wide. Pressing her ear against the door, Jesse held a finger to her lips and waited. They listened for a full five minutes, but heard nothing. She eased open the attic door and turned on the light. As before, the naked bulb cast a soft glow over the room, but this time the bulb was swaying. She checked the usual places but came up with nothing.

"Did you notice the light when we came in?" she asked.

Maggie nodded.

"It seemed to be swinging a little, didn't it?"

Maggie nodded again.

"I think Aunt Helen is trying to tell me something."

Maggie's eyes were bloodshot and she was quiet, even for 6:30 a.m., as they sat across from each other at the table.

"What are you going to do, Jess?" she asked.

"About what?"

"About living in a haunted house. You can't stay here!" Maggie said.

"Mags, I have nowhere else to go."

"You could be in danger. Aren't you afraid?"

Looking out the kitchen window, Jesse weighed that question. While the noises always startled her, and she explored the attic room with apprehension, she wasn't afraid. More and more she was convinced that the noises were somehow connected to Aunt Helen, but they didn't threaten. Each time, she was curious but not fearful.

"No, I'm not afraid, Maggie." She shifted her gaze to her best friend. "Not at all."

Maggie peered at her. "You really aren't, are you? I'd be terrified. I *was* terrified last night. I never got back to sleep! How do you feel when you hear the noise?"

"I feel…I don't know…intrigued, curious. I want to find out how it's happening, and more importantly, why. If it is Aunt Helen, and right now I have no other reasonable guesses, is she trying to communicate with me? Is it because of what Marty said and she is trying to reveal the truth about her death?"

Maggie nodded. "I've heard of stories like that. The avenging ghost."

"I'm not sure she wants vengeance, Mags. Maybe she just wants peace."

They carried their dishes to the sink and Maggie filled it with soapy water. Jesse filled their coffee cups with what remained in the pot and dumped the grounds in the trash can. Grabbing a towel, she began to wipe the orange juice glasses.

"I think it's time to pay Susan a visit," she mused.

"You'll get to see Joe, too," Maggie smiled at her out of the corner of her eye.

Jesse rolled her eyes and flicked the towel across Maggie's behind. "Maggie," she warned in her don't-mess-with-me voice. Maggie laughed.

"Well, he's very sweet and obviously quite smitten with you," Maggie laughed.

"Smitten? Really, Mags, smitten?"

"You know he is, Jess. Are you going out with him again soon?"

"We didn't 'go out,' Maggie, we went to a fish fry…together. That's not exactly 'going out.' That's eating fish while someone sits across the table from you."

"Well, when you put it like that it's about as romantic as a sack of potatoes," Maggie said. "But wasn't dancing involved? *Slow* dancing?" Maggie drew the word out.

"Yes, and he was very respectful. No pawing or hand sliding down across my ass or anything. Plus, I didn't dance just with him."

"That's right. When is Mr. Al Wyndham, heir to Wyndham Estate, going to sit across from you and eat fish?"

Jesse rolled her eyes again. "Cute, Mags. He has invited me to a Founder's Day celebration at his home. So I will drive over there, eat some fish across the table, watch some fireworks and drive home. Period."

"Speaking of fish, he'd be a great catch." Maggie waggled her eyebrows as Jesse groaned.

"There's no spark there, Mags. He's nice enough, intriguing, but I'm not attracted to him that way."

"Which begs the assumption that you *are* attracted to Joe in that way," Maggie said folding her arms in front of her and raising her chin.

Jesse felt the familiar warmth mixed with the confusion that spread through her at thoughts of Joe. "No. I'm on sabbatical for a while, Maggie. A long while. I'm still licking my wounds from the Robert debacle. Between his lies and my mother's I don't trust anyone anymore." She caught Maggie's eyes. "Present company excluded, of course."

Susan sat on her patio beneath the canopy of a spreading oak. The early July sun was high, as was the humidity. Jesse hadn't seen Joe when she pulled into the driveway, and she tried to ignore her disappointment. Walking toward the patio, she was grateful for the shade of the oak; it was going to be a killer day.

"Hi, Jesse," Susan called as she approached. "Hot enough for you? Why do we say those inane kinds of things? I suppose you should answer, 'Hot enough to fry an egg on the sidewalk,' which we will probably see on the six-o'clock news tonight."

They laughed together as Susan poured iced tea. The ice swirled around clinking against the sides of the tall glasses, beads of water forming and running down the sides. Taking a sip, the cold liquid shocked Jesse's throat and slid down to her stomach. Uncovering a tray of lemon bars, Susan held the plate out to Jesse who took one and placed it on her dessert plate. She licked the powdered sugar off her fingers.

"I love lemon bars," she murmured as she bit into one.

Susan smiled at her, then cocked her head.

"I was so pleased when you called asking to come over, Jesse. Joe was disappointed that he couldn't be here to say hello, but he had to run over to Geneva to supervise a job."

Jesse had just taken her first bite of lemon bar and was savoring the sweet-sour flavors that fought for attention from her palate. Her mouth watered as the smooth filling mixed with the flaky crust. She nodded and pressed the napkin to her mouth.

"I noticed he was gone, but that's okay, Susan; I wanted to talk to you alone," she answered.

"I suspect you have more on your mind than lemon bars, right?"

She gave a half-smile and put down her napkin. "Yes."

"Jesse, the other night I said to be sure you want the answers to questions before you ask them," Susan reminded her.

"I know. It's just been such a jolt to discover that my Aunt Helen did not die in an accident as my mother led me to believe."

Susan waited in silence for a moment.

"What do you want to know?" she asked.

Jesse sat back and turned her glass around wiping off the drops that had formed on the outside. Looking at Susan, she said, "I've just found out that Aunt Helen might have been murdered." She noticed that Susan flinched at that remark. "I want to know the truth. However painful, I need to know the truth."

"I'll answer your questions, Jesse, but I was not privy to the information gathered when they found Helen."

"I understand."

"Helen was my best friend, and I knew most of her secrets. Ask your questions, and I'll be honest with you," Susan said.

"Thank you." Jesse's voice was soft. "How was she found?"

"A neighbor, Claudia Harris, was out walking that night. She claimed she walked because her husband snored and she couldn't sleep. Actually, she was a closet smoker and that was her one chance to sneak a cigarette in at night. Her nocturnal smoking hikes took her around the road where she received free education about her neighbors via their lighted windows. I'm not saying she was a voyeur or a peeping Tom, but walking by windows at a casual pace can supply interesting tidbits. Once she was caught sitting on the hood of a car that brought her up level with a window; another time she was standing on a patio chair. She prided herself on discretion while taking great pleasure in sharing these bits of information. Kind of like Teddy Roosevelt's daughter Alice who had a pillow embroidered with, 'If you don't have anything nice to say, come sit by me.' Anyway, that night she walked by Helen's house and noticed a light on in the second story window which had never been lit. A figure seemed to be silhouetted against the light. Out of "concern" for her neighbor, she climbed a tree to look in and saw Helen..."

Susan's voice caught and Jesse saw sadness in her eyes. Looking out across the yard, Susan continued.

"Claudia almost fell out of the tree, and she began to scream, waking a neighbor who found her clutching the branch frozen in fear. He called the police who arrived shortly after."

Silent tears streamed down Jesse's face as she stared ahead. Even though she had never met her Aunt Helen, she was moved as she thought about the young woman whose life had become so desperate that she wanted to end it. Or perhaps she had somehow become such a threat that someone wanted to kill her. Jesse shuddered thinking about the fear her aunt would have lived with if that were the case. And now Aunt Helen's ghost was trying to communicate with her—at least that's what seemed to be happening. Looking at Susan, she saw tears in her eyes, too. And something else, perhaps sympathy. Should she confide in Susan about the mysterious noises she heard at night? She wasn't sure she was ready to do that; not that she didn't trust Susan, but it was rather bizarre. Susan, if put off by the notion of a ghost, might think Jesse a little strange.

"Aunt Helen must have been terribly distraught or terribly afraid if something so serious was occurring in her life. Did she say anything to you about it?"

Susan shifted in her seat and took a sip of her tea. Placing the glass on the table, she rubbed the moisture off with her thumb.

"Helen was involved with someone and I don't think it was going well. I found that out because I stopped by one day and found her crying so hard she couldn't hide it from me. She would not tell me whom she was seeing. She said it was complicated, so I assumed he was a married man."

"So someone might have harmed her if she threatened his marriage or reputation..."

"Yes, but, Jesse, murder is pretty extreme. Couldn't they have bribed her or offered her something in return for her silence?"

Jesse considered this for a while.

"How did you meet her? What was Aunt Helen like?"

Susan sat back in her chair and lowered her shoulders, the tension in her face smoothing out.

"We met in nursing school at the University of Rochester. We shared an apartment and moved through our coursework together, which made it easier and more fun than it probably should have been. Helen wasn't above a practical joke or two, and we got called on the carpet a couple of times with a warning about professionalism. We used to have parties where we'd decorate with inflated examining gloves and use IV hookups to deliver the strongest garbage can booze. Oh my gosh, the world was our oyster back then! She loved to dance and we'd hit the nightlife scene in Rochester on our limited time off. Helen dated some very nice men, but never became serious. She helped me through some hard times with a couple of men I dated, and stood by me when I was so down I considered dropping out of nursing school. When we graduated I talked her into moving here with me to work at Grayson State Hospital because both of us were fascinated with the mental health classes we took. It used to be called the Grayson Asylum for the Insane, and it was quite intimidating for us to work among the poor souls there. We lasted a couple of years and then took positions at Geneva General Hospital. That was just a 20 minute drive for us, but we had plenty of time to chat."

"Susan, do you suppose someone from the Grayson State Hospital could have been released and harmed Aunt Helen?"

"I suppose anything is possible. Most patients never left the facility because programs and treatments back then were basically to control them, not to rehabilitate them. There was little understanding of mental health issues and it was more punitive than remedial. I guess if someone were released without the appropriate treatment…"

Susan looked at her. "Jesse, you couldn't find a better friend. Helen was a loving, giving, fun person." She stopped, took a deep breath, and continued. "We were very close until she started seeing whoever she was last involved with; then she started withdrawing. When she died, I lost my best friend." Susan looked at her and then looked off in the distance. "Who would have thought…"

The high-pitched whirring of cicadas filled the silence and a gentle breeze blew across Jesse's face. The serenity of the sun-washed day belied the sadness that enveloped the women. Watching a fuzzy caterpillar inch its way across a paving stone, Jesse reflected on all that Susan had shared. Something still unsettled her. Susan obviously had no more information about her aunt's death. But she had to find out more about the events that took place that night over twenty-five years ago.

It might be time to have another conversation with Marty.

-FOUR-

Speeding along Routes 5 & 20, Jesse remembered visiting the Finger Lakes area as a child. The memory of its charm returned as she skirted Seneca Lake. Those had been some of her happiest days, waving sparklers through the firefly-lit night, toasting marshmallows until they caught fire and burned to a delicious black crisp that instantly dissolved in her mouth, swimming in the crystal clear waters of the glacier-formed lakes. Like far-off voices, memories of playing along the shore and riding in a small fishing boat with her father floated through her mind.

Brought back to the present she leaned forward and cranked up the radio. WBBF was airing a Beatle's afternoon, and she couldn't get enough.

"Can't Buy Me Love" was playing, and she sang along with the Fab Four. "Boy, that's for sure," she murmured thinking of Robert. She tightened her lips and clenched the steering wheel, the familiar anger rising within her as she drove. She floored the gas pedal and was rewarded with a shudder from her Volkswagen Beetle. Realizing it was ridiculous to even expect a surge of power from her bug, she patted the dashboard.

"Sorry, Bert, I shouldn't have even asked."

She downshifted as she contemplated how this evening might unfold. Al had invited her to Wyndham Estate for the annual Founder's Day celebration. Since many guests were invited, she could avoid the awkward first date getting-to-know-you conversation, for seeing him in his natural habitat would speak volumes. Also, she could remain comfortably anonymous.

She turned south down Route 14, pulled over, and checked the map again. Finding the road indicated, she turned into a long drive dappled by sunlight filtered through the leaves of ancient oaks. Jesse sucked in her breath when she saw Wyndham Manor rising through the trees. Constructed of red Medina limestone, the structure boasted four-stories with turrets at the front corners. Large rectangular windows with beveled glass glistened in the late afternoon sun that was beginning its descent in the west. Manicured lawns and shrubs surrounded the manor, precision clipped in each blade and branch. From the huge carved oak door, broad steps stretched outward like arms trying to envelop anyone near and guide him inside. Above the door was a Tiffany stained-glass transom window with a border of fleur-de-lis panels. Along the circular drive Jesse spotted car models ranging from Mercedes Benz to Porsche to Lincoln. She groaned when she saw valets perched and waiting at the steps.

"This ought to be good," she said patting Bert's dashboard again.

Pulling up, she put the car in neutral and set the emergency brake as a young man stepped forward and opened her door. To his credit, he never cracked a smile but simply assisted her out, climbed in and drove away. She suppressed the giggles that bubbled up, not sure if they were due to the ridiculous situation she had just faced or nerves. She had hobnobbed with crowds like this before, but Robert had always been beside her. Going it solo was uncharted territory, though she took solace in knowing what fork to use when. Hearing her name, she looked up at the front door and saw Al bounding down the steps.

"Jesse, welcome to Wyndham Manor!" He took her hand and placed a peck on her cheek. His genuine pleasure at seeing her put her at ease.

"Nice little place you've got here, Al," she said laughing as he dragged her up the steps.

"Come in, come in! The party is in full swing," he called back to her.

High oak wainscoting with raised moldings ran along the walls, and the marble floor gleamed white with veins of grays and black. Stained glass windows with the fleur-de-lis pattern marched above the wainscoting at regular intervals. Guests mingled in the rooms on either side of the foyer, and Al steered her to the room on the left. Standing just inside the door was a woman in a taupe silk pant suit, her blonde hair swept up in a beehive hairdo. Large gold hoop earrings dangled from her earlobes as she chatted with two guests. Her demeanor and the way she wore her clothes spoke of wealth, and although attractive, the sharpness of her features marked her as striking rather than beautiful. Al stopped next to her and she turned to him, smiling.

"Mother, may I introduce Jesse Graham? Jesse, my mother Monica Wyndham," Al said.

Monica Wyndham turned and held out her hand. "How do you do, Miss Graham?"

"It's a pleasure to meet you, Mrs. Wyndham. Thank you for inviting me to your Founder's Day celebration."

"Our pleasure." She paused, studying her. "Have we met before?"

"No, I just moved to Seneca Corners from Rochester."

"Jesse is the newest member of St. Bart's faculty, Mother. She is replacing Sr. Perpetua, God rest her soul."

Jesse started. She hadn't realized she was replacing a deceased nun. That would skew the holiness factor at St. Bart's. Mrs. Wyndham nodded, smiled and returned to her conversation elegantly dismissing them.

"Let's get you a drink," Al said making a path through chatting groups of people. "How about a superb Riesling from our vineyard?"

"That sounds perfect," she said as she scanned the crowd for any familiar faces. She noticed a couple of women who had been sitting at Al's table at Tony's, and it was obvious they had spotted her first. They smiled and waved half-heartedly. *I think I have "competition" emblazoned on my forehead. No worries girls, I'm not interested in Al.* Jesse smiled and waved back gaily. Sipping the wine he gave her, she was impressed by its delicate effervescence.

"Excellent," she said. He beamed at her compliment.

"My family was one of the first to introduce the Riesling grape to the United States back in the 1800s. This area was perfect for growing these grapes, and we owe much of our success to this noble fruit. We do grow other varieties as well such as our award-winning Cabernet Sauvignon."

She raised her glass. "Riesling has become a new favorite for me. I salute your ancestors." She smiled as he lightly clinked his glass against hers.

"Well, let me introduce you to them. Come with me." He crooked his arm, and she laughed and slipped hers through it. He escorted her through two rooms filled with the pleasant chatter of guests enjoying Wyndham hospitality. Finally, he swept open a door that led to a hallway lined with windows on one side and portraits on the other. Jesse scanned the pictures noting by the clothing styles that they covered at least a century. Al led her to the far end of the hall.

"Here is my great-great-great grandfather Bartholomew Wyndham. He is the patriarch who planted the original vineyard. He's a crusty looking old boy, isn't he? But we owe all of this," he spread out his arms to indicate the estate, "to him." Al blew him a kiss. "Thank you, sir." He bowed.

Leading her along the hall, he mentioned other relatives whose portraits graced the wall explaining how each was related to the other and completely confusing her. He paused beside the portrait of a corpulent man, a silver flask partially concealed in his broad hand.

"This is the Bartholomew who navigated the tricky waters of Prohibition. With great ingenuity, and a few bribes, he maintained a game room on the second floor that served liquor brought in from Canada via the lake and some well-hidden roads. There will be a test on this, you know. As a first-time guest to Wyndham Estate, you will be expected to memorize the history of each."

Jesse's eyes grew wide.

Al laughed. "I'm kidding, Miss Graham."

She drew her hand across her forehead in mock relief. "Whew!"

Laughing, Al led her to the more recent portraits, including one of three young men who looked strikingly similar.

"Ah, the current heir." He looked with affection at the faces smiling back at him. "Father, I'd like you to meet Miss Jesse Graham, Miss Graham, my father."

"Which one? Are they triplets?"

"No, although my father and Bartholomew are twins." He pointed to the two men who flanked the one in the middle.

"Another Bartholomew?" she asked. "Your family must love that name."

"'Tradition!'" he sang striking a post like Tevye. "We have always had an Albert and a Bartholomew in the family."

"Any connection to St. Bartholomew's?" she asked.

"Yes. We founded St. Bart's." He pointed back to a previous portrait. My great-grandmother did not want to send her daughters away to boarding school, so they built one close enough for them to be away but not far."

"So the Wyndham family owns the school." She looked back at the portrait and then at Al. "All of you Wyndham men look alike, so which one is your father?"

Al pointed to the young man on the left. "This is my father, Benjamin Wyndham." He pointed to the youth on the other side. "And is my uncle Bartholomew. He lives in New York City and visits occasionally. Although he's two minutes older than my father, he prefers the financial side of running the estate rather than the husbandry side." He pointed to the young man in the middle. "This was my other uncle, Albert. He was the oldest, but he died before I was born, so I never knew him."

"So why are you named Al and not Bartholomew?"

"My younger brother Bart is away at school in Germany learning the mysteries of the Riesling grape."

"So he's the heir to the estate? But you're older; aren't you the heir? Oh, no, it would be Bartholomew's son who would inherit."

Al laughed. "It is a bit confusing, isn't it? Traditionally the first son is named Albert and the second son is named Bartholomew, and so far that has worked. Uncle Bart never intended to have children, so the mantle of responsibility falls to me. Thus I am named Albert, but much prefer Al."

"Oh, you poor dear. Having to live in such luxury for the rest of your life. Let me get a tissue to wipe my tears," Jesse whimpered.

Al laughed and then cocked his head. "None of this impresses you, does it? Most women who get this tour want to know my net worth and if I'm seeing anyone seriously. But you appear considerably underwhelmed."

"I hope my underwhelmedness doesn't offend you, Lord of the Manor," she said bowing. "No, Al, I've been lucky to live very comfortably, but I have learned that the old adage is true: money can't buy happiness."

"You're quite refreshing, Jesse." Al smiled.

"You haven't seen my prickly side yet," she answered turning to head back to the party.

Chuckling, Al followed her back through the hall to the living room. Guests chatted and laughed over generous glasses of wine, and others spilled out onto the patio where they enjoyed a jazz trio playing in the shade of a large canopy. The song was one that Robert often had played, and she resisted the nostalgia that swept through her. She wondered what he was doing for the summer; he usually had several gigs booked and she had always been beside him. She wondered if Peggy had replaced her there, too.

Sensing her mood change, Al steered her toward a bar set up just inside the living room.

"I think you need a refill," he said handing her another glass of wine.

Over his shoulder, Jesse saw a striking man in his fifties enter the room; tall with dark hair graying at the temples, his handsome face held arresting blue eyes and a square jawline, an older version of one of the young men in the portrait. Sweeping his eyes across the scene, he appeared to be assessing the mood of the room. Satisfied, he smiled. Beside him stood a shorter man who appeared a bit older, stockier and more alert. He also gazed around the room, but no smile appeared. Rather he appeared annoyed at the presence of so many guests in this home.

Turning, Al followed her gaze. "There's my father. Come, Jesse. I'll introduce you."

The taller man reached for a glass of red wine from a passing server as she and Al approached him. He turned to answer the shorter man who was leaning forward, speaking quietly to him. Upon reaching them, Al spoke.

"Jesse, I'd like you to meet my father, Benjamin Wyndham. Father this is Jesse Graham."

Shifting his gaze back to Al, his father smiled, caught sight of Jesse and spilled the red wine down the front of his white shirt. Looking at her, the man next to him swore under his breath. For a moment, both stared at her, and then Al's father regained his composure and started wiping at his shirt with a napkin.

"Father, are you all right?" Al asked.

"Fine, son, fine." He extended his hand to Jesse. "How do you do, Miss...?"

"Graham. Jesse Graham. It's so nice to meet you, Mr. Wyndham." She felt warm and a bit lightheaded as their eyes met and she shook his hand. *Powerful wine*, she thought.

"Jesse just moved into the Cavanaugh House," Al said.

The man froze. His eyes glazed over, as if his mind were elsewhere. He still held her hand, and she began to withdraw it bringing him back to the moment.

"This is Fred Morton, my father's accountant and right-hand-man," Al said nodding at the shorter man. The man did not extend his hand. His eyes bored into hers as she spoke.

"How do you do, Mr. Morton?"

"Miss Graham." Nodding curtly, he turned to Al's father. "Let's get you a clean shirt, Ben."

Jesse was taken aback by the man's rudeness, but Al didn't notice. As the two men left, he took her elbow and steered her toward the patio. The cool breeze off the lake improved her sense of balance, though she was still a bit unsteady. Al began a long round of introductions which she could not have remembered on a good day, let alone after the encounter she'd just had.

She met all the important leaders of Seneca Corners, from the mayor to the pastor to the manager of the Sears and Roebuck. While none of them reacted as strongly as Ben Wyndham had, Jesse detected a curiosity from many. They scrutinized her as if trying to decide where they'd met her before. Sheriff Donoghue seemed the most surprised, and she saw him flinch when he first laid on eyes her. His eyes widened and he tossed back his

Scotch, but he regained his composure as Al approached him.

"Jesse Graham, may I introduce you to the man who keeps Seneca Corners safe from all crime? This is Sheriff Bill Donoghue."

"How do you do, Miss Graham?" His handshake was firm, and like Ben Wyndham's lingered a bit longer than necessary.

"How do you do, Sheriff Donoghue?" She wondered if she had reached the hundredth time saying that phrase today. Sheriff Donoghue stared into her eyes as if trying to discern something, or as if seeing something else. Yes, Helen must have made quite an impression on this town for so many people to be shaken by Jesse's resemblance to her. Self-conscious, she released his hand.

"What brings you to Seneca Corners?" he asked.

"I've taken a teaching position at St. Bartholomew's."

The sheriff's eyebrows shot up. "So will you be living here?"

Al spoke up. "Yes, Jesse is Helen Cavanaugh's niece. She has moved into the Cavanaugh House."

She was becoming used to people's reaction to that news. Like everyone else, Sheriff Donoghue grimaced.

"The Cavanaugh House? Is that house even habitable after all of these years? Rumors have circulated for decades that it's haunted. Maybe you should rethink that decision, Miss Graham." He looked at her with concern. "We wouldn't want anything to happen to you."

Jesse shivered but quickly composed herself. "I don't believe in ghosts, Sheriff Donoghue. It's the living who haunt me." She smiled, trying to soften her words. "I meant all the mice and spiders that were 'haunting' the place. They're all gone now, and I've had some repairs done so the house is perfectly habitable now."

"Well, that's good. If you are on faculty at St. Bartholomew's you will work with my sister, Sister Alphonse." Sheriff Donoghue said.

Jesse winced at the memory of her encounter with the nun. He displayed none of the rudeness of his sister; in fact, he seemed quite taken with her.

"Yes, we've already met. Actually, your sister was the first to welcome me to St. Bartholomew's." She tried to disguise the wry note in her voice.

Pensive, he peered down at her and nodding, he gestured with his glass. "If I can be of any assistance to you, Miss Graham, please call on me at any time. Nice meeting you." He turned and walked away.

Al introduced her to more people as they mingled on the patio. She smiled and made small talk. As she tilted her head back to sip the last of her wine, she saw Fred Morton scowling down at her from an upstairs window. Catching her gaze, he retreated and disappeared.

Sunset blazed in a glorious swirl of orange, red and mauve on the western edge of the lake. The water's fiery reflection quivered in the lapping waves as the evening crept toward dark. Shifting from the veranda, the crowd spread across the lawn and out across the dock and the shore as everyone jockeyed for advantageous viewing positions for the fireworks. Children ran through the crowd waving sparklers and shrieking with excitement while parents half-heartedly hushed them. Now Jesse sat with Al and a group of his friends on the deck of a sailboat moored just offshore.

"So you're going to teach at St. Bart's?" asked a pretty blonde who sat beside her.

"Yes," Jesse replied.

"I graduated from St. Bart's. You will love it there. I know people always make fun of nuns, but I had great teachers and they're really...well, people, you know?" She tilted her head as she made her point, her long straight hair falling across her shoulders. Jesse had spent most of the day with her, as she appeared to be one of

Al's closest friends. When introduced she said her name was Barbara, "not Barbie like the doll, *please!*" Below straight bangs, her bright blue eyes crinkled with humor as she said it indicating years of teasing.

Now they sat on cushions leaning against the side of the boat sipping wine.

"Did you teach in Rochester?" Barbara asked.

"Yes."

Barbara mulled this over, then asked, "Why would you leave the city to come to such a small town?"

Looking out at the water, Jesse didn't speak right away.

"Sorry, I didn't mean to pry," Barbara said. "It's just that Rochester has so much night life and theatre and music…"

"I know. I just needed a change."

"That's cool. Hey, have you been to Roseland Amusement Park yet?" Barbara said, changing the subject. She rambled on about childhood trips there and her favorite rides. Hearing the first boom echo across the water, Barbara cried, "Oh look! The fireworks are starting!" Jesse appreciated Barbara's sensitivity.

Fireworks usually enthralled her, but tonight each ear-splitting blast made Jesse more nervous. Perhaps the reaction people had to her residing in the Cavanaugh House had put her on edge, but she suspected it wasn't the house that posed danger. She shivered despite the warm night.

Tired, Jesse drove along Route 14 north toward Routes 5 & 20. The evening at Wyndham Manor had been pleasant with the exception of her encounter with Ben Wyndham and Fred Morton. She was pleased that she did not meet them again, although, from her seat on the sailboat, she had seen them on the shore mingling with guests during the fireworks. It had become evident in the course of the evening that Barbara hoped to be more than a friend to Al, but he was oblivious to her interest. Jesse enjoyed his company; he was funny, kind, and did not wear his wealth and station in the community with any air of superiority. Attentive to his guests, he filled empty glasses or asked after their comfort on the boat, offering pillows, sweatshirts or towels as needed. His easy-going manner put all at ease, though she realized she was out of the socio-economic stratum they all enjoyed.

She had glimpsed a car pull out and leave the estate right behind her; it followed her turn onto Routes 5 & 20. *Maybe I have a rich neighbor.* She couldn't quite make out the model, but it was low to the ground and appeared sporty. It reminded her of the Mustang Robert had given her.

When Robert had given her the Mustang convertible as a birthday gift, she was speechless.

"Get in. Take us for a ride!" he said.

Her head spun, and she was unable to conceive of such an expensive present. Shaking she laughed and cried at the same time.

"Robert, this is too much! You can't give me a *car* for my birthday. Let alone *this* car!" she said.

"Of course I can. I am. Climb in; see how it fits." He opened the door and took her hand leading her to the driver's seat. She laughed and wiped at her eyes as she climbed in and took the steering wheel.

"This is too much," she said looking up at him. His ebony hair was tossed by the breeze, and his powder blue oxford shirt was open at the collar, sleeves rolled up. She felt the familiar stirring this beautiful man always evoked. She watched him walk around the front of the car with the grace of an athlete. Climbing in beside her, he smiled and took her hand.

"Love you, babe," he said, eyes dancing.

She placed her hand back on the steering wheel and started the engine; it purred. Laughing she pulled away from the curb and sailed down Eastman Ave. heading toward the Inner Loop. They drove 490 out to Victor and Canandaigua, the top down, radio blasting. The wind whipped her thick hair and she felt as though she were flying through space. Laughing and singing with the radio, they sped along the roads. When they stopped along Canandaigua Lake, Robert pulled out a picnic basket and beach blanket he had hidden in the trunk. After eating the prosciutto crudo, smoked salmon, cheese, crackers and fruit, they sipped champagne and watched the sunset as it reflected off delicate wisps of rosy-hued clouds, darkened the sky to indigo and finally yielded the sun into the water.

"Red sky at night, sailor's delight," Jesse murmured to the disappearing sun.

"You're full of them, aren't you?" Robert said. She turned to him.

"Full of what?" she asked.

"Those old sayings. Adages. Old Saws. Call them what you will, you have one for every occasion." His voice cut the air.

Hurt, Jesse didn't answer. She squinted at the thin line of color that ran along the water on the horizon. She had never noticed that about herself, and so what if it were true? But Robert made it sound like an accusation.

"Hey, babe, I was just kidding." Robert smiled at her and chucked her chin. "C'mon, Jesse, lighten up."

She smiled at him, but her unease remained. Robert often sent mixed signals, and this was one of the times she wasn't sure quite what he meant—or felt. As if reading her mind, he stroked her cheek.

"Love you, babe," he said.

And she had believed him.

But she had gripped the steering wheel all the way back to his apartment, not sure why she was so tense. When they arrived, he pulled her to him and kissed her, and they giggled as the stick shift impeded their embrace.

"We should continue this in my bedroom," he whispered into her hair. "I have another birthday gift for you, but it requires you to wear your birthday suit."

Jesse moaned at his pun.

"You did not say that," she laughed.

Robert was a wonderful lover, and he made her birthday very special. It was three a.m. when she returned to her Mustang for the drive across town to her apartment in Irondequoit. Just months later she found him in bed with her friend.

She had resurrected the Volkswagen Beetle from her mother's garage after she parked the cherry red Mustang in front of Robert's house...on empty and with barely enough air in the tires to make the trip. She had contemplated other ideas such as setting it on fire, smashing the windshield or simply running her key up and down the sides, but decided just because he was a jerk, she didn't have to be, too. She did leave the keys in the ignition hoping someone would steal it, but auto theft didn't hit Rochester that day.

Taking the bus to her mother's, she had let herself in, taken Bert's key off one of the hooks next to the garage door, and prayed that the car would start. Sitting idle for the two years she had been with Robert was probably not good for the engine. The beauty of German engineering prevailed, and after some coaxing from her and coughing from Bert, they were on their way.

Her mind returned to the present.

"Let it go," she said aloud. How could she have believed all of his lies? "Because love is blind—oh, there I go with another 'old saw' again!"

Jesse believed her trust in love again was nonexistent. Blindsided didn't describe her pain—that physical sensation of being cut through with a knife was painful enough, but the emotional anguish, loneliness and humiliation were unbearable. Leaving Rochester had been difficult, but running into all of their friends was just too much to endure. When they saw her, they would tilt their heads to the side and crease their brows and bestow some platitude on her.

"It was not meant to be."

"You're better off without him."

"What he did was unforgivable."

Then they would head to his house for a party.

The glare of headlights in her rearview mirror brought her back to the present. The car was very close behind her and it swayed across the center line as if to pass her.

"Go ahead and pass if you're in such a big hurry," she muttered. "I think you had a few too many glasses of Wyndham Riesling."

The car continued weaving, coming even closer to her rear bumper.

"Geez, just pass me for pity's sake!" she cried.

Backing off, the car steadied its path and stayed behind her. Jesse sped up just a bit. The car inched forward again and seemed to be drafting off her Volkswagen.

"Are you nuts?" she said into the rearview mirror.

The car swung toward the center lane staying just off her bumper, then started veering back and forth in her blind spot. She could not determine the model or even color of the car because the headlights blinded her in the side mirror. This was not someone who drank too much at the party, this was intentional. She fought the fear rising within her. She pressed on the accelerator and the Beetle lurched forward with a jolt, but the car stayed with her matching her speed.

"Where the hell is a cop when you need one?" Gripped by panic, she clutched the steering wheel and pushed the accelerator to the floor. "Come on, Bert. Give it all you've got!" The cars raced. The second car slowed a bit, and Jesse realized she'd been holding her breath. Slowing down, she let out her breath in a slow steady stream, watching the car grow smaller in the rearview mirror.

Resuming the speed limit, she perceived she was just a couple of miles from her own road.

"Whew, that was close," she said.

Suddenly the car raced up behind her. She gripped the steering wheel and pressed the accelerator. Before the Volkswagen could respond, the other car came alongside and clipped the rear of her car, causing Jesse to swerve toward the trees at the side of the road. Keeping her head, she let up on the gas pedal and shifted into neutral, slowing the engine. She went airborne over the culvert landing in a grassy area. Pulling the steering wheel to the right, she skidded sideways, stopping inches from a huge maple tree and jamming her chest against the steering wheel, then ricocheting and bumping her head against the side window.

She saw the sleek black car stop where she'd left the road. Her heart raced pulsing blood through her body, its rush throbbing in her ears. Would the driver come after her? The road was deserted; there was no one to help her. But the car roared away leaving her stranded.

"Holy shit, what just happened?" Looking down, she examined herself for injuries. She touched a lump sprouting above her left temple, and her ribs throbbed from the impact with the steering wheel. Trembling, she disentangled her legs from beneath the dashboard knowing that her knees would sport ugly bruises the next day. The engine was still running, and she patted the dashboard.

"Nothing stops fine German engineering, does it, Bert?" She put it in first gear, pulled the emergency brake, and turned off the engine.

Opening the door, she climbed out to check her car for damage. Her legs wobbled and she had to hold on to the frame of the car to keep from collapsing. As if awakening, her body began to throb from the collision of human and metal. Taking a deep breath, she stopped as her ribs protested, but none appeared to be broken. She trembled at the realization of how close she had flirted with death.

Crickets chirped, the leaves were motionless, the stillness a stark contrast to what she had just experienced. She searched the trunk, found a flashlight, and walked to the back of her car shining the light on the bumper. The rear fender was dented and part of the body was creased. She rubbed the area with her hand and then patted it. Looking up and down the shoulder, she saw that the culvert ran as far as she could see in both directions.

"Well, Bert, you're going to have to camp out for tonight. I'll be back for you tomorrow as soon as I can find a tow truck to come rescue you."

Grabbing her purse, she locked the car and started walking along the roadside, trying not to think about what might happen if the black car reappeared. She kept a sharp eye out for places in the trees where she could disappear if anyone approached. Realizing that the black car wasn't her only problem out in the country on a dark night, she found a sturdy stick and picked up her pace. Surely that was someone too drunk to be behind a wheel and not some intentional attempt to harm her, wasn't it? In the light of day, she would laugh this off and realize how silly she was being.

Night sounds, unfamiliar to her city-girl ears, echoed in the darkness. Hearing the far-off hoot of an owl, she tried to imagine Owl from the Winnie the Pooh stories she loved, but when she heard the rustle of underbrush made by a large animal, Tigger became ominous. *Just keep walking, just keep walking.* Ahead she spied her road and was overwhelmed with the temptation to run, but she kept her pace steady and her eyes straight ahead. The rustling stopped and she wondered if the animal had gone away or was poised to pounce. *Just keep walking, just keep walking.* She reached her corner and turned into her road observing how dark it was at midnight. Stillness lay ahead and she hurried her pace, not breaking into a run. Off to the left she saw movement by her neighbor's house and a figure melted into the trees in the side yard. Quickening her pace again, she looked at her house and stopped. A glow came from the upstairs window. *I know I didn't leave a light on in there.* She stared at the window and then the light was gone.

"Mary, Mother of God, what else do I have to deal with tonight?" she whispered.

Taking a deep breath, she stepped up to her front door and let herself in. Dropping her keys and purse on the hall table, she tiptoed up the stairs. Reaching the top, she turned toward the front room with Marty's words ringing in her ears. *Some say she didn't commit suicide. Some say she was involved with—well, with people who could endanger her life.* Did someone kill her aunt? Was Aunt Helen so distraught that she took her own life? And now is trying to communicate with her niece? For what? Retribution? Justice? Warning? Jesse crept along the hallway, her eyes locked on the space beneath the door where a soft glow shone against the hardwood floor. If Aunt Helen were trying to reach her, she would do no harm, right? She stiffened as cold air slid from under the door. Taking a deep breath, she grasped the doorknob. She felt the cold air on her toes and looking down still saw the glow. As she turned the knob and started to open the door, the cool air dissipated and the glow disappeared. Swinging the door into the room, she saw only darkness save for the dim light from the streetlight through the trees. Cold air still hovered in the room, but it was fading. Jesse turned on the light and the overhead bulb emitted its soft glimmer.

"I'm going to find out the truth, Aunt Helen," she whispered to the room. She thought she heard a soft scraping noise behind the armoire.

"Good night," she breathed as she closed the door. A soft sigh whispered from inside the attic room.

-FIVE-

She was awakened by the doorbell followed by pounding on her door. She had been restless all night, and her mind was fuzzy from lack of sleep.

"Jesse, are you in there? Jesse? Answer the door. Please answer the door!"

Jumping from her bed, she stopped as muscles and ribs and knees protested in pain. She hobbled downstairs and flung open the door. In an instant she was in Joe's arms and he pressed his face into her hair.

"You're safe! Oh, God, you're okay," he breathed.

Jesse smelled his skin, freshly scrubbed with spicy soap and relished the strong, warm comfort of his embrace. Staying in his arms was quite tempting, but she recovered and pulled away. Wincing as she stepped back, she tried to cover it up with a wry smile.

"You must have come across Bert," she said.

"Bert?" Joe's look shifted from concern to confusion.

"My Beetle."

Concern took over again and he held her at arm's length.

"Yes, I did! Jesse, what happened? How the hell did your car end up on the other side of that ditch?"

The more she awoke, the more her body reminded her of the previous night's mishap. Her head throbbed and her body shook with the effort to remain standing in place.

"I desperately need coffee. Come on in and I'll tell you all about it."

She slogged around the kitchen in a sleep-deprived stupor fishing for coffee, cream and sugar until Joe finally eased her into a chair and poured some orange juice for her. She began relating the events of the previous night while he finished preparing the coffee pot and turned on the stove. Rummaging through her cupboards, he found cups and saucers, spoons and napkins. In her telling, Jesse kept it light, insinuating it was some drunk who had happened to be behind her on the road.

"Jess, this doesn't make sense. If it were just someone who was at the party, why didn't they stop to help when you went off the road?"

"I don't know. Maybe they didn't see me, or maybe they were too drunk to care."

Joe sat down reaching across the table to take her hands. She pulled them back and placed them in her lap looking down at them. Neither spoke for a minute, and then he noticed the lump on her head.

"Geez, Jesse, you need to see a doctor."

She brushed her hair forward in an effort to hide the swelling, but he got up and found a plastic bag that he filled with ice. He held it against her temple. Shocked by the cold, Jesse reached up to retrieve the ice bag from him. Her hand covered his just for a moment until she pulled back.

"Can you recommend a good towing company?" she asked.

Joe got up to pour more coffee.

"Jesse, I think there's more to—." He was interrupted by the doorbell and then insistent knocking.

"People have their shorts in a knot this morning," she said shuffling to the door.

Opening the door, she stopped Marty in mid-knock. He blew out a breath of relief when he saw her.

"Jesse, a report came in about an abandoned car off the road and when I checked the license and registration, I saw it was yours. That's some fancy driving, kiddo. What did you do, take a running start and leap over the ditch?" Marty's humor couldn't hide the concern in his eyes.

"Come on in, Marty. I was just filling Joe in about my midnight adventure."

Removing his hat, he followed her back to the kitchen and greeted Joe. Sitting down, he accepted the cup of coffee she offered and dumped two teaspoons of sugar in it. Stirring it, he blew across the steaming brew and took his first sip.

"So what happened last night, Jesse?" he asked after

She repeated the story as she had told it to Joe skipping the part about believing that she was intentionally run off the road. Neither man was buying it.

"If he was someone from the party, why didn't he stop to help you? Especially if he was the one who caused you to swerve off the road?"

"That's what I said," Joe agreed.

"I guess he was too drunk to notice," she said.

"This doesn't make sense," Marty said.

"That's what I said." Joe ran his fingers through his hair and looked at her. "What aren't you telling us, Jess?"

"Honestly, guys, I've told you what happened. You're suggesting that it would make more sense if someone deliberately ran me off the road." Even as she said it, she was uneasy.

The two friends looked at each other. Marty grimaced.

"I guess you're right, Jesse, but it's all so weird. I saw your fender where he rammed you. Man, he must have been trashed. Well, I can have the lab check the paint to see what kind of car it was and you can submit an accident report."

"Is that necessary? I mean it was probably a couple of kids who could get into a lot of trouble..." she wished she could convince herself. But somehow she understood that the less said about this the better.

"Even more reason to hold them accountable. This was a cheap lesson for them; someone could have been killed."

She shivered at his words and knew Joe saw it. She shrugged it off.

"It was probably just kids," she repeated.

"Well, you need to fill out an accident report; I'll call a tow truck to get you out of there. Man, you must have been flying! Maybe I need to issue you a speeding ticket, too."

She recalled her thought about needing a cop and wished Marty had shown up last night. She gladly would have paid for speeding if it meant getting rid of that other car. Somehow she wasn't ready to admit to them that her suspicions matched theirs—the encounter was intentional and aimed at her.

Marty stood and hitched up his gun-heavy belt. "Can you come down to the station this morning to file that accident report?"

"Sure, as soon as I get Bert back."

Marty's brows came together in a puzzled look.

"Her Volkswagen—she named it Bert," Joe explained.

"Uh, okay then," he answered as he put on his hat. "See you later, Jesse."

"Bye, Marty. Thanks for your concern."

Giving her a wolfish smile, he tipped his hat. "Just doin' my job, ma'am."

Jesse laughed and walked him to the door. Returning to the kitchen she found Joe pouring them each a fresh cup of coffee. Sitting down, she took the cup he offered and sipped the hot drink, savoring the caffeine kick, a little more awake. Awake enough to sense the weight of the silence between them. Butterflies quivered in her stomach as she anticipated his next words. Always intuitive, she could sense his feelings, and she wasn't ready—she knew she wasn't ready. That brief embrace when he arrived awakened her to just how vulnerable she was with Joe. Keeping her eyes downcast, she fought her mixed emotions. Yes, she was pleased that he was attracted to her, and subconsciously she knew it was mutual. But not yet. She knew what he was about to say—knew it as clearly as if he had already voiced it. Joe was about to declare his love, or at least attraction, to her. She was feeling too fragile to trust yet, and after last night, new acquaintances especially were on her "not to be trusted" list.

"I was worried when I saw your car off the road like that and you nowhere to be found," he said.

"You worry too much," she chuckled. Seeing his hurt look, she tried to soften her answer. "It's nice of you to be so concerned about me." She smiled and recognized a stirring within that she could not afford to reveal.

"Jesse, I care about you. I ..."

"Joe, please. Don't."

"But, Jesse..."

She stood and placed her cup and saucer in the sink looking out the back window at the yard. Her yard. This was her time to make it on her own—solo. She had to face whatever life threw at her, no matter how scary, no matter how difficult. If life with Robert had taught her nothing else, it was that she must depend solely on herself. He had pulled the rug out from under her, her mother had never given her support, her father was long gone. After all, who stayed around to take care of her? No, she did not need someone to take care of her—the price was too great. She would not be hurt like that again.

Turning she looked at Joe; he stared into his coffee cup. Tenderness welled up within her, but she fought it. She could not afford him; her heart was still in pieces.

"I need to get ready to go downtown." Her voice sounded flat and empty.

"Sure," Joe said, the chair scraping against the floor as he stood. He didn't meet her eyes, but turned and walked down the hall to the front door. She could have called his name. She could have made it easier, kinder. No, she couldn't.

The Seneca Corners police station was located in the courthouse, a neat two-story brick building in the center of town. Crisply edged lawns and sculpted shrubs surrounded the structure reflecting the order and compliance expected of its citizens. She angled Bert into a space in the parking lot beside the building.

"So good to have you back, buddy. Sorry you had to go through all that dragging and towing."

True to his word, Marty had sent the tow truck to Jesse's house to pick her up and take her on the rescue mission. It had been tricky for the tow truck to maneuver across the culvert and hoist Bert, easing the car across metal runners laid over the ditch. She held her breath through the whole operation, but the mechanic knew his job well. In minutes she was back in the driver's seat of her trusty Beetle. With barely a cough, Bert turned over and started down the highway.

Now Jesse's biggest dilemma was how to give an accident report that essentially should be an assault report. She needed to cherry-pick her words. Entering the building, she approached an information desk. After giving her name and explaining her reason for the visit, she was directed to a corridor to the left. Her sandals made a soft clopping noise on the highly polished marble floors, and the smell of Old English furniture polish emanated from each solid oak doorway. There was something attractive about courthouses even though the reason for being there often was troublesome. The order, the pristine condition, the sense of heavy matters being discussed behind the closed doors seeped into her being and made her feel like part of the importance via osmosis.

She came to a door with POLICE painted on its window. Peering through the glass, she saw Marty hunched over his desk, a half-eaten apple beside him. Turning the knob, she swung the door in to a rush of noises from ringing phones, clacking typewriters and hurried conversation. She approached his desk.

"Isn't that supposed to be a doughnut?" she asked.

He looked at the apple and laughed. "This is my chaser."

Jesse sat in the chair he indicated settling her macramé purse in her lap. Looking around she was fascinated by the bustle and the purpose of every person in the room.

"Busy crime life in Seneca Corners?" she asked.

"There's been a chain of break-ins recently. We think it's some young kids with too much time on their hands during summer vacation. I personally vote for year-round school which would ease up my summer schedule."

She laughed and held up her hands. "Whoa there, cowboy. This teacher needs a break from those cherubs."

Marty chuckled and stood. "Can I get you some coffee or water?"

"Water, thanks. I'm coffeed out after this morning's little get-together."

"Joe stuck around for a while, eh?" his shoulders slumped a little.

"No, no he left right after you." When he straightened, her heart sank a little.

"Oh, good…I mean, oh. Let me get you some water."

Jesse tried to compose her thoughts as to what she did and did not want to say in this report. While the car seemed intentional in its attack, why make it worse? If someone truly meant to harm her, midnight on a deserted highway was the perfect place. Why just bump her fender and leave her on the side of the road? Was it purely to scare her? Was it a prank? Or was it simply someone with too much hearty Wyndham wine in his system? If she gave just the facts without her gut reaction to them, perhaps Marty would be satisfied.

"Hello, Miss Graham."

She looked up to see Sheriff Donoghue standing beside her.

"Oh, good afternoon, Sheriff Donoghue."

"Were you a victim of our gang of vandals?" he asked.

"No, I'm here for another reason," she said.

The sheriff sat at Marty's desk, a look of concern crossing his face. "Nothing serious, I hope."

"Well, I had a little incident last night on the way home from the Wyndhams' party." Jesse paused not sure if she should relate any details before Marty took the report, but figured since it was the sheriff, she'd be all right. "I was run off the road."

His eyebrows shot up. "Are you all right?"

"Yes, thank you. I think it was kids out for a joy ride—maybe your gang of vandals on the way to their next target."

Marty returned with a plastic cup of water and a full cup of coffee for himself. "Hello, Sheriff. Can I get you some coffee?"

Sheriff Donoghue rose to relinquish his seat to the younger man.

"No thanks. Miss Graham was just telling me about her accident last night." He looked at his officer. "Get every detail down, Marty. We need to find whoever did this to her." He turned to her and held out his hand. Taking hers he smiled at her. "We will do everything in our power to solve this, Miss Graham."

Jesse withdrew her hand. "Thank you, Sheriff Donoghue."

The man nodded. "I'll leave you to it then." He walked away.

"Okay, Jesse, can you tell me what happened last night?" Marty pulled the report he had been working on out of the typewriter and inserted a clean form. As she related the events of the previous night, he quickly typed, his face a mask of concentration on her words, but his eyes never leaving the page. As she talked, his face darkened, his brows scrunching down over his eyes. When she mentioned the car backing off, then speeding and eventually hitting her fender as they sped along, he stopped and looked at her.

"This doesn't sound like some drunk weaving along the road. This guy was purposely intimidating you, and possibly attempting worse."

She brushed her fingers through her hair and looked away. "The car followed me out of Wyndham Manor. It was someone who was at the party. Who was there that would want to intimidate, or worse, hurt me? As far as I know I didn't tick anybody off. I did drink, but I was in full control. I would remember something like that."

"Was there anybody who seemed angry with you? Anything like that?"

Jesse recalled the encounter with Ben Wyndham and Fred Morton. Mr. Wyndham certainly was ill at ease upon their introduction, but that might have been because he ruined a Botany 500 dress shirt. However, she knew he spilled his wine at the sight of her. Susan told her she was the spitting image of her Aunt Helen, and her mother's old photos confirmed it. Perhaps Aunt Helen had visited Wyndham Manor and knew the family. Fred Morton was just rude, but she suspected she was not the sole recipient of his behavior. Of all the people she had met that night, those two men were the least friendly, but certainly not hostile enough to follow her in a car and endanger her.

Marty eyes were on her. "What are you not telling me?"

"It's nothing really. It's just, when I met Mr. Wyndham and his accountant, they seemed...I don't know...surprised to see me."

"Surprised like 'whoopee!' or surprised like 'what the hell'?" he asked.

She thought a moment. "The latter. Definitely not 'whoopee!'"

He mulled over her response, and she was surprised that he gave it so much consideration. She realized that beneath his fun-loving exterior, Marty was a shrewd, insightful man.

"Well, that won't go in the report, but it's a good thing to tuck away for later consideration."

"What do you mean, 'later consideration'"?

"I don't discount anything, no matter how small. Sometimes a detail can lead to other details that lead to solving a case. Something as small as, say, a victim who won't give you the whole story." He leaned across the desk towards her and smiled. "You're an open book."

She laughed. "Let me think things through. I can't believe someone would be out to harm me."

"Hello, Jesse. Marty." Al Wyndham walked up to the desk. Marty stood and shook his hand. "What are you doing here, Jesse? Checking out Seneca Corners' finest?"

"What brings you here, Al?" Marty asked allowing her to evade the question.

"Man, someone stole my car after the party last night. I had moved it out of the garage and onto the lawn so the fireworks could be stored in case of rain. I never thought to take the keys out of it—it was on my own front lawn for God's sake! Anyway, when I went to move it back into the garage after all the guests had left, it had vanished."

Jesse felt the blood drain from her face. That could have been the car that followed her.

"Was it your black Porsche 911?" Marty asked.

"Yes, such a fine machine. I hope you can find it. I only had about 1400 miles on it, and it's the finest car I've ever owned. Low to the ground, it can accelerate to 75 miles per hour in a heartbeat and prowl like a cat.

Handles beautifully, too, with power steering that can swerve past anything in its way."

Jesse shuddered and caught Marty watching her.

"So you have no idea who might have taken it? No one on the grounds saw anyone near it?"

"No, no one. I've filed a report already, so I'm sure it will be found. I just hope they don't damage it, or worse get in an accident. Probably some kids out for a joy ride. They'll abandon it when they're done. Well, I'm glad you came to the Founder's Day celebration, Jesse. I hope you enjoyed yourself."

She had recovered her composure and stood to take Al's extended hand.

"I had a great time, Al. Thanks for inviting me."

"I hope you'll come over again soon. You, too, Marty. I'll let you both know when we're going to throw our next bash."

"That would be great, Al. Thanks," Marty said, shaking his hand.

Al headed for the door; Jesse and Marty looked at each other.

"You think Al's stolen car is connected to what happened last night, don't you?" she asked.

"It sure is a coincidence." He looked at the paper in his typewriter and she knew he wished he could add that information to it. "Jesse, I want you to take extra care. This may be nothing but joy-riding teenagers, but in all my years as a cop, kids have never deliberately tried to run people off the road. Just the opposite. They look for deserted roads where they can open it up to 100 miles per hour. You need to keep your eyes and ears open. And maybe not drive alone late at night."

"I'm not going to let this random event dictate how I live my life. If they wanted to harm me, they had the opportunity to do so. I'm sure it was an isolated incident."

He pursed his lips and frowned at her. "Redheads are stubborn."

"It's the Irish in me. I can't help myself."

"How about I give you the twenty-five cent tour? I can impress you with my manly art of protecting John Q. Public."

"Sure, I'd like that." She smiled at him.

Walking through the building, Marty pointed out the interrogation rooms, the holding cells and the processing rooms on the first floor and the courtrooms on the second floor. She felt sorry for the people sitting on benches along the walls waiting to be called into court. Their expressions ranged from nervous fear to bold, self-righteous stares. None of them were going to have a good day.

As he led her down the stairs to the basement, Jesse fought the usual uneasiness she experienced when descending below ground. She focused on his description of the various rooms they would see on the bottom level. Reaching the basement, he pointed out the forensic labs, medical examiner's office, autopsy rooms and the archives. She paused in front of that door and cocked her head.

"Marty, how long do you keep cases on file in the archives?" she asked.

"Forever. We have cases in there going back to the 1700s," he replied.

"So the report of my Aunt Helen's death would be in there."

He shifted uncomfortably. "Yes." He drew the word out.

"Are the records open to the public?"

"No. I see where you are going with this. Your aunt's case was declared a suicide anyway."

"But you said there were rumors about foul play. You said she may have gotten in with some people who needed her out of the way…"

"Whoa, whoa, whoa, Miss Nancy Drew. That was all conjecture. There was an investigation and nothing was found. You need to let this go."

"I can't. I think there's more to my aunt's death than is in those reports."

"And what makes you think that?" He folded his arms across his chest.

How could she tell him about the midnight occurrences in the attic room where Aunt Helen's body had been discovered? He was a no-nonsense cop and would laugh at her "woo-woo" imaginings. No, she couldn't tell him about that any more than she could tell him about her instincts about last night.

"Jesse, you're not telling me everything."

You have no idea, Marty.

⁂ ⁂ ⁂

She half-listened to the presentation being given by Sister Anne, the principal of St. Bartholomew's. Even though she wasn't teaching summer school, she had been invited to this in-service so she could begin to meet the staff. Maggie sat beside her conscientiously taking notes, so Jesse knew if she wasn't attending to the presentation, Maggie could fill her in later. That was how they had operated in school, too. Maggie was always the conscientious student, but she generously shared notes and studied with Jesse to bring her up to speed. Not that Jesse was an academic slouch; she aced her classes and had an uncanny ability to recall information from lectures that Maggie could retrieve only by reviewing her notes. Now, while she was trying to focus on Sr. Anne, her mind was still going over the occurrences of the night the week before when someone had followed her home from Al's party and then she had seen the glowing light in the attic window.

"...and the fall class lists will be in your mailboxes by August 15—the Feast of the Assumption." The nuns laughed at the principal's comment as the meeting broke up. Several women came up to Jesse and introduced themselves, offering assistance should she need anything. She was amused to see them all in casual attire rather than their habits. A stranger walking into the room would have no idea these were Catholic sisters. They all made her feel very welcome, except of course, Sr. Alphonse who glowered at her from the corner. When Jesse saw her glare, she simply nodded at the older woman. Scooping up her notes, the nun hurried out the door.

"Your classroom will be just down the hall from mine. Do you want to see it?" Maggie asked.

"Sure!" Jesse was excited about preparing for a new school year. She had already begun lesson plans based on the curriculum she'd been given, recognizing the rigor of the Regents Diploma requirements. She remembered those three-to-four hour exams she and Maggie had sweated through, and knew she would do her best to prepare her students to succeed.

As they walked through the corridors with floors polished to a high sheen, she inhaled the familiar scent of beeswax mixed with chalk dust and the lavender soap all nuns seemed to use. Most memories of her Catholic school experience were pleasant with the exception of a Latin teacher who warned them about the dangers of wearing patent leather shoes and kissing boys. She never experienced getting knuckles rapped with a ruler or standing on one foot for half an hour. And even though she protested it, deep down she understood why she wasn't allowed to wear David Flaherty's class ring when they were going steady.

Maggie asked questions about her frightening ride home from Al's party. Her best friend was the only one to whom Jesse admitted her fear that the encounter was intentional. Maggie never questioned her assessment of the situation, merely listened and asked questions for clarity.

"Well, you know I'll worry about you, Jess, but you'll go ahead and do what you want anyway. So how can I help?"

"Mags, you are the best friend ever. Right now I'm trying to convince Marty D'Amato to let me see the archived investigation report on Aunt Helen's death."

"So you've talked with Officer D'Amato about this, right?"

"Right. He was the first person to hint that Aunt Helen's death might not have been a suicide. He said there were rumors of foul play and shadowy people in her life. I'd like to see what information, documents or photos are in that file."

"Be careful what you wish for..." Maggie said.

"You sound like Susan Riley, Mags. She keeps telling me to be careful what questions I ask."

"Speaking of Joe Riley...what is happening on that front, Jess?"

"I wasn't speaking of Joe Riley; I was speaking of Susan Riley."

"Don't dodge the question, Jesse. Are you seeing him?"

"No, Mags. I think I effectively shut that down."

Maggie stopped in the middle of the hall. Jesse tilted back her head and groaned. She turned to look at her friend. "What?"

"He seems like a good guy. What did you do?"

Jesse ran her hand across her eyes.

"I'm just not ready to be involved yet. He was getting... I don't know, all mushy."

"How? Like sending you valentines? Calling in the middle of the night? Bringing you flowers? How?"

"No, nothing like that, Maggie." She ran her hands through her hair and blew out a stream of air. "When he saw my car deserted by the side of the road and came to my house he hugged me."

"Oh my God, Jesse, he hugged you? He discovered that you were alive and well and HUGGED you? How dare he!"

"He embraced me. He held me. I was in his arms…Geez, Maggie, it was more than just a 'oh good you didn't die' hug."

"So an 'oh good you didn't die hug' would have been acceptable? But one second longer, and you kick him out?"

"It was like a 'God, I really love being with you' hug. There's a difference. Geez, Maggie, it felt so damn good. And I didn't kick him out. We had coffee and then Marty joined us because he had seen the car and had run the plates. Marty didn't hug me. Anyway, after Marty left the air turned thick with 'now I'm going to spill my guts about how I feel about you' and I wasn't ready. I wasn't rude, I just…I don't know. Whatever I did or said, Joe got the message. He left and I haven't seen him since."

Maggie continued down the hall and stopped before a classroom door. Room 36—Jesse's favorite number. Handing her the key, Maggie stepped aside and made a fake bow.

"Your kingdom awaits, m'lady."

Jesse turned the key and opened the door to a cheery room with four large windows along the outside wall and a long chalkboard on the wall opposite. The requisite crucifix hung above the chalkboard in the middle of the front wall and the American flag draped to its right. A large oak desk stood sentry in front of it and twenty-five students' desks stood at attention in neat rows across the room. The hardwood floors creaked as they walked around looking in the large built-in cabinets along the back wall.

"This room is beautiful!" Jesse exclaimed. "It's huge and bright and clean!"

Maggie smiled. "We aim to please."

"I can't wait to get my bulletin boards up and start bringing in my materials and books." She turned to her best friend. "Thank you for this gift, Mags. I haven't enjoyed anything in so long. I'm really looking forward to this year."

"I'm glad, Jess. I've been worried about you for a while. I had hoped having your own home would be fun, but it's just been work and...well, kind of scary. Any more visits from Aunt Helen?"

Jesse told her about the light she saw when she walked home after being run off of the road.

"I get the sense she's trying to tell me something, Mags."

"Be careful, Jess. Do you want to talk to Father Steve about it? Maybe he could do an exorcism or bless the house or something."

"No, I don't want to exorcise Aunt Helen; I want to understand her! I don't think I'm in any danger. I mean, it's creepy, don't get me wrong, but I'm not afraid. In fact, when she shows up, I feel such a longing, like she's pulling me toward her. It's hard to explain."

"Well, *I* feel scared, and I feel scared for you. Promise me you'll be careful."

"Pinky swear," Jesse said and the women locked little fingers. "We're twenty-eight years old. Maybe we should give up pinky swearing."

"Never," Maggie said, and the women locked fingers again and laughed.

For a moment Jesse was happy for the first time in months. She hoped it would last a while.

Jesse pushed the lawn mower through the grass in front of her house. While she'd diligently kept it a decent length, the hot afternoon made it ten times harder to mow. As she trudged behind the mower, her thoughts traveled back to the day Joe had helped her mow it all down. So far she had been successful in pushing away thoughts of him, but today she allowed herself to wallow in missing him. He had helped her tremendously, and being in his arms had been wonderful. He made her laugh and put things in perspective—he was so down-to-earth. His teasing was never malicious as Robert's had been. Oh no, now she was comparing them. *I'd better stop this train in its tracks.* Getting all nostalgic over Joe was not going to help her one bit.

Rounding the corner she saw the last patch of grass to be mowed and wiped her forehead. Her pony tail swung with the rhythm of her steps and tickled across her shoulders; wisps that had escaped hung down in auburn ringlets around her face and the back of her neck. Anticipating a nice cold beer when she finished gave her a second wind and she hurried through the last section. She swept the back sidewalk that led along the back of the house under the kitchen windows and trimmed the grass along the foundation. Collecting the mower and all of the tools, she walked to the small shed nestled in the trees. She always got nervous when opening it waiting for the onslaught of her furry friends, but everything was quiet inside. Putting away the equipment, she closed and locked the door and turned toward the house. Something inserted in the kitchen door caught her eye; she crossed the yard to look closer. A white paper was tucked inside the screen door secured by the frame. *Must be a flyer from the Knights of Columbus for their Friday Night Fish Fry.* Grabbing the note, she unfolded it and gasped. Scrawled across the page was a message.

Leave town for your own good.

The handwriting had been disguised; it looked like a child's scribble and was written with crayon. The paper was lined school paper.

Jesse's heart beat fast and she scanned the yard. She shivered despite the summer heat and was unable to move. If whoever had written the note had appeared at that moment to do her bodily harm, she doubted she could have fended him off. The sun ducked behind a cloud and she crossed her goose-bumped arms. Her mind raced. What was going on? Few people in Seneca Corners even knew her. The sun emerged and Jesse stared at the reflection off the aluminum lawn chair in front of her. The light started to ripple and shimmer. Rushing rhythms pulsed in her ears as though she was underwater, and everything faded into white. Slumping to the steps, she put her head between her knees trying to regain her equilibrium.

"Jesse? Jesse?"

She heard someone calling her from far away.

"Jesse?" the voice was more insistent now. "Jesse! What's wrong?"

Marty knelt in front of her and gently touched her shoulder. Her head still lowered, she saw his gun strapped to his belt, the metal shining in the sun. *How odd that a gun would sparkle in the sunlight like a gem. Something so violent and deadly could draw the sun to itself just as a flower or an ocean wave.* Her mind focused on the weapon; she felt herself drifting off.

"Jesse, stay with me, hon."

His voice steadied her. She roused and lifted her head.

"Are you okay?"

She nodded as her vision came back into focus.

"I need a beer," she mumbled.

He laughed. "Can you stand up? Do you need me to carry you into the house?"

She shook her head and managed to rise. Dizziness returned and he propped her up and helped her inside. The coolness of the house helped to ground her and she sat in a chair at the kitchen table.

"The beer's in the fridge," she said.

He poured a glass of water and handed it to her. "No beer until you drink all of this."

She took the glass and gulped the water. The cold liquid slid down her throat and hit her empty stomach. She shivered at the contrast to her hot, sticky skin. Marty soaked a dish towel, wrung it out, and placed it on the nape of her neck. She jumped at the effect of the cold cloth, but she began to focus.

"Thanks, Marty. That was good timing," she said.

"I was driving patrol in this area and thought I'd stop by to see how things were going. Never say there isn't a cop around when you need one. What happened?" he asked.

"I was mowing in the heat on an empty stomach," she grimaced.

"And?" he prodded.

"And I almost passed out. And there you were, my knight in shining armor."

"And?" he said again.

"And now we should have a beer."

He held out the note. "What's this?"

"Oh, I think some neighbor kids must have been playing cops and robbers." She waved the note away.

He sat down across from her. She looked at him, but he didn't speak. Rubbing the wet towel across her face and neck down to the top of her halter top, she avoided his eyes. The silence was awkward, and she shifted in her seat.

"So, do you want a beer?" she asked.

"I'm not moving until you tell me what's going on," Marty said folding his arms across his chest and sitting back in the chair.

"Nothing…"

"Don't feed me that baloney anymore. I knew something was up when I saw your car by the road. Those tire tracks didn't happen because you swerved a little. You were airborne for several seconds—which may not sound like much, but those could have been the last seconds of your life."

She shivered. "Okay." She sipped the last of her water. "We'll need beer."

"I'm on duty, Jesse, and it's only three o'clock in the afternoon."

"The sun is over the yardarm, Marty. You want the truth, I want a beer…"

He sighed and rose retrieving a bottle of Genesee Cream Ale from the refrigerator.

"I might need 12 Horse for this story." she grinned at him.

"You're getting Cream Ale." He plunked the bottle in front of her, grabbed the bottle opener from the counter and popped off the cap. "May I get you a glass, ma'am?" His voice was high and sweet, but he glared at her.

"No, thank you, miss." Jesse took a swig and set the bottle down. She laughed as he gave her a sideways frown.

"Okay, I'll tell you whatever you want to know, but I'm warning you, some of it might be hard to swallow."

"Try me. You'd be amazed what I hear on any given day."

"I gave you the facts about the car that followed me, but I didn't include how I felt about it. At first, yes, I thought it was someone who had too much to drink at Al's party, and even thought it might be some kids out joyriding. But when the driver pulled that stunt and fell back in the distance then raced toward me, I was terrified. I knew right then that this wasn't a drunk or a kid; it was someone purposely trying to scare or hurt me. I didn't want to say anything because that would make it real, you know? As if ignoring it would make it irrelevant, you know?" She shook her head and looked out the window at her freshly mowed lawn. "I just wanted a simple life away from complications. Life in the country with fresh air and no problems. Instead I get terrorized, threatened and haunted."

"Haunted? What do you mean, 'haunted'?" Marty studied her.

"Okay, you asked for it. Since I've moved into my aunt's house, I've been hearing eerie noises coming from the attic room. Scraping noises, sighing. The night of my accident, I saw a glow in the window as I approached the house. When I went upstairs to investigate, the room was freezing. I think it's my Aunt Helen trying to communicate with me. You can laugh all you want and think I'm a nut-case, but these are facts. My friend Maggie can confirm some of them." She crossed her arms and leaned back in her chair waiting for his onslaught of "policeman common sense." Instead she watched him digest her words and saw no sign of mocking in his eyes.

"You believe me, don't you?" she said in amazement.

"Jesse, my Italian grandmother had 'the sight.' She saw ghosts all the time. I didn't inherit her gift, but I sure believe in it. Too many times what she predicted came true. I actually witnessed one of her 'visits' when I was quite young. I get it," he said.

"Wow, I thought you would laugh your ass off if I told you. You never cease to amaze me, Marty." He beamed at her and sat up taller. "I think all of this is connected somehow. Susan Riley told me my resemblance to my Aunt Helen was uncanny, and photos of her and my mother bear it out. I once thought a photo of her as a little girl was me. Add that to the fact that there were rumors about her death being suspicious, and someone here doesn't want me around. I didn't want to point suspicion at Ben Wyndham, but he was obviously shaken when he met me. Maybe he knew my aunt. Maybe he knows more about what happened than he ever disclosed. I just can't imagine Mr. Wyndham jumping into his son's car for a wild ride to intimidate me."

Marty rubbed his hand across his chin. "Ben Wyndham is the richest man around here. He's always hosting outings and parties for charitable causes. He seems like a good guy; it doesn't fit for him to be your pursuer." Marty paused and thought for a moment. "Was there anyone else, anyone at all, who seemed disturbed at meeting you? Maybe not just disturbed—maybe surprised. Anything unusual?"

Jesse laughed. "Well, when I first entered several other women smiled and waved but their eyes weren't particularly friendly. I was an unwelcome addition to the Al Wyndham Dating Game. I wanted to hold up a sign that said 'Not Interested in a Relationship with Al' as reassurance."

"You're not interested in the most eligible bachelor in Seneca Corners?" His face was a mixture of disbelief and pleasure.

She looked at him and took a long pull on her beer, draining the bottle.

"Marty, look. I am not interested in anyone right now. I'm coming off a nasty break-up and I need time."

"So you and Joe aren't..." He shifted in his seat.

"No, Joe and I are not. In fact, I haven't seen him since the morning we all had coffee together." Jesse noticed an almost imperceptible smile cross his face. "*Anyone*, Marty."

She stood and rinsed out her beer bottle and set it next to the sink. Catching her reflection in the window above the sink she tried to tame the spiral curls framing her face. She pulled the tendrils at her neck up into the rubber band holding her ponytail, but to no avail. Dirt smudged her face and her halter top needed readjusting. She loosened it at her neck and retied it pulling her breasts up and in more securely. "Who could resist this sweaty woman?" she murmured to her reflection.

"You look beautiful."

His voice was a whisper and she wondered if he had even intended for her to hear it. She pretended she didn't. Turning back to the table she sat down; she noticed how serious he looked.

"What?" she asked, more an accusation than a question.

"Jesse, when I said I was patrolling the neighborhood and just stopped by, it was partially true. I also have some news for you." Marty pulled a photo out of his pocket.

She stared at the picture of a black Porsche half immersed in a pond.

"So you found Al's car," she whispered.

"Yes. And the interesting thing is that it was wiped clean of any fingerprints. None, nada, zip. Not even Al's. And there was a trace of yellow paint on the front bumper."

He looked at her; a crease formed between his eyebrows.

"This was no kid out for a joy ride or a drunk swerving down the road. This was someone intent on hurting, or at least scaring, you. And they were savvy enough to erase any evidence."

"Yeah," she whispered.

"We've called Al and told him. He's heading down to the station to verify that it's his car, but there aren't too many Porsche 911s around here."

"I don't think he's going to be happy about this," she said trying to shift focus.

"You need to take this seriously. Someone meant to scare you, or warn you, or harm you. And he means business."

"Okay. I get it. I will be vigilant and careful."

"And you'll call me if you sense any trouble, right?" His eyes bored into hers.

"Right, Officer D'Amato."

"Damn it, Jesse! I'm not kidding!"

"What do you want me to do? I can't leave Seneca Corners—I have nowhere to go! This is it for me; I haven't got anything else!" She fought back tears of fear and frustration. Taking a deep breath, she continued, her voice softer. "Yes, I will be careful. Yes, I will call you if

I sense trouble. And I am grateful for your friendship, Marty."

He softened his voice, too. "I didn't mean to upset you. You're just so damned flip about all of this."

"It's the only way I know how to cope with this craziness."

He glanced at the window and back at her. He nodded. Silence fell between them.

"Sounds like an invitation to Wyndham Estate was issued by the heir when we talked with him at the station the other day," she said attempting a lighter mood.

He relented. "Yeah, even I was included in that one. Let's see, it's late July, so their next annual event would be the Rodeo Round-Up in August. They raise money for the Equestrian Club at St. Bart's. Did you know that it was a Wyndham ancestor who started the school?"

Jesse's taut muscles began to relax as the conversation turned away from her accident. "Yes, Al gave me a quick tour of his ancestors when I was at the Founder's Day party. Somewhere in my Staff Initiation Packet was a section on the history of St. Bart's. Between making this house livable, my Aunt Helen's visits, lesson planning, and dealing with threatening motorists, I haven't given my Staff Initiation Packet its due. So what you're telling me is that I am an employee of Ben Wyndham. Interesting… You know, the next chance I get I'm going to ask Mr. Wyndham if he knew my aunt and if he knew anything about the circumstances of her death."

"Take it easy, Nancy Drew. What if it was Ben Wyndham who tried to hurt you the other night? What if the rumors of your aunt's death are true and he knows something, or worse, was involved somehow? Marching into his office demanding to know information that might be the reason you're in danger could *really* put you in danger."

"But I thought you said he was a good guy? Now you think he's involved in all of this?" She leaned across the table. Her forehead wrinkled in confusion at what Marty was saying.

"I'm not saying he was; I'm not saying he wasn't. I have learned over the years to not suspect *anyone* and to suspect *everyone*. You'd be amazed at who ends up being guilty. I like to examine everything from every angle and reserve final opinions until all the facts are in."

"Well, all the facts aren't available, are they? Lots of facts are locked up in the report of my Aunt Helen's death." Leaning back in her chair, she crossed her arms and her legs with an air of finality.

Marty blew out a long breath and shook his head. "You are tenacious."

"I'll consider that a compliment. What I'd like instead is access to my aunt's investigation." She leaned forward again and took his hand. "Please, Marty. Couldn't you slip me into the archives on some quiet Saturday afternoon when no one is around?"

He squeezed her hand and she slipped it away. He grinned at her.

"You could drive a person crazy."

"Don't flatter yourself on thinking you're the first person to tell me that, although you at least said it kindly." Jesse's heart beat faster; she was gaining ground in her battle to see the report. She knew she had to be careful, though. Marty pretty much admitted his attraction to her today; it would be very easy to press that advantage. She did not want to use him; that would be sinking to Robert's level. But she did need to encourage him and that could require some innocent flirting. Flirting lost its innocence when the other person's feelings were involved. Good humor, not flirting might be her best weapon—oh, not a good way to think where a cop was involved. Her best tool. Good humor and honesty.

"Marty, it would mean so much to me if I could see those files."

He rubbed his hands over his eyes and down his face. Shaking his head with a forlorn smile, he said, "I'll see what I can do."

Her impulse was to jump up and hug him, but she held back and instead patted his hand.

"Thanks."

Jesse's arms were loaded with two grocery bags as she unlocked the door to the ringing of her telephone. Juggling bags, keys and closing the door behind herself with her foot, she hastened to the phone on the hall table. Setting down one bag, she lifted the receiver.

"Hello?" she said.

Silence.

"Hello? Is someone there? Hello?"

Click.

Shrugging, she replaced the receiver and retrieved her grocery bag. In the kitchen she put away the refrigerated items first then the food for the pantry. The phone rang again, and she was tempted to let the person call again later. Muttering, she went to the hall and picked up the receiver.

"Hello?"

"Hi, Jesse. This is Al Wyndham."

"Hi. I guess the connection was bad when you called a minute ago," she said.

There was a pause.

"I didn't call a minute ago," Al said.

"Oh. Well, someone did and the connection was bad. So, did you get your car back? Is there much damage?" she asked.

"Yeah, I got it back. It can be repaired, but some of the interior will need to be replaced. Look, Jesse, that's why I'm calling. I feel kind of responsible for what happened to you that night—Marty filled me in on your accident."

"Why do you feel responsible, Al? Was it you chasing me down the highway?" she asked, not sure if she wanted the answer.

"No, no! Of course not! But it was my car. Geez, you could have been badly hurt!"

Jesse was tired of this conversation with yet another person.

"You are not responsible, Al. And I'm fine. Really, I am."

"Well, it was my excuse for inviting you to dinner. Will you have dinner with me? After all, it was my Porsche that damaged your car."

She suddenly pictured the ridiculous image of her Beetle being pursued by a sleek, black Porsche and she snickered.

"Does the idea of having dinner with me make you giggle?" Al asked.

"No, it was just the thought of the cars…never mind. And I don't giggle."

"Corrected and repentant. So, will you have dinner with me? There's a café in Geneva with a jazz trio on Saturday nights. It would be fun."

"Gee, I don't know, Al…"

"C'mon, Jesse. Let it be an apology from my car."

She could hear the smile in his voice. She had been working hard on the house, and an evening out would be a nice change.

"All right, Al. Yes, I'll have dinner with you."

"Great! I'll pick you up at 6 o'clock on Saturday. I look forward to it."

"Me, too. See you then." Hanging up the phone, she shook her head wondering why she had agreed to this date.

She checked the clock in the kitchen. Maggie was coming for dinner, and Jesse was grilling steaks and potatoes. Placing a pot of water on the stove, she took four ears of corn out to the back steps and sat down. She heard the front doorbell and called "Back here" around the side of the house to Maggie. Grabbing the silk, she pulled down the first corn shuck and threw it in the paper grocery bag. The silken strings stuck to her fingers and she rubbed her hands together trying to get them off.

"I hate sticky hands, Maggie; maybe you should do this," she said, hearing footsteps coming around the side of the house.

"No thanks. I hate that job."

Jesse jumped at the sound of Susan Riley's voice. She stole a glance toward the kitchen door as if Susan would know she had just gotten off the phone with Al. Why did she feel guilty? She and Joe were not dating, but somehow the guilt seeped through her.

"Didn't mean to scare you," Susan apologized.

"No, I was just expecting someone else," Jesse answered.

"Oh, I see. Well, I won't take much of your time. I needed to talk to you." Susan paused. "Joe told me about what happened to you on the road. Some kids or someone drunk...?" Susan's voice drifted off.

"Who knows? I couldn't see much in the dark, so I have no idea who it was. I know the car followed me from Wyndham Manor."

Susan thought about that for a moment. "Jesse, be careful, okay?"

Jesse looked at her friend. "Why do you say that, Susan?"

"Because I care about you..."

"No, that's not what I meant. You know what I meant."

Susan gazed out at the trees that lined the yard. "Why don't you come over for tea again?"

"That might be awkward..." Jesse hesitated.

"I see. I don't want to pry, but I knew something had happened between you two. He hasn't been himself lately. We could meet for coffee in town, or I could come over here," Susan offered. "I think we need to talk some more."

"I have a hair appointment tomorrow at 11 o'clock. How about lunch after that?"

"Perfect. I'll meet you at Woolworth's lunch counter."

"Don't you answer your door, Graham?" Maggie called as she turned the corner of the house. "I've been ringing and knocking like a maniac, but you just—Oh, hello," Maggie said spotting Susan.

Susan grinned when she saw Maggie. "So you're the dinner date, Sr. Angelina!"

"Please, call me Maggie."

"Susan, why don't you join us for supper? I have enough food here for an army," Jesse laughed.

"Thanks, but I've got a roast in the oven for Joe. I'd love to join you another time though. It was a pleasure to see you again, Sister...er...Maggie. Wow, that will take some getting used to. See you tomorrow, Jesse." Susan waved as she left the yard.

"I'll put this stuff in the refrigerator," Maggie said opening the kitchen door. "It's beer and ice cream for dessert."

"Beer and ice cream for dessert sounds perfect," Jesse said. Sitting down she picked up the second ear of corn and began shucking it. "Do you think God created corn to grow like this as a penance, Sr. Angelina?" she called into the kitchen. "I mean, I hate this job. So maybe as I get this crap all over my hands, a little 'heaven eraser' is scrubbing away some of the smudges on my soul."

Maggie walked out with two beers. "You mean those milk bottles in the *Baltimore Catechism*? I don't think there are enough 'heaven erasers' for you, Miss Graham. Four ears of corn aren't going to forgive what happened behind the Home Ec building."

"My soul is lost forever, Mags. What are you going to do up in heaven without me?"

"You forget, Jess. God is all-merciful. He'll find a broom closet for you in one of His mansions. So, any more threatening notes stuck in your door recently?"

"No, and I haven't heard back from Marty about seeing my aunt's report. I was hoping to hear from him by now." She heard the phone ring and jumped up. "Maybe that's him."

Running into the house, she lifted the receiver. "Hello?"

Silence.

"Hello?"

Click.

Hanging up, she headed back outside.

"I have to call the phone company; I think there's a problem with my line."

"What's going on?" Maggie asked as she finished shucking the last of the corn.

"Calls aren't coming through. When I answer, no one is there and then the line goes dead."

Maggie looked at her saying nothing.

"What?" Jesse asked. "It's your local-yokel phone company. I never had trouble like that with Rochester Telephone."

"We've never had trouble like that either, Jess. I'm not sure it's a problem with the phone company."

"I'll have it looked at tomorrow." She frowned at the finished corn. "Oh no, Maggie, you've stolen all of my penance!"

Maggie didn't smile. "I think you should tell *Marty* about the phone calls, not the phone company."

Jesse sobered instantly. "I know, Mags. I just keep hoping there are other explanations."

The telephone jarred Jesse awake. Stumbling from her bed, she groped her way into the upstairs hall and down the stairs to the telephone. Moonlight filtered in through the living room windows casting long shadows that trespassed into the hall where she stood. Rubbing her eyes, she tried to orient herself. She fought down panic as she wondered who might be hurt or worse—middle-of-the-night phone calls were never good news. Her mother had been in good health when she last saw her, and Robert wouldn't contact her...he didn't even know where she was. She picked up the receiver.

"Hello?"

Silence. She realized it was the person who had called before.

"Stop this high school foolishness," she said into the phone in her best teacher voice.

She heard breathing, steady, deep breathing. She hung up the phone. Standing in the moonlit hallway, she shivered. Someone was targeting her and doing his best to intimidate her...maybe more. Damn, she would not be controlled by someone else. Especially someone she didn't even know. This person was a coward. Why not come to her face to face and tell her what his problem was? If it was because she looked like her aunt, there was nothing she could do about that. Why should that threaten anyone anyway? She moved from scared to angry as she thought about the spinelessness of the person harassing her. She knew now more than ever how important it would be to see Aunt Helen's information. Then her ears pricked up.

Scritch, Scritch, Scritch.

She looked up at the ceiling where the noises originated.

"Cripes, can't I get a night's rest around here? Maybe it's time to see Aunt Helen face to ghost," she said aloud.

She tramped up the stairs to the attic room and flung open the door. Gripped by the cold, she lost her breath. Flicking on the light, she scanned the room checking every corner. As the cold eased somewhat, she walked to the armoire; the door was ajar. Pulling it open, she saw the fringe on her aunt's cowgirl jacket swaying for no apparent reason.

"Aunt Helen, what do you want to tell me?"

She heard sighing, soft and longing; it wrenched her heart. She circled the room trying to locate the sound, as her heart felt it would break with aching.

"I'm here, Aunt Helen. I'm going to find out who did this to you, I promise."

A whisper of breath breezed across her cheek, and the yearning disappeared with the cold. Jesse wiped the tears on her face with the back of her hand. Overwhelmed with exhaustion, she scanned the room once more, then returned to her bed. She slept until the morning sun streaming through her window awoke her.

-SIX-

Jesse tried to cover the dark circles under her eyes with foundation, but to no avail. Giving up, she patted on powder and brushed color across her pale cheeks. These nocturnal occurrences were taking a toll on her beauty sleep. She wrapped a tie-died headband around her hair and blotted her lipstick.

"What you see is what you get," she said to her reflection. She had never considered herself beautiful, so she was casual with make-up and hair styles. Her mother certainly hadn't affirmed her good looks, in fact, just the opposite. Any comment she did make about Jesse's appearance was critical, so Jesse was unaware of how many heads turned when she passed by. She had always viewed her mother as the embodiment of attractiveness and style, and since she had not inherited those genes, she had never aspired to glamour.

Smoothing the polka-dot crop top she wore with yellow capris and tan flats, she headed to her car, hoping her haircut would be quick since it was to trim the split ends. Anxious to hear what Susan had to say, she pushed Bert a few miles per hour over the speed limit. Two miles from town, her heart sank as she heard a siren behind her.

"Come on, cop. I was only speeding a little. Give me a break!"

Pulling over, she leaned toward the glove box to retrieve her license and registration.

"You don't need those, ma'am."

She jumped at the sound of Marty's voice. He stood beside the car with his arms folded, her face reflected in his sunglasses.

"Geez, Marty, you scared the crap out of me. Are you giving me a speeding ticket?"

He hitched up his belt. "Well, ma'am, you were exceeding the posted limit. But I'll forgive it if you go to Tony's with me on Friday night."

"I think that's called blackmail. I could report you."

"Well, that would dry up your source for any research you might want to do," he examined his fingernails.

Jesse tried to open her door, but he blocked it as a car sped by.

"I'm going to have to ask you to remain in your car, ma'am."

"Wow, you do that whole intimidating cop thing really well."

He leaned against her window.

"Something's up, Jesse. I asked Sheriff Donoghue about letting you look at the report on your aunt's death, and he hemmed and hawed for a while. Then he said he'd be happy to look at it and let you know if he found any discrepancies. When I pressed him to look at it myself, he said, 'It's best if that's all left alone.' Weird, huh?"

Her stomach tightened as she thought about Marty's words. He continued.

"He said the investigation was thorough and there was no need to revisit it. 'Let sleeping dogs lie, Marty.' was his last comment. I don't know, but I think you're on to something. Thing is, it's putting you in danger."

"But if we can get to the bottom of this and identify the person or persons responsible for my aunt's death, they will be put away and the danger disappears. If they are never discovered, I'll constantly be looking over my shoulder—if I can even stay here. Or I'll be killed."

"Don't even say that."

"Well, that appears to be the direction this is taking, doesn't it? First the car, then the note, now phone calls…"

"What phone calls?" he asked.

"Someone has been calling and hanging up. I thought it was a problem with my phone, but Maggie said I should tell you not the phone company. Well, apparently she was right because in the middle of the night last night he called again; this time he just breathed into the phone. I told him to grow up."

"Jesse, don't talk to him like that! You're just asking for it." Marty shouted.

"Asking for what, Marty? For threats? For harm? Or worse?" She stretched out of the window to get in his face. "So you see? I've got to find the answers or this harassment continues…and escalates." She sat back against the seat. A car of teens went by laughing and jeering at her. She flipped them off.

"I can cite you for public lewdness, ma'am," he said, his eyes following the car.

"Cite me for anything you damn well please. Arrest me—at least that would place me in the building I need to explore." She crossed her arms.

"Which leads me back to my blackmail. Okay, this is what I'm thinking. I invited you to Tony's because I thought that after the dancing we could head over to the court house and sneak into the Archives Room."

Her heart began to pound.

"Really? That would be great…but you could get into deep trouble over this." Jesse's eyes bored into his.

"Only if I get caught," he said. Apprehension rolled off him, and she realized the risk he was willing to take for her.

"Marty—I," she began.

"Don't say anything. Let's just make this happen."

She reached out and touched his hand that rested on the windowsill of her car. Suddenly she was filled with fear mixed with anticipation at the thought of their escapade. "Thanks, Marty," she choked out.

"I'll pick you up at six on Friday," he said, his eyes scanning the highway. "And slow down, Miss."

"You've made me late for my hair appointment, officer. I could cite you for public harassment." She waved as she drove off, his chuckle echoing in her ears.

Jesse slid into the booth across from Susan at the cafe in Woolworth's. Several people sat on the stools along the lunch counter, and more filled the booths on either side of them. Aromas of french fries and freshly brewed coffee mixed with leather from the nearby purse department. Brightly-dyed dry goods stacked in neat piles covered shelves and tables, while discriminating homemakers compared prices and discussed the merit of one tablecloth over another. Looking around the perimeter of the restaurant she felt stunned with sensory overload. Maybe her senses were just on alert because of her conversation with Marty.

"Hi, Jesse. Your hair looks great," Susan said, flashing a warm smile.

"Hi, Susan. Sorry I'm a little late."

Susan scrutinized her. "Your hair looks great, but you look like you've been working too hard on that house. You look like you need to eat lunch. A big lunch."

Jesse brushed her friend's concern aside. "It's that damn lawn. It takes forever to mow; I use up all my energy on that."

Susan's eyes were observant; she merely nodded.

After giving their orders to the waitress, Susan leaned in on the table and lowered her voice.

"I think there is more you should know about Helen."

Jesse leaned in, too. "Tell me, Susan."

"As I've told you, we were best friends. I knew all of her secrets...for a while. She was my maid of honor, and we stayed close after I was married. We tried to get the same shifts at the hospital so we could ride over together talking the whole trip there and back. When Joe was born, I didn't work for a couple of months. She started dating someone, but we didn't see each other much after that, so I never got the details. I was so busy with a new baby and juggling a work schedule that we had to make a point to get together. As we all know, if you don't make it a priority, it doesn't happen. So we drifted apart."

Jesse had listened carefully, but was growing impatient for Susan to get to the point. When the waitress brought their sandwiches and iced tea, the girl struck up a conversation with Susan asking about Joe and his construction business. It was quite evident she was more interested in Joe and any inquiry about the business was polite window dressing. They chatted and she finally asked if they needed anything else.

I need you to go away. Jesse wasn't sure if her impatience was simply so Susan could continue the story or because of the girl's obvious interest in Joe. She shrugged off the latter.

Susan leaned in again, and Jesse followed her lead, but then Susan sat back and spoke loudly. "So every fall I dig up the tulips in that part of the yard and plant some of them over by the fence."

Jesse looked at her like she was crazy, and then felt whoever was in the booth behind her shift in her seat. She turned at the sound of the woman's voice.

"Oh, hello, Susan. I didn't realize that was you behind me," said a white haired lady whose bulk flowed beyond the edge of the booth. Looking back at her, Jesse thought the way she tucked herself above and below the edge of the table surely had to hurt, but it was obvious the lunch counter was no option.

"Hello, Gert. How are your hydrangeas coming along this year?" Susan asked.

Jesse was amazed at the woman's agility as she slid out of the booth, gathered her girth into one mass and stood. Though her breathing was a bit labored, her voice boomed as she answered.

"Exquisite. Come for tea and see how that fertilizer has renewed them." Thrusting out her hand, she said. "I'm Gert Hawthorne, and you must be the new teacher at St. Bart's."

"Gert, may I present Jesse Graham?"

"How do you do, Mrs. Hawthorne?" Jesse took her hand.

"Jesse has moved into the Cavanaugh House. She is Helen's niece."

"Spittin' image." Gert said, her smile reminiscent of the Cheshire Cat. "Nice to meet you, Miss Graham. Have a lovely day, ladies." She moved along the aisle clearing just enough space to avoid spilling the mounds of folded items in her path.

"Gert was trying to get an earful," Susan laughed. "She knew I caught her and had no excuse for staying where she was."

"Boy, in small towns everybody's business is everybody's business," Jesse sighed.

"A good thing to keep in mind. Well, let me continue; now where was I?"

"You had drifted apart due to your maternity leave and Aunt Helen dating a mysterious man."

"Oh, yes. Well, when I went back to work part-time, we started riding together any time we could, which wasn't often. Helen was very closed-mouthed about her mystery man, so I assumed he was married. Finally, she admitted that she was seeing someone who did not want their relationship to be public—yet. I remember clearly that she said 'yet' and smiled when she said it. About a month later, she confessed that she was pregnant." Susan let the words hang in the air.

Jesse had been listening, concentrating on every word. At Susan's last sentence, her mind did a somersault over the meaning of those words and they spun through her head like a merry-go-round. Susan might as well have been speaking Greek for all the sense it made. Looking up, she saw her friend watching her.

"Helen loved the Wild West, and her favorite outfit included a leather fringed cowgirl jacket. When she told me she was pregnant, she referred to the baby as her little cowboy, but beneath her excitement was a layer of fear. I don't even know if she had told her lover that she was pregnant. Soon after that she moved away—not unusual back in those days for unwed mothers. I received a birth notice that read, 'announcing the arrival of my little cowhand' with the footprint and handprint of her new baby. She even named the baby after a famous Wild West character."

Every muscle in Jesse's body quivered. Her ears rang with the cacophony of every voice in the store, with the bell that rang each time a customer entered or left, with the cries of a child who had been told he couldn't have that toy, and with the blood that rushed through her veins. The world tumbled yet again into a dreamlike scene where nothing made sense.

"Wild West?" she said faintly. "Like Wyatt Earp?" She gazed at Susan. "Or Jesse James?"

Susan reached across the table and took Jesse's icy hands in her own.

"Yes, sweetie. Just like Jesse James."

Jesse sat, stunned, her world tumbling about her, yet sensations were sharp and clear—the metal-edged Formica table cutting into her forearms, the orange-red vinyl seat squeaky beneath her legs, the sun slanting in the storefront window casting bright rays across her half-eaten sandwich left on its plate, the corners of the drying bread starting to curl. No thoughts formed; she was unable to reason, as if these last words of Susan's had rendered her incapable of intelligent thought. She merely felt, and even then wasn't sure what she was feeling. She had a sensation of being down a long tunnel filled with sludge, groping to regain her footing and emerge unscathed. The only sound, her heartbeat thudding a rhythm of disbelief, and yet belief, for somehow deep within, this all made perfect sense. Somehow this was the umbilical cord connected to the sweet-misery of longing she experienced in the attic room.

Helen was her mother.

Susan's voice brought her out of the tunnel and back to the moment. "Are you okay?" Her forehead was creased with concern, her eyes soft with sympathy.

Jesse looked at her as if coming out of a trance, still unable to speak. No coherent thought formed as she looked across the table. Susan gave her time, calling the waitress over to order some coffee for both of them.

"When did you know?" Jesse asked.

"The minute I saw you."

"Why didn't you tell me right away?"

Susan looked out the window at the street busy with people bustling by and cars pulling in and out of the slant-angle parking spots.

"It wasn't my place."

"What changed your mind?"

Susan hesitated as the waitress delivered their coffee and left.

"Well, after hearing about your relationship with your...uh...mother, Eileen, it was clear she would never tell you. When Joe told me about what happened on the highway, it sounded too coincidental. I think there is lingering fallout from whatever happened to Helen, and I think you need to be careful. I never discovered who she was involved with. She was seldom secretive with me—

we shared everything—so it must have held some danger for her."

"Marty said there were rumors that it wasn't suicide. Do you remember anything about that?" Jesse asked.

"Oh, indeed I do. Rumors flew about foul play, but they were squelched and the investigation eventually ruled her death as suicide. I wasn't privy to any of the details...no one was. The night Helen died, Eileen came from Geneva to identify her sister and to pick you up. God, you were a beautiful baby. I got to hold you that night, and I saw that your eyes were already turning the same brilliant green as Helen's."

In profound sadness, Jesse's heart ached and she was surprised at her deep affection for her aunt—no her mother that she had never known. Her mother. Thoughts whirled through her head. Her whole life had been based on lies; she had never known who she really was. Was this why her mother was always so cold? Did she resent her that much? But Eileen wasn't her mother, was she? She was her aunt. Oh, it was too confusing. She was going to need time to come to terms with all of this. And what about her father...who, by the way, wasn't actually her father?

As if reading her mind, Susan spoke again.

"Eileen's husband was with her when she brought you over and told me what had happened. They had to return to Helen's to identify her...body... and they asked if I could watch you. I was despondent at the news and held you through the night. We rocked and I cried; you snuggled into me and slept, unaware of how your life had changed in an instant. Eileen and Jim arrived the next morning to take you with them. Jim adored you instantly, and you responded to him, too. When Eileen picked you up, you started to wail and were inconsolable until Jim took you. He walked with you cooing and whispering, and you settled right down." Susan looked at her, great sadness in her eyes. "I guess that was a harbinger of things to come."

Jesse nodded, still groping for some equilibrium.

The waitress brought the checks to the table and Susan scooped up both of them. Fishing through her purse, she took out a dollar and laid it beside her coffee cup and tucked a five in with the tab.

"Do you need some fresh air?" she asked. Jesse nodded again.

Stopping by the cash register, Susan settled the bill and they headed out into the sunshine. Jesse found it incongruous that the sun should be shining when she had just received such jarring news. Susan steered her toward a park across the street and they sat on a bench in silence. Jesse watched a little girl on a swing, her mother pushing her and laughing as the girl begged, "Higher, Mommy, higher!" Her squeals of delight floated over to where the women sat. Jesse looked away.

"I'm sorry to lay all of this on you, but I believed it was time you knew. You have some decisions to make, and you will need all of the information you can dig up."

Jesse was quiet for a few moments before she spoke.

"Thank you for your honesty, Susan. I understand why you didn't tell me right away, and I appreciate your sensitivity in sharing what you know. So many people have reacted so strongly upon seeing me, but it all makes sense now. Ben Wyndham was especially surprised."

"Yes, Joe told me about his reaction when Al introduced you. I suspect many people of my generation will recognize Helen in you. She was very popular in Seneca Corners. Very active in community events and fundraisers. I'm surprised some of the sisters over at St. Bart's haven't mentioned anything to you about how much she volunteered over there."

"Well, Sr. Alphonse certainly had a cold greeting for me the day I arrived. Maybe she wasn't so fond of my aunt—I mean my mother. Wow, this is going to take some getting used to!" She was steadier now, at least able to think about what Susan had told her. Absorbing that much shocking news was exhausting, and she was still tired from her disrupted sleep the night before. Suddenly her limbs were leaden, her eyes dry and tired.

"Susan, I think I need to go home and think about all of this."

"Of course, Jesse. I'm here if you need to talk, cry, whatever. Just let me know. Joe and I are not attached at the hip. If you need me, it doesn't have to be awkward."

Jesse gave her a hug. "You're a good friend, Susan. But you sure as hell have given me a lot to think about."

Maggie ripped open the bag of marshmallows as Jesse broke the graham crackers into squares. Dusk cloaked them in purple twilight, and the flames in the fire pit flickered on their faces.

"I wish I had a dime for every time someone called me 'Graham Cracker'," Jesse said with a grimace.

Maggie laughed. "You couldn't win. It was either that or 'Jesse James.' Oooh. Sorry Jess. I know that must be sensitive for you right now."

"Maggie, I am still trying to fathom that my mother is actually my aunt and Aunt Helen was really my mother. This is like a bad trip for me…and I've never tripped! My whole world has been turned upside down." She looked at her best friend. "Who am I then, Mags? All of my life has been a lie."

Maggie rose and wrapped her in a bear hug. Jesse leaned her head on Maggie's shoulder as hot tears streamed down her face.

"It's hard, not knowing who you are. What about my father-who-is-really-my-uncle? What happened to him? Mother, that is Eileen—I don't know what the hell to call her—told me he just up and left one day. What if all of that is a lie, too? Mags, I'm so confused."

Maggie held her, rubbing her back, as she cried. Ever since her conversation with Susan that afternoon, Jesse had felt as though she were tumbling through space unattached to anything, her jumbled thoughts scattered, unable to form a coherent train of thought. How could she accept the fact that the woman she'd thought of as her mother, was not? That a woman she had never known was, in fact, her mother? She wondered about Jeanie Conklin, a girl she'd been in grade school with who had found out in sixth grade that she was adopted. Was this how she had felt? Was her world turned topsy-turvy like Jesse's now was? She wished she'd been kinder to Jeanie. Not that she had been mean to her, but she never befriended her or tried to reach out to her that year.

"Mags, maybe this is karma. Maybe I'm being paid back for not being nicer to Jeanie Conklin in sixth grade." She pulled back from Maggie's hug.

"What are you talking about?" Maggie looked at her with a mix of concern and confusion. "This isn't karma…"

"Maybe it's earthly purgatory, you know. God needs a head-start with me because I've screwed up so much."

Maggie grabbed a Hershey bar and broke it into squares. "Now you're talking crazy, Jess. You need a strong infusion of chocolate. I'm doubling up your s'more." She balanced two squares of chocolate on a graham cracker and grabbed a stick, poking it through a marshmallow. "First of all, God doesn't work that way. *Merciful* God, remember? Secondly, you are not as good a sinner as you think. You give yourself way too much credit. You're a slouch compared to Marie Vallero; she did the whole first string of the football team that one night, remember? You were never that good at being bad, my friend." Jesse doubled over laughing as Maggie placed the chocolate-laden graham cracker below the golden brown marshmallow and placed another on top, expertly sliding the sweet treat off her stick. Handing the s'more to Jesse she said, "Perfection. Just like you."

Chocolate dripped down Jesse's hand as she took the offering. "Oooh, I hate sticky hands!" she cried and bit into the s'more. "But they're worth the price of this little bit of heaven."

"Just like dealing with shocking news is worth the price of truth," Maggie said.

Jesse chewed thoughtfully and stared into the fire.

"You're right, Mags. No matter how difficult it is to comprehend this, it is the truth. Not knowing the truth doesn't change it, and perhaps knowing the truth will help me to discover who I really am. Mother—that is Eileen, I don't know what the hell to call her—"

"You've already said that," Maggie interrupted.

"And I'll say it again a million times because I don't know what the hell to call her!" Her voice rose and a dog started barking in the darkness. Far off they heard a sharp command and a door slam; then the dog was quiet. Jesse continued, her voice soft. "We never were close; she was as nurturing as a prickly cactus. I wonder if she resented having to raise me? I wonder if that's why she never loved..." her voice cracked. They sat in silence staring into the flames. After a while, Maggie spoke, her voice floating on the night.

"One thing is for sure, Jess. You're going to have a lot of questions, and some of them may never be answered. That's a fact you will have to live with. But this is a starting place. Knowing the truth is a starting place."

"I can start with the circumstances of my Aunt Helen's—I mean my mother's death."

"You know, it might be better if you continued to call her 'Aunt Helen' until you sort this all out. Don't forget, someone tried to hurt you, and the only possible reason would be your connection to your aunt—mother. Geez, you're right, this is hard."

"Can't tell the players without a score card," Jesse joked, and then she sobered. "You may be right, Mags. Susan knows I'm her daughter, but does anyone else? It's just my resemblance to her that stirred memories up for someone."

"So what's your plan for tomorrow night? Marty is going to sneak you into the Archives Room?"

"Yes, after dinner and dancing at Tony's, we're heading over to the court house. Maggie, I'm so excited that I am finally going to see my Aunt Helen's file. I don't know what I'll find there, but any little item that could point me in the direction of who might have had something to do with her death, or known something that generated the rumors surrounding it, would be a place to start."

"Please be careful. You might be stirring up a hornet's nest."

"Weren't we just talking about how the truth can set you free?" Jesse asked as she slid a marshmallow on her stick.

"I hope that's all it does," Maggie sighed.

Jesse tossed and turned until well after midnight. Mentally she tried to arrange the characters that were her family, but like in a wavy mirror at a fun house, they kept shifting and melting into one another. Eileen's face but with auburn hair, green-eyed Helen reaching out to her, and her father's face blank of any features she could remember. She found it hopeless to clarify an image of any of them and impossible to determine what to call them. She agreed with Maggie that it was best to continue referring to her birth mother as Aunt Helen until she could figure out the lay of the land here in Seneca Corners. Therefore, she would continue to refer to—and think of—Eileen as "Mother." It was all so confusing.

She plumped her pillow for the twentieth time and flopped to her other side.

Then she heard the sighing. A soft hollow noise that wafted through the wall and floated to her. Almost an "ooohhh" that someone might whisper while petting a kitten. She turned over on her back and listened.

Nothing.

Did she imagine it? Her mind sparked with confused thoughts and images; why not add a visit from Aunt Helen to the mix? She heard it again. Throwing back the covers, she slipped out of bed and padded down the hall. A soft glow radiated from beneath the attic room door. She approached the door and stopped. This time was different. This wasn't her aunt, this was her mother. *Her Mother*. Her heart beat faster; she was afraid to open the door. Intense longing filled her and she pitched forward as though pushed. The sighing was eerie and mesmerizing. Straightening, she reached for the doorknob and the sighing stopped. Tendrils of cold air slipped beneath the door and brushed over her toes.

Easing the door inward, she scanned the dark room. To her right, a faint glow shimmered beside the armoire, then disappeared. Flipping on the light, she could see nothing where the apparition had been. Again the door to the armoire was ajar; Jesse approached it. One sleeve of the jacket protruded through the opening, and she opened the door wider taking out the leather coat. In the light, the soft leather glowed pale, creamy ivory. Slipping the fringe through her fingers she tried to envision her Aunt Helen wearing this, laughing and enjoying herself. Instinctively, she checked the pockets and found a clean handkerchief. The small item made Helen even more real. She looked around the room, and for the first time, she looked up toward the rafters. Still tied around a beam was a loop of rope, frayed at the end where it had been cut. Jesse's knees wobbled beneath her and bile rose in her throat. She fought down the nausea and stared at the rope that had been the cause of her mother's death. Clutching the cowgirl jacket, she trembled, wanting to run and never return to this room.

She heard the sigh echoing as if from above her and closed her eyes. *I don't know if I have the courage to do this.* Then the thought floated into her mind: *You can walk away or you can find the truth. You can live in fear, or you can face your destiny.* Recognizing this as a defining moment, she wavered between fear and defiance. Suspended between two worlds, she knew it was up to her to decide in which one to live. Straightening her shoulders, she stood tall.

"Aunt Helen—I mean, Mother, I'll need you beside me."

She heard the sighing, and the sense of longing overtook her again.

"I think that was a hug." Through her tears, Jesse smiled toward the armoire.

Marty arrived promptly at six o'clock in his pickup truck. Jesse grabbed her purse, put her Kodak Hawkeye Instamatic camera in it, locked the door and walked to the passenger window.

"You mean I don't get to ride in a police car tonight?" she teased.

"In my experience, most people don't want to do that," he said.

"I thought we could arrive sirens blaring and lights flashing," she said as she climbed into his truck.

"Tonight we're going to fly under the radar, no pun intended. I see you're dressed like Mata Hari."

Jesse looked down at her black pants cropped just above her ankles and her black cotton top. Just in case, she had a black scarf hidden in her purse. She looked at his madras shirt, unbuttoned at the collar, and khaki pants that looked casual, as if nothing were planned for the evening but a fish fry and some dancing.

"Too much?" she asked.

He looked at her sideways. "You look great. You always look great."

She smiled, "Thanks. I think this is only the second time I've seen you out of your uniform...I mean dressed, not naked...I mean in regular clothes." She babbled as she appreciated at that moment what a very good-looking man Marty was.

He laughed. "Are you trying to seduce me, Jesse? All this naughty talk?"

She flushed. "No, I meant, you look nice tonight, too."

"And I don't look nice in my uniform?" he teased.

"Yes! Yes, you do, but you look nice tonight, too. Crap, you're making me crazy, Marty."

Laughing, he backed out of the driveway and headed toward town.

Lively chatter and clanking dishes welcomed them as they entered Tony's and found the last available table in the center of the room. The restaurant was already filled with diners, people lined up at the counter, many calling "Hello" as they passed. Settling in, they waited for the waitress to appear to take their order.

Jesse's stomach fluttered so much at the thought of their plans for later that night she could hardly concentrate on their conversation during dinner. As the waitress was clearing their table, she saw Joe enter the restaurant and her heart did a flip-flop. Smiling, he greeted people as he entered, his smile disappearing when he caught sight of her with Marty. When his eyes met hers, she saw him stop in mid-sentence and freeze. She raised her hand to wave, but he turned away and she sat there with her hand stopped in mid-air. Seeing her movement, Marty looked over his shoulder and spotted Joe who had turned his back and was talking to friends at the counter. Marty looked back at Jesse who caught his eye and lowered her hand. Her pulse raced despite her effort to remain calm, and she could not stop the blush from creeping from her neck to her face. An awkward silence fell between them. Finally he spoke.

"So, there's Joe," he stated the obvious.

"Yes."

"So, didn't you say that you haven't seen him since the day after your accident?"

"Yes."

"So how is that going?"

Looking down at the table, she didn't know what to say. How was it going? She missed Joe more than she was ready to admit, and she was embarrassed that he saw her here with Marty. She thought she was cheating on him somehow, but she had made it clear she wasn't ready to be involved yet. So what was all this heart-racing, high-school blushing about? As if she didn't have enough confusion in her life, add this to her "things-to-keep-me-awake-at-night" list.

"Look, Jesse, it's as plain as the nose on your face how you care for each other. Why all this keeping-your-distance crap?" he asked.

"I'm just not ready to get involved right now," she said, her voice weak and thready.

"I don't get all that 'work through it' bullshit. If you got dumped, get over it. If you care about someone, take the risk. Sometimes it works," he looked away, "and sometimes it doesn't."

Jesse saw the look in his eyes and felt a stab of guilt. Had she been using Marty to get what she wanted after all? She hadn't thought so, but maybe that's how he saw it. God, life was just too hard. Never would she intentionally hurt him, but maybe her desperation had clouded her self-awareness.

"Marty, I'm sorry if I led you on," she said.

"No, Jesse, you never did that. Sometimes we just have feelings we didn't ask for—you know?"

"Look, about our plan. Why don't we just forget it?" she said lightly, hiding the disappointment that lay heavy in her stomach.

"No way, Nancy Drew! We are on for the Case of the Secret Files."

She laughed. "How do you know so much about Nancy Drew, officer?"

"*Ai yi yi*! Are you kidding me? I have six sisters. Nancy Drew books decorated every nook and cranny of our house."

"And perhaps landed in your hands, thus your interest in detective work."

"I will never admit to reading a sissy girl's book," he laughed. "Seriously though, Joe's my buddy. I can't just ignore him." He looked back to where Joe was still standing by the counter. "You've got your feelings, and I respect that. I can go over and talk to him where he is…"

"But it would be more normal if he sat here with you," she finished.

Marty nodded. Jesse took a deep breath. "Then I think you should invite him over to our table."

He grinned and cuffed her upper arm. "'Atta girl."

But as he started to rise, Joe turned and left. Marty looked at her and shrugged. "I guess he wasn't hungry."

Jesse nodded, fighting her disappointment.

They stayed for most of the dancing, but Jesse's increasing restlessness was becoming unbearable, so Marty called for their check.

The night breeze, heavy with humidity, rushed against her face as she walked out the door. She inhaled the fresh air that was free of smoke and the smell of beer; her spirits lifted. She vacillated between anticipation and fear at knowing she would see the report of the investigation of her aunt's death—she still must think of Helen as her aunt. But she was also aware of the risk Marty was taking to allow her access to the Archive Room. She looked at him across the seat of the pickup, his face calm, maybe even determined. But she wondered if his resolve had lessened after seeing her reaction to Joe earlier.

"Are you sure about this?" she asked, fearful of his answer.

"Positive. We're going to see what we can find out, Jesse." He looked at her, his face illuminated by the lights of the dashboard. "You may not find anything, though."

"There has got to be something," she answered. "I feel it in my bones."

He laughed. "You sound like my grandma again."

He pulled along the street and parked a block away from the courthouse under the shadow of an elm tree.

"It will look suspicious if my truck is in the parking lot while I'm off duty," he explained.

They climbed out of the truck and hurried along the street, turning the next corner where the court house loomed in front of them. Somehow it hadn't appeared so ominous in the daylight. Wind blew the leaves on the trees, causing shadows to dance on the building's façade, like grotesque marionettes. Off in the distance thunder rumbled heralding an impending storm.

"Classic," she muttered.

"Did you order the weather, Nancy Drew?" Marty whispered.

"Right. I've got God's ear," she smirked.

"It might work to our advantage. If a storm is brewing, it could cover any sound we make."

Lightning lit up the sky to the west.

"And lightning will cover the flash of any pictures I take." she said.

"Pictures? What pictures?"

"Of the report."

"You can't take pictures of the report!" Marty rasped.

"Well, I can't remove anything. How else am I supposed to study it?"

"Shit, Jesse, I didn't figure on this."

"Think about it. We can't remove the files, and there may be things in there that we need to study. You can't sneak me in every other day so I can double check information."

He shook his head. "I think you're nothing but trouble, Nancy Drew."

Jesse's heart hammered as they neared the steps to the front door of the court house. Grabbing her elbow, Marty steered her toward the back.

"This way, ma'am. I only have keys to the back entrance. Besides, we're less likely to be seen." He surveyed the street, but all was dark, quiet.

As they circled the building, she saw lights on in several first floor windows.

"That's the station. We offer twenty-four hour service to our citizens. I'm not sure who is on duty tonight, but whoever it is, it's best if they don't see me."

Staying in the shadows as they passed those windows, he led her to a small inconspicuous door at the back. Pulling out a key ring, he flipped through and settled on a bright brass key in the middle of the bunch. Inserting it, he again scanned the area, then silently turned the key, turned the door knob and pushed in the door. They hurried inside and he closed the door leaving them in the dim glow of the light of an emergency exit sign. To their right was a tall metal cabinet, padlocked. Reaching between it and the corner of the wall, Marty pulled out a Kel-Lite flashlight and clicked it on. The circular glow illuminated the concrete staircases in front of them; he led Jesse to the one going down. Seized with foreboding, she froze at the top of the stairs. She shrugged her shoulders, trying to rid herself of the anxiety. They descended to the basement as another bolt of lightning lit up the small window above them at the landing; a growl of thunder followed. With each step, the musty odor reminded her how much she disliked basements.

Her arms prickled as her stomach flipped with unease. She fought to maintain control as doubts bubbled up. What they were doing was illegal, dangerous and, for Marty, could be devastating to his career. Was she willing to put him at such risk? And why was he willing to take the risk? Guilt mixed with the unease hanging heavy in her gut.

They reached the room with "Archives" on the door, and Marty pulled out his key ring again. Then he stuck his hand back in his pocket and pulled out a separate key on its own ring. Jesse looked at him and raised an eyebrow in question.

"I don't have a key to this room," he explained. "I had to 'borrow' one from Sheriff Donoghue's desk."

"Oh my God," she whispered, her stomach dropping to her knees.

He unlocked the door, then relocked it and ushered Jesse inside. Closing it behind him, he angled the beam toward a box of gloves on a nearby table. Grabbing two he handed them to her to put on and donned a pair himself. He began swiping the flashlight along the labels on the file cabinets.

"Do you know the exact date of your aunt's death?" he asked.

"No, at least not based on what my mother told me," she said thinking of what she had learned since arriving at Seneca Corners. But based on what Susan said, she knew it was after she was born, which was July 1940. Susan hadn't said how old Jesse had been that night, only that she was an infant. She shivered as she realized that she had been right there with her mother when she died...or had been murdered. "Let's start with July 1940—the year I was born."

She saw Marty's eyes study her over the glow of the flashlight, but he didn't say anything. He pointed the light at file cabinets until he found 1940. "January and February, March and April...ah, here it is, July 1940," he said as he opened the drawer. Manila file folders crammed together, some with papers haphazardly poking out like hands raised for deliverance. He pointed the flashlight while Jesse looked at the tabs reading off case file names.

"Albertson, Andrews, Basel..." she flipped through them. Abruptly her fingers stopped searching and she froze. "Cavanaugh." Her voice was tiny. She felt tiny, as if everything in her life had funneled her to this one moment. As though she had traveled through a kaleidoscope and ultimately found the one jewel that created all the designs that had been her experience. Her hands shook as she withdrew the folder.

Marty studied her. "We don't have to do this."

She stared at the folder. "I have to. I have to know. For her and for myself, I have to know."

Taking her arm, he led her to a table beneath a small window situated high up in the wall. Lightning flashed, illuminating the room to a brilliant white and thunder rolled across the sky directly above them as if in warning. Jesse gripped the folder to keep from dropping its contents all over the floor. Sitting down, she placed it flat on the table and opened it up. Marty held the flashlight over her shoulder so she could read the account. Across the top of the first sheet was the medical examiner's report with the words "U.S. Standard Certificate of Death" in bold black letters across the top.

"It sounds so uncaring," she whispered.

"Everyone who dies gets a form with these words across the top," Marty said quietly.

"They should say, 'We're Sorry to Report Your Death', or 'We're Sorry You Died' or anything sympathetic," she said. Just cold, hard facts. Jesse knew that was how she would need to approach what she was about to see or she would fall apart. She took a deep breath and began to read.

On Line 1 the immediate cause of death was listed as asphyxia. On Line 2, compression of the carotid arteries was listed as causal, and on Line 3 bruises around the victim's neck were noted. Because she was leaning in to read, and the beam of the flashlight was so focused, she noticed a smudge on the paper where something had been smeared—or erased. Squinting at the form, she wished she could hold it to more light. Then, remembering her camera, she pulled it out, focused on the paper and snapped a photograph of it. The flash lit up the room revealing the hulking forms of the file cabinets.

Jesse examined one report after another, taking photos of each sheet. Finally, she turned a report over and stopped. She felt as if ice had been poured over her. Marty tried to hide it, but he was not quick enough, and she brushed his hand away. In front of her lay the first photo of Helen suspended from the beam in the attic room. Jesse's stomach turned over and her ears rang. She felt faint; spots floated before her eyes. *No! I will not be weak! I will face this and I will find the truth.* She heard his voice from far away.

"C'mon, Jesse, that's enough for tonight. You don't need to see these photos; they're not going to help you one bit." He took her arm to help her rise from the table, but she pulled away.

"Just give me a minute," she said.

Waiting for her to compose herself, Marty walked around down the aisle between some cabinets. He hurried back to her turning off the flashlight. Closing the file folder, he snatched it up and pulled her to her feet.

"Quick, follow me," he whispered grabbing her hand.

Groping their way to the back of the room, they hunkered down beside the last file cabinet in the corner just as a light flicked on, flooding the room in harsh fluorescent light. Footsteps sounded as someone entered. They held their breath as the person circled the front section of cabinets and started back toward the spot where they hid. Jesse was certain the person could hear her racing heart, so she closed her eyes and willed herself to be still. Marty was curled around her with his arms embracing her in a protective posture. She felt his breath against her hair and tried not to move, which might cause their closeness to be even more awkward. With the footsteps coming closer, she could hear the person's breathing, and then he muttered, "Must be mice again." She wanted to jump up and run regardless of who was standing there. She had had her fill of those furry critters; she didn't want to encounter any more right now. Eyes squeezed closed, she tried not to think about rodents as she waited for the man to move again. He stepped closer toward their hiding place, paused, then reversed his progress and headed to the door. Flipping off the light, he closed and locked the door, his footsteps echoing down the hall.

Jesse and Marty let their breath out simultaneously and moved away from each other.

"That was a close call," he whispered.

"Marty, let me just photograph what's remaining and we'll get out of here," she replied, her voice soft in the darkness.

Marty flicked on the Kel-Lite, and they went back to the table where he reopened the report. Jesse flipped through the paperwork until she got to the photos and took out her camera. She snapped pictures of the crime scene photos one by one. Gritting her teeth, she tried not to think about what she was seeing, pushing through to complete her task. She came to a photo of her bedroom as it had been then; tucked into a corner was a cradle, one tiny fist raised above the side of it. In a moment of complete clarity, she realized she was looking at herself at the time of her Aunt Helen's death. Overwhelmed with exhaustion, she sat back in the chair. Marty slipped the camera from her hand and finished photographing the three remaining pictures.

"Come on, Nancy Drew. Time to get you out of here." He straightened the papers and photos and closed the file. Leaving her to recover, he replaced the manila folder in the cabinet and returned to where she was sitting.

"You okay?" he asked, his voice just above a whisper.

Standing, she nodded. Taking her arm, he led her to the door, cracked it open, and checked the hallway. They slipped out and headed for the stairs.

Back out on the street, rain pelted them as they hurried to Marty's pick-up. Crouching over as she ran, Jesse used her black scarf to keep her hair as dry as possible, her eyes watching the pavement…so she didn't notice the car that sat just down the street from Marty's truck, its driver watching their every move.

-SEVEN-

Jesse regretted her dinner plans with Al. He would arrive soon to pick her up, but her mind whirled with all the information she had learned over the past week. Standing in front of the oak secretary in her living room, she traced the pattern of the wood with her fingers trying to settle her thoughts. A list. She needed to make a list of all the new information. Folding down the desk surface, she pulled over a chair, sat down, and reached for a pen and paper. She had thrown out all the dried up jars of ink that had been Aunt Helen's, but there were some treasures remaining: an elegant fountain pen and a letter opener with a pearl handle inlaid with lapis lazuli. The latter was fashioned like the handle of a pistol, and Jesse thought of the cowgirl jacket in the armoire…and her name. Yes, Aunt Helen had been a fan of the Wild West. Her musings interrupted by the doorbell, she closed up the desk, checked her hair in the mirror and answered the door.

Al stood on the porch holding a huge bouquet of pale pink roses. Jesse checked a grimace; she did not want romantic gestures to spoil the night. She took a deep breath and smiled at him.

"Thank you, Al. These are beautiful. Let me put them in water before we go. Come in, please." She held the door open for him to enter.

Al looked around at the rooms still in various stages of repair. He whistled.

"You've got your work cut out for you."

Jesse followed his gaze.

"Actually, I'm proud about what I've accomplished. The living room is finished, and the kitchen is workable. The dining room needs a lot of TLC though."

Al looked at her with admiration. "You are one determined woman!"

She smiled at the compliment and went to the kitchen to find a suitable empty jar to fill with water for the roses.

Al was a delightful dinner companion sharing stories of growing up at Wyndham Estate. He didn't try to impress Jesse; rather, many of his stories were humorously self-deprecating or in praise of someone else. She relaxed and, for a time, forgot about the serious issues that had invaded her life since moving to Seneca Corners. They had finished dinner and were enjoying Crème Brule and coffee for dessert as the band arrived and started setting up.

"I had hoped to pick you up in my Porsche so you could see it's not a thug," Al laughed.

"I suffered so having to ride in your Mercedes, Al," she countered.

"Jesse, I'm sorry that my car was involved in your accident."

She looked away and studied the other patrons. When she looked back at him, her voice was quiet.

"Let's not discuss my accident, Al. You don't need to feel guilty because your car was involved. Someone with sinister intentions took advantage of your trusting nature. The end. Now let's talk about the fun side of life. Tell me about Barbara."

"Oh, Barbie and I have been friends for years. We've been hanging around in the same crowd since high school."

Jesse stopped him with a cold look.

"What?" he asked.

"You've been friends for years and you don't know that she hates to be called 'Barbie'?"

"Aw, she changed to Barbara with this women's lib movement. I've always called her Barbie."

She straightened in her chair as her anger swelled.

"So you don't respect her enough to honor her request?" She glared at him.

He sat back in his chair and raised his hands, palms toward her in surrender.

"Geez, back off, Jesse. I guess I didn't realize it was so important."

"You said you prefer to be called Al to Albert. Would it bother you if I ignored your preference and called you Albert?"

He lowered his hands and shrugged.

"You're right. I guess I hadn't thought of that. I will call her Barbara from now on...at least I'll try. It's a hard habit to break."

She relented. "I guess it would be hard after many years to call someone by a different name." *Like 'mother' instead of 'aunt.'* "Sorry I became so worked up about it. Women's rights issues are important to me. Names can affect how we see people, and Barbara wants to be seen as a woman, not a little girl—or a doll." she paused. "Are you aware of how she wants *you* to see her?"

Al looked confused. "As a woman not a little girl or a doll?" he offered. He cringed a bit as if waiting for a blow to be delivered.

Jesse laughed. "I guess I let my Irish temper take over sometimes. Sorry. No, Al. Barbara wants you to see her as a *desirable* woman. Didn't you know that?"

A surprised look flickered across his face. "Barbie—ara?" he corrected. "Hmm. We've been friends for so long, I never thought of her romantically. This will sound like I'm an egomaniac, but many women pursue me. Some are pretty aggressive about it; after all, I'm the most eligible—and rich—bachelor in Seneca Corners. I've put up a pretty solid wall of defense. But Barbara?" His focus drifted off as he pondered this revelation. After a few minutes, he looked back at her.

"How do you know this?"

"It was very obvious at your Founder's Day gathering," Jesse laughed.

"Obvious to you. But sometimes an objective observer sees what people in the midst of a situation miss."

She was silent for a moment. She toyed with the idea of asking the question burning within her but knew she had to approach the topic with subtlety. She took a deep breath.

"Something else I noticed was the strange reaction your father and Fred Morton had when they met me. Do you know why?"

Al shrugged. "No idea."

"Did you notice their reactions when you introduced me?"

Al studied the ceiling as he searched his memory. He shrugged and grinned at her. "Not really. I do recall that Father spilled his wine and left to change his shirt."

"Precisely. He spilled his wine when he looked at me. And Fred Morton scowled like I carried the plague."

"Fred Morton always scowls—don't let that be a basis of your judgment. He's a good guy, though. He's been a friend of the family, and our accountant, for years. He went to school with my uncle who brought him into the business."

Jesse thought about this.

"Did your father say anything about me?"

"No. Why?"

"As I said, his reaction was quite strong."

"Maybe you just misread him. He might have stumbled and spilled his wine. Or maybe somebody bumped his arm. People were moving all through the rooms."

"You're probably right," she said. Whatever she needed to know, Al did not have the answers. She looked around the room.

Waiters moved among the tables clearing dishes and bringing wine bottles or after-dinner drinks. As the first chord played, the lights dimmed and the atmosphere transformed from dining room chatter to smooth jazz that wrapped itself around the patrons like a mist. Jesse peered through the haze of cigarette smoke sensing a stab of longing. This room could have been in Rochester several months ago, with Robert on the stage. She had sat at his gigs many times watching him with love and pride, believing she was loved in return. But his love for her had been as ephemeral as the smoke that smudged the air around her. Excusing herself, she snaked her way between tables to find the ladies' room.

Her eyes looked hollow as she stared into the mirror. The weight of melancholy on top of the recent shock of discovering her identity crushed her. Tears stung her eyes and a lump formed in her throat. Yanking paper towels from the holder, she dabbed at her eyes as she took deep breaths. *Steady girl.* Searching her purse though tear-blurred eyes, she found her compact and lipstick. Her hands trembled as she powdered her nose and cheeks. *Pull yourself together.* She willed herself to calm down as she meticulously applied her lipstick. Straightening her shoulders, she took a deep breath, satisfied by her reflection that she had improved her looks marginally and regained her composure. But she knew she could not stay here.

Returning to the table, she explained that she had a headache intensified by the smoke. Al called for the check and they left. The summer night had done little to alleviate the humid heat of the day, but at least the fresh air was a relief from the smoky atmosphere of the club. Walking to Al's car, Jesse again apologized for cutting the night short. She had, in fact, been having an enjoyable time with Al.

"How about an ice cream? My treat," she offered.

"Sure!" Al said, turning the car toward Seneca Corners.

They sat on a bluff overlooking Seneca Lake as they enjoyed their ice cream cones. Jesse was thankful for the breeze that had come up; it tossed the wisps of hair that surrounded her face. They enjoyed their cones in silence for a moment before she spoke.

"I have to be honest with you about tonight," she said.

Al looked at her waiting for her to continue.

"Al, one of the reasons I moved to Seneca Corners was to escape the constant reminders of my broken engagement. I needed to leave Rochester because I was a familiar face there, and everyone associated me with my former fiancé, Robert Cronmiller."

Al's eyebrows shot up.

"You were engaged to Robert Cronmiller? I love his mus... nevermind." He looked out at the lake. "Geez, I couldn't have taken you to a worse place than a jazz club. I'm sorry. I didn't know."

"It's okay. I should have thought it through, but I've had so much on my mind lately."

Al looked back at her. "So that's why you moved into the Cavanaugh House?"

"It was the only place I had to go. The job at St. Bart's was a Godsend, and Maggie helped me get that."

"Maggie?"

"Sr. Angelina."

"Oh! Her name is Maggie? I never knew that," he mused.

"The house belonged to my aunt, Helen Cavanaugh, and she willed it to me. I didn't know that until my twenty-first birthday, and when I caught Robert...when I broke off the engagement, I remembered that I owned this house. I needed to get away and the house needed someone to love it—a match made in heaven."

"Whatever brought you here, I'm glad." Al reached over and took her hand. "You've got guts, Jesse. I admire you." He squeezed her hand and released it.

She was touched by his sincerity.

Throwing away their napkins, they returned to the car.

"You look beat. I'll get you home," Al said.

"Thanks." She smiled at him.

They slipped into his Mercedes and he started the engine.

"So you think Barbie—Barbara thinks of me as more than a friend?"

Jesse relaxed and enjoyed the smooth ride home.

Jesse knew it was time for a conversation with her mother. Besides, she couldn't develop the photos she had taken in Seneca Corners—that would really start tongues wagging. She sped along I-490 heading north into Rochester. Having been away from traffic for a couple of months caused her to grip Bert's steering wheel a little tighter and watch other drivers a little closer. She eased off the expressway into Brighton, her stomach tight with nerves at the thought of confronting her mother. Their conversations had never been easy; civil was the most she ever hoped for. Even when her heart had been broken by Robert, Eileen's cool assessment was cruel. Her words still rang in Jesse's ears.

"I told you he was no good. Men who look like that never want someone who looks like you. Maybe if you were filthy rich he would have stayed, but he would always cheat."

Jesse had no idea what would come of the conversation she intended to have with her today. Stopping by the Rexall Drug Store, she dropped of her film to be developed. The earliest she could have the prints was three days later since she had missed the pick-up for that day. She purchased a few items and returned to her car. It was weird to be back in Rochester; she felt like a stranger already. In a way, anonymity was comforting because she did not want to run into any mutual acquaintances of Robert's. Or even any of her own friends who would know their story, too.

As she neared the house, she saw her mother's BMW 1600-2 parked in the driveway. Good, she was home. This trip might be shorter than she had anticipated. Pulling in, she took a deep breath to steady her nerves. Doing battle with Eileen Graham was daunting on a good day, but after the emotional ups and downs Jesse had been on lately, she knew she would have to steel herself for this encounter.

"Mother?" she called as she entered the marble-floored foyer. The word stuck in her throat. It had never felt natural; now it felt sacrilegious. "Mother? I'm here."

"Jesse? Is that you?" Eileen's sharp voice ricocheted down the stairs. High-heel clicks hurried across the second story floor. Jesse had never liked how hollow the house had always sounded. Noise echoed and bounced off whatever it encountered, never landing and making a home. Never nestling in and resting in the peace of a soft, cushioned surface. Everything here simply confronted what it met, the force sending it in another direction.

"Yes, it's me," she called up the stairs. "I need to talk to you."

Eileen appeared at the top of the staircase clipping a pearl earring to her lobe. "I don't have much time. I'm meeting a client at one o'clock and it's already noon."

"I think you'll want to make time for this conversation," she said watching her mother smooth her hair in the mirror at the top of the stairs. Something in Jesse's voice made Eileen stop, her hand in mid-air. She turned and looked down at her. Descending, awareness flickered in her eyes half-way down.

"I told you not to go there," she said, her voice low.

"Why didn't you tell me?" Jesse said, angry at the catch in her voice. Eileen picked up on her vulnerability and lifted her chin.

"What good would it have done? What would it have changed? Helen was dead and you were an orphan. What else could have been done?" The words cut through the air and into Jesse's heart. She wondered at the cruelty of this woman.

"It might not have changed anything, but I would have known who I am."

Eileen snorted, which would have been unladylike for some, but made her appear more dramatic. She snatched up a silver cigarette case from the coffee table and took one out. Lighting it, she tilted her head, letting the smoke miss her eyes, then inhaled deeply. Her long fingernails, the color of blood, held the slim white cigarette so elegantly that she fashioned an art of smoking.

"Who you are," she spat the words back at Jesse who wondered how anyone so beautiful could be so cold. "You are a mixed up little tart who gave it all to the wrong man and now you're off licking your wounds. But in your own inimitable way, you went to the one place that could only make you suffer more. That's who you are. You make stupid mistakes just like Helen did, and look what happened to her."

Jesse's mind reeled from the vitriol that spewed from Eileen's mouth. She had to maintain her composure. If Eileen detected any weakness, she would go for the jugular; Jesse knew that from years of experience.

"Just what did happen to her?"

Eileen paused, taken aback by the question. Recovering, she took another long drag off the cigarette then blew the smoke out slowly; Jesse watched it swirl in her mouth and nose, repulsed. Eileen clicked her nails together just beyond where she held the cigarette; she was considering what she would reveal. Jesse wondered if she were formulating the cruelest way to say it.

"What have you heard?" Eileen asked.

"Why don't you tell me what you know? Why don't you tell me the truth for once?"

Eileen went to the sideboard and snatched the top off a crystal decanter. Pouring a generous glass of Scotch she turned to Jesse. "Maybe you need a drink, dear. Oh, I forgot your peasant penchant for beer. Why not check in the refrigerator?"

"No, thanks. I just want information."

Eileen faced her, motioned for her to sit down, and then followed suit.

"Helen committed suicide and left you alone. That's all I know."

Jesse fought a grimace keeping her face blank.

"You must know more. You were there that night."

"I was there to pick you up. You were in your cradle screaming like a banshee. I couldn't make you stop. No matter what I did, you just kept crying and crying. I thought I would go mad." It was as if she were talking to herself. "Then Jim took you and immediately you settled down. Just like that. I told him I was never cut out to have children and there was the proof. But he insisted we take you. I was your aunt for God's sake. 'What kind of woman would forsake her sister's child?' he asked me. Well, I told him, 'This kind of woman. Children were never in my plan.' But there was no one else to take you. Oh, that friend of Helen's wanted to keep you, but Jim put a stop to that. And just like that my life changed." She returned to the present and looked at Jesse who remained silent. Eileen drained her glass. "We had to identify Helen's body." She closed her eyes. "It was horrible. Her face was blue, her eyes bulging out." She put her face in her hands. "Who would do that?"

Jesse was alert. "What do you mean, 'Who would do that'?"

Eileen looked up and brushed her hair back from her forehead. "I don't know. Please, Jesse, I don't want to talk about this anymore."

"You have to. I need to know the truth about that night."

"I've told you what I know."

"There's more. Tell me what else you remember."

Eileen leaned back against the sofa and closed her eyes. "I remember the room she was in—it was like an attic. She was going to finish it to use as your nursery. Thank God they had cut her down before they brought us in to identify her. It would have been unbearable to see her just hanging there."

Jesse recalled the photo she saw and shivered.

"We entered the room and she was lying on the floor right below where... There wasn't much else in the room—a chair close to where she was and an armoire off to the side." Eileen's eyes were focused inward, a journey in her memory. "Just a bare light bulb hanging from the ceiling..." She buried her face in her hands again.

"Do you remember what anyone said? Did the sheriff or a policeman tell you anything? Ask you anything?"

"Oh, Jesus, you are tenacious. Let me think. We walked in, they said not to disturb anything, as if I would touch anything in that dusty old room. As I said, they asked me to identify Helen, which was so traumatic for me. It was all so horrible." She hugged herself.

"What else? What else did anyone say?"

Eileen stared off trying to recall the scene. She straightened and looked at Jesse.

"There was something odd that I'd forgotten because I was so shaken up. When we first entered, before I saw Helen, one of the policemen asked me if Helen had any enemies. Anyone who might want to harm her. I was so confused that night, but I clearly remember saying that Helen was the white sheep of the family; everybody loved her. He took that down in his notebook, and I remember thinking I should have elicited at least a chuckle at my *bon mot*."

Jesse was both reassured and saddened by this. On the one hand, this seemed to confirm her suspicion that Helen had been murdered; on the other, how sad that she had been murdered.

Eileen looked at Jesse as if she had just entered the room. "What is going on?" she asked, suddenly alert.

Jesse toyed with not revealing anything to the woman just to maintain control, but she reconsidered since Eileen might have other useful information.

"Apparently I resemble Helen enough to stir up bad memories for someone."

"What do you mean?" Eileen studied her.

"Well, so far, I've been run off the road, received a threatening note and now strange phone calls are waking me up in the night."

Eileen's face turned ashen. As she lit another cigarette, Jesse noticed her hands shaking. After her first deep inhale, she spoke, smoke flowing from her mouth with her words.

"Take care, Jesse. Seneca Corners is a small pond with some big fish who like to throw their power around. It might be best if you came back here for a while."

Jesse's insides went cold at the thought. She would rather face the danger—and a ghost—than stay in this house one minute longer than necessary.

"I'll be fine. But I am going to find out the truth."

Eileen stubbed out her cigarette.

"Listen. Stay out of this. You have a track record of making stupid mistakes—don't add to it. Your others have been imprudent, this one could be dangerous."

"You're confirming my suspicions that Helen's death was not suicide. What else do you know?"

"I know that you're an idiot to pursue this."

"As always, *Mother*, your "affirmation" just makes me stronger." Jesse stood and leaned in toward Eileen. "I am going to pursue this, and I am going to discover the truth."

Eileen cowered from her, her eyes wary.

"Oh, and by the way, your sister haunts the house. Why not come by and say hello? She might like to thank you for covering up the truth of her death."

Jesse saw Eileen's face blanch before she turned and marched out the door slamming it behind her.

Jesse sat at her kitchen table poring over her notes on *The Merchant of Venice*. With the windows open, she could hear the crickets chirping in the darkness, the breeze, cool with its hint of looming autumn. Observing the tinges of color on the trees as she drove back from Rochester, she had a heightened sense of anticipation for fall semester, and she decided to prepare some lessons. If the trees were changing, so would her life soon. At the start of every school year, she had the sensation of being at the beginning of a roller coaster ride that would not end until June. It was non-stop with peaks and valleys and more thrills and chills than she could imagine.

She set her beer on the table and decided to recite Portia's soliloquy. If she expected her students to memorize it, she should dust off her own recitation. Closing her eyes, she began:

The quality of mercy is not strained,
It droppeth as the gentle rain from heaven
Upon the place beneath. It is twice blest:
"Does the quality of mercy extend to me?"

Jesse jumped. Her heart leapt at Joe's voice and she turned to see him washed in the glow of the mercury light from above the screen door.

"Joe."

"Hi, Jess." He stood with his thumbs hooked in his jeans pockets, the breeze tossing his hair and a half-smile on his lips. She thought there was no better way for him to appear more desirable. She came to her senses and rose.

"Come in, come in," she beckoned to him, and the screen-door creaked when he opened it, snapping back with a bang behind him. She took a beer out of the refrigerator and motioned for him to sit down. "So, are you going to help me plan Shakespeare lessons?" she asked popping off the beer cap and handing it to him.

"I think I have more hair than wit," he smiled.

"Oooh, a scholar." She laughed at his reference to *Two Gentlemen of Verona*. "I'm impressed!"

"I saw you at Tony's the other night..." his voice trailed off.

"Yeah, I waved, but I think you missed it."

"I saw it." He took a swig of beer and looked out the kitchen window as if viewing more than the blackness of night. The chirruping of crickets filled the silence. Jesse stared at her book, the line "...when mercy seasons justice" jumping out at her. She thought about what it must have been like for him seeing her there with Marty after telling him she wasn't interested in anyone, and her heart softened even more.

"Joe, Marty and I were there because he was helping me find out more about my Aunt Helen's death. It was nothing more than that."

He nodded still looking out the window. She rolled a pencil back and forth across her lesson plan.

"He was getting up to invite you to join us, but you left before he got to you."

Joe's eyes slid over to her.

"Jesse, I know I have no hold on you, it's just that..."

"I know. Marty is just a friend."

"Like me." His voice was low, filled with hope and fear at the same time. She knew he was laying himself open to her in this moment, but she still was unable to say what he wanted—and what she knew, deep down, she wanted, too.

"Like you."

He looked back out the window.

"For now." She had whispered it, but she knew he heard her. He continued staring out the window.

"Why, Just Jesse, I think I just heard the drop of a seed into the garden soil in the springtime."

"Could be, Joe, but that seed needs the fullness of time before harvest."

"'No, I will be the pattern of all patience; I will say nothing.'" He winked at her.

"*King Lear*. Very impressive."

"We had a lot of time to read during the rainy season in 'Nam."

He stood to leave. Jesse looked up at him.

"It's good to see you, Joe."

"Everything ok, Jess?" he asked.

"Interesting." She wondered how much to say. She could not reveal her visit to the Archive Room since that could cost Marty his career. But she could mention what she had learned from his mother.

He sat back down. "What?"

"Has your mother told you anything about our conversation?"

"No," he said.

Jesse was pleased that Susan had held their conversation in confidence. Trusting people had been difficult since her discovery of Robert in bed with someone else, but Susan had earned her trust. Now Jesse had to decide about Joe. Just because she was attracted to him, didn't warrant trust—she had been engaged to Robert after all. But her friendship with Joe held none of the treading on eggshells that had always been there with Robert. She'd always felt a little off kilter with him and after she left, the restoration of balance was refreshing despite her broken heart. Looking at Joe, the sincerity in his eyes compelled her to decide; she took a deep breath and a leap of faith.

"Well, it turns out that my Aunt Helen was actually my mother. You and I met a *looong* time ago on the night she died."

His eyebrows furrowed in confusion. Jesse related what she had learned from Susan and his face cleared as he understood what she had meant. When she finished, he ran his fingers through his hair until it stuck out like he'd just climbed out of bed.

Her heart skipped, her concentration momentarily interrupted.

"Man, that's a lot to digest," he said.

"Not only that, but I had a conversation with my mother—well, my aunt—I still don't know what the hell to call her! From what she said, I think the initial conclusion was that my aunt—my mother—was murdered."

"What makes you say that?"

Jesse took a deep breath.

"Eileen—that's what I'm going to call her because I cannot call her "mother" any more—said that when she arrived to identify Helen that night, the first thing the police asked was if Helen had any enemies. Now why would they even ask that if it were clearly a suicide?"

"Then how did they end up ruling it a suicide rather than a homicide?" Joe's confused look returned.

"I don't know. Somewhere in the course of the investigation, I think there was a cover-up."

"C'mon Jesse. This is Seneca Corners, not Rochester. Things like that don't happen around here."

"Okay, then why did the police even ask Eileen that? And why did she suggest I move back in with her— which will never happen—and tell me there were big fish in this little pond and I needed to be careful? Why?"

"I don't know, maybe they just weren't sure when they found her."

"She was hanging from the beam; why would they question it? Something caused them to ask that question.

Plus, why did someone run me off the road that night? And leave a threatening note? And call to scare me?"

"Whoa, whoa, whoa, Jess. What note? What calls?"

"Oh, I forgot you haven't been around. No, I didn't mean that I forgot you haven't been around—I sure noticed that, I mean, well, crap, never mind." Her face flushed and he grinned making her blush even more furiously. "What I mean is that I forgot you didn't know about those incidents."

Joe's smile vanished. "If you're being threatened, maybe Eileen is right and you should leave...just for a while, I mean. Not forever."

"But don't you see? If I don't discover the truth about this and I just leave, I can never return to Seneca Corners. No matter when I came back, the threats would continue. I have to solve this or I have to move away. Those are my choices."

He thought this over for a few minutes, and then let out a sigh. "I see your point."

"Besides that, Joe, she was my mother. How can I let her death—her murder—go unresolved? Someone, maybe many *someones*, in this town knows what happened and why. That secret needs to come to light. That secret lives within this house and it needs to be revealed. I am going to continue searching and asking questions, and I'm going to disturb some people."

"Or threaten them and make them *very* angry. You need to be careful, Jesse. You said Marty is helping with this?"

She flinched. "Well, yes, as much as he is able."

"So he knows where you are and what you're doing when you're out searching and asking questions and generally disturbing people?"

Jesse nodded not wanting to say more than was needed.

"There's nothing I can say to stop you, is there?"

She shook her head. "Not if you want me to stick around and see how the garden grows."

Joe broke into a smile that made it nearly impossible for her to resist jumping into his lap.

Marty concentrated as Jesse related her conversation with Eileen. She watched him absorb the information, his eyes moving around the room as he sorted through each detail.

"Jesse, it's S.O.P. to ask a victim's family member that question if foul play is suspected."

"Is it Standard Operating Procedure to ask a family member whether or not the victim had enemies if it is plainly a suicide?"

He squinted and shook his head. "No, in fact, that would be poor procedure."

She swallowed the bile that rose. Even though she was convinced there was foul play involved in Helen's death, each confirmation of it disconcerted her. As she had been doing throughout this search, she tried not to think of her mother as she appeared in the first photo she had seen. She would have time to grieve later; right now it was time to investigate. To everything there is a season.

"I am driving back up to Rochester to pick up my photos tomorrow. Then I will have time to sit down and pore over them, searching for any little clue," she said.

"I doubt you'll find anything. Say this was murder, and say it was covered up. Don't you think whoever covered it up would remove any sign from the report that pointed to murder? I don't know, Jesse. It's not all that easy to conceal evidence—especially with a crime photographer right at the scene."

"But, Marty, I don't think it was covered up initially, otherwise the officer wouldn't have asked Eileen that question. I think somebody showed up after and decided it should be hushed up. That's why those photos are so important. They capture the scene immediately before anyone decided to obscure things."

Marty nodded. "That also means that if anyone finds out you're poking around in this, your ass is grass."

"I know, I know, I know!" She ran her hands through her hair. "You've told me, Eileen's told me, Joe's told me..."

"Joe?"

"Yes, he stopped by last night. We talked."

"Well, it's about damn time. Too much 'I need time' shit, Jesse. Get on with life.

"It's not like we fell into bed. We *talked*, that's all."

"Geez! You two are slower than molasses in January."

"Anyway, he said to back off, too. But I reminded him, as I will you, that if I back off and leave town, there's no returning to Seneca Corners. Whatever I've set in motion, it's in motion and I'm the catalyst. As long as I live here, someone's nose will be out of joint."

"I guess you're right. Just don't do anything stupid," he paused, "without me."

She laughed.

"How about staying for supper? Maggie is coming over and we're making pasta."

"It's 85 degrees out. Why are you making pasta today?"

"I miss Rochester's Italian restaurants. I need some *manicotti*."

"Hey, you even pronounce it like an Italian—'mon-a-gaut'!" he beamed at her.

"I know my Italian pasta. Stick around."

"Well, if you pronounce it right, there's an outside chance you might even make it right."

"Ya takes yer chances," she laughed, relieved to talk about something other than Helen's death. She decided to take life easy tonight and just enjoy the company of good friends. Sometimes you had to take a break.

Maggie was washing the dishes and Marty was wiping while Jesse put away the paltry leftovers. All three had sat at the table rubbing their over-sated bellies after the meal. Marty bestowed the highest praise when he said her *manicotti* was almost as good as his grandma's. Toasting his compliment, they clinked their glasses of Chianti and sighed in contentment.

Finally needing to move they had begun the ritual of cleaning up the kitchen when the phone rang. All three stopped and looked at each other. Nodding, Marty followed Jesse into the hall to listen to the call. She lifted the receiver.

"Hello?" she said.

"Jesse, it's your mother." Her shoulders relaxed and he gave her a thumbs up and returned to the kitchen.

"Hello," Jesse's voice was flat.

"Listen, I wanted to encourage you again to leave well enough alone down there and come home for a while. You don't have to go anywhere or do anything. Just come and relax, swim in the pool, read. No need to be back in the social scene since you find that so distasteful right now."

"No, I don't want to be there. I'm fine here."

There was silence on the line for a moment, and when Eileen spoke, Jesse perceived a softness in her voice that she had never heard before.

"Listen to me. You're in over your head right now, but it's not too late to get out. Drop your insistence on finding the truth—whatever you mean by that—and come home. Darling, trust me on this one."

Darling? Where the hell did that come from? Jesse had heard Eileen use that when air-kissing her faux friends on either cheek at social gatherings. But the way she had just said it was different...as if she meant it as a term of endearment.

"You may not understand this, but finding the truth is something I must do," Jesse said, her voice firm.

Eileen sighed and Jesse heard her take a deep drag on her cigarette.

"Fine. Are you coming back to Rochester any time soon?"

"Tomorrow as a matter of fact. I have to pick up some photos."

"Swing by. I need to talk to you again. Since you're hell-bent on following this tack, I have something else I remembered from that night."

"Can't you just tell me now?" Jesse asked, dreading another encounter with her.

"No, not now. And I have something to give you."

"Fine. I'll be there tomorrow around two."

"I'll see you then."

"Bye—," she choked off the word mother. Then she heard a click.

"Jesse?" Eileen's voice startled her.

"I thought you hung up," Jesse said.

"I thought you did," Eileen said.

Silence.

"Gotta go," Jesse said and replaced the receiver. Her skin tingled with fear. She sauntered into the kitchen. Both Maggie and Marty stopped when they saw her face.

"What is it, Jess?" Maggie asked.

"That was Eileen." She looked at Maggie. "I finally decided what-the-hell-I-should-call-her. She wants to see me because she remembered something else from that night. She said she has something to give me, too. I'm heading up to Rochester tomorrow to pick up my photos, so I said I would swing by in the afternoon." She looked at them in turn. "She called me 'darling.' I think that's the scariest thing that's happened to me yet. There's something else. I heard a click on the line and thought she had hung up, but then she said something. She'd thought

I had hung up, which means she heard it, too. I think someone was listening in on my conversation."

Marty's eyes went dark and he looked away.

"Is that possible, Marty? Could someone have been listening in?" she demanded.

He looked at her and she saw the answer in his eyes. She slumped into a chair.

"This is crazy," she murmured.

"Jesse, maybe you should come stay at the convent for a while...until you figure out who is menacing you," Maggie said.

"I think that's a great idea. I agree with Maggie," Marty chimed in.

"Just what I need to add to my already overflowing bowl of worries—Sr. Alphonse lurking behind every pillar waiting to scowl at me."

"Sticks and stones. At least she won't harm you," Maggie said crossing over to her friend. She massaged Jesse's shoulders eliciting a long sigh.

"I want to stay here. This is my home now—and it feels like home. Even when Helen visits me at night; *especially* when Helen visits me at night." she said. Maggie and Marty exchanged looks.

"That doesn't spook you? Oh, sorry, no offense." He stumbled over his words.

"Not at all. I can't describe how it is when she's in that room. It's not scary for me, in fact, I feel...I don't know, warm, loved maybe, although I guess I don't know what that feels like. It's like being wrapped in a warm blanket. It's like being pulled toward something—something good."

Maggie hugged her. "You do too know what it feels like to be loved, Jess. I love you!"

Jesse squeezed her back. "I know, Mags. I love you, too. But this is different—deeper than any love I've ever experienced. I think I knew she was my mother before Susan told me."

"That's cool, Jesse. Weird, but cool," Marty said.

"So back to this phone call, Mr. Police Officer. That is possible, right?"

"Sure is. Piece of cake."

"So who would be capable of doing that?" she asked.

"Anybody who could afford the equipment."

Jesse shuddered, thinking of Wyndham Manor. There was no lack of money there. Then another thought crossed her mind.

"Or the local authorities," she said.

Marty looked at his hands. "Yes, or the local authorities."

-EIGHT-

Jesse sped along I-490, ideas playing leap frog in her mind. As some things got clearer, others got more muddled. She moved facts around like pieces in a puzzle where you slide tiles to form a picture. But none of these pieces were creating a picture, they were creating more of a puzzle. Perhaps her mother's information would be a key to the solution. What was it that Eileen wanted to give to her?

Glancing in her rearview mirror, she spotted the same green sedan that had been following her along Route 96 since before the town of Victor. She chided herself for being suspicious. This was the main route to get to Rochester from the Finger Lakes area; thousands of cars traveled it each day. Zipping into the right lane, she angled over to the Brighton exit too fast for the green car to make the same move. Relieved, she watched it fly by toward downtown. *I'm getting paranoid.*

Stopping by the Rexall Drug Store, she went in to pick up her photos. When she gave the clerk her envelope stub, he disappeared into the back room. After several minutes, he returned with an older man wearing a suit and tie. Introducing himself as the store manager, the man motioned for her to follow him to the back room.

"We have an alert on your photo order," he said.

Jesse's stomach turned.

"Why?" she asked widening her eyes and tilting her chin down hoping to look as innocent as possible.

"Your subject matter is...ah...quite provocative," he answered.

"Oh, I see," she laughed hoping her nervousness didn't show through her attempt at lightheartedness. "I'm taking criminal justice classes at Monroe Community College. We have to, y'know, investigate real cases and file a credible report based on our findings. Y'know, the teacher gives us each a file for one hour and we have to reach a conclusion. We can take photos to study as a follow-up, but he only gives us a week, and that's not very long especially if you have to wait for your pictures to be developed, y'know? And he won't let us share information, which is so unfair. So I only have until Monday morning to go through these and figure out what happened and write up the report and I don't think that's fair. We should have two weeks at least, and I'm going to write that in my evaluation at the end of this class..." As she blathered on, she saw his eyes grow bored with her explanation. He stepped back and held up his hands.

"All right, all right, all right, miss. It's just that the nature of your photos was so disturbing." He scrutinized her, rethinking her explanation. She sensed his doubt and began again.

"I know. I got the grossest case of all, and I can hardly stand to look at some of these photos, but he said I would have to get used to this if I wanted to work in the criminal justice system and maybe I should just be a nurse or a teacher or stay home and raise children like a woman is supposed to do, but I think that is biased thinking, don't you? I wanted to tell him that but he's the teacher and I don't want to get a bad grade...," Jesse never realized how fast she could talk or how easily she could lie. Both disturbed her, but her blouse was soaked with sweat and she wasn't sure how much longer she could carry off this charade. Her best chance was to be unbearable. "Don't you think that's unfair, Mr...Mr..."

"Very well, take your photos and go." He thrust the envelope into her hands and edged away.

"Thanks. Wish me luck on my final grade," she called to his back as he retreated to his office.

Relieved, she took the photos to the counter, paid for them and hurried to her car. Slipping into the driver's seat, she made the sign of the cross and murmured, "Bless me Father for I have sinned. Maggie's going to love hearing about the whopper I just told. She'll say a novena for me. Maybe two." She started the engine and headed to Eileen's.

Trying to imagine where this conversation would lead, she again recalled the way Eileen had called her "Darling" the night before. She had never heard that softness in Eileen's voice; it had sounded sincere. How different their relationship would be if that tone had been the norm. But she had no fantasies about Eileen's motherly love; it was non-existent. Whatever the woman had to tell her must be important for a change like that.

She pulled in beside Eileen's car and tucked the photos under her seat remembering the green car she had seen on the highway. Getting out, she locked the car, again wondering why since little crime made its way into Brighton's safeguarded neighborhoods. She waved across the yard at a woman tending her garden, headed to the front door and stopped. The front door was ajar. Her neck crawled as if an army of ants marched up it, and her heart pounded. Despite the safe neighborhood, Eileen never left the house unlocked whether inside it or out. Jesse tried to rationalize that Eileen might have left it open knowing she would arrive, but she knew that would never happen. She scanned the front of the house seeing the symmetrical flower beds—equal numbers of rhododendron and hydrangea with clusters of impatiens on either side—and neatly clipped hedges. Even the porch furniture was angled precisely as if marked on a stage. The balance mocked as if daring her to ruin the perfection…but someone already had, for the door opened a little wider with a breeze. Jesse waited to see if Eileen would step through to greet her, and snorted at that image. Her stomach heaved with dread as she approached the porch and climbed the steps.

Pushing in the door, she inspected the front hall. The white marble gleamed, reflecting the afternoon sun that streamed in through the door's sidelights. Fresh flowers towered out of a crystal vase on the cherry table, and umbrellas stood guard in a stand by the door. Everything was eerily normal.

"Mother?" she called up the stairs, her voice echoing. She wandered through the living room and dining room, the silence a palpable entity that throbbed in her ears. "Mother?" Swinging the kitchen door, she peeked around it not expecting to see Eileen in the kitchen since the woman's forays into that room were solely for more ice for her drink. She passed through to the family room with its floor to ceiling windows and white French doors out to the gardens. She could hear the humming of the pool filter's motor as she stepped through the door, but all else was quiet. She inched to the pool, feet leaden, dreading what she might discover there. A bright pink raft floated in the aqua water, bumping against the ladder at the deep end, and Jesse closed her eyes before she dared peer into the water. Nothing.

Despite the warmth of the sun, goose-bumps broke out on her arms as she re-entered the house. She had never felt comfortable in this house, but this was the first time she had ever felt afraid. She passed through the family room and moved toward the stairs. "Mother?" she called. Maybe Eileen had been in the shower when she arrived. "Mother. Eileen, I'm here." She heard a note of desperation in her voice. Reaching the top of the staircase, she walked to the bedroom door as memories of

Eileen's voice whispered in her mind: "Never, I repeat never, come into my bedroom without my permission." Jesse had been scolded more than once as a child, the temptation of colorful make-up and glistening jewels irresistible. The time she doused herself and several dolls with Eileen's most expensive perfume led to the locking of the door. She hoped it was locked now. She hoped Eileen would ream her out when she opened the door and stepped inside. She hoped against hope. She knocked. "Mother? Are you in there?" She knocked again. "Mother? It's Jesse." Silence. Taking a deep breath, she tried the knob; it turned smoothly in her shaking hands. She edged the door in and skimmed the room, her eyes halting at the bed. She choked back a scream, and her knees gave out dropping her to the floor. For a moment she could not breathe, and bile spilled into her throat. Through the black dots that swam before her eyes, she saw Eileen's body sprawled across the bed, her face hanging over the side. Her face mottled, her eyes bulging and reddish staring at her. Her face just like Helen's.

Jesse slapped her hand to her mouth to stem the vomit until she got to the bathroom where she flung herself over the toilet and emptied her stomach. She retched until dry heaves convulsed her, and then she sank to the floor and pressed her forehead against the cool marble. Tears streamed down her face and her hair clung to her cheeks and neck. When threats of nausea subsided, she dragged herself to her feet, caught sight of herself in the large mirror, and gasped at how pale she was. Cop shows always warn against tampering with anything at the crime scene, but she risked jail time by wetting a wash cloth and wiping her face. Then she cupped her hands under the cold water and rinsed out her mouth. Her mind careened with confused thoughts and images. She dreaded passing through the bedroom again.

Screwing up her courage, she reentered the room trying not to look at Eileen's face. She did note that there had been a struggle; the bed clothes were messy and Eileen's dress was ripped. It seemed absurd that she had one shoe on and one off. Jesse winced with guilt as the thought *She would never be caught dead like that* floated through her mind. The telephone receiver was knocked off its cradle, and when she lifted it to listen, there was no dial tone. She replaced the receiver and picked it up again, her back to the bed. Her stomach lurched, but she fought it down. Hanging up the phone, she murmured, "Come on. Please work." She feared the wires had been cut and was paralyzed with the realization that whoever did this could still be in the house. She forced herself to move. "Please," she whispered as she lifted the receiver once more, relieved at the sound of the dial tone. With trembling fingers she dialed "0" and tapped her fingers waiting for the operator to answer. It rang three times. "Pick up, oh God, somebody please pick up."

"Number please," a flat voice came through the line.

Jesse's voice caught, her throat dry. She tried to speak, but no sound came out.

"Number please."

"Please help me." Her voice was a whisper.

"I'm sorry, did you say 303? You'll have to speak louder." Irritation was replacing boredom.

Jesse took a deep breath, and then she heard the front door close.

"Help me. Please help me." Her voice shook with panic.

The operator came to life. "What is your address? Are you all right?"

Jesse was frozen. Did someone just come in or leave?

"Please don't hang up. I need to lock the door." She ran across the room and flipped the bolt, then wedged a chair against the door handle and ran back to the phone.

"My mother has been murdered. I think someone is still in the house."

"What is your address, please?" The operator's voice was steady.

"262 Winding Brook Parkway in Brighton. Please hurry. He may still be in the house." Jesse fought down rising panic and tried to stop shaking. Looking out the front window, she saw the neighbor still weeding her garden. The scene was surreal; how could that be? How could something so ordinary be occurring just yards away while she stood in a room with her mother's—rather her aunt's—dead body. Averting her eyes, she skirted the edge of the bed and went into the bathroom and got sick again. She pressed the cold washcloth to her mouth to stifle her sobs. She tried to calm down and listen for any noise inside the house, but she heard nothing. Curling up on the floor, she soon found herself in a fetal position with the washcloth against her mouth. Though she was repulsed by the scene, the urge to look was irresistible and she surveyed the adjoining room. Lying on her side, her mind was unable to focus on any one element, instead merging everything into a collage of obscenity. Stillness owned the house, the silence a vacuum swallowing up any sign of life. She tried to calm her trembling by taking a deep breath, but she could only manage a shaky shallow one. The silence hurt her ears. The jarring ring of the telephone sent a jolt through her and she bumped her head on the clawfoot tub. Rubbing it, she found a lump forming as she ran to grab the phone.

"Hello?" her voice seemed to come through a hollow tube.

"Is this the Graham residence?"

"Yes."

"This is the Brighton Police Department. Did you call in an emergency?"

"Please get over here. My mother is dead and I don't know if the person who killed her is still in the house.

Please, please hurry," Jesse had to drag her words out her teeth were chattering so. Didn't they realize the urgency?

"Someone will be right there, ma'am. You must stay in the house."

"I am locked in the room with my mother. Someone else may still be in the house."

"You're in the room with the deceased? Were you there when it happened?"

"NO. Please just hurry and get here. Please!"

"Someone will be right there, ma'am," he repeated. "Do you want me to stay on the phone with you?"

"Yes, oh, yes, please." She heard a siren in the distance. "I think I hear them coming. Thank God."

"They should be arriving soon. Can they get in?"

"The front door was open when I arrived, but I heard it close a few minutes ago. I don't know if someone is still here or not."

"Stay where you are. I'll radio them to break down the door if necessary. Stay where you are, do you hear?" His voice grew firmer, and Jesse realized that she could become a hostage if the murderer was still in the house.

"Yes. I hear. I will."

The siren was loud, insistent as the police car pulled up to the house. She saw red lights pulsing off the wall opposite the front windows. Her shaking increased, and she started crying again. Realizing she was close to hysterics, she closed her eyes and began to count her measured breaths. An image formed from her earlier inspection of the room—she remembered a small, white piece of paper protruding from beneath Eileen's shoulder. Opening her eyes, she hurried to the bed and kneeled beside Eileen, her stomach overturning as she slid her hand along the woman's body. She heard noises as the police tried the front door to no avail. She knew she would have to hurry and retrieve the paper before the police entered the room. The sharp edge of the paper slit her finger; she flinched and drew back her hand. *Damn.*

She sucked the drops of blood and used her other hand to grasp the paper and pull it from beneath Eileen's body. No need to leave her blood at the scene of the murder. She heard what sounded like bodies thudding against the front door, or perhaps feet trying to kick it in. *You boys don't understand; Eileen bought only the finest solid oak for her grand entry.* Then a shot echoed through the house and she jumped. She figured they had blasted through the lock. Hearing footsteps on the stairs, she tucked the paper into her pocket. Hastening to the door, she removed the chair, unlocked the door and flung it open. Two uniformed police officers pointed their weapons at her and she raised her hands.

"Please, help me...my mother..." Her legs gave out and she collapsed to the floor.

Looking past her, they saw Eileen's body on the bed and looked at each other.

"Who else is in the house?" one asked.

"I don't know. I heard a door slam after I arrived, so whoever did this must have still been here."

The taller of the two nodded to the other who left to search the house. Replacing his gun in its holster, the officer who remained pulled out his radio and requested the medical examiner. Hearing another siren, Jesse looked out to see a fire truck pull up. Jumping off the truck, men scrambled to get lifesaving equipment and a gurney then raced into the house. Jesse slumped onto the end of the chaise lounge and watched them run into the room.

The police officer approached her and pulled out a small notebook.

"Miss...uh..."

"Graham. Jesse Graham."

He scribbled her name. "And this is your mother?"

How to answer that? *No officer, I always thought she was my mother but...*

"Yes," she whispered.

"I'm sorry, Miss Graham." He tipped his hat.

"Thank you officer."

The shorter policeman returned and shook his head indicating he'd found no one else.

"I'm going to have to ask you to leave this room, Miss Graham, but I need you to remain in the house."

"Of course." Jesse's bones felt weary and her head ached. She left the room and went down to the kitchen. Looking in the refrigerator, she found a beer and popped the cap off. Taking a deep swallow, she walked into the living room unprepared for the scene outside. Flashing lights lit up the afternoon and more neighbors than she thought could fit in the area craned their necks along the curb. Catching sight of her through the broken front door, one called, "There's the daughter. Do you think she did it?"

Jesse blinked.

"Did what?"

"I don't know. Whatever the police are here for."

She shuffled back into the kitchen and sat at the table staring ahead. Her shaking had subsided enough that her teeth were no longer chattering, but her arms and legs were still weak and wobbly. She took another gulp of beer and listened to the noises upstairs. The second officer who had searched the house came into the kitchen.

"Want a beer?" she asked raising her bottle as if he hadn't understood the question.

"No thanks. I'm on duty." He touched his fingers to the brim of his cap.

"So no one else is in the house?"

"No sign of anyone," he said.

"That's good," Jesse said with relief.

"No one but you in here, ma'am."

Jesse stiffened. He turned and left the kitchen.

The medical examiner and crime scene photographer arrived soon after the fire department. Jesse greeted them at the door aware of the insanity of the situation. It wasn't as though she was hosting a party, yet there seemed to be a need for some kind of ritual or formality. Maybe pretense of routine would keep her from dissolving into a puddle on the floor. She led the two men upstairs and saw the bustle of activity in the room. Having retrieved a crime scene kit from the patrol car, the officers were dusting for fingerprints and sketching out the scene. She imagined them drawing the bed with the outline of the twisted form of Eileen. Seeing her, the taller officer stepped to the door.

"I'll have to ask you to wait downstairs, Miss Graham." He closed the door.

Jesse returned to the kitchen and was disappointed to find no more beer in the refrigerator. Looking around, she spotted the tea kettle on the stove and shrugged.

"Next best thing," she said to no one.

Filling the kettle, she then found a tea bag and set it in a mug. Her legs began to shake again, so she sat at the table. Surely she would awaken from this hellish dream. Why would Eileen have been murdered? She remembered the click on the phone the previous night. Someone knew that she was coming up to Rochester and that Eileen had information for her about Helen's death. That knowledge had cost Eileen her life. What had she intended to give Jesse? She remembered the slip of paper in her pocket. Listening to the noises from upstairs, it was evident the authorities were busy at the moment. She pulled out the paper.

It was ivory card stock with Eileen's initials in script on one side. Leave it to her to put a clue on socially acceptable stationery. No wonder it gave such a nasty paper cut. Jesse flipped the paper over and saw an address: 418 Gibson St. Geneva. She tried to make sense of its meaning. Whose address was this? Was it a business of some kind? Was this even the item Eileen was going to give her, or was it an appointment for later today? Jesse shuddered at the realization that what had started as an ordinary day filled with appointments for Eileen had ended so brutally. *Carpe diem.*

"Excuse me, Miss Graham."

She jumped at the sound and dropped the paper. The taller officer stood at the door to the kitchen. He stooped to pick up the note for her, and Jesse panicked thinking it must be sending off some kind of "major clue" vibrations. He glanced at the paper and paused. Jesse's heart beat faster. Staring at her, he handed back the paper.

"Thank you," she managed to squeeze out.

"I'll need you to come down to the station with me, Miss Graham."

She frowned in bewilderment. "Why, officer?"

"We'll need you to file a report—just routine."

Jesse nodded and looked around. "I don't even know where my car keys are…"

"We'll drive you there, Miss Graham."

"My car is just out in the driveway."

"We'll need to take you, ma'am."

She looked at him and his eyes bored into hers.

"Do you think I…?"

"Routine, ma'am."

"If it's routine, why can't I drive my own car there?" Jesse's voice was rising with alarm.

"You've had an awful shock, ma'am. It would be better if you didn't drive right now."

"I'm fine."

The police officer placed his hands on his hips and shifted his weight.

"All right, ma'am. You were the only person in the house with the deceased. We're going to have to ask you some questions."

She stood and faced him. "I wasn't the only person in the house. The door was ajar when I arrived, and I heard a person leave after I found my mother's body." Her voice rose with each word. She was shaking with anger and fear. "You can't possibly think that I would do this—,"

"Take it easy ma'am."

"How could you think I would do such an awful thing?" Jesse was shouting now.

The police officer took handcuffs off of his belt; she fell silent.

"There are two ways this can go, Miss Graham. I don't think you want your neighbors seeing you led out in cuffs."

She felt as though she was tumbling through space. Backing up, the chair bumped against her legs and she collapsed into it. Elbows propped on the table, she buried her face in her hands and stifled a sob.

"This can't be happening. This is a nightmare," she rasped.

"That's better, Miss Graham. We'll be down shortly to drive you over to the station."

The shrill whistle of the tea kettle sliced the air.

The constant ringing of telephones, click-clack of typewriters and bustle of people made Jesse dizzy as she sat in the Brighton Police station. She had given her report to the tall officer and then again to a police stenographer. They repeated questions, sometimes wording them the same way, sometimes reworded as if to disguise the intent. She tried to remain focused and calm, realizing that anxiety or confused answers could increase their suspicion. She was alarmed by the fact that they actually believed she might have murdered Eileen.

After a while, a police woman took her down a narrow hall to an interrogation room with a one-way mirror that didn't fool anybody. She wondered how many people stood behind it assessing her guilt. Some of them probably thought she was a Lizzie Borden with a different modus operandi. Buzzing overhead, fluorescent lights reflected in her stale coffee as she stared into the cup. Always independent, Jesse had faced most of her childhood and adolescent trials alone. She had learned early on that in any given situation Eileen's advice would be "pull up your bootstraps and don't cause a scene." Right up through her recent break-up with Robert she had worked through challenges on her own and coped very well. But never had she felt more alone than at this moment. Maybe Eileen wasn't June Cleaver, but at least she had been there. Their relationship was strained at best, but she had had a mother...sort of. Now people actually suspected her of killing Eileen. The implications overwhelmed her. If they believed that, she would go to trial, be sent to prison, maybe even face the death penalty. She trembled. Aware that she was being watched, she sat still and tried to breathe evenly. *How does one appear innocent? What movements do authorities look for that convince them someone is capable of murder? Maybe I should stand up and do a song and dance routine.* The thought made her snort a half-smile which she quickly erased from her face. This was not a time to laugh, and her warped sense of humor was not her friend right now.

The door opened and a burly man came in and sat across from her.

"Miss Graham, I am Detective Holden. How are you doing?" His voice was kind, but dark brows frowned above his steely eyes. He moved smoothly despite his hulking size. When he laid the file folder on the table, his sleeves inched back revealing a generous expanse of dark hair traveling from the back of his hands, up his sleeve to his forearms.

"I'm not doing so well today, Detective Holden. How about you?" A mixture of anger and sarcasm rose from nowhere and Jesse knew she would have to stifle it.

He snorted and opened the file folder. "No, I don't suppose you are doing very well. That was quite a tough spot for you to be in, locked in a room with your deceased mother. Not knowing if someone else was in the house waiting to do you bodily harm." He watched her.

She crumbled, all her bravado melting away. She couldn't speak and the two sat staring at each other. Detective Holden motioned to the mirror and the policewoman walked in and set down a box of tissues next to her.

"Thank you," she murmured to the woman's back as she exited. She wiped her eyes and blew her nose, then looked around for a trash can. There was none, and Detective Holden glanced around, too, and then motioned for her to put the dirty tissue on the table. Instead Jesse tucked it into her lap to dispose of later. She hoped it would be on her way out the door.

Detective Holden looked down at the file in front of him and then at her.

"So how did you and your mother get along, Miss Graham?"

Her stomach dropped. If she told the truth of their relationship, it would appear even more likely that she could have killed Eileen. If she lied about it and they questioned others who disclosed the coolness between them, it would look like she covered something up. Maybe a few Hail Marys were in order right now. Oh, that Mary had been her mother! The prayer started running through her brain: "Hail Mary, full of grace..." and Jesse sent it up silently. She sat up straighter and looked Detective Holden in the eye.

"My mother and I were not close, Detective Holden. She was a business woman first and motherhood fell somewhere on her priority list after manicures. But I did not hate her, and I did not kill her." She took a deep breath. "Mother is—was—a highly respected woman in the community and I admired her accomplishments while

I longed for her nurturing. I found out at an early age that was not something she could give, so I adapted."

Detective Holden pulled out a cigarette and offered her one. She shook her head "no." Pulling out a Zippo lighter with a police decal etched on it, he flipped it open, brushed his thumb against the wheel to strike the flint and the flame erupted. His eyes never left her. He held the lighter to his cigarette inhaling deeply, turning the tip crimson. Shifting to replace the lighter in his trousers, he blew smoke up and away from her.

"So you don't smoke, Miss Graham?" he asked.

"Never started. I'm glad based on what medical experts are finding." The question was so mundane in this claustrophobic room. "You ought to quit, Detective," she added.

"I've tried. Never happen. Too much stress in this job. Your mother smoked though, correct?"

"Yes. She liked the new Virginia Slims cigarettes. 'You've come a long way, baby' and all that it implied. Before that, she smoked Kents."

Detective Holden made a note in the file.

"The officer who searched the house for the intruder found nothing to suggest anyone had been there except you."

Jesse felt the eyes of those behind the glass as if they radiated heat beams at her face. She wondered if she were making unconscious movements or facial expressions that might implicate her. She sighed. All she could do was be honest.

"When I arrived, the door was ajar; Mother would never leave it unlocked let alone open. She was a security fanatic; she even considered investing in an alarm system, but she never did. When I entered, I didn't see or hear anyone, so I searched the house looking for her. She wasn't on the first floor, so I went upstairs. Her bedroom door was closed, but not locked; I went in...and I saw her..."

Detective Holden took a long drag on his cigarette and waited.

"I was sick so I ran to the bathroom and threw up a few times. I know I disturbed the crime scene, but I had to wash my face so I used one of her washcloths. Sorry."

A trace of a smile crossed his face. "That's okay, Miss Graham. I doubt that messed up any evidence."

"Oh, good." She let out a sigh. "While I was on the phone with the operator, I heard the front door slam and realized someone had been in the house. I was scared so I locked the bedroom door and called for help. Wait a minute. Our neighbor was out in her garden—she must have seen who it was!" Jesse sat forward as relief flooded her. "You can ask her about it!"

Detective Holden stubbed out his cigarette.

"We did question her, and she didn't see anyone but you enter or exit the house."

She slumped back in her chair.

"Miss Graham, you have the right to remain silent, you have the right to legal counsel. Anything you say can be used against you in a court of law. Do you understand this, Miss Graham?"

"Oh my God," she whispered. "This is just crazy. This is insane." She looked at Detective Holden. "Don't I get one phone call?"

"Maggie, it's Jesse." Her voice broke.

"Hey, Jess. I can hardly hear you." The sound of Maggie's voice shattered the last of her resolve and she started to sob.

"Jesse? Jesse? What's wrong?" Maggie pleaded.

"Maggie, my mother has been murdered," she sobbed.

"I know, you told me…"

Jesse stole a look at Detective Holden who sat nearby listening.

"*Eileen*, Maggie. Eileen has been murdered." she turned away wishing for privacy. This situation was getting more complex by the minute.

Maggie was silent for a moment.

"Maggie, are you there?"

"Where are you?"

"I'm at the Brighton Police Station. They're holding me for suspicion in my mother's death." She fought down panic because saying the words made it even more real. "Maggie, this is my one phone call. I need a lawyer—they've read me my rights for God's sake." She looked at Detective Holden who was watching her.

"Holy Jesus," Maggie whispered. Jesse wasn't sure if her friend was praying or swearing.

"Maggie." Her voice broke again. "I need you." Hot tears streamed down her face; she shifted away from the detective and brushed them away. She could never remember a time in her life when she had uttered the words, "I need you."

"I'll be there as soon as I can. Don't worry, you are going to be all right, I promise," Maggie said. Jesse knew her friend well enough to hear that Maggie was as frightened as she was.

Hanging up the telephone, she turned back to Detective Holden.

"Are you going to put me in a holding cell?" she asked remembering a terrifying women's prison movie she'd seen. Fresh tears stung her eyes as she tried to still her trembling.

His elbow propped on the desk, Detective Holden rested his chin against his fist and stared at her.

"Motive," he said through his fist.

"What?" She gaped at him.

"Motive. What could be the motive for your mother's death?" Leaning back, he flipped open his lighter and lit another cigarette. Jesse knew that from that moment on whenever she heard that clicking sound she would be transported back to this police station. He drew the smoke in and let it dance around in his mouth before breathing it out his nose.

"Robbery?" she asked, an uneasy suspicion taking root in her mind.

"Nothing was taken. In fact, nothing was touched."

"Revenge?"

"You said she was highly respected in the community."

"Attempted rape?"

"There were no signs of attempted sexual assault."

Jesse stared at the wisps of smoke rising around his head. She realized there was a question that she hadn't asked yet, and the fact that she hadn't made her look even more suspicious. But she already knew the answer, didn't she? Because she had seen crime scene photos of Helen. She thought it best to ask the question anyway. Her eyes bored into his.

"How was my mother murdered?"

Shifting in his chair, Detective Holden took another deep drag on his cigarette. "It's interesting that you're finally getting around to that question, Miss Graham. I expected you to ask it much sooner than this."

Jesse weighed how much to reveal about her familiarity with this kind of murder. The case of Helen's death was old and had been established as a suicide. To divulge her knowledge of anything else would require an explanation of how she had access to the file, and that would implicate Marty. She could tell Detective Holden about the threats to her life, about the phone call with someone listening in, but what if that had been the authorities? Hadn't Marty gotten uncomfortable when she posed that as a possibility? She wasn't sure the good-old-boy system would see a problem with that. She had to tread carefully.

"I think she was strangled." She shuddered remembering the scene. "I didn't see blood, so it wasn't a stabbing or gunshot. And her face..." Jesse swallowed and closed her eyes. "Her eyes bulging out like that. I assumed she had been strangled."

"Yes, the petechiae—purplish spots on her eyes—could indicate asphyxia or strangling."

When he said the word "asphyxia" she recalled the image of Helen's death certificate. The same method to kill both sisters. Coincidence? Doubtful. That meant the murderer was still around...and still murdering. She shivered.

"So you think I grabbed my mother, wrestled with her and strangled her? You give me a lot of credit for upper body strength."

"The autopsy will take a few days. We don't know if your mother had any drugs in her system that might help a person of smaller stature overcome her."

Jesse looked away. "Jesus," she whispered.

"When will your friend Maggie arrive, Miss Graham?"

"She's driving up from Seneca Corners, so probably about an hour."

"Well, we won't put you in a holding cell for now. You can wait right here." Detective Holden rose, closed the file folder and took her coffee cup. "I'll see that you get some fresh coffee."

Crossing her arms on the table, Jesse rested her head on them and closed her eyes. Every bone and muscle ached from tension and trembling. Surely five hours must have passed since she'd called Maggie, but glancing at her watch she saw that only one had. Detective Holden had brought fresh coffee as promised and a stale sandwich from a vending machine. Her stomach convulsed at the sight of it, but she tried to eat a bite or two knowing she would need her strength if the holding cell was in her future.

Hearing the door open, she raised her head and Maggie's voice preceded her into the room. The sight of her best friend in her full regalia of black habit with veil, white linen gimp, cincture and rosary was more than she could bear. Such goodness in the midst of such violence. Jumping up, she knocked the chair over backwards and ran to Maggie who wrapped Jesse in her arms and held her.

"Oh, Jess! Are you okay?"

The last sinew of resolve melted away. Jesse burst into tears and sobbed on her friend's shoulder. Maggie held her and brushed her hair back, whispering soft words of encouragement that didn't register in her brain. A primeval sense of safety pulsed through her as if Maggie's presence would somehow erase any danger. Her legs quivered beneath her, weak from fear and hunger, and she started to slip to the floor. Maggie supported her and sat her back on the chair. The chair that Joe had turned back upright. She felt his arm against her back before her eyes slid up to meet his.

"Hey, Just Jesse," he smiled.

"Hey," she whispered. Despite all she'd been through, her heart did that teeny-bopper flip-flop that always accompanied Joe's presence. Despite the terror of the fate that awaited her, she longed to be wrapped in his arms and comforted. It was official. She was nuts.

Detective Holden had been standing in the doorway in deep conversation, and he gestured for the other person to enter ahead of him. Marty peeked around the corner and he flashed a crooked smile at her. Dressed in his uniform, he hefted his belt laden with his gun and handcuffs as he stepped into the room followed by Detective Holden.

"Do you need a police escort everywhere you go, lady?" Marty asked.

Giddy with gratitude, she laughed, then sobbed. She was losing it. The arrival of these three friends was going to make her fall apart and melt into a puddle on the floor that they could mop up and squeeze out into a pail. Well, at least she wouldn't end up in women's prison being someone's bitch.

"Marty," she breathed.

"You sure make the best use of a phone call. What is this, a costume party for good guys?" Detective Holden smirked as he sat across from her. "Your policeman friend has been giving me some background on what's been swirling around you for the last couple of months. Why did you never think to mention all that in the interrogation, Miss Graham?"

Jesse looked at Marty, then back at the detective. "I didn't want to get...that is, there is nothing official to tell."

"You filed a police report with the Seneca Corners police department, did you not? Someone tried to run you off the road? You've been getting threatening phone calls and notes? You heard a third party on the line during your phone conversation with your mother last night? A conversation in which you mentioned the time you would arrive at her home here in Rochester, did you not?"

Jesse nodded dully. It had been too confusing to determine what she could and could not tell Detective Holden, but Marty had resolved all of that. She glanced up at him and smiled; he responded with a wink. Nothing he had relayed implicated him or even mentioned their late-night foray into the Archives Room. But it was enough to make it obvious that her life had been threatened. She felt the detective's eyes on her and looked at him.

"Miss Graham, did it ever occur to you that perhaps your mother was not the target of this attack?"

Jesse shuddered at the logic of his question. That could be so, but Eileen was already dead when she arrived. Why didn't the person wait for her and then kill her as well? He was still in the house; she'd heard him leave. She had been completely vulnerable. Besides, whoever listened to that phone call knew she'd planned to arrive around two-o'clock. Why arrive early and kill Eileen if she were the intended target? No, either this was meant as a warning to her, or Eileen was even *more* of a threat to whoever killed Helen. She ran her hands up and down her arms to stem the goose-bumps.

"Do you need a sweater, Jess?" Maggie asked.

She shook her head still trying to make sense of what had happened to Eileen.

"Just to let you know, we did find a fresh cigarette butt in the fireplace that was not a Virginia Slims, so apparently someone else had been in the house. Your mother must have known the person and let him in because there was no sign of forced entry. Do you have any idea who it might have been, Miss Graham?" Detective Holden asked.

"No. None," she answered.

"Is there anything else you can tell us that might help the case? Any little detail at all?"

"I wish there was, Detective. Oh..." she paused.

"What is it?" he encouraged.

"On my way up here, I noticed a green car that had been following me since before I drove through the town of Victor. I didn't think too much of it since that's a main route into Rochester, but the car seemed to hang behind me. I don't know, maybe it's nothing. Maybe I'm paranoid since my accident a while back."

Detective Holden wrote a note in the file. "Do you know the make or model?"

Jesse shrugged. "Maybe a Buick or Oldsmobile...I'm not sure. When it passed me, I noticed that it had chrome trim along the side and nice wheels. Fancy. That's all I noticed."

"When it passed you? I thought it was following you."

"It was. At least I thought it was, so I shifted into the right lane and took my exit quickly. Another car was in the lane so the green car couldn't get over in time to make the exit behind me. That's when I saw it from the side."

Detective Holden stared at her for a moment. "Anything else?"

She shook her head.

"We're going to release you to the Three Musketeers here, but you may be called in for more questioning as the investigation proceeds. We have your contact information, so you're all set to go. But a word of advice, Miss Graham. What happened to your mother was cold and calculated. This person is ruthless, and based on what Officer D'Amato has told me, you may be a target, too. Be careful."

She stood. "Thank you. I will keep that in mind, Detective Holden." She and the others headed for the door.

"Oh, and Miss Graham?"

"Yes?"

Detective Holden stood and smiled at her. "You're one tough cookie."

Jesse nodded her thanks and walked out the door.

-NINE-

Jesse's head lolled as Maggie drove her Beetle along Route 5 & 20. Dozing intermittently, she tried to stay awake by conversing but was overcome with exhaustion. WBBF played softly on the radio and Maggie hummed along. Jesse had been relieved to find her photos still tucked under the driver's seat; now she clutched them in her hands still somehow fearful that they might disappear. Her gut told her these photos would reveal something that had been overlooked—or covered up.

Images of the afternoon played in her mind, shifting from Detective Holden's face to the first police officer's to Eileen's with her bulging eyes and gaping mouth. She shuddered awake. Maggie reached over and patted her knee.

"We're almost there, Jess. How are you holding up?"

"Barely. What a day, Mags. What a shitty day."

"No doubt. We'll stop by your house and pick up a change of clothes and toiletries."

"Why? Just drop me off."

"You might be in danger. We thought it best if you stayed at the convent for a while."

"No way! Nobody's going to scare me out of my own home."

"Jesse, be reasonable."

"I am being reasonable," she shouted.

"I can see that," Maggie murmured.

Jesse settled back against the seat and snorted. "I want to be in my own house, Mags. I *need* to be in my own house. If someone wanted to hurt me, he had the perfect opportunity this afternoon when I was alone at Eileen's. Why didn't he kill me then? Because I don't think he wants me dead. At least not yet."

"Oh that's reassuring, Jess. 'Not yet.' So how long do we wait until he *does* want you dead?"

Jesse stared out the window at the trees, shadowy shapes in the dark. How could these things be happening? She was still numb from the trauma of the afternoon, but she knew the fact of Eileen's death would hit her soon. She wondered what her grief would be like. Would she mourn at all for the woman who had raised her despite her lack of maternal instincts? Right now she didn't feel anything but bone-tired. She saw her road up ahead and shivered. What would she find at her house? Would she be safe there?

She almost shut her eyes as Maggie turned the corner, fearing the house might be burned down or surrounded by gunmen or... but she saw the house as she had left it, looking ordinary. Except for the glow from the attic window. Then that was gone. She glanced at Maggie to see if she had noticed it, but her friend was concentrating on the road. Jesse saw the beams of Joe's truck's headlights behind them as they pulled into the two-track driveway.

Unlocking the front door, she swept it open and they all piled into the house. Joe and Marty separated to search the place from top to bottom while the women headed to the kitchen to fix sandwiches. Jesse pulled out four beers and flicked the caps off with the churchkey. Taking one bottle, she tipped it up and guzzled a hefty draught. She felt Maggie's eyes on her.

"Take it easy, Jess," she murmured.

"I don't think this is a 'take it easy' kind of day, Mags." She gulped another swig of beer.

Maggie laid out slices of bread and swiped them with mayonnaise and mustard. She layered each with ham, cheese, tomato and lettuce and cut them in half. Placing them on paper plates, she scooped chips out of the Charles Chips can and deposited them beside the sandwiches. Setting the plates on the table, she positioned a beer beside each, except for Jesse's whose bottle was already empty. She poured a tall glass of water, setting it at Jesse's place then filled the tea kettle and put it on the burner to heat.

"Sr. Angelina, your disapproval can be detected from way over here," Jesse said opening the refrigerator to claim another beer. She felt lightheaded after drinking the first one so fast on an empty stomach.

"I don't think getting falling down drunk is the way to handle this," Maggie said sitting down at the table.

"Well, excuse me, Sr. Angelina, but you find your mother's body, fear for your life and then get arrested as the prime suspect in one afternoon and see if you don't guzzle a couple of Gennys!" Swaying a bit, she tipped her bottle at Maggie and then took a generous swallow.

"Just sit down and eat something, Jess," Maggie urged.

"The hell I will, Sr. Angelina! Oh holy sacred woman. I don't have to do anything I don't damn well want to do. And I don't want to do this!" She finished her second beer in one gulp and then pounded the bottle on the table startling Maggie who stood and put her hands on Jesse's shoulders.

"Jess, it's okay now. You're okay now."

Jesse looked at her through blurry vision, tottering. Exhaustion and drinking so much so fast rendered her woozy. She started to shake.

"Mags, I was so scared. Eileen was dead and she looked so…dead. I thought I would end up in prison. I thought I was going to…" She burst into tears.

Maggie pulled Jesse into her arms and let her cry. Joe and Marty came through the kitchen door from their reconnaissance of the back yard and stood watching the women. Maggie nodded her head slightly and Joe stepped over to her. The tea kettle whistled and Maggie released a sobbing Jesse into Joe's arms. She sunk into him and he held her, gently pressing his face against her hair. Her sobs subsided replaced by short gasps. Settling down, she pulled away and realized through hazy eyes that it was Joe's arms that held her.

"Holy crap! I can't hug you. I don't have the strength to hold myself back!"

The others froze not knowing how to react to her words. Joe smiled down at her.

"Don't worry, Just Jesse. I'll protect you from yourself."

She turned scarlet and they all laughed.

"C'mon, let's eat! *Mangiate, mangiate!*" said Marty.

Joe helped Jesse into her seat then sat down.

Once she had some food in her stomach, she was somewhat able to take them through the events that had occurred that afternoon. She relived her terror as she related the time she had spent in Eileen's bedroom; she had to stop several times to compose herself. She remembered the dread she'd suffered in the police station when she realized they suspected her of the murder, and she shuddered at the potential consequences. As her retelling became more punctuated with yawns, Maggie suggested they gather some of her things and head over to the convent.

"I'm not going to the convent, Mags, but thank you. I want to stay here."

"Jesse, I'm worried about your safety…"

"I'll stay with her," Joe said.

"I don't think so, Joe," Jesse answered.

"Maggie is right. We don't know who this guy is or whether or not he is around here right now," he argued.

Jesse looked at the darkness outside her kitchen window and shivered.

"Joe's right," Marty added. "This guy could be waiting for an opportunity to get to you."

"So I endanger Joe, too? Why does that make sense?" she asked then sipped her tea.

"We have a quorum here, Jesse. Either I stay with you or you enter the convent." Joe's eyes sparkled with amusement.

She saw the futility of any further argument. "Fine. You can sleep on the couch, Mr. Bodyguard."

The others laughed, rising to clean up. Maggie filled the sink with soapy water, and Jesse picked up a dish towel to dry but Marty took it out of her hands.

"You need to rest for now," he said grasping her shoulders and sitting her down at the table.

She yawned—so wide she thought her jaw would dislocate. "Thanks, everyone. You don't know how much it means to me that you all showed up to rescue me today."

"Yeah, we were Jesse's posse," Marty laughed.

She yawned again and watched with tired eyes as her friends took care of her. *Maybe needing somebody once in a while is okay.*

Watching Marty and Maggie leave in her Beetle, Jesse bore an odd sense of loss as her beloved car drove away. Joe stood beside her and she felt his eyes on her. What had she done, agreeing to let him stay the night? Sure he said he'd sleep on the couch while the others were here, but now that they were alone, would his expectations change? She didn't want to meet his eyes. She didn't want any more emotions to possess her tonight. She was too weak, too exhausted, too vulnerable.

She turned off the porch light.

"Are you sure?" His voice was soft.

Here it comes. He's going to make his move now.

"Yes, I'm sure." she stated.

"I was just thinking that having the porch light on might offer a little more security," he said.

"Oh, is that what you meant?" she blurted.

He hid a half-smile. "Yes, what did you think I meant, Just Jesse?"

She couldn't believe that her face was hot from blushing. For goodness sake—she was twenty-eight years old!

"Sorry, Joe. I'm just tired…it's been a rough day."

He stepped toward her taking her shoulders. "It's okay. Detective Holden was right—you are one tough cookie." He brushed his lips across her forehead. "If you need me, just whistle. 'You know how to whistle, don't you?'"

Her soft laugh was muffled by the nearness of his chest. "Oh, Shakespeare *and* classic films. You are a renaissance man."

"A jack-of-all-trades, Jess. Good night." He released her.

"Good night, Joe."

She turned and climbed the stairs.

The sound was different tonight. Rather than sighing, it sounded more like weeping, a soft keening noise like a far off wounded animal. Jesse heard it through hazy dreams and hangover stupor. It took a moment for her to rouse enough to realize what it was. Unearthly, eerie, ethereal, tonight the sound evoked disquiet rather than longing. Helen was mourning the death of her sister. Or perhaps welcoming her to the realm of those who had passed to the other side.

She untangled her legs from the sheets and slipped out of bed. Remembering that Joe was asleep downstairs, she tiptoed to the attic room door. As she stood outside it, she felt the icy fingers reach beneath the door to wrap around her toes. Her chest was heavy with feelings of the usual peace that Helen's visits brought conflicting with a sense of foreboding. Immobile with fear, she was reluctant to open the door—she had never experienced this before. She listened for any movement downstairs, but all she heard was the soft weeping from within the attic room. Gripping the knob, she pushed the door in, entered, and was greeted with a blast of icy air that almost knocked her over. It slammed the door behind her and drove icy chills through her. Off in the corner by the armoire, she saw the glimmer of light that she knew was Helen. But the other sensation was violent, filling her with dread.

Eileen had decided to visit Jesse's new home.

Gasping, she tried to breathe as Eileen's fury ripped around the room, silent but fierce. She turned toward the door, but felt bolted to the floor. Hearing Joe on the stairs, she tried to cry out, but no sound emerged from her dry throat. She heard him calling her name as he ran into her bedroom. His voice rose with concern not finding her in her bed, and he continued calling as he neared the attic room. She stumbled forward as the angry force of Eileen halted when he opened the door. She sank to her knees shaken by the tempest.

"Jesse? Jesse? Are you all right? Why are you in here?" Joe's sleep-addled brain was still trying to awaken. He came over and knelt beside her. She crumpled into his arms; his strong hands rubbed her back, then stopped. Looking up at him, she saw his eyes widen and she followed his gaze to the armoire.

"Joe, meet my real mother, Helen Cavanaugh."

She heard his soft intake of breath.

The dim glow shimmered a soft rosy gold before it faded.

Jesse groped toward consciousness. Her head pounded and her mouth tasted like the bottom of a two-seater outhouse. Rolling over, she stopped when she saw Joe propped up asleep in the rocking chair. Rays of the sun poking through the gap in the curtain emblazoned his red hair with golden highlights reminiscent of a Celtic warrior...or Opie Taylor, both of whom she loved. She warmed at the sight allowing desire to smolder for a moment. If her breath hadn't reminded her of a bad summer at Girl Scout camp, she might have tried to seduce him. *What the hell am I thinking? Am I still drunk?*

She closed her eyes to stem the throbbing in her head and groaned. Dizzying images from the previous day reawakened the gut-wrenching fear she had lived through the afternoon and evening before. Running her hands through her thick hair was comforting, and she evened out her breath, trying to let go of the fear. Her friends had come when she needed them. Needing people was not a bad thing. This was a new concept for her. They had asked for nothing in return; there was no cost, no pound of flesh—or even an inch of flesh—required. She stared at the ceiling for a moment until she became aware of being watched. She looked across at Joe whose eyes were soft and warm as they studied her

"Good morning," she said sure that fire erupted from her dragon's mouth.

His smile was slow and drowsy, causing warmth to surge through body parts Jesse had been effectively ignoring of late. It felt delightful. *Steady, girl.*

"How did you sleep? Or should I say did you sleep at all?" he asked.

"I did sleep—quite well, considering all that happened yesterday." She needed to speak as little as possible until she could brush her teeth. "How about you? Looks awfully comfy in that rocking chair."

He laughed and sat up, stretching, lifting his arms above his head to reveal his flat belly and downy reddish golden hair that ran in a line to the top of his jeans.

Lord, help me, she thought.

"Well, let me rustle up some chow…" she said angling her mouth in a different direction from where he sat.

"Wow, Seneca Corners has brought out the cowgirl in you," he laughed.

"I just might get me a rootin', tootin' six shooter." She pretended to draw two guns from an imaginary holster.

He sobered. "That actually might be a good idea."

The grimness of the last day's events crashed in on their moment of levity, and she fell silent. Hadn't there been an old revolver in the armoire with the cowgirl jacket? Did she truly need one? If she had a gun, would she use it? Her mind travelled to Eileen's bedroom. If Eileen had owned a gun, would she still be alive today? Jesse hated guns; she shivered at the thought of using one. But maybe Joe had a point. He couldn't stay here every night—not without dire consequences if he looked like this in the morning. She could agree to have a gun; then he wouldn't worry so much about her. She stopped. He worried about her. Robert never worried; he was very nonchalant about her comings and goings. *Damn,* she was comparing them again. Looking at Joe she knew there was no comparison. Even in the short time she'd known him, she knew he was a far better man than Robert could ever hope to be. All the more reason for him not to stay another night.

"Maybe you're right."

He looked at her with bemusement. "Somehow I'm not convinced."

Her stomach growled and she wanted to crawl under the covers and hide. "Well, that was ladylike," she said feeling the color in her cheeks.

"You are a woman in need of food, Just Jesse. You hit the shower and I'll rustle us up some grub."

She rolled her eyes. "What have I started?" she laughed. She watched him stand and stretch again, rubbing his eyes like a little kid. He smiled at her, turned and left the room. She let out the breath she was holding. No, he definitely could not stay another night.

As Joe was drying the last dish, Jesse wiped the kitchen table and counters. Breakfast had been comfortable and easy with him, no pretense, no preening. Just Joe. As they cleaned up, he had asked her to go over the previous day's events since she was a little tipsy during the telling the night before. In the course of retelling, she remembered the slip of paper she had retrieved from beneath Eileen's body.

"Oh my gosh, there's a clue I forgot about!" She told him about the address that Eileen had written down. "I need to get that out of my pocket." She started toward the hall stairway and turned. "Come on up. I've got something else to show you."

"Yeah, I've heard that one before," he chuckled; she glowered at him. "Sorry," he mumbled barely hiding his smile. "I just like to pull your chain once in a while."

Jesse swatted his arm and laughed. "C'mon. I think you'll approve of this."

First she stopped in her room to reclaim the note, and then she headed for the attic room. Joe's footsteps slowed as he saw where she was going.

"Um, Jesse, are you sure you want to stir things up in there again?" he dragged the words out.

"Helen has never appeared during the day; of course Eileen had never appeared before, so maybe I don't know all the ghost rules." She pressed her ear to the door. Hearing nothing, she turned the knob. He lagged behind near her bedroom door.

"Are you afraid, big manly man?" she teased.

"Sometimes fear is a very judicious emotion," he reasoned.

Jesse swung the door in and looked about the room. Sunlight slanted through the window lighting up dust motes that danced on the air. Looking very mundane, the room was still. She went to the armoire noticing that the door was ajar again. Joe stepped into the room scrutinizing every corner.

"Joe, this door is always open after Helen's visits. I think she's trying to convey a message through it."

"I didn't believe in ghosts until last night, but I don't think they convey messages."

"Then why do they bother to hang around? Ghosts are people who have passed but have unfinished business here on earth. Or maybe they don't know they're dead."

"Well, I think Eileen figured that out and she was exceedingly irritated about it," he replied looking over his shoulder.

Jesse opened the door and took out Helen's cowgirl jacket. "Wouldn't this be perfect to wear to the Rodeo Round-Up?" She shook it so that the fringe danced and swayed.

He ran his fingers along the leather and hummed. "This is one nice jacket. Your aunt had excellent taste."

"My mother," she sighed, tracing the seams along the back of the coat.

"Right, your mother." His voice was gentle. "In addition to his critter control business Erik is also a taxidermist. He might be able to restore this with some saddle soap and TLC," he murmured still holding the fringe. "Jesse, this is a classic. You would look great in it—try it on."

She took the jacket off the hanger and slipped into it. Flexing her arms and shoulders, she was amazed at how perfectly it fit.

"I must be built just like her. This is too cool!" She spun around and looked at herself in the beveled mirror on the door of the armoire. Years had skimmed away some of the silver paint on the back of the glass, but Jesse could see well enough to know that she looked great in the jacket. She also saw Joe beaming at her delight in the coat.

"Why, ma'am, you look right purty in that there get up," he drawled.

"Why thankyee kindly, sir. And looky here." Reaching into the armoire, she took out a box and lifted the cover. Lying in a bundle of rose colored silk was a Colt revolver. Her heart thumped as she hefted it from the box. The gun felt awkward in her hand, heavy and clumsy. Joe took it from her, checked that the chambers weren't loaded and aimed it toward the window, siting it.

"You're full of surprises, Just Jesse." He handed it to her and winced when she took it by the barrel. "You need some lessons."

She replaced the gun in the box. "I need some bullets."

"Lessons first is my suggestion," he laughed. "I can offer some if you like."

He turned and began to examine the armoire. He ran his fingers along the panels on the doors as he smoothly swung them open and shut on their brass hinges. His eyes traced the contours of the piece running along the raised trim and the fan embellishments at the top of each door. He leaned to one side and brushed along the dovetail joints visible at the back corner. Opening the doors, he tapped along the sides and across the top shelf. The metal bar held hooks that slid along the bar to accommodate clothing. Jesse looked over his shoulder at the interior of the armoire admiring his obvious knowledge of its quality.

"Jesse, this is an amazing piece of furniture. The details and craftsmanship are superior."

For some reason, she felt proud. Perhaps because her mother had a good eye for well-made clothing and furniture. Perhaps because for the first time in her life she was proud to have such a discerning mother. In any event, it cheered her to be proud of her mother.

Joe frowned. "There's something off…"

The phone rang and she hurried to the downstairs hall to answer it.

"Hello?"

Silence.

Click.

Her stomach lurched. Whoever this was, it was the same person who had killed Eileen. The thought of that person on the other end of the line—connected to her somehow—made her shiver. When Joe appeared, she still stood with the receiver to her ear staring ahead. He took it and replaced it on the cradle.

"You okay?"

"It was him. Joe, it was him—the guy who killed Eileen," Her voice rose with panic.

He took her into his arms and she buried her face in his chest.

"Jesse, you've seen ghosts in this house, you've received threatening notes and strange phone calls. I think it might be time to move out of the Cavanaugh House."

She recoiled at the thought of leaving; the sensation seemed to come from somewhere else—someone else. Helen wanted her to stay…needed her to stay. And Helen would protect her. She moved away from his embrace and shook her head.

"I have my six-shooter. I'll be okay." She knew he wouldn't accept her belief that a ghost would be her guardian. But she knew it was true.

Joe shook his head in resignation.

"Fine. Your first shooting lesson is today."

Jesse maneuvered Bert down the street as she examined house numbers. The map that she carried showed the city of Geneva hugging the northeast corner of Seneca Lake, and the city was laid out in a basic grid pattern. Finding Gibson Street had been simple enough as it was just two blocks from Main Street. Now she searched for number 418—the address Eileen had written on her ivory calling card. There it was—a modest Cape Cod with a small flower bed in front. What was the significance of this place? She parked her car across the street and scrutinized the home. No car was parked in the driveway, but there was a two-car garage. People could be inside. The afternoon was overcast, but no lights illuminated the windows. Not having thought this through, she wondered what her next move should be. She hadn't expected the address to be a private home. What had she expected? She had no idea. For some reason, Eileen thought she needed to know about this place. Well, all she could do was knock on the door and ask if the residents knew Eileen Graham.

Climbing out of the car, she grabbed the notebook and pen she'd brought along and crossed the street. Two rocking chairs and a table sat on the porch. She noticed that they were askew, not aligned as Eileen's had been. The flower bed was randomly planted with more attention to varieties enjoyed than perfect placement. She already liked these people. But she still didn't quite know how to introduce the topic of Eileen...and her murder. What was the connection between these people and her death? Jesse hoped she would soon find out. She rang the bell and waited. No answer. She tried a couple more times, but it was obvious the people were not at home.

Disappointed, but unwilling to give up this easily, she decided to shop in Geneva and return near supper time; surely they would be home by then. She was anxious to find out how this piece of the puzzle fit.

She drove down Main St. until she found a stationery store, parked and went inside. Her favorite kind of store. Perusing the aisles, she purchased supplies for her classroom, plus some notecards, a selection of greeting cards, and a large magnifying glass. Although she'd had the crime scene photos developed as 8 x 10s, the few she had studied had details that were too small to distinguish. She wanted to see everything. After making her purchase, she returned to her car and drove back to Gibson St.

Pulling up to the Cape Cod, her heart skipped a beat when she saw a light on in the front room. The afternoon had grown gloomier, with a northwest breeze hinting of rain. She sat staring at the house and from within her came a stirring of anticipation. She didn't know what secret would soon be revealed, but knew it would be significant. Inexplicably, that hope rooted her to the seat of her car. Forcing herself to move, she opened the driver's door as if pushing a one thousand pound weight. *Why do I feel like this when I'm on the brink of answers?* She trudged across the street, overcome with lethargy, her limbs heavy burdens. The wind picked up, tossing her hair around in a red frenzy, and she forced herself to hurry up the steps. The doorbell loomed before her, and it was an effort just to raise her hand to ring it. From within the house Jesse heard the echo of the Westminster Chimes stirring a memory deep within her. A gust of wind rose as the door opened, and her hair blew across her face.

"May I help you?" a man's voice asked.

Jesse brushed her hair back in place and heard a gasp.

"Oh, my God." The man's voice was a hoarse whisper.

She looked into clear, blue eyes wide with shock. The man was in his fifties with dark hair, distinguished gray at the temples. His face was square and handsome, laugh wrinkles evidence of someone who enjoyed life. His reading glasses perched on top of his head, and a book was tucked beneath one arm. As she looked at him, sounds played in her memory: waves on a beach, a child's giggles, a lawn mower. And she knew.

"Daddy?"

Rain splattered against the windows as Jesse sipped her wine. Lamplight lent a soft glow to the comfortable living room. While the fireplace held no fire, birch logs were arranged in anticipation of the first cool autumn evening. The overstuffed furniture had done its duty over the years, with one cushion on the end of the couch sagging beside a reading lamp—the owner's favorite perch. Stacks of books climbed along that end of the couch, each waiting for its turn to be read. She did not remember living here, though Jim Graham told her she had for a few years. He was a professor of English Literature at nearby Hobart and William Smith College. For the past twenty-four years he had been searching for her.

He was staring into the cold fireplace, digesting the news of Eileen's murder. "That poor woman," he murmured.

Jesse studied him as he assimilated the news. She traced his profile with her eyes and tried to place it on her vague memories. She had been very young, and their times together had been precious, of that she was sure. His face held a kindness found only in victims who have lost someone dear and understood that pain in others. She basked in gratitude, even extending to Eileen whose last act on earth was to bring her to this man.

Jim turned and looked at her. "My God, I can't believe you are sitting right in front of me!" His smile was contagious, and then he sobered. "Are you all right?"

"Yes, I am."

"But it sounds like you're in danger, too. Why is that?"

"Are you sure you want this whole story?"

He nodded. Jesse took a deep breath and began her tale at the point where she had moved into the Cavanaugh House. As she talked, he nodded in response to her account. Occasionally, he would ask for clarification, but for the most part he sat in silence just listening. She decided not to include Helen's haunting of the house, unsure of how open he might be to such events. She concluded with her decision to look up the address on Eileen's card.

"I think this is what she wanted to give me. She knew I would be arriving soon, and I believe she had it with her for that reason."

"That makes sense, though removing it from the crime scene could cause trouble down the road. But I have a question, Jesse. What encouraged you to pursue this investigation you've mounted? Why not just allow the police to investigate the threats? You seem emotionally entwined in this somehow."

She shifted her eyes to a window where rain drizzled down the screens in zigzag patterns. How could she explain her emotional connection? Her innate sense that Helen needed both her death to be recognized as a murder and someone brought to justice? The longing Helen conveyed to her and her loving response to a woman she had never known? Only by revealing the hauntings did all of this make sense.

"Hold on to your hat; there's more to the story." she took another deep breath and began.

Although she concentrated on her words, Jesse noticed that at no time did Jim Graham appear incredulous or mocking. His eyes bored into hers throughout the telling, never looking away, never revealing disbelief. When she finished, he was silent. After a moment, he nodded.

"You believe me?" her voice rose in wonder. While she knew all of this to be true, she wondered if she would believe it had she not experienced it herself.

"Of course I believe it," Jim laughed. "Jesse, I teach English Lit.—there are ghosts all over the place, Shakespeare, Dickens, you name it. A common cultural belief doesn't just spring from the mind of various writers like Athena from the head of Zeus unless there is some basis for it. Yes, I believe in ghosts, both in fiction and non-fiction."

"Wow," she whispered.

Jim rose and took her glass. "Follow me into the kitchen and I will make you the best omelet you have ever tasted."

The kitchen was dated with white metal cabinets and black and white square floor tiles. Avocado green appliances were the sole testament to any updates, and a small oak table claimed the center of the room. Airy and bright despite the gloom of the day, the kitchen drew her into its embrace.

Jim pulled out a cutting board and chef's knife, placing them on the counter.

"Would you like to do the chopping honors?" he asked as he pulled onions out of a basket.

"Sure," she grinned taking the onions.

Jim added green peppers, mushrooms and garlic to her pile and retrieved a pan from the cupboard beside the stove. "So what shape did you find Helen's house in when you first arrived?" he asked.

Jesse regaled him with the story of the million mice. They chatted and laughed companionably as they prepared dinner together. The aroma of onion, garlic, and chives swirled around her as she set the table and refilled their wine glasses. With a flourish, Jim slid two perfect omelets onto their plates and they sat down to eat.

"You've been through quite an ordeal since you moved to Seneca Corners," Jim said.

"True," she said sampling her dinner. "You were right; this is the best omelet I've ever tasted!"

Jim laughed, "Well, I had to endure my own cooking for a long time, so I decided I would teach myself to cook." He paused, and the bright, airy kitchen became imbued with the suffocating sensation of unanswered questions and lifelong hurts.

"Why did you leave us?" Jesse's voice was soft; she sounded like a little girl.

Jim let out a long breath and sat very still for a moment. She was unsure whether he was gathering his thoughts or suppressing anger. He looked down and stared at his hands folded in his lap. Jesse waited, silent. Rain pattered on the windows marking the time as Jim contemplated his response. When he looked back at her, she noticed his eyes shiny and sorrowful.

"I don't believe in speaking ill of the dead, Jesse, but in this instance, I think you need every shred of information you can garner. I never left you. Eileen left me and took you with her." He smothered a break in his voice and cleared his throat. "I searched for you for months, but I had no idea where she went. The police couldn't trace her, so I hired a private detective. He found her car at the Trailways Bus Terminal; a ticket seller recognized her picture and remembered you with your red hair. She had purchased tickets to New York City, so the detective travelled there and tried to discover her whereabouts, but to no avail. After a couple of years, he gave up, too. Eventually, so did I."

Jesse remembered the loathing in Eileen's voice when she told her that her father had deserted them, and now she wondered if it were directed inward. Despite what Eileen had told her, Jesse never had hated him. Perhaps living with that woman allowed even her child's mind to understand why a person might leave. Once again, her world and what she had believed about it was thrown into chaos.

"You looked for us?"

"For years. I couldn't believe it when I saw you standing on my doorstep today. You look just like Helen."

"That seems to be the source of all my woes," she winced. "Eileen wanted me to find you. I believe your address is what she wanted to give me, but why? She knew I was trying to find out the truth about Helen's death. Do you know something about that night that would help?"

A faraway look came over Jim's eyes as he cast his mind back to the night Helen was killed. "It was so long ago. Let me think." He closed his eyes for a few minutes. "My main memory is of you crying in the cradle in Helen's bedroom. Eileen bounced you and, well, shall we say 'encouraged' you to quiet down, but you just yelled louder. It was so chaotic. I took you and your crying lessened until it stopped. I'll never forget your eyes looking up at me—most baby's eyes are very dark, but yours were already hinting at emerald. You had downy red hair; God you were a beautiful baby." He smiled at her. "And you've grown into a beautiful woman."

Jesse warmed at his compliment. Eileen had never told her she was beautiful—just the opposite, always pointing out flaws. What would she be like today if she had grown up with this kind of affirmation? How could this man have been taken from her life? Of all the cruel things Eileen had done, taking this man from her life was the cruelest.

"What else do you remember? When did you go into the attic room?"

Jim closed his eyes again. "After you quieted down, we took you to the home of Helen's best friend to stay while we returned to identify Helen. The officer led us to that room. Helen's body was on the floor…the rope was still around her neck." He spoke slowly as if walking through the scene once more. "He asked us if Helen had any enemies, anyone who might do this to her. We both said no. He instructed us not to touch or disturb anything in the room, but there wasn't much in there…a chair, a large piece of furniture off to the side, perhaps it was an armoire? Maybe some boxes set in one corner." He opened his eyes and looked at her. "That's about all I can remember."

"Was anyone else there besides the police officer?" she asked.

"Yes, there were two police officers. I don't remember their names, but they were both pretty young, maybe rookies. Soon after we arrived, two more men came in—a photographer and the coroner."

Jesse mulled over his account for a moment. "Your description matches what Eileen told me. So my question is, if Helen committed suicide, why would they ask you if she had any enemies?"

"That struck me as odd, too. And yet, her death was ruled a suicide."

"I have photos of Helen's crime scene—don't ask how I got them," She held up her hands as if to stop any questions. "Would you be willing to look at them to see if they jar any more memories for you?"

"Sure, if you think it might help. But, Jesse, I'm worried that your probing this incident is disturbing a hornet's nest. Maybe you should just turn everything over to the police."

"The police aren't interested. They told my friend Marty, who I told you is on the force, to just leave it alone. Did you know Ben Wyndham?"

Jim laughed. "Anyone within the Finger Lakes region knows of him."

"Do you think Helen knew him?"

"What are you getting at?"

Jesse described Ben Wyndham's reaction to seeing her and Fred Morton's apparent aversion to her. "That was the same night someone tried to run me off the road. Someone in Al Wyndham's sports car. Marty said anybody could tap my phone if they had the funds to do it. I think these threats are coming from that house."

Jim grunted. "You might be disturbing a very *big* hornet's nest. But from what I know of Ben Wyndham he's a fine person. I don't see him murdering innocent women or threatening them either."

"Funny thing about men who seem like nice guys. Sometimes they turn out to be rats." She took a sip of wine.

"So when are you going to tell me about him?" Jim asked.

"Him who?" She raised her eyebrows in innocence.

"Him who broke your heart and sent you running to a decrepit haunted house in Small Town, USA?"

"You're pretty insightful."

"I read a lot," he laughed. "Some stories never tire of being told."

Jesse was surprised at how little emotion she experienced in the retelling of the Robert tale. She remembered a time recently when she could barely think about him without crying, but now that pain seemed so distant. Perhaps threats on your life put things in perspective rather quickly. As she finished, she braced herself for the kind of insulting remarks Eileen would have hurled at her.

"He didn't deserve you," Jim said.

She shook her head trying to make sense of his statement. Wasn't it the other way around? Didn't Eileen say she didn't deserve Robert? She cocked her head looking at Jim. "What?"

"He didn't deserve you; you were too good for him."

"I think you got that backward."

Jim nodded. "I see. Eileen spread her pixie dust all over you. She had a way of making people feel small and worthless. You turned out pretty well despite her poison. I'm telling you, men like Robert use their good looks and wealth to prey on people, use them and discard them. You are too good for him. Too beautiful, too intelligent, too good. Period."

Jesse's heart warmed at the thought that this man, who should have raised her, believed she was all of those things. Now he was back in her life, and she wasn't sure how to handle that fact.

"I...I don't know...I mean, I know I called you 'Daddy' at the door because all these memories flooded my brain at once, but I don't..." she stammered.

Jim covered her hand with his. "Call me Jim—at least for now. Maybe someday you'll find another name. There's no rush; we've found each other at last. I hope we can continue to be in each other's lives, but I leave that up to you."

"I'd like that...Jim. Thanks."

Jesse prepared to leave and turned back to him. "I'll be heading up to Rochester to arrange Eileen's funeral as soon as they release the body. I'll let you know about the funeral arrangements."

"I'd like that, thanks." Jim walked her to the door. "Drive safely...geez, I sound like a father."

She grinned. "I like that."

Starting her car, she drove to the end of the street, pulled over and burst into tears.

-TEN-

Light rain tapped against the windows as Jesse peered at the photos spread out on the table. Using her best guess, she had arranged them in chronological order starting with the one of Helen still hanging from the beam. Marty used the magnifying glass she'd bought in Geneva to scrutinize the pictures for details they might otherwise miss. She had to steel herself to inspect them; the sight of Helen's bloated, darkened face, bulging eyes and protruding tongue had caused her to lose her dinner. Marty doubted the wisdom of her examination of the pictures, but she insisted. His sudden cry made her jump.

"Holy shit!" he shouted.

"What is it? What did you find?"

"Sheriff Donoghue was one of the two police officers that found the body...sorry, Jesse, found Helen." He pawed through the other photos looking for one depicting the second officer. Finding it, he aimed the magnifying glass over the policeman's nametag. "Here he is. Officer Walter George. Hmmm. That rings a bell..."

She leaned over his shoulder looking at the photos of the two men. "If Sheriff Donoghue was there that night, he could have been the one who asked Eileen and Jim if Helen had any enemies. If he wasn't the one who asked, he was right there when Officer George asked them. He would know everything about that night. *Everything,*

Marty. So why did he tell you to drop it? To stop asking questions?"

He shook his head. "I don't know. It's all so weird."

Jesse thought for a moment. "Maybe someone changed the report after he filed it. Doesn't it go through some kind of process? Like being passed on to a senior officer?"

"Sure, he'd submit the report to the sheriff who might make changes based on later evidence that turned up. Then Donoghue would have gotten it back to verify the report and file it."

She rummaged through the photos, now in a mess on the table. She found the one she sought. "Remember this one, Marty? It's Helen's official death notice. The night we were in the Archive Room I noticed that this looked like it had been altered. See? The photo shows it, too. Something has been erased."

"Evidence tampering is pretty serious stuff."

"What if someone higher up changed Sheriff Donoghue's report and then ordered him to keep quiet about it? Or maybe he never even knew."

"If someone intimidated him into being quiet about it, Donoghue sure wouldn't want it found out after all these years. Especially since he's now the sheriff," he said.

"I think Ben Wyndham is involved in all this. Maybe he paid someone off. Or with all his power around here, maybe he threatened people."

"I don't know, Jesse. Ben Wyndham is an okay guy…"

She gave a sharp laugh. "I keep hearing that. When I do, I picture Robert: charming, rich, a people magnet. The unwashed masses never want to believe that their benefactor might have feet of clay." Her voice was harsh and bitter. She was surprised that her anger had returned, but thinking of how wealth and influence might have led to Helen's death made her remember how easily Robert manipulated—and hurt—anyone who stood in his path.

Marty looked at her for a moment. "You need to let go of that. How does your bitterness hurt Robert? It doesn't; it just hurts you."

Jesse sat back against her chair and folded her arms, pouting. "Pretty righteous talk, D'Amato. You're beginning to sound like Sr. Angelina."

"But I let you drink beer if you want to."

She looked at him out of the corner of her eye and saw the gleam in his. "You tick me off, D'Amato," she smirked. Sitting up, she grabbed another photo. "Let's get back to work."

She was holding the first photo in the sequence: Helen still suspended from the rafter. Off to the side stood a chair. Jesse studied the photo unsure about why it puzzled her. Suddenly she exclaimed. "That's it!"

"What? What's it?" Marty asked looking up from the photo he was studying under the magnifying glass.

"Look. See that chair? Would they have moved that chair?"

"No, everything must be left just as it's found at a crime scene."

She felt a stab of guilt at the note she took from beneath Eileen's body.

"So they would not have slid it over or turned it upright?" she asked.

"No. They shouldn't have."

"Look at the chair. Helen could not possibly have stood on that chair to hang herself. Her legs couldn't reach it from where she is. And if she had kicked it away, it would have turned over."

Marty studied the photo, letting out a low whistle.

"You're on to something, Jesse," he murmured.

"Marty, those two officers knew that Helen never committed suicide. I think there was something in her original death certificate to prove that."

Maggie had insisted on accompanying her to Rochester to claim Eileen's body and make the funeral arrangements. Jesse filled her friend in on the discoveries she and Marty had made while examining the photos.

"Jesse, that means Sheriff Donoghue has known all these years that Helen didn't commit suicide. No wonder he reacted to you like he did when he first met you. Didn't you say he appeared surprised?"

"Not as surprised as Ben Wyndham, but yes, he was shocked to see me, too. I think Helen must have known many of Seneca Corners' leading citizens. Susan did tell me that she was very involved in community service, and from what I've heard of Ben Wyndham, he is quite the philanthropist." She checked her rearview mirror and her voice took on a darker tone. "We've got company, Maggie."

Maggie started to turn her head, but Jesse stopped her. "Don't turn around. We need to pretend we don't notice the green...Buick maybe...that is following me to Rochester once again." Her insides twisted at the memory of what had happened the last time that car followed her, and she fought the image of Eileen lying dead, sprawled across her bed.

"What should we do?" Maggie said.

"Nothing. We're headed to a coroner's office. I assume there will be police clambering all over the place. If this guy wants to follow me there, let him. I'll have him arrested on the spot."

"Arrested for what? You have no proof that he murdered Eileen."

"Well, arrested for following me...on suspicion of his involvement with her death...for scaring the shit out of me...I don't know, Maggie, there must be a crime in there somewhere." She watched as the green car slipped behind the car directly behind her Beetle. "Maggie, somebody's after me." Her voice was low with fear.

Sighing, Maggie folded her arms. "It's time for you to join the convent, Jess."

She didn't want to admit that Maggie might be right. At least in the sense of staying as a visitor, not staying permanently. *God help us all!*

Jesse pulled off the Brighton exit and drove to the coroner's office. She watched as the green car, still a few car lengths behind her, slowed and then sped past the building. Her heart lurched. Although the driver had turned his head away, she recognized him.

"Maggie, that was Fred Morton."

"Are you sure, Jess? He drove by pretty fast."

"I would bet my life on it." They looked at each other both struck with the unintended meaning of her comment.

Jesse was surprised at the depth of her sadness when she looked at Eileen's body. She signed the papers and the coroner informed her that "the deceased" would be transported to the Wilson Funeral Home right away. Shaking his hand, she thanked him as she left, wondering why she did so—but the circumstances seemed to call for some kind of formal gesture.

She struggled with the bizarre sensation that filled her as she drove to the funeral home. Did all of this actually happen? The events of just a few days ago seemed a distant memory...or a terribly bad dream. She juggled all these thoughts as she drove until Maggie interrupted her reverie.

"Any sign of the green car?"

She sat up straighter in her seat, realizing she had been ignoring Maggie. Checking the rearview mirror, she shook her head.

"You mean Fred Morton, don't you?" she said.

"Jesse, don't jump to conclusions until you are absolutely certain," Maggie warned.

"Mags, I am absolutely certain…about ninety percent absolutely certain."

"You know that's a mathematical impossibility right?" Maggie laughed.

"I'm an English teacher, Mags. You do the math."

Jesse pulled into the sweeping driveway of the funeral home and ignored the valet who stood at the entrance. *I'm not going to put Bert through that humiliation again.* Pulling into a parking space, she took a deep breath.

"Let's get this over with," she said as she opened the driver's door.

She hated funeral homes with their thick carpets and elegantly appointed décor. She would much prefer an all-out Irish wake where everyone drank too much Guinness and brawls broke out. That's how the dead should be honored—with life and all of its warts. But Eileen would roll over in her grave, were she there yet, if everything wasn't tastefully done. Following the specter who had greeted them, they passed the viewing rooms to the office. The scent of roses and lilies floated on the air accompanied by a muted rendition of *How Great Thou Art.* Jesse thought she would suffocate.

The owner greeted them with solemnity and offered his condolences. Then he sat down and addressed the business at hand and what their budget might be. So much for sympathy; there was money to be made. When he checked his records, he found that Eileen had enrolled in a funeral package. He straightened and cleared his throat when he realized it was the Eternal Happiness version and suddenly he could not do enough.

Maggie helped to plan the funeral vigil and Mass, for which Jesse was grateful since she hadn't attended church in so long that she would have no idea where to begin. Then Jesse selected the handouts for the liturgies, the holy cards with the obituary and the flowers from her to be laid on the casket at the viewing. By the time they were finished, she felt she'd run a marathon. Her head spun with emotion and confusion; Maggie took her keys and let her sit back and close her eyes a bit in the car. They still had appointments with Eileen's accountant and the manager of Graham Designs.

Her worst hangover had never been this bad.

Eileen's accountant peered at them over reading glasses perched at the end of his nose. Although the formal obituary had not been published yet, news of Eileen's death was making the rounds. This man looked sincerely shaken by the event, and the sympathy in his voice was matched by the sadness in his eyes. Jesse had always thought that accountants were heartless number-crunchers, but this man did not fit the stereotype at all.

With heaviness, he pulled out Eileen's files and opened them. Poring over the documents, he explained each. Maggie took notes while Jesse nodded dumbly. What was clear to her was that she was Eileen's sole heir and a hefty trust was hers. She had never questioned Eileen about her financial situation; her lifestyle confirmed her wealth. She had been generous with Jesse who had never lacked for material possessions, and in fact, always had the best. College tuition had been paid, as had that for graduate school. Money had never been an issue for Jesse. When she left Robert, she was determined to make it on her own; she had left her savings in the bank in Rochester withdrawing just enough to get her settled in Helen's house—another gift to her. Her attention drifted back to the accountant who was now addressing Maggie more than Jesse.

"The monthly payments cease on her death," he said.

She stirred. Monthly payments? Was this child support that Jim never told her about? Her thoughts cleared. Had Jim somehow known at least how to send money for her?

"What monthly payments? From whom?" she asked.

"I don't know the source; I have merely recorded the income. You would have to ask the bank for more information, though they may not be able to give it to you," he said, his voice gentle. "You've had a significant amount of information to consider today, Miss Graham. Perhaps we can schedule another appointment to continue our discussion and make arrangements for the transfer of the trust fund."

She nodded, her mind awash with the details surrounding Eileen's life...and death.

Visiting Graham Designs was daunting. Jesse's entrance had been a flurry of air kisses from all of the staff and a babble of high pitched condolences and freely flowing tears. Apparently Eileen had been a decent employer, for most of the women were genuinely moved to grief. Viola Schumacher was managing to keep scheduled projects running, but it was clear that without Eileen's vision and drive, Viola would not maintain the level of success the business had enjoyed. Ushering Jesse and Maggie into Eileen's office after an appropriate amount of sympathy had been expressed, Viola asked one of the staff to bring them tea. They chatted about what a wonderful woman Eileen had been and how devastated all of her clients were upon hearing about her death. Viola asked her polite questions about how she was coping without asking the burning questions about the circumstances surrounding Eileen's passing.

The tea arrived in finest porcelain, accompanied by scones fresh from the oven. Cinnamon and allspice filled the room with comfort, and Viola did the honor of pouring. Jesse's finger barely fit in the delicate handle of her teacup, so she grasped it with her hand instead. Besides, was she supposed to raise a pinky when she sipped? She just didn't know.

"I suppose you want to go over the books," the woman said, then raised her pinky and sipped her tea.

Jesse sighed. She didn't know how much more she could handle in one day. Maggie came to her rescue.

"Jesse has had a full day today. Could she take the files with her and peruse them at her leisure?"

Viola had offered the books as a courtesy and was taken aback that Jesse would even want to look at them. "Of course," she said raising an eyebrow and sitting straighter. Brushing an imaginary piece of lint from her silk shantung skirt, she twitched her head in a defensive nod. "Eileen kept a duplicate set of records; I'll give you one to take with you."

"Thank you, Viola. It's not that Jesse doesn't trust..." Maggie let her voice fade into the meaning. "She is trying to understand Eileen's assets and sort through her financial picture." Maggie's genuine smile put the woman at ease.

Viola looked more relaxed. "Of course."

They chatted a while longer and then took their leave, a banker's box of records in Jesse's arms.

Their final stop was the bank. Jesse wasn't ready to tackle Eileen's home yet. They waited for the bank manager to finish with his customers. The bank was sterile, marble floors echoing transactions that depositors tried to conceal in whispers. The vault stood open behind a barred gate revealing safe deposit boxes marching along in neat rows. Jesse watched a teller help a customer access her box, each of them inserting a key and opening the small door. The customer slid the box out and disappeared into a small room inside the vault. She sat up, alert.

"Maggie, I need to get into Eileen's safe deposit box right now."

"Why?"

"Access to her safe deposit box ceases on her death. Her obituary hasn't been published yet, so maybe the bank doesn't know about it. At least no one but the manager since I told him why I needed to meet. I have her key on my key ring, and I am on the account." She jumped up and hurried to the teller nearest the vault. Maggie followed. Jesse requested access to the box, and the teller drew out the signature card. Jesse's eyes darted to the manager who was still deep in conversation with the customers. The teller looked at the card and paused. She looked at Jesse. Jesse's heart sank; it must have already been flagged.

"Do you have identification?"

Relieved, Jesse pulled her wallet out of her large macramé purse and showed the woman her driver's license. The woman handed her a pen and indicated where to sign. As Jesse did so, she sneaked another peek at the manager's office. Still talking.

The woman led Jesse and Maggie into the vault and inserted the bank key into the door of a large safe deposit box. Jesse inserted her key and opened the door. She slid the box out and hefted it, carrying it into one of the small rooms. The teller closed the door for them.

"Maggie, this is heavy. How big is your purse?"

Maggie lifted her small bag. "Nuns don't need big purses, Jess."

"Mags, go get that beach tote in my back seat. Eileen stashed a lot of stuff in here. If I don't get it out now, it will be months before I can access it."

Maggie hurried out and Jesse's heart pounded. She didn't know the penalty for accessing a dead person's safe deposit box, but it was probably a situation Marty would not be able to get her out of this time. She opened the box and inspected the contents; jewelry boxes, bearer bonds, stock certificates, silver coins, birth and death notices, and other papers tucked inside a manila envelope. She stuffed what she could into her bag, but not all of it would fit.

"Come on, Maggie," she whispered. The clock in the vault ticked a slow droning sound, making it seem like an hour had passed. Finally, she heard the barred vault door being unlocked and Maggie's voice politely thanking the teller. Her friend hustled into the small room and handed Jesse the large, striped beach bag. Jesse plunked the remaining items in and pulled the drawstrings.

"It looked like the manager was finishing up with the people in his office. We'd better hurry," she whispered.

She pushed the bag into Maggie's arms and added her purse.

"Run these out to the car, Mags, and then join me back inside." Maggie looked startled, but took the bags and headed for the barred door. Jesse replaced the safe deposit box in its opening and called the teller over. Smiling, the woman opened the barred doors and Maggie hurried out to the car. The teller placed her key in the lock and secured the safe deposit box back in place. Jesse stepped out of the vault and saw the manager escorting the couple to his office door. He caught sight of her as she walked away from the vault area, and he raised an eyebrow.

"Oh crap," she murmured. "Busted."

The customers asked another question, but the manager's eyes lingered on Jesse as he answered them. At last, saying their good-byes, the couple left and he approached her.

"Sorry to keep you waiting, Miss Graham. I am so sorry to hear of your mother's death." His eyes flicked over to the vault and back to her. Seeing that she carried nothing, he relaxed and motioned for her to come into his office. Maggie had slipped back in and was sitting innocently in a chair in the lobby.

"I would like my friend Sr. Angelina to join us, if that is all right," Jesse said.

Turning, the manager looked for a nun but found only Maggie.

"I am not in my habit today," she smiled at him.

He escorted them both into his office clearly delighted to grace it with such a holy woman.

Numbers danced before Jesse's eyes, and she knew without a doubt that with all she had faced in one day she was too overwhelmed to comprehend this information. Was it just hours ago that she had viewed Eileen's body in the morgue? The bank manager had presented all of Eileen's accounts and assets to her just as the accountant had earlier. All the information ran together in a cacophony of financial gobbledygook. Maggie was attentive and continued to take notes. Jesse knew that without her, the day would be like one of her childhood finger-paint pictures where all the colors merged into a dull brown. Then she remembered the point Eileen's accountant had mentioned about the monthly deposit.

"Mother received a monthly deposit," she said.

The manager looked at a statement. "Yes.'

"Who was it from?" she asked.

"The statement lists it as Bremen Investments, Ltd."

"A corporation? Not a person?" she asked, disappointment filling her heart.

"Yes, a corporation. It would be a hefty sum for an individual to pay out each month," he said, his smile hinting at condescension.

Jesse hadn't thought to ask the amount. It had been at that point that the accountant had wrapped up the meeting in deference to her exhaustion. She assumed it was a few hundred dollars in child support from Jim.

"How much was it each month?"

"Five thousand dollars."

Jesse's sharp intake of air caused her to begin coughing. Maggie patted her on the back, and the manager poured a glass of water from the metal pitcher on his desk and offered it to her. She gulped it trying to calm herself. Jim Graham did not have the resources to pay that kind of money. What was it? Investment income? Dividends? Eileen was a savvier investor than Jesse had imagined.

"Was it investment income? Was is profit from her business? What was this money?" she asked.

"Mrs. Graham's accountant would know that more than I," he replied. "I just know the amount and when it started."

"When did it start?" she asked.

"The banker leafed through a pile of papers. "Let's see, hmmm." He flipped through some more. "Ah, here it is. The first payment was made in August 1940."

Stars swam in the blackness filling Jesse's eyes.

Scattered across the kitchen table, the contents of Eileen's safe deposit box looked like a pirate's treasure. Jesse and Maggie stared at it in wonder.

"Jess, this is tens of thousands of dollars' worth of possessions. Maybe hundreds. You need to get your own safe deposit box," Maggie said in a low voice as if someone might be listening.

"Geez, Maggie, I had no idea how much Eileen was worth. Where did she get all of this? That's the question, isn't it? Not just this stuff, but the monthly deposits. I doubt that coincidence played any part in the fact that these payments started the month and year Helen died. Who besides Ben Wyndham would have the resources to pay her off like this?"

"Jesse, you're jumping to a lot of conclusions there," Maggie cautioned.

"Then offer another explanation, Mags. What other source could there be?"

Maggie shook her head and sighed. "I don't know."

"I'm going to confront Ben Wyndham and demand an explanation. Maybe he wasn't the one who actually killed Helen, but I'll bet Fred Morton was in on it," she said.

Maggie's eyes grew wide and her mouth gaped. "Are you nuts, Jesse Graham? After you confront him, what do you plan to do? Outrun him? If he did kill Helen and Eileen, or had Fred Morton do it for him, and you reveal that you know it, why would he then not kill you, too?"

"I'll do it in a public place—like at the Rodeo Round-Up. That would be perfect because there will be so many witnesses. How could he wiggle out of it? He can't kill me in front of everybody." Her voice rose with excitement. "Then Marty can arrest him and Fred Morton, and I will be safe at last."

"Have you lost your mind? You can't accuse someone of murder because they might have, possibly, maybe sent your mother—aunt—whatever the hell she is—money!" Maggie was shaking with rage.

Jesse stared at her usually serene friend. "Did you just swear, Sr. Angelina?" She made the Sign of the Cross.

"This isn't funny, Jesse. Your life is in danger and if you don't care, at least respect the fact that I do." Maggie's eyes glistened and her hands balled into fists; she stood and leaned toward Jesse. "You think you can just cavalierly run around like a detective and then publicly accuse the most powerful man in central New York of murder and dance off unaffected? If he is involved, you're dead. If he's not involved, you're guilty of slander. I don't want anything to happen to you. Don't you realize the danger you're in? Don't you care? Well I do, damn it all." Maggie was shouting now, tears streaming down her face. She wiped at her eyes looking around for a tissue. Finding a napkin on the counter, she wiped her eyes again and blew her nose. "And I'm sorry I swore. Twice." She plopped back down in her chair.

"You're going to burn in hell for that, you know," Jesse said.

"Don't try to lighten the mood, here. I am furious with you," Maggie snapped.

The two women sat in silence, both staring at the items on the table. Jesse hadn't realized how frightened Maggie was for her. The knowledge that people cared about her brought ambivalence. On the one hand, it was reassuring and comforting to know someone else cared; on the other, letting people into her life had ended in pain too many times. But if she couldn't believe that Maggie truly cared, then there was no one in the world she could trust.

Her voice was a whisper. "I'm sorry, Mags. I didn't realize how scared you were about all of this."

Maggie nodded but said nothing.

"I won't confront Ben Wyndham. I promise."

Maggie nodded again.

"I need to find out the truth, though. Do you understand that?"

"I guess so, but couldn't you just let the police handle it?" Maggie begged.

"The police aren't interested in Helen's death, and Eileen's death is related somehow. Who knows if the police will solve it. I don't know what the common denominator is, but I think it's the murderer. If it's not Ben Wyndham, then it's Fred Morton. Maybe he's doing the dirty work for his employer."

"If so, these are dangerous men and you need to stay as far away from them as you can," Maggie said. "Why don't we just skip the Rodeo-Round-up?"

"Are you kidding? I want to wear my mother's jacket. Face it, Mags, where else in Seneca Corners could I wear that?"

"It isn't funny." Maggie used her "teacher voice."

"Yes, Sr. Angelina."

Maggie shot her a severe look. "I'm serious."

"Well, I can't hide in my house for the rest of my life. Besides, you said yourself the Rodeo Round-Up will be public, so he can't hurt me."

Maggie sighed. "You're impossible."

"Plus, I'll have my holy sister friend with me." She smiled. "Now I'm going to get the soap."

Maggie's brow furrowed looking over Eileen's items displayed on the table.

"Soap? What for?"

"To wash out your potty mouth," she teased.

Maggie lowered her brows into a frown. "Bitch."

Jesse laughed.

Jesse sank into the mauve sofa positioned before the casket. Maggie sat on her left, Joe and Susan on her right. Jim sat behind her, and his presence brought a calm that she desperately needed. All the other chairs were filled with Eileen's former employees, clients and a sprinkling of friends she had socialized with through Robert. Sitting in the very back row was Robert himself, drawing more of a crowd than Eileen. Upon arriving he had approached her with open arms and a contrived look of sympathy.

"Jesse, my love, I am so sorry." His voice invited onlookers.

She had ignored his invitation to embrace and shook his hand causing him to awkwardly lower his other arm. She felt shaky seeing him for the first time since she had broken off their engagement.

"Hello, Robert. Thank you for coming." Her voice was ice.

"Jesse, I—." He stopped, seeing Joe approach.

"You must be Robert," Joe said, standing beside Jesse.

Robert looked from one to the other.

"You don't waste time, do you?" Robert smirked.

"At least I waited until the engagement was broken, Robert."

He flinched. "Touché." He bowed. "I am sorry about Eileen's death. What a horrible thing to happen."

"Thank you, Robert," she said hearing sincerity in his voice.

At that point the funeral director had appeared to escort her to the sofa so the vigil service could begin.

The overpowering scent of flowers sickened her. Bouquets and arrangements covered the front wall surrounding the casket and then trailed down either side of the room. Jesse had to admit that the funeral director had worked a miracle on Eileen's appearance so it could be an open casket service. She stared at the woman's make-up-caked profile; the lipstick color was all wrong. Eileen would never have worn Peachy Pink; she was more a Vivid Vermilion sort of woman.

Her mind wandered over the events of the last few weeks as people droned the rosary. She could not concentrate on Hail Marys right then and offered up a prayer of contrition. Images drifted through her mind and she tried to make sense of them. Her awareness returned to her surroundings and she listened to Maggie's kind voice as she participated in the rosary.

"The fourth Sorrowful Mystery: The Carrying of the Cross. Hail Mary, full of grace the Lord is with thee...," her friend's gentle voice intoned.

Jesse closed her eyes and let her mind float on Maggie's voice, lyrical and reverent. Peace enveloped her and tears slipped from beneath her eyelids and streamed down her face.

Every time the phone rang, Jesse was loath to answer it, fearing silence at the other end. Picking up the receiver this time, she was relieved that it was Marty; he spoke fast with excitement.

"Hey, Jesse, remember I said the name of Officer Walter George rang a bell?"

"Yeah, I remember."

"Well, his name came up during a meeting today. They have something called the "George Rule" and I never put it together before. I thought they just used George as a generic kind of name to mean 'everyman' like John Doe or something. Turns out, it was named after this cop. This "George Rule" says that if we see a fellow officer struggling under the stress of the job, we have certain procedures to follow to get him help. Apparently this guy had a nervous breakdown and attempted suicide because of the stress of his job."

She knew before she asked the question. "When did he have this nervous breakdown?"

"Let me check my notes." She heard notebook pages flipping. "Here it is. Whoa, Jesse. He was put on medical leave in October of 1940. That's…"

"…that's just a couple of months after Helen was murdered," she finished for him. "What happened to him?"

"He was committed to the Grayson State Hospital. As far as I could find out, he's still there."

She slid down the wall and sat on the floor. "Holy crap." What went on all those years ago to drive a man over the edge? She had heard terrifying stories of the Grayson State Hospital and the treatment of patients there. What mental state was Walter George in today? Twenty-eight years after Helen's death? What did he know? If he knew something about that night, could he remember it?

"I have to go to Grayson State Hospital," she said as she stared at the wall across from her seat on the floor.

"Jesse, I don't think that's a good idea."

"You know, I'm tired of hearing that from everybody, Marty. Nobody likes my ideas, but nobody else has family members being murdered."

Jesse navigated Bert up a broad drive that cut through manicured lawns sprinkled with brick buildings of different sizes and hues. Innocuous names like The Meadows, Forest Hall, and Glenview suggested a college campus, but the small square building called The Morgue clarified any such misconception. All of the windows in The Meadows building were barred, so she decided that was her destination. Ringing the buzzer at the front door yielded no results, so she headed over to Glenview, the oldest building on site. As she approached the front entrance, she read the plaque proclaiming it to be "a haven for the distressed soul."

Trying the door, she opened it and entered. After approaching several people, she found the person who could grant her permission to visit Walter George. He handed her over to an energetic young man, apparently some kind of intern.

"I happen to be familiar with this case," he explained as she followed him back to The Meadows. "Part of my internship included his case study. Apparently he was not cut out to be a police officer because one particularly nasty crime scene pushed him over the edge. He exhibited the typical anxiety and dissociation evident in such cases, but intensive...ah...therapy," he stole a glance at her seeming to assess her understanding of his remark, "appeared to worsen his condition. Eventually, he became non-responsive and withdrew into silence. While patients often recover from nervous breakdowns, he did not, so the diagnosis stood. Ah, here we are." He fumbled with a large key ring until he found the correct key, inserted it and opened the door.

Jesse once again felt like Alice tumbling down the rabbit hole. While a window to her right admitted sunlight, a long dark corridor stretched in front of them with doors along either side. Voices called out from behind the doors, some audible, some animal-like sounds that wrenched her heart and turned her stomach.

"Help me, please, help me."

"Mama. Mama. Mama.

"Get me out OF HERE! GET ME OUT OF HERE!"

And then a shriek made her realize the truth of the term "blood-curdling" for she was sure her blood had done just that. Her knees went weak, and she doubted she could walk along the dim hallway.

"Our patients are particularly lively today," her escort beamed. "Perhaps they sense your presence."

She tried to still her trembling.

The young man passed through a door marked "Office" and beckoned her to follow. The normalcy of the room she entered sharpened the madness without, and she was astonished at the business-like atmosphere of the secretaries and staff. She shook her head as if to try to marry the two images within the same building. The young man pulled a file, had her sign a waiver indicating that she would not hold them liable for any injury inflicted during her visit, and grabbed a key ring from a hook behind the long main counter. The shaking that started in her knees was now a full-body tremor, and Jesse hoped she would not embarrass herself with an accident somewhere along the way.

They exited the office to the cacophony of weeping, swearing and moaning she had heard before. The intern straightened his shoulders and strode down the hall. She wondered who he was trying to convince. They climbed the stairs to the second floor and an identical hallway wrapped in gloom.

"It's not as bad as it sounds," he said over the noise. "If I were to open all of these doors, you would see most of them simply sitting on their beds staring into space. Many of the calls are residual actions from before their…uh, treatments."

Jesse's mind flashed to stories of electroshock therapy, frontal lobotomies and other secretive remedies. Her skin crawled as if the mournful cries were slithering beneath it, worming their way into her very being. She jumped at a shriek that erupted through the door they were passing.

"I think they know you're here," he sniggered.

She wondered at the sanity of the man she followed. *What if this is one of those situations where an inmate gets loose and poses as a doctor? What if he locks me in one of these rooms?* Gripped by fear, she could barely continue on. Certainly the staff would have recognized him as a patient while they were in the office—wouldn't they? Bile rose in her throat and the urge to run almost overtook her. *Stop it, Graham. Pull yourself together. You need to see Walter George and find out what he knows about that night.*

"I don't know what good it will do you to see Mr. George; he has been mute and withdrawn for a long time. In his file there are notes about communicative activity initially in his stay, but nothing for the last twenty-seven years. There was one nurse he offered up a few words for, though when she left, nothing. But you're welcome to try. Mostly he sits and stares at the window."

He stopped before a door and pulled out the key ring.

"You'll stay with me, won't you? You'll stay in the room, right?" she asked.

"Of course, Miss Graham. We never know what our patients might do, so we never leave visitors alone with them."

Jesse wasn't sure whether or not his statement was reassuring. What would this encounter be like with Walter George? Would he be like a vegetable now? Would he be violent? Would he even be able to communicate if he did know something?

The door swung open and the intern led her into an austere bedroom furnished with a metal bed, a wash basin, toilet, chair and table. Walter George sat on his bed staring out the window as her escort had predicted.

"Mr. George, you have a visitor," he boomed as if the man were deaf.

Walter George slowly turned his head in their direction. When he caught sight of her, his face contorted with fear and he screamed.

"No, no, no! I didn't do it! I swear I didn't do it! He made me. He forced me. Leave me alone! Stop coming to my dreams! Leave me alone!"

His voice was shrill, a cornered animal facing certain death. He scrambled up the bed to the corner farthest from where she stood, his legs and feet kicking at the bedclothes as if trying to back away farther, eyes wide with terror, mouth twisted with screams.

The intern was shocked by the man's reaction and for a moment stood agape. Regaining his senses, he pulled Jesse into the hall and locked the door behind them. Nearby residents who heard Walter's cries joined in shrieking, sobbing, and calling in a symphony of terror. Walter's screams continued, his voice rasping from strain. Jesse's escort looked at her with a mix of fear and confusion.

"That is quite remarkable. Nothing in all of his years of treatment has caused such a violent reaction in Mr. George."

She leaned against the opposite wall pressing her forehead into the dull green paint. Her breath came in short gasps as she fought down panic.

"Can we please leave here?" she whispered.

"Of course. Follow me, Miss Graham."

He grasped her elbow and steered her down the hallway. Walter George's voice trailed off behind them. Jesse's legs wobbled beneath her like a toddler's, and she was grateful for the intern's assistance. Walking down the stairs, she gripped the railing, steadied by the cold metal. By the time they reached the front door, she was composed enough to walk unassisted.

"Well, I'm sorry you didn't get to talk to Mr. George. I know you were hoping to discover some information of great significance to you. I'm sorry you were unable to learn anything."

"Thank you for your assistance," she said as she shook the young man's hand finding that it was sweaty and a bit unsteady as well.

"You are most welcome. Again, I am sorry you did not discover anything."

Jesse walked to her Beetle.

Oh, but you are mistaken. I learned something quite significant. In spite of her shaky legs and still-pounding heart, she smiled to herself.

-ELEVEN-

"What the hell were you thinking?" Maggie paced back and forth in the living room. "Jesse, are you crazy?"

"No, but if I were, I hope you wouldn't lock me up in that place." Jesse took a swig of beer. "Settle down, Maggie. I went there. I'm home. I'm fine."

"Oh good God in heaven, what will you do next?"

"Well, I promised I wouldn't confront Ben Wyndham, so we can check that off our list," she laughed.

"AHHHHH! Jesse be serious!" Maggie yelled.

"Look what I found out! Doesn't that count for something? Walter George was there with whoever murdered Helen. He said, 'He made me. He forced me.' Surely Ben Wyndham's money could bribe a young police officer. A rookie who doesn't make much money. Or maybe he intimidated Walter. Maybe Ben knew something about Walter that he wanted to keep hidden…"

"Oh, that wild imagination is going to get you into trouble. You have no proof of anything. You heard the ravings of a mad man. Come on, Jesse, get real! You have to let this go." Maggie stopped pacing and stood before her friend. "Please. Just let it all go."

"No, I won't. I can't! Why would Walter fly into a raging terror? Because I look just like Helen! Don't you see? He thought I was her ghost, which is ironic considering her ghost is around—,"

She was cut off by Maggie's loud sigh.

"Stop. Please stop trying to bring humor into this. There is nothing funny about it! I can't live in fear for your life if you are going to continue to take reckless chances like this. I'm sorry, Jesse, but I can't just sit by and watch you destroy yourself."

Maggie grabbed her purse and stomped out the front door slamming it behind her.

"Maggie?" Her voice was tiny. Her heartache was huge.

Jesse was creating a grammar lesson on comma usage figuring if the day was going to be so painful, why not go for broke. The doorbell brought her to her feet in an instant and she ran to it and flung it open.

"Maggie?"

Based on Joe's reaction, her disappointment must have been evident. He looked down at himself, arms fanned out, then looked at her apologetically.

"I don't have the right equipment, and I sure as hell am not holy enough. Sorry."

"No, that's okay. I mean, I just thought it might be Maggie."

"By the look of your swollen eyes and red nose, I'd say you two had a falling out."

She shrugged. Joe pulled her into his arms and held her.

"It's okay, Just Jesse, you can cry. You don't have to be a tough cookie all the time."

His tenderness was like a lever opening a dam, and she released the tears she'd been suppressing. Succumbing to his embrace, she sobbed against his tee shirt until dark spots of salty tears stained it. His chin rested on her head as she cried and somehow that comforted her as she yielded to vulnerability in a way she had never before allowed. Wrapping her arms around his waist, she tucked into him needing his warmth and his strength. Gradually, her need became more primal and she wanted to lie with him, to take him into herself completely. Need became desire and she slowly raised her face to his, looking into his eyes then dropping her gaze to his lips. She perceived a shift in him; he pressed his finger to her lips.

"Not now; not like this," he whispered. "I'll hold you for as long as you like, but when I make love to you for the first time it will be when you won't regret it later."

"Joe…" Her voice rasped with need.

He leaned his head in and brushed his lips against hers; she felt his desire and understood how strong he was being for her.

"It will be wonderful, Just Jesse, but it won't be now." He kissed her forehead and held her tighter. Burying her face in his chest once again, they stood together for several more minutes.

"I need a beer." Her voice was muffled against his shirt.

"What did you say? 'Joe, you're a dear'?" he teased.

Jesse pulled her head back looking up at him, loving the playful sparkle she saw in his eyes.

"Time for a Genny," she said.

Holding his hand, she led him to the kitchen where she popped the caps off two bottles. He sat at the kitchen table and studied her.

"Tell me what happened with Maggie."

"We had a fight. It would probably bore you; boys get bored with girl things."

"Nothing you do could ever bore me, Jess." His voice was soft.

She felt a stirring deep within that made her knees weak. She sat in the chair across from him and he took her hands.

"Tell me."

She related the argument she'd had with her best friend, trying to sound like the injured party, but even in the retelling she acknowledged that Maggie was right.

"I know I'm driven by this thing, Joe, but Helen needs to be avenged. It's important to her."

She stopped, realizing what she had said. He had listened quietly to her until this last sentence. She knew she had revealed too much.

"What do you mean?" His brows furrowed and he released her hands and sat back. He tilted his head as if listening more closely.

"I know you'll think I'm crazy, but I can sense Helen's emotions. At first I felt total love and warmth, then an urgency to discover the truth, and then, I don't know…trust. I think she trusts that I will find her killer and bring him to justice. I know it sounds crazy, but I feel all of this from her."

Joe stared at his empty beer bottle turning it around in his hands. He was silent for several minutes, and then he placed his bottle on the table and looked her squarely in the eyes.

"If you had said that to me a few weeks ago, I would have believed that you were certifiably nuts. But I saw Helen—I sensed something, too. When I first entered the room it was electric with…I guess anger. But when that left—I guess that was Eileen—there was such a peace, warmth. I get what you're saying. But I also understand where Maggie is coming from. I'm worried about you, too. I think you've taken some dangerous chances, but I can't tell you what to do. No one can. You have to follow your heart, Jesse. If it's saying find this bastard, then so be it. That doesn't mean we're not going to worry about you. But know this: I am here for you. Whatever you need."

She reached across and took his hands. "Thank you."

"Listen, one reason I came over was to take another look at that armoire. Something about it has been bugging me and I think I realized what it was. You said Helen doesn't come around during the day, right?"

She laughed. "I also said I don't know all of the ghost rules."

They climbed the stairs and entered the attic room. The late afternoon sun streamed in, casting two rectangular patterns from the front windows on the floor. The wide floorboards were gray with age, and Jesse thought how beautiful they would be if sanded and polished. She looked around the room as if for the first time realizing what a lovely study it would make.

Following Joe to the armoire, she watched him examine it again, running his hands along the sides and taking out a measuring tape to calculate its depth. He opened the doors and measured the interior depth and murmured.

"This is what had me puzzled. The interior depth is six inches less than the exterior. Why?" His hands explored the back panel and he rapped against the wood. Stooping to study the inside, he cocked his head away from the pole used to hang clothing. He slid his fingers along the seam where the shelf was tucked high in the back and stopped.

"There's a latch."

As he spoke, she heard a sound like a window sliding open.

"Look in here, Jesse." His voice caught with excitement. "There's a secret compartment."

She squeezed in next to him and he took her hand placing it in the opening.

"Helen had some secrets, it seems," he whispered against her ear. The sensation of his breath combined with his closeness threatened to put her over the edge. But her curiosity won out as she peered into the space that stretched from the floor of the armoire to the base of the shelf and across the width. Joe moved out so she could explore the hidden opening.

"There's something in here," she said, her voice muffled by the enclosed area. Her hands grasped a box and she pulled it out. Blowing dust off it, she saw the name of a hat company inscribed across the lid. Easing it off, she peeked inside fearful that something alive might jump out at her. "Ugh!" She brushed spider webs off her hands and tried again. Tissue paper crinkled and crumbled as she lifted it out revealing a cloche hat of soft, grey felt with a wide red arrow-shaped ribbon.

"Why would she hide this hat?" Jesse wondered aloud.

Digging through the tissue paper, she touched something hard. Riffling through the tissue, she pulled out a stack of letters tied with a red ribbon. Her heart skipped like a stone across a calm lake. She sat down on the floor in front of the armoire and stared at the letters.

"Oh, wow," Joe whispered.

"She hid these letters for a reason. Reading these might answer some of our questions." Her voice was soft with wonder. She felt immobile knowing that whatever the letters revealed would affect her life. Helen had been murdered, of that Jesse was sure. Whatever she read in these could name her killer. She shivered.

"Is there anything else in there?" he asked.

Jesse knelt and leaned into the armoire. At first she didn't find anything, but then she ran her hand along the back wall and fingered a piece of paper pinned or taped to it. Tugging, she released it and pulled out a large Victorian valentine. She crawled to the sunlit area by the windows where she was barely able make out the faded pink roses and yellow ribbons held by two cupids. The card opened like saloon doors, and inside a saccharine verse floated above a signature.

"Forever yours, B."

Jesse gasped. "Look, it's signed B—as in Ben! As in Ben Wyndham!"

Joe examined the card and handed it back to her.

"Could be, Jesse, but we don't know that for sure."

"I know, I KNOW, I KNOW! But everything points to him!"

"Circumstantial evidence."

She ran her fingers through her hair in frustration.

"How do I prove it? How can I find the truth?" she moaned.

"Maybe you could start with these letters." He ruffled the stack.

The age-yellowed letters sat in the middle of the kitchen table still tied with the faded red ribbon. The grain of the oak table ran in fingers along the wood, all pointing at this stack so heavy with consequence. Musty and brittle with age, the letters would require a delicate touch and Jesse knew she would have to handle them carefully. She filled the tea kettle with water, placed it on the burner and lit the stove. Stepping to the cupboard she fished out two mugs and deposited a teabag in each. She felt Joe's eyes on her as she moved and knew he wondered at her procrastination. How could she explain her reluctance, after all of her searching, to read these letters? Setting the mugs on the table, she fetched the sugar bowl and spoons knowing that neither she nor Joe needed them. She sat down and looked at him.

"I know I'm stalling, it's just that once I look at these…"

"Jess, it's okay. When you're ready, you'll read them. Tonight might not be the time."

She thought about this. Could she leave them undisturbed, unread through this night? No, she knew she couldn't. Whatever she discovered in these letters would answer many questions. Were they questions she wanted answered? She gazed out the window. The setting sun blazed red and orange on the horizon. Sunset came much earlier now, in mid-August, and the nights cooled down. The mutability of nature; nothing remained the same.

This summer had been dramatic for her with all of the changes—and danger—in her life. Somehow she had narrowed her focus to this one mission: to find Helen's killer. And Eileen's. Was it possible that in a few short months she had gone from living in the lap of luxury, to deception by Robert, to moving into the Cavanaugh House, to discovering her real mother—well, her ghost—to investigating a murder, to this moment where the answer could lie before her, written in the hand of a murderer? To Joe who sat across from her, patiently allowing her to work through this process in whatever way she needed?

Reaching out, she picked up the packet and drew one end of the ribbon. It started to untie, then broke off leaving her with a knot. She poked at it trying to untie it until Joe pulled out his jackknife and opened the blade. He did not cut the ribbon; he looked at her with his eyebrows raised. She nodded; he cut. The ribbon fell away.

The envelopes were not addressed and stamped to be delivered by mail; instead each had "Helen" written in neat script on the front. The envelopes had been opened with a letter opener and Jesse suspected it was the very one that sat in the roll top desk in the living room. The one with the pearl handle inlaid with lapis lazuli. The one Helen had used to open these letters. Jesse lightly blew into the first envelope bowing out the sides and creating a small plume of dust. She tapped out the letter and unfolded it gently. Written on one sheet of ivory stationery, it contained a brief note that she read aloud.

January 14, 1939

Helen,
How can I find words to speak what rests within my heart? When you are near, all darkness vanishes and hope wells up within me. From the first time we worked

together at the Charity Christmas Ball, I knew that my life would be bleak and meaningless if you were not in it. Yes, my love, there are complications that must be confronted and dealt with, but all of this is possible if the result is a life spent with you. We must meet for I cannot bear to be away from you for a day. Please find it in your heart to grant me but a few moments to bask in your beautiful smile and hear the angelic sound of your voice.

I await your answer, my heart torn between the anguish of "no" and the rapture of "yes" from you.

Always yours,
B

Silence filled the kitchen as the voice from long ago echoed through the years. Jesse released her breath slowly and placed the letter on the table.

"Helen's lover. It must be the first letter he sent to her," she said.

"Yes, and it sounds like there were barriers to their being together."

She replaced the letter in its envelope and reached for the next one.

"There is no postal stamp to indicate the date, but I assume these are in chronological order."

She lifted out the second letter whose message was similar with a declaration of love, a promise to overcome the obstacle to their happiness, and a request to meet. The next five were the same, and Jesse began to fear that all she would discover was the initial "B."

As she carefully opened the seventh letter, her heart began to pound.

November 26, 1939

Dearest Helen,

Can it be true that at this time of Thanksgiving we have so much to be thankful for? I ask your patience a little longer, for I am preparing to end the engagement, but my darling, I must not break it off during the holiday season. Had she not been so ill and then traveled to the Continent for the autumn season, I would have ended it immediately, but to do so now by letter would be cowardly.

Ah, do I hear you remarking that keeping you waiting this long is cowardly? So it is, and I regret my immersion in the traditions of my upbringing. I pray that you will forgive me and continue to be patient for soon we will be together forever. Especially, now my love with the wonderful news you bring to me. A child! Our child! Miracle of miracles my heart sings out in joy.

Let us meet in our usual place, my love. My heart swells with anticipation of holding you once more.
Your devoted love,
B

Tears ran down Jesse's cheeks.
"My God, this was written by my father."

Jesse stood before the armoire in the attic room assessing her outfit. It was fitting to view herself in this mirror while she tried on Helen's cowgirl jacket, now expertly restored by Erik. Her hands slid over the sleeves, caressing the supple smoothness of the leather. Erik was able to restore the natural ivory color and repair some of the faded and worn creases. Her green eyes danced with delight at the sight of herself in her mother's jacket. Since the afternoon was warm, she'd dressed in a long, flowing flowered skirt and a white peasant blouse. Not exactly a western look, but her boots gave a nod to the rodeo theme. She had braided her hair, pulling the plaits forward to rest against her collarbone. Laughter bubbled up as she twirled before the mirror. The day promised to be pleasant—late summer warmth with a cool evening, and time spent with Joe. She looked forward to seeing Al again, even though Joe didn't care for him, and she wondered about their history. She had enjoyed her dinner with Al, until the jazz trio brought back memories of Robert. But if Joe disliked him, there must be a reason.

Her thoughts drifted to Ben Wyndham, and her gaiety disappeared. She knew she would see him today, and she wondered how she would feel. Was he the "B" of Helen's letters? It made perfect sense since he referenced the "traditions of my upbringing." What else could that mean but that he had to follow the dictates of being the son of the owner of the richest estate in the Finger Lakes region? What had been the obstacle to their happiness? Engagement to another who was a fitting match? The fact that Helen was a middle-class, small-town girl unsuitable for life in the upper echelons of the social strata? Jesse filled with anger at the injustice. She didn't like Ben Wyndham, and if he was indeed her father—what? If that were true, her dislike didn't change a thing. She studied her face in the mirror. Auburn hair framed her oval face, green eyes staring back. Her skin was fair as porcelain. Did she inherit any of these traits from him? Based on people's reaction to her, not a one—she was all Helen. She smiled at that.

"We don't need anyone else, right?" she whispered to Helen. The image of Joe popped into her mind and she shrugged with resignation. "I am your daughter. Hopeless. What was it like for you to love this man and be forbidden to see him? How did you endure all the lonely nights? Not being able to tell even your best friend Susan about him?"

A breeze caressed her face though no window was open. Tears blurred her image in the mirror. She warmed as a soul-crushing rush of deep love ran through her heart.

"You loved him that much." Somehow Jesse understood.

Hearing the doorbell, she hurried downstairs and opened the door. Joe leaned on the doorjamb, arms crossed, cowboy hat pulled down, peering at her from beneath its brim. Wearing a checked shirt and blue jeans that hugged his hips and thighs just enough, he stood with one foot propped over the other balanced on the toe in brown leather cowboy boots polished to a russet sheen. Jesse caught her breath at the sight of cowboy perfection.

"Howdy, pardner," she drawled.

"Ma'am." He touched his finger to his hat.

Her heart fluttered. *No fluttering hearts, no fluttering hearts* she scolded silently.

"Let me get my purse and we can mosey on down the road," she laughed.

When she returned to the door, Joe offered his arm and escorted her to the car.

There was more than one kind of danger in her life right now.

Wyndham Estate had been transformed to the Old West with a façade of a street with a saloon, general store, barn and hotel. People in various attempts at western wear strolled the grounds, some in authentic livery, some in chaps, others in blue jeans, cotton shirts with embroidered yokes, bolo ties and bandanas around their necks. The air was festive with games—horseshoes, target practice, hoop rolling and horseback riding. Caught up in the excitement Jesse realized how much she needed this escape from the investigation of Helen and Eileen's murders and the frightening events surrounding them.

Spotting them, Al approached and greeted them.

"Jesse, Joe, I'm so glad you came today!" His smile was warm and he gave her a peck on the cheek. She sensed Joe stiffen a bit.

"Hello, Al. Wow! This is quite the extravaganza!" she said.

Al looked around at the grounds, a grin covering his face. "We love this event—and it's for such a worthy cause. The Equestrian Club is known throughout the Eastern Seaboard. That program is one of the reasons many of our students attend St. Bart's."

Jesse recalled her student teaching experience several years earlier in Rochester's inner city and the students there who couldn't afford warm coats. She shrugged the thought away and tried to regain the excitement of the day.

"That's wonderful. I'm looking forward to being on staff there."

"It's good to see you again, Jesse. I enjoyed our dinner and ice cream," Al said.

"Me, too," she said, wanting to kick herself. She'd never mentioned the date to Joe. Well, it wasn't actually a date…it was just sitting across the table from Al and eating. But she detected an increased tension in Joe who had been silent all this time, standing off to the side.

"So, Joe, how is business?" Al asked turning to include him in the conversation.

"Going well, thanks, Al."

There was an uncomfortable silence, and then Al took her arm to lead them toward the façade.

"Through that saloon door is the refreshments area. We have some sarsaparilla, beer, and, of course, wine."

"Of course," she laughed. Her laugh was cut off by the sight of Fred Morton. He was dressed in his usual dress shirt, tie and slacks. *No sense of fun in him. It's probably common among murderers.* Jesse turned back to Al who was opening the saloon doors for them. They passed through the façade to a bar fashioned like one found in a western saloon and stepped up to it.

"I'll have a sarsaparilla in a dirty glass, Black Bart," Al said as he tipped his cowboy hat back. Jesse laughed, but she saw Joe's blank expression. She ordered a Riesling and Joe ordered a beer.

"How about a go at horseshoes?" Al asked.

"You don't have to worry about us, Al, we can fend for ourselves," Joe said, his voice even.

She was startled by his demeanor. She had never seen him like this, bordering on rude.

"Joe, Al is just being a good host," she said.

Al drained his glass and set it on the bar.

"It's okay, Jesse. I should check on how the barbeque is coming along anyway." He nodded to her and looked at Joe as he passed him.

"What the hell was that all about?" she hissed.

Joe slid his eyes away from Al and stared ahead.

"Nothing." His voice was flat.

"Like hell, nothing."

"Just leave it."

She wanted to protest, but she saw the resolution in his eyes and knew he would reveal nothing about his animosity toward Al right then. Joe turned and leaned against the bar nursing his beer. Sipping her wine, Jesse looked around at the people enjoying the late summer day. She always felt nostalgic in August with all the indicators that summer was coming to a close: red and orange-tipped leaves, coolness in the breeze, earlier sunsets and cool nights. And the start of a new school year.

"Carpe diem," she whispered.

"What?" Joe asked looking at her. "Hey, I'm sorry. When the time is right, I'll tell you the whole sordid tale. But we're here to have fun and get those St. Bart's girls a good ride." He waggled his eyebrows and Jesse slapped his shoulder. "Let's go toss some horse shoes." Taking her hand, he led her back out the saloon doors.

As they walked toward the horse shoe pits, Jesse saw a lively game of baseball in the far field. She stopped and gawked. Playing outfield were the Sisters of St. Joseph, some of them dressed in their black and white habits. She watched a teenaged boy hit a pop fly and was astounded to see Sr. Alphonse in her full attire, cleanly catch the ball for the third out. A whoop went up from the nuns as they scurried off the field. Jesse laughed out loud.

"Now I've seen everything! Sr. Alphonse playing baseball?" Her laughter subsided as she spotted Maggie dressed in a yellow blouse, a mid-calf brown suede skirt, cowboy boots...and her veil. "Joe, I need to talk to Maggie."

He winked at her and they approached the bench where the nuns were taking their seats. Maggie looked up as they approached and put her mitt on the bench. She took a few steps toward them and waited.

"Hi Mags," Jesse said standing awkwardly in front of her best friend. This is where they would normally hug and she would make some snide remark about Maggie's fielding abilities. Instead silence hung between them They needed forgiveness and one willing to be the first to offer it. After a moment, both spoke at once.

"Mags, I'm sorry."

"Jesse, I was harsh..."

They laughed, then hugged, then cried.

"You were right, Mags. I was being reckless, and I didn't consider your concern for me. I'm just not that used to having people around me who truly care."

Maggie glanced at Joe who smiled.

"I shouldn't have been so insensitive, Jess. You have been dealing with more in two months than most people deal with in a lifetime. Forgive me?" Maggie said.

"Nothing to forgive." Jesse hugged her friend again. "Your fielding stinks, you know."

"I was born to pray not play," Maggie said striking a pose with hands folded and eyes toward the sky.

"Lord, help us," Jesse laughed.

"Hey, I'm up to bat, gotta go." Maggie grabbed a bat and hurried over to home plate. While her swings were sincere, she struck out in three pitches returning to the bench to the magnanimous cheers of her teammates.

"You're a better fielder than batter," Jesse called. Maggie resumed her angelic pose and they all laughed.

As the sun slipped into the far rim of Seneca Lake, old-fashioned lanterns strung about the property and stationed on tables winked on, illuminating the lawns of Wyndham Estate. Voices were muted by the dewy grass, but voices of the revelers by the shore echoed off the water. The evening air was cool and humid, so Joe retrieved Jesse's leather jacket from his truck.

"Now I'll look like a proper cowgirl," she laughed as she slipped it on.

A dance floor had been set up with lanterns strung around the perimeter and a band perched on varying levels of hay bales. Tuning his instrument, the fiddler leaned his ear near the strings as he plucked them, the guitarist laid out picks selecting one to strum with, and the drummer tested each drum and cymbal. Tables covered with blue and white checkered tablecloths and mason-jar candles had been scattered around the edge of the dance floor and were now crowded with people, their faces illuminated by soft lantern light.

Jesse looked around her table at the people, so recently placed in her life, who had become such dear friends. Joe sat beside her watching the musicians tuning up. Marty and Maggie were deep in discussion about the finer points of batting skills. Susan sat on the other side of her, and when Jesse looked, she knew the woman had been studying her.

"Quite some adventure you've been having, I hear," Susan said, her voice low.

"Has Joe been keeping you up to date?"

Susan nodded.

"Susan, you never knew who Helen was involved with at the end, did you?"

"No, as I told you, I was busy with juggling a new baby and my job, so we didn't see each other as often. I did suspect she was seeing someone—you know how people newly in love can't hide it." She glanced at Joe and hid a smile. "I knew there was someone in her life, but she wouldn't discuss it." Susan paused and tilted her head as if listening. "You know, I do remember her saying something about revealing something soon...something wonderful. I don't know if she meant her lover or her baby." Susan took Jesse's hand. "Maybe both." She smiled.

"Did she ever mention Ben Wyndham? Anything at all?"

Both women looked over to the family table near the dance floor. Jesse noticed Ben's arm resting across the back of Monica's chair; they looked like any happily married couple. They were engaged in conversation with another couple sitting across from them, all of them laughing, enjoying the night. Fred Morton sat at the table, too, his eyes scouring the crowd, a dour expression on his face. *Every party has a pooper; that's why we invited you...* When his eyes met hers he started and quickly looked away. Jesse shivered as goosebumps covered her arms.

"Who is that other couple with the Wyndhams?" she asked Susan.

"Oh, that's his brother, Bart...short for Bartholomew."

Jesse's mind raced. Another "B" name—maybe it wasn't Ben Wyndham who was involved with Helen, maybe it was his brother. She was aware that Susan had continued talking.

"There's always been a Bartholomew in the family, thus the name of the academy. It's a long tradition for the second oldest son to be named Bartholomew."

Jesse thought about this. Oldest. "Traditions of my upbringing." Had he been Helen's lover? And her father? As the eldest due to Albert's death, he would be the Wyndham heir—even more reason to adhere to the dictates of tradition.

"Why haven't I seen him before?" Jesse asked, her eyes never leaving the back of his head.

"He lives in New York City and leaves the actual running of the estate to Ben. He's always here for the Rodeo Round-Up since he is the 'patron saint' of St. Bart's. Finance is his forte, so he works with all of their investors, accountants and bankers on Wall Street."

Jesse remembered Al telling her that while he introduced her to his ancestors at the Founder's Day party. She also remembered Jim saying that Eileen had purchased tickets to New York City. Was she going there to meet with him? Did Eileen know that Bartholomew Wyndham was Jesse's father and so should have custody of her? She couldn't tear her eyes off him. As if feeling her stare, Bartholomew Wyndham shifted in his seat and turned in her direction. Studying him, she looked for any feature they might share, but he resembled Ben so strongly that she could easily confuse the two of them.

"He's the oldest?" Jesse asked.

"Albert was the oldest, but he died in a car accident..." Susan looked at Jesse as Joe swept her out of her seat for a dance.

"C'mon, Miss Kitty, it's time for the two-step," Joe laughed.

The music swirled around Jesse's thoughts as the dance floor crowded with people, among them Al and Barbara, gazing into each other's eyes. Jesse smiled to herself hopeful that her hint to him was the catalyst for this romance. Joe took her hand as he led her to the dance floor.

Jesse had never done the two-step so she had to concentrate on his instructions in order not to cause a dance floor collision. Once she got the hang of it, they glided around the circle with the others: *fast, fast, slow, slow.* She loved the freedom that dancing brought, the rhythm of the music seeping into her muscles, urging them to move with the beat. Joe was an excellent dance partner, leading her with firm, certain moves that eased her into each step. She laughed as he twirled her, the fringe from her jacket swirling around her as if caught up in her delight. They circled the dance floor, and as they passed the Wyndham table, Jesse saw three men looking up at her, mouths agape, eyes wide.

The music ended and Joe led her back to the table where it was all she could do not to look across at the Wyndhams. She had obviously made some kind of impression, but she didn't know whether that was a good thing or not. Out of breath they sat down with the others and each took a long sip of their beers.

"You two cut quite a mean figure out there," Marty laughed.

"She's light on her feet, that's for sure," Joe said as he squeezed her hand.

Jesse joined the lighthearted fun, but as she looked around the table at her friends, she was able to glance at the Wyndham table where the ladies were absent and the men sat with their heads together in deep discussion.

The evening continued with dancing and light conversation, and Jesse again was gratified at this circle of friends who truly cared for her. There was no pretense here, no posturing, just honest, down-to-earth people with

generous hearts. After consuming several beers, she rose
to visit the ladies room—a permanent structure near the
pool that for tonight sat behind a façade of outhouse
doors complete with crescent moons. She wove her way
through the tables into the darkness of the out-lawns,
aiming for the lanterns that glowed by the "outhouses." A
narrow path led through tall thickets as she approached,
and suddenly her arm was jerked as she was pulled aside
against a thick bush away from the light of the lanterns.

"What the hell do you think you're doing coming here
dressed in that jacket?" a voice hissed, spittle hitting her
ear. She opened her mouth, but he clapped his hand
across it, turning her cries into dull moans dampened by
the night. She tried to pull away, but his grip tightened.
"Are you trying to get yourself killed, too? You already
look just like her, now you're flaunting her clothes—
clothes that have meaning, you little fool."

Jesse's heart pounded and she squirmed trying to get
away. As she turned, she caught sight of Fred Morton's
face close to hers, his eyes stormy, his mouth twisted in
anger. She heard footsteps approaching and he released
her; she lunged back to the path into the arms of Sheriff
Donoghue.

"Whoa! What are you doing?" he gasped. "Oh, I see, a
little necking in the dark?" His eyes scanned the bushes,
but Fred Morton was gone.

"Oh, thank God," she said. "You came just in time."

He took her arm as if to lead her through the shrubs
back to the party, but nature was insistent at this point
and she turned toward the ladies room. Standing before
her was Joe.

"Everything okay, Jesse?" he asked.

She ran to him and his arms went around her.

"Yes, I'm fine. Thanks."

Sheriff Donoghue coughed and then chuckled. "Just as
I suspected—a little kissy-face in the dark. You two

behave yourselves, now. Hear?" Tipping his hat, he walked back toward the festivities.

"Jesse, what happened?"

"Oh my God, Joe! Fred Morton grabbed me. He threatened me and asked why I dressed in this jacket." She was shaking and leaned into him for support.

Joe looked back toward the party.

"We need to tell the Wyndhams. They need to know what kind of man works for them." His voice was terse.

"We can't. What if they are the ones who put him up to this? What if he's acting on their orders?"

Joe looked at her in the moonlight, his eyes full of concern. Brushing a strand of her hair back, he started to speak, stopped and nodded.

"What do you want to do, Jesse?"

"Right now?" she asked.

He nodded.

"Go to the ladies' room."

When Jesse and Joe returned to the table, the others were gathering their things to leave. The band had announced the last song for the evening, and couples were melting into each other, evidence of romantic connections made that night. Maggie and Marty avoided looking at each other, and Joe understood by Jesse's slight nod that she wished to forsake the tradition and leave.

Driving home, Joe again voiced his concerns about her remaining alone in the house.

"I'll be fine. I've got my six-shooter, remember? I'm all cowgirl tonight. Any varmints try to rustle me out of my house, I'll git 'em right between the eyes."

He looked at her out of the corner of his eye. "Maggie is right. You are very stubborn. I could stay again."

"I don't think that would be a good idea." She looked out the window.

He walked her to the door and as she opened it, he followed her in.

"We never got our last dance." His voice was low.

Jesse smiled. "One dance."

In the living room Joe thumbed through her record collection. Selecting one, he slid the vinyl disc out, turned on the record player and placed the record on the turntable. Jesse watched his movements, slow and deliberate, and knew he would be a good lover. He turned to her and opened his arms; she placed one hand on his shoulder and her other hand in his. "When a Man Loves a Woman" floated out from the speakers, and they began to sway together.

"You are a romantic, Mr. Riley," she whispered.

He held her closer and pressed his lips against her temple. They danced past the lamp she had lit upon entering, and Joe flicked it off. The glow from the front porch light was all that illuminated the room, and the darkness surrounded them in a solitary world of desire. He released her hand and slipped his arm around her waist; she slid her free hand up around his neck.

"It will be like this, Jess, our first time together. But there will be no fear for your life, no threat of danger. All we'll be concerned with is making love."

His words stirred passion deep within her, and she knew he could have her that night if he wished.

"Will that be the start of our garden?" she teased.

Joe leaned back and looked at her, his eyes smoldering with desire. He leaned toward her and his lips found hers. Soft at first, his kiss became more intense and their dancing halted as they pressed against each other. As his hands swept across her back, pulling her closer, she melted into him. He traced kisses down her throat; she moaned. Finally, he rested his forehead against hers, and tried to stem their passion.

"I think the garden is tilled and ready." He kissed her forehead and released her. "I'd better go now."

Holding his hand, she walked him to the front door.

"Seriously, Jesse, keep that six-shooter nearby. Your aim stinks, but you at least know which end not to point at yourself."

She laughed and cuffed his shoulder. "You said I was getting better."

"Better is a relative term. Good-night."

Joe kissed her lips again, and the fire within her rekindled.

"Good-night," she whispered.

It was the sighing that woke her. Jesse listened with her eyes closed trying to get her bearings. The sighing was different than it had been earlier, even before Eileen's death. There was an urgency to it, an intensity that she had never heard before. Listening for a while, she knew that Helen wanted to see her; she arose from the bed. The night had cooled the house, so she grabbed her robe off the hook on the door and slipped it on as she listened to Helen's sighs.

That's when she heard the other noise, the soft clicking of a lock being picked. Her skin prickled with fear as she cocked her head to listen. There was no mistaking the sound. She opened the drawer in her bedside table and lifted out the Colt. Slipping it into her robe's pocket, she tried to determine what to do. If she went to Helen, she would be trapped in the attic room...the room where Helen had been murdered. She had to get downstairs so she could escape out the back door.

Trembling, she opened her bedroom door and started for the stairs. Craning her neck, she looked at the front door, but didn't hear anything. Had she imagined it? She held the railing and hurried down the dark stairs keeping her steps light and avoiding the areas that squeaked. As she reached the third step from the bottom, she heard the noise at the lock right in front of her. Her heart jumped and she almost lost her footing. Whoever murdered Helen and Eileen was breaking into her house at this moment, intent on doing the same to her. Would he make it look like she hanged herself as he did with Helen? Wouldn't that make sense? Woman moves into haunted house and kills herself the same way? "Such stuff as *movies* are made on."

Jesse dashed down the last steps and along the hall. Reaching the kitchen, she pressed her back against the wall. Moonlight flooded in through the curtain on the kitchen door. She heard the rustle of the front door opening and held her breath. Surely he could hear her heart pounding in her chest. Hearing his footstep on the bottom step—the squeakiest of all—she was relieved at his soft curse. *Good, he still thinks I'm asleep upstairs.* She listened to the silence. Was he still on the stairs? Was he afraid to continue up the stairs for fear of waking her, so he would wait down here? Perhaps come into the kitchen?

She knew it was her chance to make her escape. Poised to run to the kitchen door and out into the yard, she halted at the sight of a shadow moving outside the kitchen door blocking her escape. Had two of them come to kill her? In a panic she took a deep breath to calm her nerves. Her hand clasped the gun in her pocket and she knew in the clarity of that moment that she couldn't kill someone. *Just wound him. Just wound him.*

The man on the stairs decided to give it another go, and she heard him test and then go up the next step. The figure at the back door tried the knob, finding it locked. His shadow hunched forward, and she heard jangling like a key ring. To her horror, she heard a key inserted into the lock. Trembling, she darted to the basement door, opened it and pulled it closed behind her just as the man entered the kitchen. She dared not turn on the basement light, so she flattened her back against the wall and inched her way down the stairs. *I hate basements.* A cobweb brushed against her face, and she fought the urge to scream. Wiping it away, she continued her descent. As her feet touched the cement floor, the door above her opened. Her heart stopped. Bathed in the moonlight streaming through the kitchen door, the figure stood at the top of the stairs. Running his hand along the wall, he found the light switch and flipped it on, flooding the cellar with fluorescent light and revealing her cowering at the bottom of the steps. She looked into the eyes of Fred Morton and then pulled out her gun.

Jesse started to speak, but the sound came out as a croak. Clearing her voice, she said, "Stand back or I'll shoot." She pointed the gun at him, both hands clutched around it, shaking.

Fred Morton's eyes never left her as he descended the stairs, his hands also holding a gun.

"You have really done it, Miss Graham. It's bad enough that you move here looking just like your mother, but then you stick your nose where it doesn't belong. Do you know how many cages you've rattled? You have no idea. The minute you moved here you were marked for murder. I can't believe you've lasted this long."

Jesse realized that there was something about facing certain death that makes a person braver in the last minutes, something that begs for clarity of mind. Maybe Fred Morton was going to kill her, but she wanted some answers first.

"So which of the Wyndham brothers is my father? Which one did Helen love?"

Fred Morton raised his eyebrows. "Well, you are a good little detective, aren't you?"

"How could he kill my mother if he loved her? The letters he wrote spoke so sincerely of his love for her. Was it all a lie?" Her mind flashed with a picture of Robert. So beautiful, so wealthy, so deceitful. Why wouldn't the Wyndham brothers be just like that?

"She kept the letters?" Fred Morton asked. "Of course. She would." He thought about that then focused on Jesse again. "What do you mean which one killed her? They didn't kill her."

"Oh, so it was you, then," She raised the gun to his chest level as he descended to the floor. She backed up out of his reach.

"So you have the mystery all figured out, do you, Miss Graham? The big, bad rich boys killed your mother? Tell me why."

She held the gun steady. "He was engaged. Helen was pregnant with me which would spoil all of his 'heir to the estate' plans. She was a middle-class nobody who wouldn't fit in with his 'king of the hill' lifestyle."

Fred Morton stepped closer to her, and Jesse wavered, the gun almost slipping out of her hands. He waved his gun at her, clearly in control. "Put that thing away before you hurt somebody with it." He motioned with his gun at her. His voice got louder, "Put it away."

She jumped, but did as he said tucking the gun back into the pocket of her robe.

"Now we're going to get out of here," he said.

"I don't think so, Morton. Drop your gun; put your hands in the air," said a voice at the top of the stairs. Startled, Fred Morton swore and dropped his weapon. Looking up, Jesse saw black shoes and blue uniform pants coming down the stairs.

"Sheriff Donoghue, thank God!" she breathed. The police officer descended the stairs, never taking his eyes off of the other man.

"Donoghue, you don't want to do this," Fred Morton said.

Jesse's mind raced to one of her hypotheses, that the Wyndhams had either bribed or threatened Sheriff Donoghue to be silent about Helen's death. Would he cave again, giving into their wishes and allowing her to be killed? Could he have gained enough courage over the years to stand up to them? She breathed a sigh of relief when he came and stood beside her, pointing his gun at the other man.

"Thank God you're here," she repeated. "Sheriff you need to arrest this man for killing my mother, Helen Cavanaugh. I think Ben Wyndham is involved, too, or maybe his brother." Her words tumbled out faster than she could think. She stopped. Gaping at him, she realized that Sheriff Donoghue must have been the man breaking in her front door; the thought struck her like a blow to the gut. He had been involved in this all along. With despair, she turned to look at him, his face a garish mask in the unforgiving fluorescent light. He was staring at her.

"You look just like her, you know. She was so beautiful. When I first saw you, I thought she had come back to me, had finally realized that it was my love she wanted, not his." Still looking at her, his eyes took on a faraway look. "I loved you so much, Helen. Why wasn't that enough?" Softening, his eyes travelled over her hair, down her neck and along her body; she shivered with revulsion. Seeing her reaction, his mood darkened. "So, you still despise me, do you? You'll pay for this rejection. If I can't have you, no one else ever will!"

Slamming his gun back in its holster, he sprang at her and gripped her throat. He turned blocking her from Fred Morton's view. She pulled at his hands trying to wrest them away but to no avail. She heard Morton shout, "Stop!" but Donoghue's grip tightened, and Jesse saw stars swimming before her eyes. Blackness started to overtake her, and she heard Fred Morton yell again. Releasing her, Sheriff Donoghue grabbed his gun, spun around and fired at him. She heard Morton cry out as blood spurted across the wall beside him. The sheriff turned back to her and grabbed her throat. Instead of trying to break his grip, Jesse put her hand in her robe pocket and pulled the trigger.

The gunshot blasted in her ears and hurt her hand as the gun recoiled. Sheriff Donoghue's eyes bulged in surprise as he looked at her in wonderment before he slid to the floor, doubled over in pain, and passed out. In shock, Jesse stood gaping at the two men, but common sense took over and she kicked the sheriff's gun out of his reach. Hearing footsteps on the stairs, she looked up to see Joe and Marty staring at her.

-TWELVE-

Flashing red lights reflected off the living room walls and the static of police radios crackled in the night. Jesse sat covered in a blanket on the sofa beside Joe who wrapped his arm around her. Her trembling had subsided, but every once in a while it began to overtake her again. Images from the evening ran through her mind: the lively dance floor, Fred Morton grabbing her on the path, the romantic dance with Joe, awakening to Helen's sighs—a warning that someone intended to do her harm. Helen. She had never made it to the attic to see her. Instead she ended up in the basement, almost ended up dead.

Two ambulances had just arrived to transport Sheriff Donoghue and Fred Morton to the hospital in Geneva. The medics brought in the gurneys and headed to the basement. Fred Morton had suffered a gunshot wound just below his collarbone which missed his heart and passed through cleanly, so he would be treated and released in a few days. Sheriff Donoghue's wound was more serious as he had been shot in the torso; they were waiting to hear if any vital organs had been damaged.

The first gurney came through bearing the unconscious sheriff, his face as pale as the sheet he lay on. Jesse's stomach flipped at the thought that she had injured someone so severely. She looked away unable to watch as the gurney rolled by, afraid she might vomit, but forcing it down. The next gurney came up carrying Fred

Morton; he looked equally pale, but was conscious and talking. He had them stop in the living room, and he looked at her.

"You saved my life, Miss Graham. Thank you." He dipped his head as they rolled him out to the ambulance.

Jesse nodded silently realizing she owed him the same thanks. Her brain still could not comprehend that it was Sheriff Donoghue who had killed Helen and Eileen. So many questions floated around in her mind.

Joe patted her shoulder. "How about a beer?"

"I think I need a cup of tea," she answered surprising even herself.

"Just what the doctor ordered," Susan said carrying in a tea pot and cups on a tray. She set the items down on the coffee table and poured tea into the cups passing one to each of them. "How are you doing, Jesse?"

"I'm not quite sure yet." She sipped her tea. "I'm trying to sort all of this in my mind. Susan, did you know how Sheriff Donoghue felt about Helen?"

Susan thought for a moment. "I do remember that they dated for a while, but Helen was very popular. She dated quite a few men, none of them seriously, though. I mean, she didn't talk about Bill Donoghue any more than the others." She pursed her lips. "Hmmm. I do remember that she broke it off, though. She said he made her uneasy."

Jesse shivered remembering her fear in his presence earlier.

"He must have pursued her quite zealously from what he said to me. No wonder her affair with...whomever...drove him over the edge. But I still have so many questions left unanswered. Who was Helen in love with? How is Fred Morton involved—it must be through the Wyndhams, but which one? Which begs the question, who is my father?"

Joe squeezed her shoulder. "Those questions will keep. You need some rest."

"I doubt I can sleep tonight," she said, still dazed.

Marty came in from the front yard as the last police car pulled out of the driveway.

"Sheriff Donoghue's wound is serious, but Fred Morton's wound should heal just fine."

"Marty, if Sheriff Donoghue...if he doesn't make it, will I be arrested for murder?" Jesse couldn't believe the specter of a woman's prison was rearing its ugly head again. Trembling, she nestled closer to Joe who held her tighter.

"Relax, Jesse. This was unmistakably a case of self-defense. Fred Morton is a witness, and so are the bruises on your neck."

"Just like Helen's and Eileen's," she murmured.

Marty nodded.

Susan collected the cups and put them on the tray. Carrying it to the kitchen, she called over her shoulder, "You could stay at our place tonight, Jesse."

Joe tipped her face toward him. "But you're not going to, are you, Just Jesse?"

She smiled at him. "No, I'm not."

He kissed the top of her head. "Stubborn" he breathed into her hair.

"The danger is over now, Joe. The bad guys are locked up tight." She smiled up at him.

"Bad guy. Sheriff Donoghue was in on this alone," Marty said.

"No, Marty. He had assistance from Walter George, whose guilt drove him insane."

"You're right. If Donoghue strangled Helen, as he did Eileen and tried to do to you, he would have needed help to hang Helen's body from the beam in the attic. He must have coerced Walter George to hold her body while he threw the rope over the rafter and then suspended her there."

Jesse felt sick at the image.

"Sorry. Maybe we can discuss this more tomorrow," Marty apologized.

"Good idea," Joe agreed.

Jesse yawned and pulled the blanket tighter. Laying her head on Joe's shoulder, she mumbled an "Uh-huh," and yawned again.

Susan returned from the kitchen and picked up her purse, and looked at her. "You look pretty settled in there. Does that mean you're not coming with us?"

"With you, Mom. I'm staying here tonight," Joe said.

"Mmmmhmmm." She pursed her lips. "I suppose that's better than Jesse staying here alone tonight."

"Mom, it's fine. I'll sleep on the couch...or something," he said flashing his mother a smile.

"I think it's a good plan. I'll be over in the morning," Marty said.

"I'll bring breakfast around nine," Susan added planting a kiss on Jesse's cheek. "Try to sleep, honey." She brushed a wisp of hair from her face.

Jesse's heart fluttered at the tender gesture. *So this is how a mother acts.*

"Thanks, Susan," she said over the lump in her throat. Though Jesse heard it, no one else seemed to hear the sigh emanating from the attic room.

The house was quiet at last as Joe and Jesse climbed the stairs. The stillness wrapped around the two as they entered her bedroom. Turning toward him, she melted into Joe's embrace surrendering to his tenderness. His hands rubbed her back and kneaded her shoulders and neck. She relaxed into his ministrations until he wrapped her in his arms again and she nestled into his chest. Exhaustion could not temper her desire for him, and she raised her head and looked into his eyes. Slowly their lips met and heat spread through Jesse as their kiss deepened, but her arms slid down to her side as fatigue engulfed her. He eased her onto the bed chuckling.

"Time for your pj's. Where are they?" he asked.

"Really? My pj's? How could I not be ready for this moment?" she said through a yawn. "Where's that order from Frederick's of Hollywood?"

"Don't tease me like that, Miss Graham," he scolded. "Now, where are they?"

Jesse looked down at what she was wearing: an oversized Buffalo Bills jersey and athletic shorts. "I am wearing them."

He laughed. "Your attempt to seduce me is thinly veiled, Miss Graham."

"I should have sent that order in weeks ago." She yawned again.

Joe turned down the bed and she crawled in. He covered her up and sat in the rocking chair. Jesse looked at him through sleepy eyes.

"No, Joe. Come over here." She held out her arms.

Hesitating at first, he finally rose and stood by the bed. She smiled up at him, took his hand and pulled him down beside her. He lay down and she curled up against him immediately falling asleep.

Jesse heard it first. The soft sighing caressed her like gentle waves on a beach. Joe's arm was still around her, and she lightly moved it so she could slip out of bed. Her movement woke him, and his eyes widened when he heard the sound. She started to rise, but he pulled her back down.

"You don't have to go in there, you know," his voice was soft and insistent.

She laughed and tousled his hair. "It's okay, Joe. It's just Helen now. You stay here if you like."

Climbing out of bed, she found her slippers and robe and opened the bedroom door. She saw the soft glow beneath the attic room door, and pushed it in. Entering the room, she was wrapped in a peaceful warmth; a rosy glow shimmered near the armoire. She watched as the glow took on the ethereal form of a woman. Jesse could just make out her long, curly hair and a sweet smile playing at her lips. She understood at last why people had reacted to her as they had—she felt she was looking in a mirror.

"Mother," she whispered.

Helen's smile widened as she raised one arm as if to wave. Her essence flickered, the rosy hue vanishing. Jesse caught her breath and stumbled as if something supporting her had been removed. She stepped toward the armoire, but all was dark. The serenity still possessed her, but she knew that Helen was gone; at last, she was at peace. Though Jesse was happy that she had brought Helen peace by finding her murderer and bringing him to justice, she was saddened to know that Helen would no longer visit her in the stillness of night. She reached out to the spot where Helen had appeared and a misty coolness evaporated at her touch.

"Rest in peace, Mother," she said as tears ran down her cheeks.

The aroma of freshly brewed coffee and smoky bacon woke Jesse from a deep slumber. Leaden and sand-filled, her eyes resisted opening, so she lay with them closed enjoying the enticing aromas. She heard muted voices floating up from the kitchen and knew that Susan had arrived with breakfast. Lingering another minute she savored the knowledge that people who cared for her were gathered in her kitchen, and that she was safe. She stretched and opened her eyes, looking around her bedroom as if for the first time. This had been Helen's room, and she herself had been here as an infant. Her tiny eyes had scanned these walls then just as she was doing now. Life was very strange—she heard Joe's laugh—and wonderful.

Climbing out of bed, she put on her robe against the cool morning and headed downstairs. Joe was at the stove poking at the sizzling bacon with a fork while Susan cut up melon. Neither was aware she had entered, so she stood for a moment watching mother and son joke and tease as they worked side by side. Her heart swelled with an unknown joy. *I get it. This is how it's supposed to be.*

"Good morning," she said feeling just a little out of place in her own kitchen.

They both turned and smiled, Joe looking so much like his mother.

"Good morning, sleepy-head," he said, greeting her with a quick kiss.

"How did you sleep, Jesse?" Susan asked as she placed the bowl of fruit on the table.

"I slept very well, thank you," she said accepting a mug of steaming coffee from Joe.

"After her visit with Helen," he added.

Jesse stole a quick glance at Susan.

"Yes, Joe told me about Helen's ghost. I wasn't surprised; rumors of this house being haunted are legend around here. It's just hard for me to imagine her..." Susan's voice trailed off.

"I know. It's hard to believe she stayed here all of these years, but she was waiting for someone to bring justice for her murder," Jesse said. As she watched Susan wipe her eyes, she wondered how she would feel if it had been Maggie who had died so young. She embraced Susan, the two women crying together. "I am sure of one thing—Helen is at peace now."

Susan smiled through her tears. "Thanks. I needed to know that."

Releasing her, Jesse picked up her cup of coffee, inhaled the comforting aroma, and took her seat at the table. She rested her face in her hands letting the steam from the coffee infuse her senses. Eyes closed, she listened to the reassuring sounds of Susan and Joe finishing breakfast preparations. How her life had turned around. She realized how perfunctory her relationships had been up to now, even her relationship with Robert. She would never have allowed herself to be as vulnerable with him as she had been with Joe. Most of her friendships had orbited around Robert and his world. Maggie had been the only constant, the only deep and abiding relationship in her life…until now. She raised her head and looked at Joe. Was she ready to commit to him yet? She needed time to figure that out. Routine life with daily stresses that normal people deal with—not ghosts and murderers. She understood that the urgency and danger she had been living in could create a false sense of being in love, and she needed time to discover what being with him was like when she had papers to grade and students to manage. But as she watched him work beside his mother, she knew it would be hard to back off now. As if sensing her eyes on him, he turned and winked at her. Yes, she would tumble into bed with him that minute if she could. She sighed. A hopeless romantic, just like her mother. Her *real* mother, Helen.

Marty arrived in time to finish off the last two pieces of bacon and a slice of toast with Susan's homemade strawberry jam.

"Sheriff Donoghue had surgery last night; they had to remove his spleen. They removed the bullet, and he's expected to make a full recovery," Marty said, licking the jam off his fingers.

Jesse released a deep sigh as though she had been holding her breath all night in anticipation of the news of his condition. "So I won't be sent to a women's prison?"

He laughed. "No, you won't."

Relief surged through her. "Thanks, Marty."

He patted her shoulder and smiled at her. "I should be thanking you, Nancy Drew. You're the one who figured all of this out, solved the case. You are one determined woman; I never want to get on your bad side."

They all laughed and Joe nodded vehemently. "You are so right."

Marty continued. "Anyway, Sheriff Donoghue will be questioned when the drugs from the surgery wear off. You'll need to come to the station to make a statement, and Detective Holden from Rochester will need to interview you, too. Are you up for all of that today, Jesse?"

She nodded. "Yes, I want to get this over with as soon as possible."

"Well, there will be a trial. You will be called to testify, but that's months down the road," he explained.

"How is Fred Morton?" she asked.

"He had surgery to repair the injured muscles from the bullet wound. The doctors want to keep him a day or two to treat him with IV antibiotics to guard against infection. He'll recover completely barring any complications from the wound," he said.

"I'd like to visit him. I need to thank him for trying to save my life, but I also have a boatload of questions for him."

"That can be arranged, no problem," Marty said.

"Has Sheriff Donoghue said anything?" Jesse asked.

"No, he was unconscious before surgery, and he hasn't come out of the effects of the anesthetic yet. He'll be questioned later today, but it might be a longer process than just one interview."

"Marty, thanks for all you've done to help me with this. I know I pushed you a little ways past legal…," she said.

He raised his eyebrows in mock disbelief. "A little? If Donoghue had caught me with the key to the Archive Room, my ass would have been grass, *amica mia!*" Then he laughed. "Actually, that was pretty fun, sneaking around with my Kel-Lite in the dark."

"We had a couple of tense moments there, didn't we?" Her face was serious as she recalled her fear that night.

Marty sobered. "Who knew we were dealing with murder?"

"Helen did," she answered.

Jesse disliked the smell of hospitals as much as the smell of funeral homes. The sharp scent of disinfectant and rubbing alcohol mixed with the earthy human aromas from the unfortunate patients who were ill or injured permeated the air, and she wondered if she could filch a doctor's mask to block some of the odors. She and Joe walked along the hallway following the "blue line" on the floor which led to the post-surgical ward. They passed rooms with patients lying in various states of distress and recovery. She heard someone moaning and shivered as she recalled her visit to the Grayson State Hospital. At least no one here was crying to be released. But then lunch hadn't been served yet.

They found Fred Morton's room and knocked. A nurse opened the door and stood aside so they could enter. She followed behind them and continued checking the IV line and recording numbers on a chart. After fluffing his pillow and straightening his sheets, she left, leaving the room filled with their presence and the quiet that precedes unanswered questions.

Fred Morton peered at them through drowsy eyes. Jesse was surprised at his pallor; obviously his wound was more than superficial. His face was slack in drug-induced relaxation, but she could see his eyes trying to focus and stay alert. Questions burned within her, but it was obvious that he would not be able to answer them today. Walking to his bedside, she leaned in so she could keep her voice low. His eyes followed her as best they could.

"Thank you for saving my life," she said, her voice soft.

A small smile played at the corner of his lips. He nodded slightly, closing his eyes in answer. Fighting to reopen them, he tried to speak.

"Shhh, just rest," she said. "I'll come back tomorrow."

His eyelids drooped, fluttered, then closed as his breathing deepened.

Jesse slumped with disappointment as they left the room. She had hoped to find answers today, and Fred Morton held many of those answers. As they walked back down the hall, she spotted a police officer standing guard outside a room, and she guessed it was Sheriff Donoghue's. She needed to see him. Whether to assure herself that she hadn't killed him or to face her worst nightmare in the light of day with no threat, she didn't know. She just knew that she felt compelled to see him with her own eyes and know that she was safe now.

She walked up to the officer who blocked her entrance.

"I need to see Sheriff Donoghue," she said.

"Sorry, ma'am, he is not allowed visitors."

"You don't understand, I need to see him," Jesse's voice wavered as she feared yet another disappointment.

"Sorry, ma'am, not even family members are allowed to see the sheriff today."

"I'm not family, for God's sake!" She pulled the collar of her blouse back to reveal the bruises where Sheriff Donoghue's fingers had clutched her neck.

Shocked, the officer took a step back, but then resumed his stance in front of the door. "I'm sorry, ma'am…"

"I'll escort Miss Graham into the room, officer," came a deep voice from behind her, and the image of an interrogation room leapt to Jesse's mind. Turning, she looked into the shrewd eyes of Detective Holden who held out his badge to the officer. The young man stepped aside and they entered the room.

"I'm here to follow up on your mother's murder in Rochester," Detective Holden said. "Your friend Officer D'Amato thought it might be connected."

Jesse nodded.

The blinds were drawn so that shafts of sunlight edged between the slats, providing muted illumination punctured by the green lights from the machines clustered at the head of the bed. A rhythmic beep from the heart monitor harmonized with a soft snore from the patient who lay propped on pillows against the raised hospital bed. His arms lay atop the blanket that covered him, one handcuffed to the metal side bar. Jesse couldn't help but stare at the meaty hands that had tried to strangle her the night before. She shuddered at the memory, and Joe put an arm around her waist. Looking at the sheriff's face, she saw the same pallor that had been evident on Fred Morton's face, but the sheriff's held a grayish tinge around the edges. Breathing deeply, he was sleeping, his face the antithesis of the angry, twisted mask it had been the night before. The darkness of the room and the alien atmosphere of the hospital created an eerie aura. Jesse wondered if she were dreaming and none of this had happened. Then she touched the tender spots on her neck where the bruises showed, turning black and blue today, and reality flooded her. Looking at Sheriff Donoghue resting peacefully brought relief; somehow she had needed to see for herself that he had not died.

"Well, Miss Graham, you certainly were persistent in discovering the truth of Helen Cavanaugh's death," Detective Holden said, his voice cutting into the quiet of the room.

Sheriff Donoghue roused at the sound of his voice and slowly opened his eyes. Jesse's stomach clenched. His eyes drifted over to her, and widened.

"Helen? Helen? Have you come to me at last? I loved you..." his voice drifted off as he succumbed to the medication.

She began to tremble, and Joe wrapped his arm around her shoulder.

"Are you ready to leave, Jess?" His voice was soft, soothing her mind. She nodded and he led her out of the room. Detective Holden followed.

"Are you all right, Miss Graham?" His deep voice was touched with compassion.

"Yes, thank you."

"If you are up to it, I would like you to come to the police station this afternoon so I can get your account of what happened last night. I may have some questions from your Rochester visit, too. Are you up to that today? It would save you a trip up to Rochester later."

"Yes, that would be fine. I'll get to the station around two o'clock if that's convenient."

"That would be great," he replied.

Jesse's eyes traveled from the door to Detective Holden's. "I didn't kill him," she whispered. "I didn't kill anyone."

"I know." His smile was kind.

"I haven't gotten my answers yet, but I know I will soon," she said, her voice sounding far away.

"I have no doubt. See you later, Miss Graham." Detective Holden walked away from them toward the elevator.

She collapsed against Joe, and he led her to a bench where they sat down. The noises of the hospital swirled around them: doctors being paged, nurses pushing wheelchairs, interns wheeling gurneys, elevators arriving with a ding of a bell, someone weeping.

Jesse was not weeping. She leaned her head against Joe's shoulder and smiled.

They picked up a pizza and brought it back to the Cavanaugh House for lunch. Joe opened a couple of sodas and they sat in the back yard enjoying the late August day. Hearing a car arrive, Jesse circled the side of the house to see who had stopped by, expecting Marty, Maggie or Susan. To her delight, Jim Graham got out of his Chevy and walked toward her.

"I heard the news this morning, so I thought I would come and check on you. How are you doing, Jesse?"

She neared him as he spoke, uncertain how to greet him—a hug, a handshake, a simple hello. But he solved her dilemma when he embraced her with a quick hug and then stepped back.

"I was extremely worried about you, you know. I finally found you after all of these years; I sure didn't want to lose you again."

She noticed that his eyes glistened and he was checking the emotion in his voice. She hugged him back.

"You can't get rid of me that easily," she laughed. "Come and have some pizza with us."

Leading him to the back yard, she wondered just how she would introduce him to Joe.

Again, Jim solved the problem by extending his hand to Joe as he said, "Hi, Joe, I'm Jim. Jesse's long-lost-sort-of-father."

Joe smiled and pumped Jim's hand. "She has told me all about you, sir. It's a pleasure to meet you."

"Please, no 'sirs.' Just call me Jim," he laughed.

Joe pulled up another chair and opened the pizza box. Jim claimed a piece and took a hearty bite. "Mmmmm. I timed this visit just right," he mumbled around his mouthful.

Jesse brought a soda for him from the kitchen and returned to her seat.

"So fill me in on the details. What happened last night?" As he looked at her, he noticed the bruises, now dark black and blue, on her throat. "Holy shit, Jesse, he tried to kill you."

Her hands instinctively reached for her neck touching the tender tissue. "It was pretty scary, Jim. All that time I thought it was Ben Wyndham, or Fred Morton working on his behalf, and it was Sheriff Donoghue. Did you know that he was in love with Helen?"

"I've been racking my brain all morning trying to make sense of this since I heard it on the news. As you have surmised, Eileen and Helen were not close, so we didn't socialize much even though we just lived in Geneva. If Helen confided in Eileen, I was never privy to their conversations. I do know that Helen was a beauty, and very popular. I suspect many men were attracted to her."

"That's what I keep hearing, but not even her best friend Susan knew all of her secrets."

"Do I hear my name being taken in vain?" Susan's voice floated ahead of her out the kitchen door. Stepping out onto the back porch, she carried a dish of brownies. Jim rose as she approached the table and pulled another chair out for her. "I brought stuff for sandwiches, but I see you've eaten. I put it all in the refrigerator." Sitting down, she looked at Jim and her eyes grew wide. "Jim Graham, is that you?"

Jim nodded and smiled at her. "Hello, Susan."

"Why I haven't seen you since the night..." Susan broke off looking at Jesse.

"It's okay, Susan. I'm fine with it," she said.

"How are you? I mean how have you been?" Jesse had never seen Susan flustered before, but she noticed the color rise to the woman's cheeks.

Jim grinned as he leaned toward Susan. "I was going to ask you the same thing. I saw you at Eileen's funeral, but we didn't have a chance to speak. Are you still working as a nurse?"

"Part-time now. I've been getting Mike's pension since he died, so I was able to cut back to part-time."

"I'm sorry to hear about your husband's death," Jim said, his voice soft.

"Yes, he died four years ago. It was cancer; I couldn't get him to quit smoking," she shrugged her shoulders still carrying the weight of sorrow. She pulled herself up straighter, and looked at Jesse. "How did it go at the hospital?"

Jesse caught her up on the events as they polished off the pizza and soda.

"I want to go back and see Fred Morton as soon as possible. I think he will be able to answer all of my questions. You know, last night when Sheriff Donoghue was breaking into the front door, I was hiding in the kitchen. Fred Morton opened the back door with a key. How did he get a key to the Cavanaugh House?" She stopped for a moment. "And why was he there?"

Jesse couldn't help but sweat as she sat in the Seneca Corners police station. Memories of her night in the Brighton station came flooding back and with it her fear of imprisonment. Detective Holden sat across from her taking notes on a pad in a pool of light from the gooseneck lamp. The click-clack of typewriters and ringing phones surrounded them, but that pool of light pulled them together into a private world of their own. Joe sat beside her, his arm resting on the back of her chair. He had been with her through all of this; even when she had rebuffed him, she suspected that he kept an eye out for her. But that could not be the basis of a relationship. She had to see how they maneuvered together in the rhythmic grind of a daily routine. She did not want to be in an unbalanced relationship ever again— but right now she needed Joe, she knew that. However, her fragility and his protection did not a lasting relationship make. How would they be on a day when she had her period and things didn't go well for him at work? That was what made for lifelong loving—the gritty, no make-up, unwashed, underbelly of everyday life.

Detective Holden was finishing up with his questions. He scribbled Jesse's last response and then looked at her squarely in the eye.

"Is there anything else you can tell us about the day you found your mother's—that is Eileen Graham's body? Anything you might have noticed but didn't think was important?" His eyes bored into hers.

She shifted in her chair remembering the slip of paper in Eileen's hand. She raised her eyebrows innocently. "No, I don't think so."

"When we interrogated you that afternoon, you said in your statement that Eileen wanted to give you something. That was the reason for making the trip to Rochester. Is that so, Miss Graham?"

"Yes."

"You had no other reason for traveling up to Rochester that day?"

"I had to pick up some personal items. I have a Volkswagen Beetle, so transporting my belongings from Rochester to my house in Seneca Corners has taken several trips." Her palms were sweating and she rubbed them on her jean shorts.

"So you were picking up personal items like clothing, small appliances. Maybe photos?"

Her armpits were starting to sweat. "Yes, things like that."

Detective Holden looked at her.

"It's interesting to me that you found your father right after Eileen's death. How did you get so lucky, Miss Graham?"

Jesse took a deep breath. "Okay. I found a slip of paper with an address on it. I suspected it was what Mother—I mean Eileen—wanted to give me since it was right…um…near her. So I took it." She raised her chin slightly. "She meant for me to have it. If she hadn't been killed…" Her voice caught, and she was surprised at her grief for Eileen.

"So the slip of paper was near her? You didn't have to disturb the scene to retrieve it, right?"

"Right. I did not have to disturb the scene," She couldn't believe she could lie so blatantly. She didn't dare look at Joe because for all of her mental posturing about assuring a healthy relationship, she would be devastated if he thought ill of her. If he knew she was a liar, could he ever trust her?

"Miss Graham, I believe you might have, shall we say, taken some liberties in your investigation of this crime. But you solved it, and I have to say, you've got pluck. But you're going to put away your Sherlock Holmes cap and go back to being an ordinary citizen, right?"

"Right," she answered with gusto. This time she was not lying. She never intended to get caught up in an investigation like this again.

Detective Holden stood and stretched out his hand to her. "It was a pleasure meeting you, Miss Graham. May you and Mr. Riley here have a very happy and boring life together," he said as he shook first her hand and then Joe's.

Jesse's face reddened as the blush crept up from her neck. "Oh we're not…that is, we aren't…"

Detective Holden looked from her to Joe. "Too bad. Life is short; *carpe diem*. Good-bye, Miss Graham."

Hiding behind cascading red hair, Jesse looked at the floor as they walked out of the station. The heat still burned in her face, and she didn't want Joe to see how disconcerted she had been by Detective Holden's remark. They walked to his truck, their hands not touching, silent. He started to open her door, but hesitated. He took her face in his hands.

"You've been through an awful lot, Just Jesse. You don't need to make that kind of decision right now. Let's just see how things progress. Okay?"

She blew out a breath of air. She nodded; he kissed her cheek and opened her door.

-THIRTEEN-

Maggie was sitting on the porch step when Joe pulled up to the Cavanaugh House. She flew to the truck and opened Jesse's door practically dragging her out. Laughing, Jesse accepted Maggie's bear hug and returned it with equal enthusiasm.

"Jesse, are you okay? Oh my God! Look at the bruises on your neck! He could have killed you." Maggie babbled all the way into the house, tears flowing. "I didn't hear the news until this afternoon; we had a meeting right after Morning Prayer, so I never saw the newscast until after lunch. I got here as quickly as I could." Maggie's veil was crooked from the bear hug she had bestowed. Jesse laughed straightening it for her.

"I'm fine, Mags. But I'll tell you it was the worst night of my life!"

Joe popped the caps off three beers and they sat out in the backyard. Jesse summarized all the events, including today's hospital visit and her trip to the police station. Weariness overtook her in the retelling, and she relaxed with the effects of the beer. Joe pulled out the grill and found some Zweigle's White Hots in the freezer.

"Saving these for a special occasion?" he joked.

"Actually, I was," She pretended to pout.

"I can't think of a more special occasion than you being out of danger," he said as he lit the charcoal.

Maggie jumped up from her seat. "Oh, I brought over a cake to celebrate, too." She hurried out to her car and returned with a cake that read *'L'chaim.'* Jesse was puzzled.

"It means 'to life' in Hebrew. I didn't know how else to fit 'I'm so glad you didn't get murdered' on a cake." They all laughed.

"Well, it's very ecumenical, Mags. I love it! *L'chaim!*" she said and they clinked their beer bottles together.

Marty arrived a little later bringing his mother's lasagna. "At one time in my youth whenever Mama made lasagna, I'd ask who died. It was her signature dish for funerals and grieving families. I think it's great she made it for you to celebrate your life, Jesse. This could be a whole new direction for her."

"*Grazie*, Marty, and thank your Mama for me, too," she laughed.

Later, as Jesse tossed the salad, she looked out the kitchen window to see Susan and Jim arrive together. A smile played at her lips. *Isn't that sweet?* Susan's face was glowing and Jim's eyes seldom left her. Jesse looked out at these people now so important in her life. She felt different inside, finally not alone, maybe able to begin to trust.

"Hey, Just Jesse, the hot dogs are ready!" Joe called to her.

She opened the door and brought out the salad, placing it on the table heaped with all the dishes, including Susan's potato salad. Laughter mingled with wine and beer and friendship. She wondered if she had ever felt this good in her life.

Fred Morton's eyes were closed, his body free of IV tubes and monitors. Hearing Jesse enter, he opened his eyes. They looked at each other for a moment, neither knowing how to begin. The room was redolent with the scent of flowers, and Jesse noticed an enormous floral arrangement of roses, orchids and lilies sitting on the table. She sneezed.

"It is a bit much, isn't it?" Fred smiled.

"Sorry, I think it took my olfactory nerves by surprise," she said. "How are you?"

"A little sore, but I'm going to live, you know?" he shrugged and then winced from the movement. "How are you doing?"

She imitated his shrug. "I'm okay." She smiled. "I'm going to live, you know?"

They laughed.

"Thank you," she said, her voice thick with emotion. "You saved my life."

"I think we saved each other," he said.

"I'm sorry that I thought it was you who wanted to kill me…" she began then stopped.

"I thought as much. I guess I wasn't handling things in the best way."

"Why did you follow me to Rochester those times? You looked so suspicious."

"I'm an accountant. What do I know about tailing people?"

They laughed again. Then Fred sobered and spoke.

"When you showed up at Wyndham Estate for the Founder's Day party, you set a lot of wheels in motion. I've never seen such a close resemblance before. I know it's a cliché, but you are the spitting image of Helen."

"So you knew my mother?" she exclaimed.

Fred looked at her with sadness in his eyes.

"So you know that she was your mother and not Eileen? Oh yes, I knew Helen very well." His voice was barely audible. He stared at her for a moment, then looked down at his hands.

A tingling started in her stomach then fluttered through the rest of her body to her fingertips and toes. A sensation that signaled truth, that she was hearing the truth. With a sudden start she realized that Fred Morton had been in love with Helen. How could he be the one? His name started with F not B! She was afraid to ask the question; she was now afraid to hear the truth. She had been so suspicious and had disliked him for so long, how could she turn that around in an instant? But hadn't she been on a quest for the truth? Reality was what it was. Wishing for or against something didn't make it so. Finding the truth was the first step, facing it was next, and dealing with it could take years. She took a deep breath.

"You were in love with her." It was a statement, not a question, because she already knew the answer.

Fred was silent for a moment, his eyes focused on memories. "Yes."

It was her turn to be silent as she weighed the consequence of her next question.

"Were you lovers?" The implication of her question was obvious to both of them, and sounds that had been white noise now filled the room, marking the time between question and answer. The murmur of voices in the hall, the muted paging of a doctor, footsteps passing the door. Ordinary people proceeding with mundane tasks wrapped around the imminent discovery of Jesse's history. Time oozed along like honey being poured from a jar and she was suspended on the silence. Feeling Fred's eyes on her, she looked up at him.

"Jesse, look in the mirror and you will see how beautiful Helen was. She was beautiful inside and out. Every man who knew her fell in love with her." He shifted, pain evident in his eyes.

She wondered if it was just physical pain; judging by the sadness in his eyes, she thought not.

"Look, Mr. Morton, I can come back when you are better…" she said trying to keep the reluctance out of her voice. Ambivalence tumbled within her: hunger for knowledge of her heritage and fear of confirmation of her new suspicion.

"We've been through a lot together; just call me Fred."
His smile was weak but sincere.

"Okay…, Fred," she laughed, feeling awkward. She
noticed how warm his eyes were when he smiled.

"I know you must have a lot of questions. I will
answer whatever I can. Shoot. Oh, sorry, poor choice of
words," he laughed and then winced.

"Were you lovers?" she repeated her question, not as
reluctant as she had been for the potential answer.

"I loved Helen, but her heart belonged to someone
else. No, Jesse, we were not lovers, but we were very
close friends."

"Then who is my father?" She felt like a child asking
for a Christmas toy. Her heart full of hope, but afraid to
hope for too much.

Fred looked at her with kindness. "I said I would
answer any question that I could, but that is not my
question to answer."

Her heart sank and she burned with disappointment.
She nodded, mute.

A nurse entered and told Jesse that visiting hours were
over for the morning. She would have to leave.

"I'm getting sprung from this joint later today, Jesse,"
Frank said in his best Bogart imitation. Then he smiled,
his eyes dancing at her laughter. "Could you visit me at
Wyndham Estate later this evening? Say 6:30—before the
dinner hour? I know you have more questions, and I may
be able to answer those at least."

"Yes, of course. I'll swing by later, Fred." She looked
at him and saw the sincerity in his eyes. He reached out a
hand and she took it to shake, but he held hers for a
moment. "Looking at you, it's a little like having Helen
around again." He smiled at her.

As Jesse walked along the hospital corridor, she saw the same police officer stationed outside Sheriff Donoghue's room. Approaching him, she stopped.

"How is Sheriff Donoghue today?" she asked.

Recognizing her, the cop relaxed and uncrossed his arms.

"He's stable, ma'am," the young man said.

The door opened and Sr. Alphonse stepped out. Seeing Jesse, she straightened and halted. Emotions played across the nun's face: dislike, anger, and fear. She chose anger and leaned in toward Jesse.

"What are you doing here?" she snarled.

"I was just asking about your brother's condition," Jesse said, taken aback. Nuns still intimidated her, and nuns full of vengeance reminded her of the Furies.

Sr. Alphonse's eyes bored into hers. "Your mother brought all of this on. She played fast and loose with men, and my brother lost his heart to her. The hussy!" Her face twisted with loathing as she spit out her words. "Her wantonness warped my brother until he was senseless. She brought on her own end and I say good riddance. May she burn in hell!"

Fire started in the pit of Jesse's stomach as anger spread through her. She leaned into the nun forcing her to shrink backwards. "Don't you ever speak of my mother that way again." her voice was low, ominous in its intensity. Trembling with controlled rage, she spewed out her response to the woman. "She was nothing like that and you know it. What happened to your brother was tragic; what he did to others was sinful. How dare you condemn my mother for your brother's sins." Jesse simmered with fury. "And if I remember my *Baltimore Catechism* correctly, you just committed a sin by damning Helen. You'd better get back to St. Bartholomew's in time for confession, *Sister*." She snarled her disrespect. "That's a *mortal* sin, and you'll be the one burning in hell." Jesse glared at the woman's wide eyes and then turned on her heel to leave.

She couldn't help noticing the police officer's smile.

Jesse's heart fluttered as she steered Bert along the sweeping drive that led to Wyndham Manor. It was just past 6:30 as she had intended; she had wanted to be fashionably late. *Okay so it's 6:32. At least I don't look overly anxious.* But her quickening heartbeat confirmed her apprehension. She parked Bert on the circular drive grateful that full-time valets were not the norm. Checking the rearview mirror, she smoothed her hair and freshened her lipstick.

The walk up to the massive front door was intimidating enough, but when a butler answered in full regalia, her knees started to tremble. The man ushered her into the foyer with its imposing staircase, solid with carved oak wainscoting and thick carved balusters that ran up to a landing where it angled and disappeared above her head. A suit of armor nestled against the staircase, and she observed how short it was, about her height. *I could take you.* She tried not to gawk as they crossed the hall to the other side where a large door was tucked into a deep recess. Pressing down the brass handle, the butler swept the door in and stood aside for her to enter.

The western sun streamed in through French doors that were open to a veranda, the late summer breeze billowing the taupe silk draperies. The palate of the room was muted neutrals accented with fresh flowers in a burst of color. Jesse paused at the door, uncertain whether she should remove her shoes before stepping onto the plush carpet. Two Chesterfield sofas upholstered in white Italian leather sat opposite each other sharing a mahogany coffee table. Propped up on Jacquard pillows, Fred Morton reclined on one of the sofas.

"Forgive me if I don't get up," he said beckoning her to sit on the other sofa.

Keeping her shoes on, she entered the room and asked, "How are you tonight?" Her question was sincere. Her impression of Fred Morton had reversed causing her even to assess his physical features differently. Instead of seeing his eyes as dark and suspicious, she saw intelligence and warmth. She realized that what she had interpreted as anger the first time he saw her was probably just shock. She sat across from him as the butler reappeared carrying a tray with wine glasses, a bottle of Riesling and club soda. Setting the tray on the table, he poured her a glass of wine and Fred a glass of soda, then he glided out of the room, a skill developed over years.

Fred raised his glass to her and said "*Salute.*"

She rose leaning over to clink her glass against his. "*L'chaim*" she answered.

Fred smiled at her. "Yes. Indeed. 'To life.'"

Jesse sipped her wine savoring the delicate flavor. She began to relax due in part to Fred's calm presence. She glanced at him and he spoke.

"So, you had more questions for me," he said.

"Yes. When you first saw me at the Founder's Day party, I thought you were angry. Your reaction was pretty intense, as was Mr. Wyndham's."

Fred thought about that for a moment.

"You were quite a surprise, that's for sure. As I've told you, you look just like Helen, so I knew the minute I saw you that you were her daughter. Was I angry?" He pondered that question for a moment. "No, not angry. More like a jumble of many emotions because your presence here was going to stir up some old secrets that many wanted left in hiding. But it was a shock because all the love I'd had for Helen rushed back as if it were mere days since I'd seen her instead of years."

"Why did you follow me to Rochester?"

"As I said, Jesse, your presence resurrected some very well-kept secrets. Any of us who knew Helen couldn't believe she would kill herself. The investigation seemed rushed and then there was that weird business with the one cop who found her."

"You mean Walter George," she offered.

"Was that his name? Yeah, I think it was. He was sent off to a mental hospital after his breakdown, and no one ever heard of him again. Bill Donoghue became almost a recluse until Ginny married him, but they were never very happy. She always seemed like a scared rabbit. Rumors flew about Helen's death, and Claudia Harris's account about finding her kept getting stranger and stranger until no one knew what to believe. We always suspected Bill knew something about Helen's death that he wasn't telling, but we couldn't prove anything. Then when you appeared, all of that mystery and sorrow came to the surface. When we heard about what happened to you after the Founder's Day party, we knew you needed to be protected."

Jesse noticed his shift from "I" to "we" and she stopped him.

"Who is 'we'?" Before you were saying 'I' and now you are saying 'we'," she said.

He glanced at her and shrugged. "Ben Wyndham. He was worried about you, too. We kept an eye on you, on your house. I followed you to Rochester, fearing that whoever had tried to run you off the road might do so again. We began to suspect Donoghue after we saw him around your house one night." He looked at her and held up his hands. "Don't get me wrong, we didn't watch you all the time, but we'd take a ride down your street every so often. One night Donoghue was coming around the side of your house carrying some kind of tool kit. All your lights were out except maybe a nightlight or reading lamp in the upstairs front room."

Jesse smiled to herself realizing he had seen Helen's emanations.

"Anyway, the night of the Rodeo Round-Up, we kept an eye on him and noticed he was watching your every move. When you put that cowgirl jacket on, he almost choked on his beer. Helen loved that jacket; she wore it all the time. His eyes were glued to you wherever you were—on the dance floor, at your table, getting refreshments—he was watching. When you left your group of friends to use the ladies' room alone—by the way, I thought women always went in groups—anyway, he took off right after you. I think the jacket set him off. I got to you first, but my manners aren't always the best. Instead of warning you, I think I scared the shit out of you, no pun intended."

She laughed. "You did. I already was convinced that it was you trying to kill me, that it was you who had followed me after the Founder's Day party, and you who was tapping my phone…"

"Ah, so that's what he was doing the night we saw him by your house."

"Yes, so he knew I was heading to Rochester to see Eileen. He must have thought that she was going to give me valuable information about Helen's death when what she was actually going to give me was my father's address." She stopped realizing she was back to her biggest question. "The only father I ever knew." She looked at Fred, her meaning clear in her eyes.

"Jesse, the answer you want is not one that I can give you," Fred said, his voice quiet.

"But I can."

Ben Wyndham stood at the French doors.

Jesse rose from the sofa and looked at the tall, handsome man framed by the sinking sun. His white shirt was opened at the collar, the sleeves rolled halfway up his forearms, and he held a glass of wine. He wore khaki pants and brown leather loafers, his suntanned skin completing the picture of a healthy, vibrant man. His dark hair was graying at the temples and his chiseled features confirmed why Helen would fall in love with him.

Entering the room, he stood before her. The furrow between his brows signaled the pain that filled his eyes. "You may want to sit down." His voice was soft.

Trembling, she lowered herself to the couch and waited for him to continue.

"Jesse, I am not your father."

The room seemed to tilt and move at the impact of his words. Jesse lost all equilibrium and impulsively grabbed the arm of the sofa to maintain her balance. She had been so sure. In all of her puzzling out of solutions, Ben Wyndham had been the lone conclusion. She regained her senses and looked at him. Her mind was grasping for clarity; once again everything she had believed to be true was like a house of mirrors.

"My older brother, Albert, was your father."

She tried to comprehend his statement, but was unable to make sense of it.

"Albert? But the letters were signed with the initial 'B'," she said. Her mouth was dry and his words echoed in her mind.

Ben smiled slightly. "My parents insisted we use our full names, but among ourselves and our friends, we used our nicknames: Ben, Bart and Bert. Helen called him Bert."

Jesse nodded.

"He told me he fell in love with Helen at first sight, but she knew he was engaged. For months she resisted all his attempts to win her. His fiancé's family and ours were lifelong friends, so their betrothal was made practically at their births. He wooed Helen persistently for months until he won her over; she admitted she had fallen in love at first sight, too. Albert had planned to break his engagement immediately but his fiancé became seriously ill and then travelled to Europe to recuperate. He had believed he could neither break it off while she was ill, nor by letter while she was overseas.

"While his fiancé was in Europe, Helen and Bert became lovers. She became pregnant. They thought it best if she went away to have the baby—you, Jesse—and when she returned they would be married. Bert broke his engagement, and my parents were furious with him. Father alleged Helen wasn't a...suitable match."

Jesse balked at that remark, and she sat forward spilling her wine in her lap and on the white sofa. Jumping up she looked around for a napkin and Ben leapt up with her. Lifting a vase off the side table, he slipped the linen cloth from beneath the large floral arrangement and started to lean forward to help her, then stood upright, his face red. He handed her the napkin; she wiped at her yellow capris and then dabbed the wine off the sofa's cushion. Embarrassed, she busied herself at the clean-up longer than necessary, trying to regain her composure. A year's salary wouldn't cover the cost of replacing this piece of furniture.

"Jesse, don't worry about the sofa, it's fine," Ben said.

"I think I got all the wine off it. If you need to have it cleaned or replaced..." her voice drifted off unable to wrestle with the reality of that option at the moment. Why not add one more catastrophe to the mix?

Ben touched her arm and reached for the napkin. "It's okay, Jesse. Really." He smiled and gestured for her to sit on a dry area of the sofa. He walked to the side table and dropped the damp napkin on it. He paced as he continued his story.

"Finally in August, Helen returned to Seneca Corners, and Bert was ecstatic. He bought a cradle for you and put it her bedroom. Planning to finish and decorate the front room for your nursery, they put an armoire in there. They were going to announce their engagement at the Rodeo Round-Up."

He stopped walking and rubbed his eyes with his open palms. Jesse's trembling tensed her muscles, but she resisted moving, not wanting to break his thoughts or spill her wine again.

"She arrived a week before the Roundup. Their relationship still wasn't public; they wanted to surprise everyone at the party. Bert visited her that evening to plan their future; the next day he got the news that she had committed suicide. He couldn't believe it—wouldn't believe it until he saw her for himself. On the way home from the morgue, he ran into a delivery truck and was killed instantly." His voice caught. "They never determined whether it was an accident or…

"Helen's suicide didn't make sense; they had made plans for a life together. She wasn't depressed at all, just the opposite. The investigation was cursory though, because all the evidence pointed to suicide."

The room was silent save for the drone of a lawn mower far out on the property. Jesse shifted in her seat, her mind whirling with the revelations Ben Wyndham had just disclosed. Ben Wyndham had not been the love of Helen Cavanaugh's life. Ben Wyndham was not her father. The eldest son, Albert Wyndham was her father, and she would never know him. At last she had the answer for which she had been searching, yet all she felt was numb.

Ben came out of his reverie and returned to the present.

"With all that happened, everyone thought it best for Helen's sister to raise you. Eileen and Jim had come the night of her death and taken you with them. When Albert died the next day, it just made sense that you would stay with them."

Jesse felt like a spring tightly wound, her muscles ached with tension. She sat with her arms wrapped around herself, her shoulders hunched forward as if warding off the information her body did not want to receive. A headache throbbed in her temples dulling the sound of the clock striking seven o'clock. She wondered at the pace this story had taken. Surely it was midnight. But the sun still streamed in lighting the room with a rosy pre-sunset glow. The lawn mower had completed its task and now birdsong replaced its drone. She took a deep breath and tried to relax her taut body, easing back into the luxury of the sofa.

"I'm sorry, Jesse." Ben sat at the end of the sofa with his forearms resting on his knees. He stared at his hands, clasped and hanging loosely.

She wasn't sure why he apologized. Was it because he knew she had believed he was her father? Was it because the story was so sad? Was it because she was now officially an orphan? Even at age 28, that realization unsettled her. Unsure of his meaning, she was unsure how to respond. "It's okay," didn't seem appropriate. "You should be," didn't either. So Jesse sat in silence trying to absorb the fact of her parents' deaths.

Ben rubbed the back of his neck and sat back. He blew out a stream of breath and rubbed his eyes.

"Jim and Eileen were good at keeping us updated about you for a while; I think it was more Jim than Eileen."

Jesse snorted softly and Ben looked at her, puzzled.

"I imagine it was," she said.

"Father would not hear of having you stay with us. He disapproved of what Albert did, shirking his duty to Wyndham Estate and all, and I believe he blamed Helen for Bert's death. He set up an account for you in Eileen's name that would allow you to live comfortably and be raised in a style suitable to a Wyndham. After Eileen left Jim, she sent account information in order to continue the monthly deposits."

"Ah, that's where all that money came from," she said.

Ben nodded. "Father believed he was fulfilling his duty to you without interrupting the Wyndham lineage. You see, Wyndham men had always sired male heirs—eldest *sons*. You were a daughter; he didn't know how to handle that and probably believed it would be wrong to pass the estate on to a female. I know that was ludicrous, but no one could convince him otherwise. I think Mother always carried a sense of guilt and regret for not including you in the family. By the time they had passed, we didn't know where you were. I know Jim Graham tried to find you for a long time."

Fred Morton had been silent all this time; he spoke.

"Ben helped finance a private detective that Jim hired," he said to her.

Ben waved his hand dismissively. He looked at Jesse, his eyes full of compassion.

"I know this is a tremendous amount of information to digest. If there is anything I can do—anything at all…I feel so badly." His voice trailed off.

Jesse felt bolted to the sofa. It seemed she should make some polite comment and then leave gracefully, but she was paralyzed with shock, confusion, sorrow and any number of emotions that pin people to their seats. Fred Morton came to her rescue—again.

"Well, for now you could pour her a little more wine, Ben," his voice held a hint of levity.

As if startled that he hadn't thought of it himself, Ben reached for the wine bottle on the coffee table. Picking up her glass, he poured wine into it, then refilled Fred's and his own. He returned to his seat and took a generous sip of Riesling.

Sipping hers, the cool liquid slid down her throat relieving the dryness. Her thoughts were jumbled, and she had difficulty settling on one concept. She said the one thing she could think of to say.

"I don't know what to say."

Ben nodded. "I know. It's a lot to comprehend, Jesse. Take your time; there is no hurry. Ask anything you want. But there is one more thing you need to realize. Albert was the eldest, so as Albert's child, you are the heir to Wyndham Estate."

But her mind was blank. No questions arose, no thoughts coalesced, no opinions formed. Sensory stimuli were warped and surreal. The birdsong sounded off-key, the sunlight was harsh, the wine tasted sour. She just wanted to crawl into her bed and pull the covers over her head.

"I think I need to go home now," she whispered. "I think I need some time."

"I understand," Ben replied. "I'm sorry."

Again Jesse wondered why.

Jesse lay in the dark staring at the ceiling, so exhausted that she could not fall asleep. Straining her ears, she listened for any sound that might be Helen. All was silent. She missed Helen's nocturnal visits. Tears streamed down either side of her face and dropped onto her already dampened pillow. Loneliness wrapped her like a shroud. She was an orphan. She was alone. She was a Wyndham. She was the Wyndham heir.

She hadn't considered that as yet. Its magnitude was more than her brain could handle. She actually did have a family—how strange that felt. They didn't feel like family, not the way Susan and Jim did. Not the way Maggie and Marty did. And Joe. She smiled in the dark. No, she was not alone at all.

She rolled over to her side and plumped her pillow. Snuggling into it she closed her eyes and relaxed into the comfort of her bed. Yawning, sleep began to overtake her, and as she drifted off she thought she heard a sigh.

-FOURTEEN-

Lesson plans covered her kitchen table as Jesse looked up passages in *Romeo and Juliet*. Finding the quote she sought, she took the pencil from between her teeth and jotted down the scene and line number on her plans. School would begin the next Tuesday, and she couldn't believe summer was over already. And what a summer it had been!

Hearing the doorbell, she went to the front hall, thinking someone had arrived early for her Labor Day barbeque. When she opened the door, she was greeted by a huge bouquet of flowers hiding the slight figure of the delivery boy. Poking his head around the blossoms, he asked, "Miss Graham?"

"Yes," she confirmed.

He pressed the flowers into her arms, tipped his cap and walked back to his truck.

Inhaling their scent, she smiled guessing that Joe must have realized what a stressful day she'd had the day before. She walked into the living room, set the flowers on the coffee table, lifted the small envelope from its holder and opened it.

Jesse,
Welcome to the family...finally.
Ben Wyndham

She reread the message twice to ensure its meaning. She looked at the flowers and ran her fingers lightly across the soft petals of deep pink roses, pink alstroemeria, green fuji mums and baby's breath. Deep within, she felt peaceful for the first time in a long time. She returned to the kitchen to put away her school work when the doorbell rang again.

Opening it this time, she found Joe leaning against the door jamb as he had the night of the Rodeo Round-Up, cowboy hat pulled down, arms crossed, striking a sexy stance.

"Afternoon, ma'am," he drawled.

Jesse laughed. "Howdy, cowboy."

He straightened and smiled at her. "It worked the other night. I got you to dance with me." He jumped down the porch steps and retrieved a six pack of Genesee beer and a package of Zweigle's White Hots. Hopping back up on the porch he held them up. "I wanted to treat you to dinner."

"You romantic," she said.

She stood back so he could enter and he stopped when he spotted the flowers. Looking at her with eyebrows raised, he cocked his head toward the living room.

"Not as romantic as some, I see." His forehead creased with worry.

Jesse snatched the note and gave it to him to read.

He let out a low whistle.

"So Ben *is* your father?" His eyes took on a faraway look as he processed that. "That would make Al your brother?"

"It will take some explaining, but no, Ben is not my father, so Al is not my brother. What is it about Al that sets you off, Joe?"

He shrugged. "It's hard to explain." He looked at her and his eyes softened. "You're not the only one who has trouble trusting sometimes, Just Jesse."

She nodded. "I understand. I hope someday you will trust me enough to tell me."

"I trust you, Jess. Let's sit down." He led her to the couch and pulled her down beside him. Sitting next to her, he took a deep breath and began.

"My dislike of Al goes back a long time, and I'm not very proud of it. When we were in school, Al and I were both contenders for varsity quarterback. I was faster and could block pretty well, too. All the guys thought I was a shoe-in for the position since I was a senior. But we needed new uniforms and equipment that year; we got everything we needed plus an update of our locker and shower rooms. With Wyndham money. Al, an underclassman, was named first-string quarterback. It seemed more than coincidental to me. I've grown up with ambivalent opinions about the Wyndhams all of my life. On the one hand they are the economy of the area; without their money there would be no Seneca Corners. Many of my father's best paying construction jobs were on Wyndham land, and so are many of mine. On the other hand, I grew up seeing Al treated differently than the rest of us. He was the golden boy. I was very jealous of the Wyndham wealth and how easy life was for the brothers. I'm not proud of that."

He stopped talking and looked at her. He looked away and when she took his hand, he patted hers and then released it.

"We went to different colleges, and I was glad to get away from the Wyndham influence for a while. When I returned to take over the business, I was called up for active duty and was sent over to Vietnam." Joe leaned forward, his elbows on his knees. "Paul Ryder, my best friend since kindergarten, was in Da Nang with me before we were sent out to units in the jungle. Paul was killed." He looked down at his hands. "The Wyndham boys served their hitch in comfy offices at the Pentagon"

Neither spoke for a few moments. He continued.

"None of this was Al's doing, and I know that. He probably didn't ask his father to buy all the football gear so he could be the quarterback. He didn't have the influence to stay out of Vietnam. It wasn't him. But he became the symbol of Wyndham wealth and how it could point your life in a better direction than most people can access. When my father died, I resented that Al still had his father, like it was something he could control."

He dropped his face into his hands and spoke, his voice muffled. "As I said, it's not something I'm proud of. It's like a snake coiled up inside of me that rises like a cobra to strike out in resentment."

Jesse rubbed his back and shoulders.

"You've lived in the shadow of the Wyndhams your whole life. It's understandable why you would resent them."

Joe rubbed his face and sat back. "But Al has never done anything to me personally. I imagine he doesn't even know that I dislike him, or if he does, he doesn't know why."

"But *you* know why. And facing that and understanding it can help you to heal from it...if you want to. I understand how it feels to dislike someone who has hurt you, whether intentionally or not. I know that repulsive sensation in the pit of my stomach when that person is near. But I know my resentment only hurts me, not the other person."

He looked at her. "And now you're a Wyndham."

She sat back as if she'd been pushed. "Do you resent me now, too?"

His eyes searched her face, tracing a line from her hair to her lips and back to her eyes.

"You know how I feel about you, Jesse. Nothing will change that."

She hesitated, not certain what to say or do.

"Joe, I have no interest in the Wyndham fortune. I just want to live a simple, peaceful life with no ghosts or murders in it." The realization of how much she cared for him overwhelmed her in that moment, and tears blurred her eyes. "But I want you in it."

Joe wrapped her in his arms and held her. She felt safe and loved as she never had before. Tipping her face to his, he kissed her deeply.

Just then Susan and Jim pulled in. Joe looked out the front window and then down at Jesse. He kissed the end of her nose and smiled.

"Mom's bringing a ton of food as usual."

They went to the car to help unload the items, and she saw that he was right. Susan handed her a cake and bottle of wine to carry. Jim hefted a cooler from the trunk, and Joe carried in macaroni salad while Susan used hot pads to grab the baked beans.

"It's a moveable feast," Jesse laughed. "Susan, you always work too hard when I host a gathering."

"My pleasure, sweetie," Susan said brushing her cheek with a light kiss.

As they all sat in the backyard, Marty and Maggie arrived at about the same time. Settled in, each with a beverage of choice, Jesse relayed the conversation from the night before.

Jim patted her shoulder. "I'm glad you finally have answers to all of your questions, Jesse. It's rather, well, complicated for you, isn't it?"

She nodded. "Ben told me that I am the heir to the Wyndham Estate." Out of the corner of her eye, she saw Joe sit back and look down. "I don't think I've absorbed that yet, but I don't think it will affect my life. I have no interest in the estate, and Ben is doing just fine with it."

Marty lurched forward. "Jesse, you're rich. You can buy anything you want—a Mustang..."

She winced at that.

"... a Porsche, hell you could buy a Maserati!"

She laughed. "I don't think so, Marty. I'm going to stick with Bert." She gasped. "Oh my God! I named my car after my father and I didn't even know it! Does anyone think that's weird?"

"Jesse, you've had a ghost living in your attic and solved a twenty-eight-year-old mystery—oh, and survived an attempt on your life. Nothing seems weird anymore," Maggie said.

They all burst out laughing except Joe who had become quiet. No one noticed except Jesse.

"I guess you're self-employed now, Jess, since you own St. Bart's," Maggie said.

She made a face. "I don't own it, Mags, but I might make some personnel changes." She related her encounter with Sr. Alphonse at the hospital. Looking at Maggie, she raised her eyebrows looking innocent.

"Am I going to burn in hell for saying that to a nun, Sr. Angelina?"

Maggie laughed. "There is no sin in speaking the truth, my child. But it will be awkward with you two working together. Frankly, I'm glad you put her in her place."

"*Cin-cin*," Marty said, raising his glass to Jesse.

Even Joe laughed and joined in that toast. She felt his mood lighten throughout the rest of the evening. He smiled at her often, but was unusually reserved with her. He was the grill master and made a great show of cooking the white hots to perfection: blackened just enough with split skins.

As they sat around the table sharing food and laughter, Jesse realized that she was not alone at all. These people had become her family. She looked at Jim, the only father she had ever known and when he caught her eye, she smiled and he winked in return. He and Susan found many reasons to touch the other's hand when they talked, and the happiness in their eyes more than hinted at a blossoming romance. Marty kept the conversation animated, and sometimes naughty, with his sense of humor. Maggie kept him in check when he got too bawdy, though she laughed as hard as the others.

Jesse's heart swelled with joy as she watched the interaction and deep affection among these friends. She sent up a silent prayer of gratitude to the God she sometimes doubted. But not at this moment; at this moment she knew *Someone* was looking out for her.

Joe lingered after the others had left, and Jesse sat beside him on the back steps. Leaves rustled in the trees, and they had put on jackets to ward off the evening breeze. In the distance they heard the muted hooting of a barn owl and surrounding them, crickets chirruped. She hated to see the sun setting so much earlier, but she loved summer nights that wrapped her in indigo peace under the stars.

She studied Joe.

"You were kind of quiet for a while there tonight."

He looked out at the shadowy forms of the trees and took a sip of beer.

"Was I?"

"Yes. When I was talking about being a Wyndham."

He was silent for a few moments.

"That's going to change your life whether you want it to or not, Jess. You will have responsibilities and you'll socialize with different people now. Things will be different."

"Things don't have to be different."

"But they will be." He turned his head to look at her. The light from the porch caught his eyes and she thought she saw them glisten with moisture.

"Joe, I have no interest in becoming a Wyndham in the sense you mean. I saw a glimpse of that world with Eileen and Robert, and honestly, I don't fit the description. I like a more simple life. With people I care about. People I trust." She looped her arm through his. "It's been a crazy, scary, bizarre summer. I can't believe we've known each other for just a couple of months. I've never felt so cared for as I do since I met you. I can't make any promises right now; we have to see what happens when life settles down."

Joe looked back out at the trees. "But you're willing to see what happens?"

"Yes."

He stood up. "I have something for you." He walked to his truck at the front of the house and came back with an enormous, clumsily wrapped present. "It's not as romantic as those flowers you got."

He set it on the ground in front of her and Jesse tore open the wrappings. The light gleamed off the handles of some kind of implement. She looked at Joe and tilted her head in question.

"What is it?" she asked.

"It's a tiller. In case you ever want to start a garden."

Warmth spread through her heart; she stood up and kissed him.

"A garden takes a lot of trust, Joe. I kinda like that idea, but I'll need some help."

-ACKNOWLEDGEMENTS-

I would like to acknowledge all those who helped me as I wrote *The Cavanaugh House*. First and foremost, thanks to my beloved husband Rich who rode the crazy roller coaster of emotions with me on a daily basis. Also, thanks to my beta readers, daughter Kate Bode and friends Tina Jacobs, Linda Kaczmarek, Janet Martyn, Deborah O'Neill Cordes, Luana Russell, H.J. Smith and Sarah Yoder. Thanks to Officer Jai Mahabir for his expertise on all things criminal, and to my lifelong friend Mary D'Aloisio Flowers for helping Marty with his Italian.

I would like to acknowledge Boris, my muse and co-creator. As real as you who are reading this, Boris has been with me every step of the way in writing *The Cavanaugh House* as well as all my other novels, poems, blogs, articles and presentations. He inspires me, whispers in my dreams and flows through my fingertips as I sit and create. I thank you, Boris, and I can't wait for our next adventure.

-ABOUT MUSES-

Muses were a regular part of instruction for my high school literature students. The opening lines of *The Odyssey* can be translated, "Sing to me, O Muse..." But that context made a muse ancient, distant and unreachable to me. After viewing Elizabeth Gilbert's TED.com talk on Creativity, I realized that muses were very present to us today. I was aware of inspiration from outside of myself as I revised *Love's Destiny* and wrote *Love's Spirit*, but it was during the writing of *The Cavanaugh House* that I was formally introduced to my muse, Boris.

Whatever your creative passion is, and you do have one, sit in silence for a moment before you begin working and acknowledge your muse. Allow him/her to flow through you and inspire your creation whether it be writing, music, art, auto mechanics, engineering... whatever. Just listen. And if you listen carefully, you might even learn your muses's name. I did.

Made in the USA
Middletown, DE
11 September 2020